NW

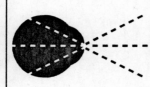

This Large Print Book carries the
Seal of Approval of N.A.V.H.

NW

ZADIE SMITH

THORNDIKE PRESS

A part of Gale, Cengage Learning

Detroit • New York • San Francisco • New Haven, Conn • Waterville, Maine • London

Thorndike Press® Large Print Core.

The text of this Large Print edition is unabridged.

Other aspects of the book may vary from the original edition.

Set in 16 pt. Plantin.

LIBRARY OF CONGRESS CATALOGING-IN-PUBLICATION DATA

Smith, Zadie.
  NW / by Zadie Smith.
    pages ; cm. — (Thorndike Press large print core)
  ISBN-13: 978-1-4104-5458-4 (hardcover)
  ISBN-10: 1-4104-5458-4 (hardcover)
  1. Planned communities — England — London — Fiction.
2. Social isolation — Fiction. 3. London (England) — Fiction.
4. Large type books. I. Title.
  PR6069.M59N84 2012b
  823'.914—dc23

                                                    2012035906

Published in 2013 by arrangement with The Penguin Press, a member of Penguin Group (USA), Inc.

Printed in Mexico
3 4 5 6 7 17 16 15 14 13

For Kellas

When Adam delved and Eve span,
Who was then the gentleman?

— JOHN BALL

■■■■

VISITATION

■■■■

1.

The fat sun stalls by the phone masts. Anti-climb paint turns sulphurous on school gates and lampposts. In Willesden people go barefoot, the streets turn European, there is a mania for eating outside. She keeps to the shade. Redheaded. On the radio: I am the sole author of the dictionary that defines me. A good line — write it out on the back of a magazine. In a hammock, in the garden of a basement flat. Fenced in, on all sides.

Four gardens along, in the estate, a grim girl on the third floor screams Anglo-Saxon at nobody. Juliet balcony, projecting for miles. It ain't like that. Nah it ain't like that. Don't you start. Fag in hand. Fleshy, lobster-red.

I am the sole
I am the sole author
Pencil leaves no mark on magazine pages. Somewhere she has read that the gloss gives

you cancer. Everyone knows it shouldn't be this hot. Shriveled blossom and bitter little apples. Birds singing the wrong tunes in the wrong trees too early in the year. Don't you bloody start! Look up: the girl's burned paunch rests on the railing. Here's what Michel likes to say: not everyone can be invited to the party. Not this century. Cruel opinion — she doesn't share it. In marriage not everything is shared. Yellow sun high in the sky. Blue cross on a white stick, clear, definitive. What to do? Michel is at work. He is still at work.

I am the
the sole
Ash drifts into the garden below, then comes the butt, then the box. Louder than the birds and the trains and the traffic. Sole sign of sanity: a tiny device tucked in her ear. I told im stop takin liberties. Where's my cheque? And she's in my face chattin breeze. Fuckin liberty.

I am the sole. The sole. The sole
She unfurls her fist, lets the pencil roll. Takes her liberty. Nothing else to listen to but this bloody girl. At least with eyes closed there is something else to see. Viscous black specks. Darting water boatmen, zig-zagging. Zig. Zag. Red river? Molten lake in hell? The hammock tips. The papers

flop to the ground. World events and property and film and music lie in the grass. Also sport and the short descriptions of the dead.

2.

Doorbell! She stumbles through the grass barefoot, sun-huddled, drowsy. The back door leads to a poky kitchen, tiled brightly in the taste of a previous tenant. The bell is not being rung. It is being held down.

In the textured glass, a body, blurred. Wrong collection of pixels to be Michel. Between her body and the door, the hallway floorboards, golden in reflected sun. This hallway can only lead to good things. Yet a woman is screaming PLEASE and crying. A woman thumps the front door with her fist. Pulling the lock aside, she finds it stops halfway, the chain pulls tight, and a little hand flies through the gap.

– PLEASE — oh my God help me — please Miss, I live here — I live just here, please God — check, please —

Dirty nails. Waving a gas bill? Phone bill? Pushed through the opening, past the chain, so close she must draw back to focus on what she is being shown. *37 Ridley Avenue* — a street on the corner of her own. This is all she reads. She has a quick vision of Michel as he would be if he were here, examining the envelope's plastic window, checking on credentials. Michel is at work. She releases the chain.

The stranger's knees go, she falls forward, crumpling. Girl or woman? They're the same age: thirties, mid-way, or thereabouts. Tears shake the stranger's little body. She pulls at her clothes and wails. Woman begging the public for witnesses. Woman in a war-zone standing in the rubble of her home.

– You're hurt?

Her hands are in her hair. Her head collides with the doorframe.

– Nah, not me, my mum — I need some help. I've been to every fuckin door — please. Shar — my name is Shar. I'm local. I live here. Check!
– Come in. Please. I'm Leah.

Leah is as faithful in her allegiance to this two-mile square of the city as other people are to their families, or their countries. She knows the way people speak around here, that *fuckin,* around here, is only a rhythm in

15

a sentence. She arranges her face to signify compassion. Shar closes her eyes, nods. She makes quick movements with her mouth, inaudible, speaking to herself. To Leah she says

– You're so good.

Shar's diaphragm rises and falls, slower now. The shuddering tears wind down.

– Thank you, yeah? You're so good.

Shar's small hands grip the hands that support her. Shar is tiny. Her skin looks papery and dry, with patches of psoriasis on the forehead and on the jaw. The face is familiar. Leah has seen this face many times in these streets. A peculiarity of London villages: faces without names. The eyes are memorable, around the deep brown clear white is visible, above and below. An air of avidity, of consuming what she sees. Long lashes. Babies look like this. Leah smiles. The smile offered back is blank, without recognition. Sweetly crooked. Leah is only the good stranger who opened the door and did not close it again. Shar repeats: you are so good, you are so good — until the thread of pleasure that runs through that phrase (of course for Leah there is a little pleasure) is broken. Leah shakes her head. No, no, no, no.

Leah directs Shar to the kitchen. Big hands on the girl's narrow shoulders. She watches Shar's buttocks rise up and against her rolled-down jogging pants, the little downy dip in her back, pronounced, sweaty in the heat. The tiny waist opening out into curves. Leah is hipless, gangly like a boy. Perhaps Shar needs money. Her clothes are not clean. In the back of her right knee there is a wide tear in the nasty fabric. Dirty heels rise up out of disintegrating flip-flops. She smells.

– Heart attack! I was asking them is she dyin? Is she dyin? Is she dyin? She goes in the ambulance — don't get no answer do I! I got three kids that is home alone innit — I have to get hospital — what they talking about car for? I ain't got no car! I'm saying *help me* — no one did a fuckin thing to help me.

Leah grips Shar's wrist, sets her down in a chair at the kitchen table and passes over a roll of tissue. She puts her hands once more on Shar's shoulders. Their foreheads are inches from each other.

– I understand, it's OK. Which hospital?
– It's like . . . I ain't written it . . . In Middlesex or — Far, though. Don't know eggzak'ly.

Leah squeezes Shar's hands.

– Look, I don't drive — but —

Checks her watch. Ten to five.

– If you wait, maybe twenty minutes? If I call him now, he can — or maybe a taxi . . .

Shar eases her hands from Leah's. She presses her knuckles into her eyes, breathing out fully: the panic is over.

– Need to be there . . . no numbers — nothing — no money . . .

Shar tears some skin from her right thumb with her teeth. A spot of blood rises and contains itself. Leah takes Shar again by the wrist. Draws her fingers from her mouth.

– Maybe *The* Middlesex? Name of the hospital, not the place. Down Acton way, isn't it?

The girl's face is dreamy, slow. Touched, the Irish say. Possible that she's touched.

– Yeah . . . could be . . . yeah, no, yeah that's it. The Middlesex. That's it.

Leah straightens up, takes a phone from her back pocket and dials.

– I'LL COME BY TOMORROW.

Leah nods and Shar continues, making no concession for the phone call.

– PAY YOU BACK. GET MY CHEQUE TO-MORROW, YEAH?

Leah keeps her phone to her ear, smiles and nods, gives her address. She mimes a cup of tea. But Shar is looking at the apple blossom. She wipes tears from her face with the fabric of her grubby t-shirt. Her belly-button is a tight knot flush with her stom-ach, a button sewn in a divan. Leah recites her own phone number.

– Done.

She turns to the sideboard, picks up the kettle with her free hand, fumbling it be-cause she expected it to be empty. A little water spills. She replaces the kettle on its stand, and remains where she is, her back to her guest. There is no natural place to sit or stand. In front of her, on the long windowsill that stretches the room, some of the things of her life — photos, knick-knacks, some of her father's ashes, vases, plants, herbs. In the window's reflection Shar is bringing her little feet up to the seat of her chair, holding her ankles. The emergency was less awkward, more natural than this. This is not the country for making a stranger tea. They smile at each other in the glass. There is goodwill. There is nothing to say.

– I'll get cups.

Leah is naming all her actions. She opens the cupboard. It is full of cups; cups on cups on cups.

– Nice place.

Leah turns too quickly, makes irrelevant motions with her hands.

– Not ours — we rent — ours is just this — there's two flats upstairs. Shared garden. It's council, so . . .

Leah pours out the tea as Shar looks around. Bottom lip out, head nodding gently. Appreciative, like an estate agent. Now she comes to Leah. What's to see? Wrinkled checked flannel shirt, raggedy jean shorts, freckled legs, bare feet — someone absurd, maybe, a slacker, a lady of leisure. Leah crosses her arms across her abdomen.

– Nice for council. Lot of bedrooms and that?

20

The lip stays low. It slurs her speech a little. Something is wrong with Shar's face, Leah notices, and is embarrassed by noticing, and looks away.

– Two. The second's a box. We sort of use it as . . .

Shar meanwhile burrows for something else entirely; she's slower than Leah, but she's there now, they're in the same place. She points her finger in Leah's face.

– Wait — you went *Brayton?*

She bounces on her chair. Elated. But this must be wrong.

– I swear when you was on the phone I was thinking: I know you. You went Brayton!

Leah perches her backside on the counter and gives her dates. Shar is impatient with chronology. She wants to know if Leah remembers when the science wing flooded, the time Jake Fowler had his head placed in a vise. In relation to these coordinates, like moon landings and the deaths of presidents, they position their own times.

– Two years below you, innit. What's your name again?

Leah struggles with the stiff lid of a biscuit tin.

– Leah. Hanwell.
– Leah. You went Brayton. Still see anyone?

Leah lists her names, with their potted biographies. Shar beats a rhythm on the tabletop with her fingers.

– Have you been married long?
– Too long.
– Do you want me to call someone? Your husband?
– Nah . . . nah . . . he's over there. Ain't seen him in two years. Abusive. Violent. Had issues. Had a lot of problems, in his head and that. Broke my arm, broke my collarbone, broke my knee, broke my fuckin face. Tell you the truth —

The next is said in a light aside, with a little hiccupping laugh, and is incomprehensible.

– Used to rape me and everything . . . it was crazy. Oh well.

Shar slides off her chair and walks toward the back door. Looks out on the garden, the parched yellow lawn.

– I'm so sorry.
– Ain't your fault! Is what it is.

The feeling of feeling absurd. Leah puts her hands in her pockets. The kettle clicks.

– Truthfully, Layer, I'd be lying if I said it's been easy. It's been *hard*. But. Got away, you know? I'm alive. Three kids! Youngest is seven. So, some good came, you get me?

Leah nods at the kettle.

– Got kids?
– No. A dog, Olive. She's at my mate Nat's house right now. Natalie Blake? Actually in school she was Keisha. Natalie De Angelis now. In my year. Used to have a big afro puff like —

Leah mimes an atomic mushroom behind her own head. Shar frowns.

– Yeah. Up herself. Coconut. Thought she was all that.

A look of blank contempt passes over Shar's face. Leah talks into it.

– She's got kids. Lives just over there, in the posh bit, on the park. She's a lawyer now. Barrister. What's the difference? Maybe there isn't one. They've two kids. The kids love Olive, the dog's called Olive.

She is just saying sentences, one after the other, they don't stop.

– I'm pregnant, actually.

Shar leans against the glass of the door. Closes one eye, focusing on Leah's stomach.

– Oh it's early. Very. Actually I found out this morning.

Actually actually actually. Shar takes the revelation in her stride.

– Boy?
– No, I mean — I haven't got that far.

Leah blushes, not having intended to speak of this delicate, unfinished thing.

– Does your mans know?
– I took the test this morning. Then you came.
– Pray for a girl. Boys are hell.

Shar has a dark look. She grins satanically. Around each tooth the gum is black. She walks back to Leah and presses her hands flat against Leah's stomach.

– Let me feel. I can tell things. Don't matter how early. Come here. Not gonna hurt you. It's like a gift. My mum was the same way. Come here.

She reaches for Leah and pulls her forward. Leah lets her. Shar places her hands back where they were.

– Gonna be a girl, definite. Scorpio, too, proper trouble. A runner.

Leah laughs. She feels a heat rising between the girl's sweaty hands and her own clammy stomach.

– Like an athlete?
– Nah . . . the kind who runs away. You'll need one eye on her, all the time.

Shar's hands drop, her face glazes over once more with boredom. She starts talking of things. All things are equal. Leah or tea or rape or bedroom or heart attack or school or who had a baby.

– That school. . . . it was rubbish but them people who went there. . . . quite a few people did all right, didn't they? Like, Calvin — remember Calvin?

Leah pours out the tea, nodding fiercely. She does not remember Calvin.

– He's got a gym on the Finchley Road.

Leah spins her spoon in her tea, a drink she never takes, especially in this weather. She has pressed the bag too hard. The leaves break their borders and swarm.

25

– Not running it — *owns* it. I go past there sometimes. Never thought little Calvin would get his shit together — he was always with Jermaine and Louie and Michael. Them lot was trouble . . . I don't see none of them. Don't need the drama. Still see Nathan Bogle. Used to see Tommy and James Haven but I aint seen them recent. Not for time.

Shar keeps talking. The kitchen slants and Leah steadies herself with a hand to the sideboard.

– Sorry, what?

Shar frowns, she speaks round the lit fag in her mouth.

– I said, can I have that tea?

Together they look like old friends on a winter's night, holding their mugs with both hands. The door is open, every window is open. No air moves. Leah takes her shirt in hand and shakes it free of her skin. A vent opens, air scoots through. The sweat pooled beneath each breast leaves its shameful trace on the cotton.

– I used to know . . . I mean . . .

Leah presses on with this phony hesitation

26

and looks deep into her mug, but Shar isn't interested, she's knocking on the glass of the door, speaking over her.

– Yeah you looked different in school, definitely. You're better now innit. You was all ginger and bony. All long.

Leah is still all of these things. The change must be in other people, or in the times themselves.

– Done well, though. How come you aint at work? What d'you do again?

Shar is already nodding as Leah begins to speak.

– Phoned in sick. I wasn't feeling good. It's sort of general admin, basically. For a good cause. We hand out money. From the lottery, to charities, nonprofits — small local organizations in the community that need . . .

They are not listening to their own conversation. The girl from the estate is still out on her balcony, screaming. Shar shakes her head and whistles. She gives Leah a look of neighborly sympathy.

– Silly fat bitch.

Leah traces a knight's move from the girl

with her finger. Two floors up, one window across.

– I was born just there.

From there to here, a journey longer than it looks. For a second, this local detail holds Shar's interest. Then she looks away, ashing her cigarette on the kitchen floor, though the door is open and the grass only a foot away. She is slow, maybe, and possibly clumsy; or she is traumatized, or distracted.

– Done well. Living right. Probably got a lot of friends, out on a Friday, clubbing, all that.
– Not really.

Shar blows a short burst of smoke out of her mouth, and makes a rueful sort of sound, nodding her head over and over.

– Proper snobby, this street. You the only one let me in. Rest of them wouldn't piss on you if you was on fire.
– I've got to go upstairs. Get some money for this cab.

Leah has money in her pocket. Upstairs she walks into the nearest room, the toilet, closes the door, sits on the floor and cries. With her foot she reaches over and knocks

28

the toilet paper off its perch. She is rolling it toward her when the doorbell goes.

– DOOR! DOOR! WILL I?

Leah stands, tries to wash away the redness in the tiny sink. She finds Shar in the hallway, in front of a shelf filled with books from college, drawing her finger along the spines.

– You read all these?
– No, not really. No time nowadays.

Leah takes the key from where it sits on the middle shelf and opens the front door. Nothing makes sense. The driver who stands by the gate makes a gesture she doesn't understand, points to the other end of the street and starts walking. Shar follows. Leah follows. Leah is growing into a new meekness.

– How much do you need?

There is a shade of pity in Shar's face.

– Twenty? Thirty . . . is safe.

She smokes without hands, squeezing the vapor out of a corner of her mouth.

The manic froth of cherry blossom. Through a corridor of pink, Michel appears, walking up the street, on the other side. Too hot — his face is soaked. The little towel he keeps for days like this pokes from his bag. Leah raises a finger up in the air, a request for him to stay where he is. She points to Shar, though Shar is hidden by the car. Michel is short-sighted; he squints in their direction, stops, smiles tensely, takes his jacket off, throws it over his arm. Leah can see him plucking at his t-shirt, trying to shed the the remnants of his day: many tiny hairs, clippings from strangers, some blonde, some brown.

– Who that?
– Michel, my husband.
– Girl's name?
– French.
– Nice looking, innit — nice looking babies!

Shar winks: a grotesque compression of one side of her face.

Shar drops her cigarette and gets in the car, leaving the door open. The money remains in Leah's hand.

– He local? Seen him about.
– He works in the hairdressers, by the station? From Marseilles — he's French. Been here forever.
– African, though.
– Originally. Look — do you want me to come with you?

Shar says nothing for a moment. Then she steps out of the car and reaches up to Leah's face with both hands.

– You're a really good person. I was meant to come to your door. Seriously! You're a spiritual person. There's something spiritual inside you.

Leah grips Shar's little hand tight and submits to a kiss. Shar's mouth is slightly open on Leah's cheek for *thank* and now closes with *you.* In reply, Leah says something she has never said in her life: God bless you. They pull apart — Shar backs away awkwardly, and turns toward the car, almost gone. Leah presses the money into Shar's hand with defiance. But already the grandeur of experience threatens to flatten into the conventional, into anecdote: only thirty pounds, only an ill mother, neither a murder, nor a rape. Nothing survives its telling.

– Mental weather.

Shar uses her scarf to blot the sweat on her face, and will not look at Leah.

– Come by tomorrow. Pay you back. Swear to God, yeah? Thanks, seriously. You saved me today.

Leah shrugs.

– Nah don't be like that, I swear — I'll be there,
serious.
– I just hope she's OK. Your mum.
– Tomorrow, yeah? Thank you!

The door closes. The car pulls off.

3.

It is obvious to everyone except Leah. To her mother, it is obvious.

– How d'you get so soft?
– Seemed desperate. She was.
– I was desperate on Grafton Street and I was desperate on Buckley Road, we were all desperate. We didn't go robbing.

Static cloud of sigh. Leah can well imagine: the snowy fringe flutters, the floral bosom lifts. A well-feathered Irish owl her mother has become. Still in Willesden, perched for life.

– Thirty pounds! Thirty pounds for a taxi to The Middlesex. It's not that to Heathrow. If we're giving money away you might chuck some in this direction.
– Might still come back.
– Christ himself'll be back quicker than she will! Two of them here on the weekend. I saw them coming down the road, ringing on bells.

33

Knew them straight off. Crack. Filthy habit! See them down our end every day, by the station. Jenny Fowler on the corner opened the door to one of them — said she was high as a kite in the sky. Thirty pounds! That's your father in you. No-one who had my blood in them would fall for something so idiotic as that. What's your Michael saying?

Easier, finally, to permit *Michael* than to hear *Meeee-Shell* swill round the mouth like the taste of something dubious.

– He says I'm an idiot.
– Well that's no less than what you are. You can't con *his* people so easy.

All of them are Nigerian, all of them, even if they are French, or Algerian, they are Nigerian, the whole of Africa being, for Pauline, essentially Nigeria, and the Nigerians wily, owning those things in Kilburn that once were Irish, and five of the nurses on her own team being Nigerian where once they were Irish, or at least Pauline judges them to be Nigerian, and they're perfectly fine as long as you keep an eye on them every minute. Leah puts her thumbnail to her wedding ring. Pushes the band hard.

– He wants to go round there.
– And why shouldn't he? You were robbed on

34

your own doorstep by a gypsy, weren't you?

Everything translated into its own terms.

– Nope. Sub-continental.
– Indian, you mean by that.
– Somewhere in that region. Second genera-
tion. English, to listen to.
– I see.
– From school! Crying on my doorstep!

Another static cloud.

– Sometimes I think it's because there's just the
one of you. If we'd had more you might have
learned more about people and how people really are.

No matter where Leah attempts to begin,
Pauline returns to this point. The whole
story gets run through: from Dublin to Kilburn, a rare Prod on the wing, back when
most were of the other persuasion. Heading
for the wards, though, like the rest of the
girls. Flirted with the O'Rourke boys, the
brickies, but wanted better, being so auburn
and fine-featured and already a midwife.
Waited too long. Nested at twilight with a
quiet widower, an Englishman who didn't
drink. The O'Rourkes ended up builder's
merchants with half of Kilburn High Road
in their pockets. For which she would have

put up with a bit of drink. Thank God she retrained. (Radiography.) Where would she be otherwise? This story, once rationed, offered a few times a year, now bursts through every phone call, including this one, which has nothing at all to do with Pauline. Time is compressing for the mother, she has a short distance left to go. She means to squeeze the past into a thing small enough to take with her. It's the daughter's job to listen. She's no good at it.

– Were we too old? Were you lonely?
– Mum, please.
– I only mean you'd have a better understanding of human nature. Now, any news? On that front?
– On what front?
– On the grandma front. On the ticking clock front.
– Still ticking.
– Ah, well. Don't worry too much, love. It'll happen when it happens. Now is Michael there? Can I speak with him?

Between Pauline and Michel there exists nothing but mistrust and misunderstanding except in this blessed alignment, once rare, now more frequent, in which Leah has been an idiot and this fact forms a coalition between natural enemies. Pauline excited and pink and sweary. Michel exercising his little store of hard-won colloquial-isms, treasure of any migrant: *at the end of the day, know what I mean, and if that wasn't enough, and I says to him, and I was like, that's a good one, I'll have to remember that one.*

– Unbelievable. Wish I'd been there, Pauline, let me tell you. I wish I had been there.

To avoid listening to this conversation Leah steps into the garden. Ned from up-stairs is in her hammock, which is commu-nal and so not her hammock. Ned partaking of the herb under the apple tree. Lion hair graying now, gathered in an ignoble elastic band. An ancient Leica rests on his stomach, awaiting the sunset over NW, for the sunsets in this part of the world are strangely vivid. Leah walks up to the tree and makes the vic-tory sign.

– Buy your own.
– Quit.
– Evidently.

Ned places a smoke between her splayed fingers. She takes it in hard, harsh against the throat.

– Pace yourself. From Afghanistan. Psychotro-pic!
– I'm a big girl.

– Six twenty-three today. It's getting longer and longer.
– Until it gets shorter.
– Whoah.

Almost anything Leah says to Ned, no matter how factual or obvious, he finds philosophy in it. A serious smoker, time congeals around him. Simple things take on a stretched-out significance. It seems to Leah that he has been twenty-eight since they met, ten years ago.

– Hey, did your visitor return?
– Nope.

It goes against the grain of Ned's optimistic nature. Leah watches him fail to find a story that will fit.

– On time. Real beauty.

Leah looks up. The sky has gone pink. The Heathrow flight paths streak white against it. In the kitchen, Michel is enjoying himself.

– That's a good one. I'll have to remember that one. Jesus Christ himself!

4.

The young Sikh is bored. His turban leaks sweat. He looks down at his father's counter where a pocketful of change is trying to add up to ten Rothmans. A cheap fan whirrs pointlessly. Leah is also bored, watching Michel squeeze pastries that will never please him, that will never be as good as they were in France. This is because they are made in the back of a sweetshop, off Willesden Lane. Real croissants may be purchased from the organic market, on a Sunday, in the playground of Leah's old school. Today is Tuesday. From her new neighbours Leah has learned that Quinton Primary is a good enough place to buy a croissant but not a good enough place to send your children. Olive hoovers up the crumbs from the sweetshop floor. Olive is somewhat French, like Michel. Her grandfather was a champion in Paris. Unlike Michel she is not fussy about croissant. Orange and white, with silky Restoration ears. Ridiculous, adored.

– and need to see a proper doctor. A clinic. We keep trying. And nothing. You're thirty-five this year.

Said Frenchly: nussing. Once they were the same age. Now Leah is aging in dog years. Her thirty-five is seven times his, and seven times more important, so important he has to keep reminding her of the numbers, in case she forgets.

– We can't afford clinics. What clinic?

The small figure at the counter turns. She smiles at Leah first before anything else — out of the instinct that pairs recognition with happiness — and then a moment later, remembering, bites her lip and puts her hand to the door, making the little bell ring.

– That's her. That was her. Buying the fags.

Leah expects a clean escape. Shar is out of luck. They both are. An elderly woman of dimension heads in as Shar attempts to leave. They do the awkward doorway dance. Michel is quick and bold and can't be stopped.

– Thief! You're a thief! Where's our money?

Leah grips the finger that's pointing and pulls it down. Each red freckle has flared and a flush is working up her neck, flooding her face. Shar stops dancing. Shoulder-charges the old dear out the way. Runs.

5.

Leah believes in objectivity in the bedroom:
Here lie a man and a woman. The man
is more beautiful than the woman. And for
this reason there have been times when the
woman has feared that she loves the man
more than he loves her. He has always denied this. He can't deny that he is more
beautiful. It is easier for him to be beautiful.
His skin is very dark and ages more slowly.
He has good West African bone structure.
Here is a man lying across a bed, naked.
Brigitte Bardot in *Contempt* lay on a bed,
naked. If only the man were like Brigitte
Bardot, who never had children, preferring
animals. Then again, she became inflex-
ible in other areas. The woman tries to talk
to the man who is her husband about the
desperate girl who came to the door. What
does it means to say the girl lied? Is it a lie
to say she was desperate? She was desperate
enough to come to the door. The husband

can't understand the woman's preoccupation. Of course, he is missing a vital piece of information. There is no way for him to follow the submerged, feminine logic. He can only try to listen as she speaks. I just want to know if I did the right thing, says the woman, I just can't work out if I

But here the man stops her to say

– the plug for the thing on your side? Mine's gone. But there's nothing to do. It's the usual. A crackhead. A thief. It's not so interesting. Come here, and

When they met, the man and the woman, the physical attraction was immediate and overwhelming. This is still the case. Because of this unusual, acute attraction, their chronology is peculiar. The physical came first, always.

Before he spoke to her he had already washed her hair, twice.

They had sex before either knew the other's surname.

They had anal sex before they had vaginal sex.

They had dozens of sexual partners before they married each other. Dance floor romances, Ibiza flings. The nineties, ecstatic decade! They were married though they needn't have married, and though both

43

had sworn they never would be. It is hard to explain — in that game of musical chairs — why they should have stopped, finally, at each other. Kindness, as a quality, had something to do with it. Many things were easy to find on those dance floors, but kindness was rare. Her husband was kinder than any man Leah Hanwell had ever known, aside from her father. And then of course they had been surprised by their own conventionality. The marriage pleased Pauline. It calmed the anxieties of Michel's family. It was pleasing to please their families. Beyond this, the proper names "wife" and "husband" had a power neither party had expected. If it was voodoo, they were grateful for it. It allowed them to stop dancing round chairs without ever admitting they were tired of it.

Things moved quickly.

They had one pregnancy before they married, two months into their relationship, which they terminated.

They were married before they were friends, which is another way of saying:

Their marriage was the occasion of their friendship.

They were married before they noticed many small differences in background, aspiration, education, ambition. There is a difference between the ambitions of the poor of the city and the poor of the country, for example.

Noting such differences, Leah was in some sense disappointed in herself that they did not cause real conflict between them. It was hard to get used to the fact that the pleasure her body found in his, and vice versa, should so easily overrule the many other objections she had, or should have had, or thought she should have had.

– Her mum could be dead. She could be dealing with that and just forgot. She might have put it through the door and it gets caught up with the junk and Ned throws it out. Maybe she just can't put her hands on that sort of money at the moment.
– Yes, Leah.
– Don't do that.
– What do you want me to say? The world is what it is.
– Then why're we even trying?

To be very objective about it, it is the woman's fault that they never discussed children. For some reason it had never occurred to her that all this wondrous screwing was heading toward a certain, perfectly obvious destination. She fears the destination. Be objective! What is the fear? It is something to do with death and time and age. Simply: I am eighteen in my mind I am eighteen and if I do nothing if I stand still nothing will change I will be eighteen always. For always. Time will stop. I'll never die. Very banal, this fear. Everybody has it these days. What else? She is happy enough in the moment they are in. She feels she deserves exactly what she has, no more, no less. Any change risks fatally upsetting this balance. Why must the moment change? Sometimes the woman's husband cuts a red pepper down the middle and pushes the seeds out into a plastic bowl and passes her a courgette for cubing and says:

Dog.
Car.
Flat.
Cooking together, like this.
Seven years ago: you were on the dole.
I was washing hair.
Things change! We're getting there, no?

The woman does not know where there is. She did not know they had set off, nor in which direction the wind is blowing. She does not want to arrive. The truth is she had believed they would be naked in these sheets forever and nothing would come to them ever, nothing but satisfaction. Why must love "move forward"? Which way is forward? No one can say she has not been warned. No one can say that. A thirty-five-year-old woman married to a man she loves has most certainly been warned, should be paying attention, should be listening, and not be at all surprised when her husband says

– many days in which the woman is fertile. Only, I think, three. So it's no good to just say "oh, it'll happen when it will happen." We're not so young. So we have to be a bit more, I mean, military about it, like plan.

Objectively speaking, he is correct.

6.

We are the village green preservation society. God save little shops, china cups and
virginity! Saturday morning. ALL KINKS
ALL DAY. Girl. You really got me going.
You got me so I don't know what I'm doing.
On Saturday mornings Michel helps the
ladies and gentlemen of NW look right for
their Saturday nights, look fresh and correct, and there, in the salon, he is free to
blast his treacly R&B, his oh baby oh shorty
till six in the mawnin till the break a' dawn.
On Saturday mornings she is free! God save
Tudor houses, antique tables and billiards!
Preserving the old ways from being abused.
Protecting the new ways for me and for you.
What more can we do? Stomping around in
pajama bottoms, singing tunelessly. Ned is
in the garden. Ned approves of loud music
of white origin. He sings along. Well I tried
to settle down in Fulham Broadway. And I
tried to make my home in Golders Green.

In this weekend abandon there is always something manic and melancholy: the internal countdown to the working week already begun. In the mirror she is her own dance partner, nose to nose with the reflection. The physical person is smiling and singing. Oh how I miss the folks back home in Willesden Green! Meanwhile something inside reels at the mirror's news: the gray streak coming out of the crown, the puffy creases round the eyes, the soft belly. She dances like a girl. She is not a girl anymore. YOU REALLY GOT ME. YOU REALLY GOT ME. YOU REALLY GOT ME. Where did the time go? She only realizes the doorbell has gone when Olive begins barking madly.

– My mum had a heart — a heart attack? Five . . . pounds.

This girl has hair burned flat by a curling iron. Either fat or pregnant. She looks down dully, puzzled by frantic Olive weaving between her legs. She looks up at Leah and laughs. HA! Too far gone to remember her lines. She turns clumsily on her heel, a dancer executing a move too late. Heads back down the path to the street, swaying and laughing.

7.

Apple tree, apple tree.

Thing that has apples on it. Apple blossom.

So symbolic. Network of branches, roots.

Tunneling under.

The fuller, the more fruitful.

The more the worms. The

more the rats.

Apple tree, apple tree. Which way is

Apple. Tree. forward? Tick, tock.

Three flats. One apple tree. Freehold, leasehold.

Heavy with seed.

In the tree-top. When the bough breaks,

the baby will

Dead man's ashes. Round the roots,

in the roots?

Hundred-year-old apple tree.

Sitting on your laurens.

Under an apple   tree. Have a *little* boy?

New branches. New blossom.   New apples.

Same tree?

Born and bred. Same streets.

Same girl? Next step.

Appletreeapple

Trunk, bark.

Alice, dreaming.

Eve, eating.

Under which nice girls make mistakes.

Michel is a good man, full of hope. Sometimes hope is exhausting.

– which I've always believed. Look: you know what is the true difference between these people and me? They don't want to move forward, they don't want to have nothing better than this. But I'm always moving forward, thinking of the next thing. People back home, they don't get me at all. I'm too advanced for them. So when they try to contact me, I don't let this — I don't let drama in my life like that. No way! I've worked too hard. I love you too much, this life. You are what you do. This is how it is. I'm always thinking: is this me? What I'm doing? Is this really me? If I sit and do nothing I know

51

that makes me nothing. From the first day I was stepping into this country I have my head on correctly; I was very clear: I am going up the ladder, one rung at least. In France, you're African, you're Algerian, who wants to know? There's no opportunity, you can't move! Here, you can move. You still have to work! You have to work very hard to separate yourself from this drama below! This is my point: I don't like to let it in. But this is what *you* do, perfect example, this girl, *you* let her in — I don't even know what is in your mind — but I don't allow this drama in. I know this country has opportunities if you want to grab them, you can do it. Don't eat that one — worm hole, right there, see? Look at your mother — we are not such great friends, but please look at what she did: she got you out of that nightmare over there, into a proper place, proper flat, mortgage . . . Of course, your skin is white, it's different, it's more easy, you've had opportunities I didn't have. The redder ones don't taste so good. We're all just trying to take that next, that next, next, *step*. Climbing that ladder. *Brent Housing Partnership.* I don't want to have this written on the front of a place where I am living. I walk past it I feel like *oof* — it's humiliating to me. If we ever have a little boy I want him to live somewhere — to live *proud* — somewhere we have the freehold. Right! This grass it's not my grass! This tree is not my tree! We scattered your father round this tree we don't own even. Poor Mr. Hanwell. It breaks my heart. This was your father! This is why I'm on the laptop every night, I'm trying to do this — because it's pure market on there, nothing about skin, about is your English perfect, do you have the right piece of university paper or some bullshit like this. I can trade like anyone. There's money to be got out there, you know? Market is so crazy right now. That's what nobody tell you. I keep thinking what Frank said at the dinner: *the smart guys get right back in the game.* It's crazy not to try to get some of it. I'm not like these Jamaicans — this new girl, Gloria, whatever is her name, up there, she still has no curtains. Two babies, no husband, taking benefits. I'm married, where's my benefit? When I have children, I knew, I said it to myself: I'm going to stay by this woman that I love, that I really love so much, I'm going to always be with her. Come here. The bottom line is like this: I was never just OK to sit on my laurens and take charity, I never was interested in that. I am an African. I have a destiny. I love you, and I love where we are going together! I'm always moving toward my destiny, thinking of the next achievement, the next thing, taking it higher, so we, so *both of us,* can make that next–

– Laurels.

– What?

– Laurels. And you rest on them, you don't sit on them. You sit on your arse.

– You're not even listening.

It's true: she is thinking of apples.

53

8.

Elsewhere in London, offices are open plan/ floor-to-ceiling glass/sites of synergy/wireless/gleaming. There persists a belief in the importance of a ping-pong table. Here is not there. Here offices are boxy cramped Victorian damp. Five people share them, the carpet is threadbare, the hole-punch will never be found.

– of money coming in. Question: how did this get so far down the line without intervention? I'd really like to know. Checks and balances, people! Because when you do it like this you're handing our heads metaphorically on a plate, to them, meaning my head also. And the next thing you hear: efficiency savings. Not meaning reusing the teabags. Meaning your job and mine. Which is exactly how

Here a nation's bad bets morph into a semblance of the collective good: after-school play groups, translation services, garden

clearance for the elderly, quilting for pris-
oners. Five women work here, their backs
to each other. Further down the hall, the
rumor of a man — Leah has never seen
him. This work requires empathy and so at-
tracts women, for women are the empathic
sex. This is the opinion of Adina George,
Team Leader, who speaks, who will not stop
speaking. Adina's mouth opens and closes.

Tooth gold tooth tooth gap tooth
tooth tooth
TONGUE
Tooth tooth tooth tooth chipped
tooth filling

Former prison guard, social worker, local
councilor. How did she get anything done
with those talons? Long and curved and
painted with miniature renderings of the
Jamaican flag. Clawed her way up through
the system. Born and bred. Is wary of those,
like Leah, whose degrees have thus installed
them. To Adina a university degree is like
a bungee cord, lowering in and pulling out
with dangerous velocity. Of course, you
won't be here long. Look, I don't want to
give you projects you're not going to be here
to finish . . .
Six years have gone by: such things aren't

55

said anymore. It occurred to Leah today, when Adina referred to her as "the graduate," that no-one — not the institution that conferred it, not her peers, not the job market itself — has a higher estimation of the value of her degree than Adina.

– which is essential for the smooth running here. The decision-making is obviously about relatability and yeah, empathy, and a personal connection but it's also about follow-through and visibility in the sense of value for money, that we get to be conscious of via a process of paperwork. Paperworkpaperworkpaperwork. In the current climate every i has to be dotted and every t crossed so when I am put in a position, as Team Leader, by the people upstairs I can say: yup, fully accountable. Here's x, y and z, fully accountable. Not splitting the atom, ladies, I should hope.

Question: what happened to her classmates, those keen young graduates, most of them men? Bankers, lawyers. Meanwhile Leah, a state-school wild card, with no Latin, no Greek, no Maths, no foreign language, did badly — by the standards of the day — and now sits on a replacement chair borrowed six years ago from the break-room, just flooded with empathy. Right foot asleep. Computer screen frozen. IT nowhere to be seen. No air-conditioning. Adina going on and on, doing that thing to language that she does.

– This was a question of communication? A blockage between parties. Who should have a tighter grasp on how their behaviors are impacting others?

This too will pass. Four forty-five. Zig, zag. Tick. Tock. Sometimes bitterness makes a grab for Leah. Pulls her down, holds her. What was the point of it all? Three years of useless study. Out of pocket, out of her depth. It was only philosophy in the first place because she was scared of dying and thought it might help and because she could not add or draw or remember lists of facts or speak a language other than her own. In the university prospectus, an italic script over a picture of the Firth of Forth: *Philosophy is learning how to die.* Philosophy is listening to warbling posh boys, it is being more bored than you have ever been in your life, more bored than you thought it possible to be. It is wishing yourself anywhere else, in a different spot somewhere in the multiverse which is a concept you will never truly understand. In the end, only one idea reliably retained: time as a relative experience, different for the jogger, the lover, the tortured, the leisured. Like right now, when a minute seems to stretch itself into an hour. Otherwise use-less. An unpaid, growing debt. Along with a feeling of resentment: what was the purpose of preparing for a life never intended for her? Years too disconnected from everything else to feel real. Edinburgh's dour hill-climb and unexpected-alley, castle-shadow and fifty pence whisky chaser, WalterScottStone and student loan shopping. Out of her mouth: a two-syllable packing company Socrates, a three-syllable cleaning fluid Antigone. Never, never forgotten: the bastard in that first class, sniggering. I AM SO FULL OF EMPATHY, Leah writes, and doodles pas-sionately around it. Great fiery arcs, long pointed shadows.

– Questions? Problems?

A pen breaks noisily. Plastic shards, a blue tongue. Adina George looks over and glares but Leah is not responsible for the Albanians. She has a mouth full of pen but she is not responsible for the Albanians nor their misappropriation of funds meant for a Hackney women's refuge. That was on Claire Morgan's watch. Although Leah has a blue tongue and a fancy degree and a hot husband and no offense, but for the women in our community, in the Afro-Caribbean community, no offense, but when we see one of our lot with someone like you it's a real issue. It's just a real issue that you should be aware of. No offense. (Brighton weekend, team-building exercise, hotel bar, 2004.) What kind of issue exactly was never made clear. *Sweet Love* sang Anita Baker, and Adina fell over a chair trying to get to the dance floor. Blockage.

Leah spits plastic shards into her hands. No questions or problems. Adina sighs, leaves. The folder-shutting and bag-packing begin with an eagerness no different from when they were all six years old and the bell rang. Maybe that was the real life? Leah plants her feet on the ground and pushes back in her chair. Lifts and coasts to the filing cabinet and this is the most enjoyable thing that has happened today. Bump.

– Oi! Fuckssake, Leah. Careful!

The great swell of it. Leah is nose to Tori's belly-button and observes how this innermost thing now thrusts out, marking a physical limit. Beyond this point we can't continue and be human.

– Just be careful. You coming or what? Last day drinks. You got the e-mail?

Piled up in a corner of the Internet with

the bank statements, student loan remind-
ers, memos from management, maternal
epics, in that place where not to be opened
is not to exist. She knew perfectly well there
was an e-mail and what it was about, but she
is on the run from people in Tori's condition. She is on the run from herself.

– Me, Claire, Kelly, Beverley, Shweta. You're
next!

Tori counts the names off on swollen fingers. She's in the final stages. Her face has
a leonine cast, the cheeks puffed up, newly
prominent. A big cat's smile. Predacious.
Leah stares at the thumb meant to represent
her.

– Trying. It's not so easy.
– Trying's half the fun.

A room full of women laughing. Some
shared knowledge of their sex to which Leah
is not party. She puts her hands either side of
the bump, and smiles, hoping that this is the
sort of thing that normal women do, women
for whom trying is half the fun and "you're
next" does not sound like the cry of a guard
in a dark place. Then they get going, a traditional round in which no voice is separated
from the other and Leah lays her head on

the desk and closes her eyes and lets them take the piss:

Specially when he looks like yours. And he's so lovely.

He's so lovely your Meeshell. Lovely way about him.

Bev, d'you remember when we was round Leah's that time and my car window weren't working and Meeshell got on his knees with a wire coat hanger? After I'd been telling Leon about it for a MONTH.

He's proper sensitive. Proper family orientated.

Whenever I'm thinking: where did all the good brothers get to? I think, breathe: at least there's Meeshell.

Yeah but they're all already taken!

HAHAHAHAHAHAHA   By the white girls!

Nah, don't be like that. Leah she's only messing with you.

Don't mess with Leah! Not her fault Leon's a useless bastard.

Leon's all right.

(Bloody useless. "Leon, what you doing tonight? "Chillin with my man dem." He's always bloody "chillin.")

Leon's all right.   Seriously tho, you're lucky.

She gets a blow dry thrown in!

A man *who can do your hair*. That's paradise right there. He can do cain row, he can do extensions . . .

Kelly, what she need cain row for? She's not Bo Derek.

HA!   (Nah, Leah, no offense —
                       sorry that's funny tho.)

I'm talking about he's a professional. I'm talking about
he can do any kind of hair.
And he's straight. Innit!

Innit!   Hahaha   Innit, yeah. (He best be!)

That's what kills me! Best of both worlds! You have
though. You don't know you're born.

She doesn't, she doesn't know she's born.

You don't know you're born.

You don't. You don't know you're born.

Finally, five o'clock. Leah looks up. Kelly
slaps the top of her desk.

– Quittin' time!

Same joke every day. A joke you can make
if you are not Leah, if you are not the only
white girl on the Fund Distribution Team.
In the corridor the women spill out of every
room, into the heat, cocoa buttered, ready
for a warm night out on the Edgware Road.
From St. Kitts, Trinidad, Barbados, Gre-
nada, Jamaica, India, Pakistan, in their for-
ties, fifties, sixties, and yet busts and butts
and shiny legs and arms still open to the

sexiness of an early summer in a manner that the women of Leah's family can never be. For them the sun is fatal. So red, so pale. Leah is wearing long white linen everything. Looks like a minor saint. She falls in step. Passes the scene of the crime, a wastepaper bin filled with vomit and tucked behind a pot-plant in the break room because the bathroom was too far.

9.

From A to B:

A. Yates Lane, London NW8, UK

B. Bartlett Avenue, London NW6, UK

Walking directions to Bartlett Avenue, London NW6, UK
Suggested routes

A5	**47 mins**
2.4 miles	
A5 and Salusbury Rd	**50 mins**
2.5 miles	
A404/Harrow Rd	**58 mins**
2.8 miles	

Turn **left** on Yates Lane	40 feet
Head **southwest** toward	
Edgware Rd	315 feet
Turn **right** at **A5/**	
Edgware Rd	1.6 miles
Continue to follow A5	

Turn **left** at
A4003/Willesden Ln   0.7 mile
Turn **left** at **Bartlett Avenue**   0.1 mile

Destination will be on the left
Bartlett Avenue, London NW6, UK

These directions are for planning purposes only. You may find that construction projects, traffic, weather, or other events may cause conditions to differ from the map results, and you should plan your route accordingly. You must obey all signs or notices regarding your route.

10.

From A to B redux:

Sweet stink of the hookah, couscous, kebab, exhaust fumes of a bus deadlock. 98, 16, 32, standing room only — quicker to walk! Escapees from St. Mary's, Paddington: expectant father smoking, old lady wheeling herself in a wheelchair smoking, die-hard holding urine sack, blood sack, smoking. Everybody loves fags. Everybody. Polish paper, Turkish paper, Arabic, Irish, French, Russian, Spanish, News of the World. Unlock your (stolen) phone, buy a battery pack, a lighter pack, a perfume pack, sunglasses, three for a fiver, a life-size porcelain tiger, gold taps. Casino! Everybody believes in destiny. Everybody. It was meant to be. It was just not meant to be. Deal or no deal? TV screens in the TV shop. TV cable, computer cable, audio-visual cables, I give you good price, good price. Leaflets, call abroad 4 less, learn English, eyebrow wax, Falun Gong, have you accepted Jesus as your personal call plan? Everybody loves fried chicken. Everybody. Bank of Iraq, Bank of Egypt, Bank of Libya. Empty cabs on account of the sunshine. Boom-boxes just because. Lone Italian, loafers, lost, looking for Mayfair. A hundred and one ways to take cover: the complete black tent, the facial grid, back of the head, Louis Vuitton–stamped, Gucci-stamped, yellow lace, attached to sunglasses, hardly on at all, striped, candy pink; paired with tracksuits, skin-tight jeans, summer dresses, blouses, vests, gypsy skirts, flares. Bearing no relation to the debates in the papers, in parliament. Everybody loves sandals. Everybody. Birdsong! Lowdown dirty shopping arcade to mansion flats to an Englishman's home is his castle. Open top, soft-top, drive-by, hip hop. Watch the money pile up. Holla! Security lights, security gates, security walls, security trees, Tudor, Modernist, postwar, prewar, stone pineapples, stone lions, stone eagles. Face east and dream of Regent's Park, of St. John's Wood. The Arabs, the Israelis, the Russians, the Americans: here united by the furnished penthouse, the private clinic. If we pay enough, if we squint, Kilburn need not exist. Free meals. English as a second language. Here is the school where they stabbed the headmaster. Here is the Islamic Center of England opposite the Queen's Arms. Walk down the middle of this, you referee, you! Everybody loves the Grand National. Everybody. Is it really only April? And they're off!

11.

So close to home, just on Willesden Lane. Strange convergence. She is leaning into a broken phone box, chewing the stick of an ice-lolly. Thick shattered glass, cuboid shards, all around. A few yards from Cleopatra's Massage Emporium. Leah opens her eyes wide to store the details for Michel, which is one of the things marriage means. Drawn to the wrong details. Baggy gray track bottoms, off-white sports bra. Nothing else, no top. No shoes! Breasts small and tight to her body. It's difficult to believe that she has had children. Perhaps that was a lie as well. A neat waist you want to hold. She is something beautiful in the sunshine, something between a boy and a girl, reminding Leah of a time in her own life when she had not yet been called upon to make a final decision about all that. Desire is never final, desire is imprecise and impractical: you are walking toward her, at great speed you are walking toward her, and then what? And then what? Leah is quite close before she is spotted in return. It's been three weeks. Shar drops the receiver and tries to cross the road. The traffic is rush hour frantic. At first Leah is grateful to be without Michel. Then her face turns into his face and his voice comes out of her throat or this is a marital excuse and it is her own voice in her own throat:

– Proud of yourself? *Thief.* I want my money.

Shar cringes and slips through the traffic. She is running toward two men, tall and hooded, with hidden faces, standing in a doorway. Shar enfolds herself in the taller. Leah hurries on home. At her back she can hear the ricochet of incomprehensible abuse, aimed at her, a patois like a machine gun.

37

Lying in bed next to a girl she loved, years ago, discussing the number 37. Dylan singing. The girl had a theory that 37 has a magic about it, we're compelled toward it. Websites are dedicated to the phenomenon. The imagined houses found in cinema, fiction, painting and poetry — almost always 37. Asked to choose a number at random: usually 37. Watch for 37, the girl said, in our lotteries, our game-shows, our dreams and jokes, and Leah did, and Leah still does. Remember me to one who lives there. She once was a true love of mine. Now that girl is married, too.

Number 37 Ridley Avenue is being squat. Squatted? The front door is boarded up. A window is broken. Human noise from behind torn gray nets. Leah moves from the shadow of a hedge to the forecourt. Nobody spots her. Nothing happens. She stands with one foot hovering off the ground. What would she do with 37 lives! She has one life: she is en route to her mother's, they are going shopping for a sofa. If she stands here staring much longer she will be late. In the front bay window: Mickey, Donald, Bart, a nameless bear, an elephant with its trunk ripped off. Fabric faces against dirty glass.

12.

– You took your time. Feeling OK? You look a bit peaky. We'll take the Jubilee, will we?

Pauline steps out of her front door back-ward pulling a tartan shopping bag on wheels. Always a little older than expected. Smaller, too. From the street it must look like human perfectibility: each generation im-proves upon the last. Fitter, healthier, more productive. From the owl rises the phoenix. Or rise only to descend again? Longer and longer until it's shorter.

– Worried about you. You seem all through yourself.
– I'm fine.
– And if you weren't you wouldn't tell.

What's to tell? On the look-out for her, still, almost a month later. Expecting her out of this shop, from behind this corner, by that phone box. The girl is more real to Leah in

her absence than the barely signifying bump
that is with her all the time, albeit hidden by
a sweatshirt.

– I've only this blouse on and I'm sweating like
a pig already. It's not natural.

The Hindu Temple has the colours of a
block of Neapolitan ice cream and is essentially the same shape. A block of Neapolitan
ice cream with two upturned cones at either
end. Old Hindus stream down the front
steps, unconvinced by the warm spell. They
wear their saris with jumpers and cardi-
gans and thick woolly socks. They look like
they have walked to Willesden from Delhi,
adding layers of knitwear as they progress
northwards. Now they move as one to the
nearest bus stop, a crowd that takes in Leah
and her mother, carrying them along.

– That's lucky. We'll hop on. Save time.
– Anyone over the age of thirty catching a bus
can consider himself a failure.
– Sugar, I've left my pass! What's that, love?
– Thatcher. Back in the day.
– One for Kilburn tube, please. Two pounds!
She was a terrible cow. You can't remember,
I remember. Today this is Brent. Tomorrow it
could be Britain!
– Mum, sit there. I'll sit here. There's no space.
– Front of *The Mail*. Today this is Brent. To-

morrow it could be Britain! The cheek of some people. The rudeness of them.

Sat opposite, Leah stares at a red bindi until it begins to blur, becomes enormous, taking up all of her vision until she feels she has entered the dot, passing through it, emerging into a more gentle universe, parallel to our own, where people are fully and intimately known to each other and there is no time or death or fear or sofas or

– and may have had our differences, but he loves you. And you love him. You should get on with it. Council's set you up very nicely really, you've a little car, you've both got jobs. It's the next thing.

You're next. It's the next thing. Next stop Kilburn Station. The doors fold inwards, urban insect closing its wings. A covered girl on her mobile phone steps on as they step off and disturbs the narrative by laughing and dropping her aitches and wearing makeup but Pauline is anyway compelled to say what she always says, with elegant variation, depending on the news cycle.

– Just two people kissing, this is Dubai — facing twelve years each. It's just not permitted, you see. It's ever so sad.

But this sadness is quickly outstripped by another, more local, sadness. A dirty gypsy girl and a tall fella doing the herky-jerky dance by the self-service machines. Pauline breathes on Leah's ear.

– I'm grateful no child of mine ever did any of that.

A quick parade of past delights flicks through Leah's mind, the memory of which is almost intolerably pleasurable: white and brown, natural and chemical, pills and powder.

– I don't see that there's anything funny about it. Ach, I can't believe I left it at home. I always have it in this pocket.
– Wasn't laughing at that.

Travelcardtravelcardtravelcard.

– What's she saying, poor love?
– Selling their travelcards, I think.

Very sad, but also an opportunity for a saving. Pauline reaches up to tap the fella on his shoulder.

– How many zones? How much do you want for it?
– One day travelcard. Six zones. Two pound.
– Two pounds! How do I know it's not some fake?

– *Mum.* It's got the date on it, Jesus!
– I'll give a pound, no more.
– All right, Mrs. Hanwell.

Look up. A jolting form of time travel, moving in two directions: imposing the child on this man, this man on the child. One familiar, one unknown. The afro of the man is uneven and has a tiny gray feather in it. The clothes are ragged. One big toe thrusts through the crumby rubber of an ancient red stripe Nike Air. The face is far older that it should be, even given the nasty way time has with human materials. He has an odd patch of white skin on his neck. Yet the line of beauty has not been entirely broken.

– Nathan?
– All right Mrs. Hanwell.

Good to see Pauline flustered, the sweaty tips of her hair curling up her face.

– Well how are you, Nathan?
– Surviving.

The shakes. Been sliced, deeply, on his cheek, not long ago. It's an open, frank face, still. Not pretending anything. Which makes it all much harder.

– How's your mother, your sisters? You remem-

ber Leah. She's married now.
– Is it. That's good, yeah.

He smiles shyly at Leah. Aged ten he had a smile! Nathan Bogle: the very definition of desire for girls who had previously only felt that way about certain fragrant erasers. A smile to destroy the resolve of even the strictest teachers, other people's parents. At ten she would have done anything, anything! Now she sees ten-year-olds and cannot believe they have inside them what she had inside her at the same age.

– Long time.
– Yes.

Longer for him. About once a year she sees him on the high road. She ducks into a shop, or crosses, or gets on a bus. Now missing a tooth here and there and there. Devastated eyes. What should be white is yellow. Red veins breaking out all over.

– Here's that pound. You take care of yourself now. Remember me to your mother.

Quickly through the barrier, bumping into each other in their haste, and then quickly up the stairs.

– That was horrible.

78

– His poor mother! I should stop in on her one of these days. So sad. I'd heard, but I hadn't seen it with my own eyes.

The train pulls in and Leah watches Pauline regard it calmly, step forward to the yellow line. This realm of Pauline's — the realm of the so sad — is immutable and inevitable, like hurricanes and tsunamis. No particular angst is attached to it. Normally, this is bearable; today it is obscene. So sad is too distant from Pauline's existence, which is only disappointing. It makes disappointing look like a blessing. This must be why news of it is always so welcome, so satisfying.

– You carried a torch for him, I remember. Went inside for a few years, later on, I think. He's not the one who killed somebody, now, no, that was somebody else. Sectioned, was he? At one point? Beat his father to a pulp, that much I'm sure of. Though that man had it coming or something like it.

Leah lifts two free papers from the pile as the train pulls out because reading is silent. She tries to read an article. It is about an actress walking her dog in a park. But Pauline wants to read an article about a man who was not really who he said he was, and she wants to talk about it, too.

– Well, if you will claim to be infallible! Say what you like about our lot but least we don't claim to be infallible. Men of God, are they? Those poor children. Lives ruined. And they call it religion! Well, let's hope that's an end to the whole business once and for all.

Seeing as how they are speaking to the whole carriage, Leah mounts a mild defense, thinking of the smell of the censer, the voluptuous putti babies, the gold sunburst, cold marble floor, dark wood carved and plaited, women kneeling whispering lighting candles InterRailing nineteen ninety-three.

– Wish we had confession. Wish I could confess.
– Oh grow up, Leah, will you?

Pauline turns the page with violence. The window logs Kilburn's skyline. Ungentrified, ungentrifiable. Boom and bust never come here. Here bust is permanent. Empty State Empire, empty Odeon, graffiti-streaked sidings rising and falling like a rickety rollercoaster. Higgledy piggledy rooftops and chimneys, some high, some low, packed tightly, shaken fags in a box. Behind the opposite window, retreating Willesden. Number 37. In the 1880s or thereabouts the whole thing went up at once — houses, churches, schools, cemeteries — an optimistic vision of Metroland. Little terraces, faux-Tudor piles. All the mod cons! Indoor toilet, hot water. Well-appointed country living for those tired of the city. Fast forward. Disappointed city living for those tired of their countries.

– Vol-can-ic air-borne ash man-i-fest-a-tion?

Pauline enunciates each syllable carefully, doubtful of its reality, and brings the photo too close to her daughter's nose. Leah can make out only a great swirl of gray. Maybe this is all there is to see. The matter is also discussed by the hipsters opposite. *Gaia's revenge,* says the girl to the boy. *Give it out long enough you get it back.* Pauline, always alive to the possibility of a group conversation, leans forward.

– No fruit or veg in the shops, they're saying. Makes sense if you think about it. Of course, it's an island we're on here. I always forget that, don't you?

13.

– Finished with the computer?
– Need to wait till they close.
– It's almost seven o'clock? I need it.
– It's not seven online. Why don't you get on with your own things?
– That's what I need it for.
– Leah, I'll call you when I'm done.

Currency trading. The exploitation of volatility. She can only understand words, not numbers. The words are ominous. Add them to that look Michel has, right now, of arrested attention. Internal time stretched and stilled, inattentive to the minutes and hours outside of itself. Five minutes! He says it irritably whether thirty have gone by or a hundred or two hundred. Pornography does that, too. Art, too, so they say.

Leah stands behind Michel in the darkness of the box room. Blue shimmer of the screen. He is two feet away. He is on the other side of the world. Why don't you get on with your own things?

She has the idea that there are a lot of things she has been waiting for weeks to do and now she will do them with the bright quickness of montage, like the middle section of a movie. In the living room the TV is on. More blue light in the hallway. In the box room, the computer plays angry hip hop, a sign that things are going badly. Sometimes she says to him: have you lost it? He becomes furious, he says it doesn't work that way. Some days I lose, some days I win. How can he be losing or winning that same eight thousand pounds, over and over? Leah's only inheritance from Hanwell, their only savings. The money itself has become notional, a notion materialist Hanwell — who kept his real paper money in a cardboard box in a mahogany credenza — would never understand. No more does Leah understand it. She sits on a chair in the open doorway between kitchen and garden. Toes in the grass. The skies are empty and silent. Outrage travels from next-door's talk radio: It's taken me fifty-two hours to get back from Singapore! A new old lesson about time. Broccoli comes from Kenya. Blood must be transported. Soldiers need supplies. Much of the better part of NW went on holiday, for Easter, with their little darlings.

Maybe they will never return. A thought to float away on.

Ned clonks down the wrought-iron steps, looking up at the sky.

– Really weird.
– I like it. I like the quiet.
– Freaks me out. Like *Cocoon.*
– Not really.
– Town was totally empty. Arbus at the Portrait Gallery with no crowds. Awesome. Real experience.

Leah submits to Ned's long, excited description. She envies his enthusiasm for the city. He does not pass his time with his ex-countrymen in their suburban enclaves, cracking beers, watching the rugby: he does everything to avoid them. Admirable. Exploring the city alone, seeking out gigs and talks and screenings and exhibitions, far-off parks and mystery Lidos. Leah, born and bred, never goes anywhere.

– is really about integrity of like a, like a, like an idea? Blew me away. Anyway. I'm starving. Gonna go up and make myself some pasta and pesto. Listen, I'll leave you a couple to be getting on with.

He sets three on the window sill, pre-rolled. She looks at them lined up in the flat of her palm. She smokes the first quickly, to the orange cardboard butt. Olive chases rustlings through shadows. Then the second. The upstairs windows are open: Gloria screaming at her children. You nah listen! Me nah got all day to tell you da same damn ting over and over! Leah calls to Olive, who comes lolloping. Leah scoops her in both arms. Shammy leather skin. Vulnerable little ribcage with a gap for every finger. Wrong to love a dog so much, says Michel, who has wrung the necks of chicken, slit the throat of a goat. Olive's throat between Leah's hands — how could a child be held with any more tenderness? Post-Olive it is easy to believe in consciousness of animals. Even the bubble-breathing crabs in the fishmonger's have taken on a tragic aspect. Yet she eats them all, still. What a monster she is. Don't let me come over dere and box you! She smokes the third.

It gets dark slowly, then suddenly. Fairy lights wrapped student-wise in the apple tree. Contact lenses so dry it's hard to see. Beyond the tree, the fence, the railway, Willesden. Number 37. It is from this direction that her father walks toward her. He comes no closer than Ned's failed rosebush. He wears a hat.

How's your little dog, he asks.

Leah finds she can answer him without opening her mouth. She tells him about all the things Olive has been up to since he died, last November, every little thing, all the little things! Even the dullest detail of the dog's day entertains him. He says, dear oh dear, and brushes the crumbs off his ratty blue cardie, chuckling. He is dressed exactly as they dressed him in Morehurst, except this trilby she's never seen before, which is the only word Leah knows for the old style of hats. He has a white stain on his thigh, like semen, crusty in a ridge of his faded brown cords that no one has bothered to clean. Those pretty Ukrainian nurses who never stayed long.

Behind here it's nothing but bleedin' foxes, says Hanwell, sadly.

It's really an epidemic. That is, they were always there, in the same numbers as they are now, but now it is called an epidemic. A recent headline in *The Standard,* NORTH-WEST FOX EPIDEMIC, and a photograph of a man kneeling in a garden surrounded by the corpses of foxes he'd shot. Dozens and dozens and dozens of them. Dozens and dozens! says Leah, and that's how we live now, defending our own little patch, it didn't used to be like that, but everything's changed, hasn't it, that's what they say, everything's changed. Colin Hanwell tries to listen. Really he isn't very interested in foxes and what they might symbolize.

Well, I can see how they got that impression, says Hanwell.

What?

I say I can see how they would have got that idea, the way you carry on.

What?

If you tell me you're happy, says Hanwell, you're happy and there's an end to it.

The talk turns to other matters. You never get your own pillowcase back from laundry. The really important things is that Chef Maureen accepts your frozen wheat-free lasagnas, that you might be allowed to eat these while others have their dietary requirements ignored and as a consequence shit blood and have convulsions and contract hiccups that never stop. Yes, concedes Leah, yes, Dad, perhaps. Perhaps shitting blood is worse than symbols and sadness and the global situation. You can't speak to doctors like that, whispers Hanwell, you might be overheard, you never know when they'll come by. You just have to pray that they do.

Leah begins to feel she is in control and that she might shape what remains of this meeting to her own satisfaction. She starts to make her father say things, directing him, moving his arms and manipulating his expressions, first innocently, and then with deliberation, so he says I love you, you know. And then: Love, you know I've always loved you. And: I love you don't worry it's nice here. And even: I can see a light. After a while he looks strange doing it and Leah feels ashamed and stops. And still he stays, and by doing so holds out the delicious possibility of madness, such a lovely indulgence. If she didn't have this everyday life to go to with its admin and rent and husband and work she could go mad! Why not go mad!

And remember to lock the gate with the water pressure where the gas is hot in the oven of the plug to switch it off when you leave it using only red onions and a pinch of cinnamon then getting back before you need to use a minicab — *without* drinking, advises Hanwell.

She can't make him come any closer. Yet his hand seems to be in her hand and his cheek is on hers and Leah kisses his hand and feels his tear in her ear because he was always such a sentimental old fool. She presses his hand between her hands. They are autumn dry. She can feel the pulpy bruise of the persistent wound, in the center of his hand, still not healed because at a certain age these things stop healing. It is purple and fills now with blood, scraped so lightly, so insignificantly, months and months ago, on the edge of the games table in the community room. The skin fell away. They rolled it back and taped it in place. But for all of that last year it stayed purple and full of blood.

Leah says, Dad! Don't go!

Hanwell says, Do I have to go somewhere?

Michel says, Computer's free!

14.

A great hill straddles NW, rising in Hampstead, West Hampstead, Kilburn, Willesden, Brondesbury, Cricklewood. It is no stranger to the world of letters. The Woman in White walks up one side to meet the highwayman Jack Sheppard on the other. Sometimes Dickens himself comes this far west and north for a pint or to bury someone. Look, there, on the library carpet between Science Fiction and Local History: a knotted condom filled with sperm. Once this was all farm and field with country villas nodding at each other along the ridge of this hill. Train stations have replaced them, at half-mile intervals.

It's a little more than a month since the girl came to the door — late May. The horse chestnuts look fine in their bushy fullness, though everyone knows they have blight. Leah is on one side of the Brondesbury ridge, climbing in the glare, unaware of who or what rises to meet her. She is so surprised she resorts to a reflex emotion: contempt. Cuts her eyes at the girl the way kids used to do at school. Coming so late and so close to Shar's face it is a gesture more violent than intended. If Michel were here! Michel is not here. Leah attempts a last second side-step, hoping to pass by. A little hand grabs her wrist.

– OI. YOU.

Her head is uncovered. Thick black hair falls free everywhere. In between its cloaking folds, Leah spies a catastrophic purple yellow black eye. Water weeps out of it, tears or something else involuntary. Leah tries to speak but only stutters.

– What you want from me? What you want me to say? I robbed you? I'm an addict. I stole your money. All right? ALL RIGHT?
– Let me help, maybe I can . . . there are places that . . . that help.

Leah cringes at her own voice. How feeble it is! Like a child pleading.

– I aint got your money, yeah? I've got a problem. Do you understand me? I AINT GOT NOTHING FOR YOU. I don't need you and your bredrin fuckin with me every fuckin day.

Pointin, shoutin. I can't take no more of it to be honest with you. What you want from me? Want me on my knees?

– No, I . . . Can I help you, somehow? Can I do something?

Shar releases, shrugs and turns, wobbles, almost falls. Her eyes roll up in her pretty head. Leah puts out a hand to steady her. Shar pushes it roughly aside.

– Take my number. Please. I'll write it on this. I work with, I'm connected to, a lot of charities, through work, you know, that could maybe . . .

Leah pushes a crumpled envelope into Shar's pocket. Shar puts her finger in Leah's face.

– Can't take no more. Can't take it.

Leah watches her stumble over the peak and down.

15.

On the 98, a woman sits opposite with a baby girl on her lap. She presents a pack of illustrated cards to the child for the purposes of stimulation. Elephant. Mouse. Teacup. Sun. Meadow, with moo cows. The child is particularly stimulated by the card with a human face. It is the only card for which she reaches out, giggling. Clever Lucia! Her fat fingers claw at it. Then she reaches up to her mother's face with the same violence. No, Lucia! The child threatens tears. Some things are people, explains her mother, and some things are images and some things are soft and some things are hard. Leah looks out the window. The rain is relentless. The planes are back in the sky. Work is work. Time has ceased being uncanny. It is just time again. She has taken some literature from work, from the literature cupboard. Professional organizations offering professional help. This is "as much as you can do."

Now it is time for the addict "to make their own decisions." Because "nobody can force anyone else to get the help they need." Everyone says the same things. Everyone says the same things in the same way. Leah gets off at Willesden Lane and starts walking quickly but the bus pulls up beside her and stalls. She has the lower deck as an audience as she doubles up over a hedge outside of a church. Vomit that is mostly water, indistinguishable from the rain. This church of her childhood, in which she was a Saturday Brownie, has been converted into luxury apartments, each with its own section of jaunty stained-glass window. Outside, a gathering of sporty little cars parked where once there was a small graveyard. The bus lumbers off in the direction of the high road. She straightens up, wipes her mouth with her scarf. Walks briskly with one hand gripping an inadequate umbrella and rain trickling down her right sleeve. Number 37. She flicks through the leaflets quickly like a good girl at a post-box checking the postage is sound before pushing them through.

She had hoped to find another method. Some old wives' remedy that might be discreetly applied at home using everyday products from the bathroom cabinet. Anything else will be expensive. Anything else will show up on the joint account. On-line she finds only moralists and no practical advice at all besides the old horror stories from the pre-moral past: gin baths and hat pins. Who has hat pins? She is here instead, with an old credit card from college days. Strange place. No place. Could be a dentist, a chiropractor. Private medicine! Plush sofas, glass-topped coffee tables, privacy. No clipboard. No-one to ask:

a) Is it your own decision to undertake the procedure?
b) Do you have someone to take you home after the procedure?

Here is a girl to ask whether she would like

a glass of water, how she would like to pay. That is all. Money avoids relationship, obligation. It is quite different. Back then she was nineteen, the university nurse organized everything. She sat with a kind ex-lover in their summer skirts on the edge of the hospital bed, legs dangling, like little girls scolded, and the thing that interested them most was the workings of anesthetic.

– It seemed like he held my wrist, said ten, nine, eight and the next second — *the next second* — was just now, was you kissing my forehead.
– It's been two and a half hours!

In its way, a greater revelation than the confusing lectures on consciousness, on Descartes, on Berkeley.
Ten nine eight. . . .
It's been two and a half hours!

No book could ever have convinced her as that day did. Ten nine eight . . . oblivion. Kind girl! It was more than she needed to do. One of the advantages of loving women, of being loved by women: they will always do things far beyond the call of duty. Ten nine eight. Back to life. Kiss on the forehead. And also a child's transfer, half rubbed off, on the wall in front of her eyes. Tigger and Christopher Robin and Pooh, all missing their heads. Spare bed in the children's ward? She remembers only ten nine eight — the painless death-rehearsal. A useful episode to recall in moments of mortal fear. (In small planes, in deep water.) That first time, she was two months gone. The second time, two months and three weeks. This is her third.

The receptionist is limping across the room. Sprained ankle, grubby white bandage flapping. Leah flushes. She is ashamed before an imagined nobody who isn't real and yet monitors our thoughts. She reprimands herself. Of course, all this was not a question of her own non-existence, of course, but rather of the non-existence of another. Of course. Yes, that's what I meant, what I meant to think, of course. The sort of thing normal women think.

– Mrs. Hanwell? In your own time.

16.

– Not relevant? What do you mean? How could you tell me that whole story and not mention the headscarf?

Natalie laughs. Frank laughs. Michel laughs hardest. Slightly drunk. Not only on the Prosecco in his hand. On the grandeur of this Victorian house, the length of the garden, that he should know a barrister and a banker, that he should find funny the things they find funny. The children wheel manically round the garden, laughing because everyone else is. Leah looks down at Olive and strokes her ardently, until the dog is discomfited and slinks away. She looks up at her best friend, Natalie Blake, and hates her.

– Leah . . . always trying to save somebody.
– Isn't that your job?
– Defending someone is very different from saving them. Anyway, I mostly do commercial these days.

Natalie crosses one bare leg over the other. Sleek ebony statuary. Tilts her head directly to the sun. Frank, too. They look like a king and queen in profile on an ancient coin. Leah must stick to the shade of something Frank calls the gazebo. The two women squint at each other across an expanse of well-kept lawn. They are annoying each other. They have been annoying each other all afternoon.

– I keep bumping into her.
– Naomi, stop doing that.
– She was at school with us. It's hard to believe.
– Is it? Why? Naomi stop it. Come away from the barbecue. It's fire, hot, come here.
– Never mind.
– Sorry, tell me again. I'm listening. Shar. Don't remember the name at all. Maybe it was during our "break"? You were hanging with a load of people back then I never met.
– No. I never knew her in school.
– Naomi! I'm serious. Sorry — so, wait: what's the issue?
– No issue. Nothing.
– It's just in the scheme of things it's not very . . .
– "She said, trailing off."
– What? Naomi, come here!
– Nothing.

Frank comes over with the bottle, as expansive with Leah as his wife is brusque. His face is very close. He smells expensive. Leah leans back to let him pour.

– Why is it that everyone from your school is a criminal crackhead?
– Why's everyone from yours a Tory minister?

Frank smiles. He is handsome his shirt is perfect his trousers are perfect his children are perfect his wife is perfect this is a perfectly chilled glass of Prosecco. He says:

– It must be comforting being able to divide the world in two like that in your mind.
– Frank, stop teasing.
– Leah's not offended. You're not offended, Leah. Of course, I'm already divided in half, so you understand for me it's hard to think this way. When you guys have kids, they'll know what I mean.

Leah tries now to look at Frank in the manner he seems to intend: as a projection of a certain future for herself, and for Michel. The coffee color, those freckles. But aside from accidents of genetics, Frank has nothing to do with either Leah or Michel. She met his mother once. Elena. Complained about the provincialism of Milan and advised Leah to dye her hair. Frank is from a different slice of the multiverse.

– My mother-in-law in her wisdom says if you want to know the real difference between people do the health visitor test. Ring the bell, and if they lay on the floor and put the lights out, they're no good.

Michel says:

– I don't get this. What does it mean?

Natalie explains:

– Sometimes people don't want to open the door to Marcia, they're worried it's connected to social work, or the benefit office. They want to be off the radar, basically. So if my mum ever rings your bell, for Godssake don't lie on the floor.

Michel nods seriously, taking this advice to heart. He can't see it, as Leah does. The way Natalie taps her finger on the garden table and looks at the sky as she speaks. He can't see that we're boring them, and they wish they were free of us, of this old obligation. He won't shut up, he says:

– These people, they would lie on the floor. They're on Ridley Avenue. And we work it out that they're all living in a squat, together, on Ridley Avenue, maybe four or five of these girls who are working on the streets, ringing door-bells, and there are some guys, too, we think.

Pimps, probably. But this is the stuff you deal with every day. I don't need to tell you it, you know it. You must see people like this every day, every day, right? In court.

– Michel, honey . . . It's like asking a doctor at a party about a mole on your back.

Michel always speaks sincerely, and it is strange that exactly this trait — highly valued by Leah in private — should so embarrass her in public. Nat is following the progress of Spike as he toddles in a flowerbed. Now her attention swings back to Leah and Leah takes its measure: serene, a little imperious. Insincere.

– No, I am interested, go on, Michel, I'm sorry.
– This other one, this guy, he's also from your school. He asked her for money a few weeks ago on the street.
– That's not what happened! He's talking about Nathan Bogle. He was selling travelcards. You know how he does that, you've seen him do that, at Kilburn, at Willesden sometimes?
– Hmmm.

It's humiliating being the cause of so much abject boredom in your oldest friend. Leah is reduced to bringing up these old names and faces in an attempt to engage her. Frank says:

– Bogle? He the one who was caught for heroin importing?

– No, that was Robbie Jenner. Year below. Bogle wasn't in that league. He dropped out to become a footballer. Spike, please don't do that, baby.

– And did he? Become a footballer?

– Huh? Oh — no. No.

Perhaps Brayton, too, no longer exists for her. It's gone, cast off. She is probably as surprised to have come out of Brayton as it is surprised to have spawned her. Nat is the girl done good from their thousand-kid madhouse; done too good, maybe, to recall where she came from. To live like this you would have to forget everything that came before. How else could you manage?

– He was a sweet kid. His mum was St. Loo-shun. St. Looshee-yan? All our mums knew each other. Very nice looking, very mischievous. Played the drums? Quite well. He sat next to Keisha. Back when she was Keisha. I was very jealous about that, when I was eight. Innit, Keisha.

Natalie chews at a nail, hating to be teased. She dislikes being reminded of her own inconsistencies. Leah dares herself to put it a little stronger: hypocrisies. Leah passes the old estate every day on the walk to the corner shop. She can see it from her back yard. Nat lives just far enough to avoid it. Anyway all meetings happen here, at Nat's house, because why wouldn't they. Look at this beautiful house! Leah blushes as an illegal word thrusts itself into her mind, Shar's word: coconut. And then Michel speaks, and makes it perfect.

– You changed your name. I forget that you did this. It's like: "Dress for the job you want not the one you have." And it's the same with names, I feel.

Ruined for Leah, though, by this depressing *I feel,* which he only ever says here, in this house, and which is embarrassing. Natalie's eyes widen; she lunges at a change of subject, which children always seem to provide.

– Michel, you can help me: what should I do about this?

Nat grabs two handfuls of Naomi's hair and demonstrates the knots by trying to pass her fingers through the nest of it as the child squirms beneath.

– She won't let me touch it, so I should give it to you to shave off, right? She can come in to the salon tomorrow and see you and get it all shaved off.

Naomi cries out. Michel answers the question, kindly, carefully, sincerely. Advising against drastic action, he recommends hairfood and coconut oil. Even after so many years in this country the English fondness for torturing children with irony remains strange to him. Nat keeps her bright smile pinned to her face.

– OK, OK, Naomi. NAOMI. Mum was only joking . . . No-one's going to . . . yes, plaiting it in the evening should help, Michel, thank you . . .

Frank says:

– At my school there was no such thing as "school holiday." My mother never saw me till Christmas.

His wife smiles sadly and gives him a kiss on his cheek:

– Oh, I bet there was. Knowing your mum she just probably never came to pick you up.

Not so funny, says Frank. Pretty funny, says Natalie. Leah watches Nat accept a daisy chain that Naomi has begun. Split a stem with a thumbnail, thread the next daisy through.

– I'm not sending my children to a boarding

school. Completely alone in a class of thirty white kids. You'd have to be crazy.

– Our children. Twenty white kids. Didn't do me any harm.

– You're wearing loafers, Frank.

Not so funny, says Frank. Pretty funny, says Natalie. Often Leah tries to diagnose a sickness here, between these two — something rotten, something virulent — but the patients persist in leaping from their beds and wisecracking. Kissing each other on the cheek.

– You're breakening it!

Leah looks at the daisy chain. Naomi is correct: Nat has breakened it. Now Spike finishes the job, snatching it and scattering the pieces back over the lawn. The screaming starts up. Leah assumes the bland smile of child appreciation. Frank stands up and gathers a kicking child under each arm.

– They'll be going to church school, for our sins.

Frank's default mode with Leah is a sort of self-parody. Leah thwarts him by faking innocence, forcing him to spell out whatever he is trying to say obliquely.

– Church school? Already?

Natalie says:

– It's all ridiculous: it's a free school, but apparently we need to start going to church. Put the effort in now. Otherwise they won't get in. Somewhere not too stressful, I hope. What's that one Pauline goes to?
– Mum? Maybe she goes once a month. To St. Somewhere, I don't know it. I'll ask, if you want.

Frank releases his children and sighs.

– Isn't it your turn soon?

Michel takes that one. His topic, his realm. A conversation now begins about the inside of Leah's body and how, if Michel had been listened to, it would have been far busier these past few years. Leah concentrates on Natalie. She is here in her body but where is her mind? At work? In some glamorous extra-marital passion? Or just wishing these people would leave so she could get back to her real life, family life?

– Damn! The banana bread. I forgot about it. Naomi, come and help me serve it up.

Leah watches Natalie stride over to her

beautiful kitchen with her beautiful child. Everything behind those French doors is full and meaningful. The gestures, the glances, the conversation that can't be heard. How do you get to be so full? And so full of only meaningful things? Everything else Nat has somehow managed to cast off. She is an adult. How do you do that?

– So . . . Michel. How's it going, man? Let's get an update. How is the hair business? Do people still . . . in a bad economy?

Frank's face registers the mild panic of being left with his wife's strange friends.

– Actually, I am moving into your region, Frank, in a small way.
– My region?
– Day trading. On the Internet. After we spoke last time, you know, I bought a book and . . .
– You bought a book?
– A guide . . . and I've been trying a little myself, small amounts, just to begin.

Frank's face suggests a further explanation is needed, he detects an improbability somewhere. It is a very subtle form of humiliation but it will still be passed from Michel to Leah in some converted form, like a liquid turning to a gas, later today, or tomorrow, in an argument, in bed.

– Well, Leah's father left her, us, a small amount.

– Oh, OK! Well, a small amount is a good place to start. But now look, I don't want to be responsible for you losing your shirt, Michel . . . I work for one of the big boys, you see, and we have a sort of safety net, but when it comes to individual traders, you know, it's worth remembering that —

Leah sighs, loudly. It's childish but she can't help it. Frank turns to Leah with a pacifying, weary smile. He places a corrective finger on her shoulder, a little tap.

– Michel: all I was going to say is it's worth signing on with an online site, like *Today Trader,* or something like it, and playing with fake money first of all, get in the swing of things . . .

– Can I be excused? I think Olive needs a shit and I don't want her to do it on your perfect lawn.

– *Leah.*

– No, no, no, it's fine. Michel, we've known each other a very long time, Leah and I. I'm used to her funny ideas. Spike, why don't we take Olive to the corner and back, before she goes home. Let's go find some bags, OK?

Leah and Michel are left sitting in the grass, cross-legged, like children. This house makes her feel like a child. Cake ingredients and fancy rugs and throw cushions and upholstered chairs in chosen fabrics. Not a futon in sight. Overnight everyone has grown up. While she was becoming, everyone grew up and became.

– Why do you treat me like an idiot all the time?
– What?
– I ask you a question, Leah.
– I didn't mean to. I just can't stand him talking down to you like that.
– He didn't. You did.
– Who is she? Who is this person? This bourgeois existence!
– Bourgeois, bourgeois, bourgeois. I think this is the only French word you know. You've become one of these English people . . . who hate all their friends.

Frank re-emerges through the French doors. If Frank were more observant he might catch them in their Punch and Judy mode, frozen in attitudes of disgust and fury. But Frank is not terribly observant, and by the time he looks up they are what they always seem to be: a happy couple in love.

– Do you know where the lead is?

Behind him, Nat strides back out, looking serene, unreadable. Naomi is hitched up on her hip like the baby she was not too long ago. Her wild afro curls shoot out in a million directions. Leah observes Michel staring at the child. He has an expression of deep longing on his face.

17.

– Auntie Leah! Auntie Leah! Mummy says SLOW DOWN.

Leah stops, looks back. There is no-one and then round a corner Nat appears, sighing dramatically. The buggy is empty, Spike is in her arms, Naomi is tugging at her t-shirt. Gulliver, about to be pinned to the ground by Lilliputians.

– Lee, you sure this is right? Doesn't look right.
– End of this road. On the map it sort of winds round and back on itself. Pauline said it's hard to find.
– I can see the magistrates' court and . . . a roundabout? Kids, stay close, stay in. It's like walking the hard shoulder on the motorway. Nightmare. Kennedy Fried Chicken. Polish Bar and Pool. Euphoria Massage. Glad we took the scenic route. This can't still be Willesden. Feels like we're in Neasden already.
– The church it what *makes* it Willesden. It marks the parish of Willesden.

– Yeah but where is it? How does Pauline even get here?

– Bus, I spose. I dunno.

– Nightmare.

The road winds. They find themselves on a thin strip of pavement with a bollard at the end, clutching the children as the cars zoom by either side. To their right a foreclosed shopping arcade and a misconceived office block, empty, every other window broken. To their left, a grassy island nestled beside a dual carriageway. Intended as a green oasis, it is a fly-tipping zone. A water-logged mattress. An upturned sofa with ripped cushions, foully stained. More eccentric items, suggesting lives abandoned in a hurry: half a scooter, a decapitated Anglepoise, a car door, a hat stand, enough rolled-up lino for a bathroom floor.

In a pause between cars they run as one animal across the wide road, and then release each other, panting, hands on knees. Advised to "take it easy" for forty-eight hours, Leah feels a lightness in her head. She turns away, lifting her head slowly, and spots it first: an ancient crenellation and spire, just visible through the branches of a towering ash. Another twenty yards and the full improbability of the scene is revealed.

A little country church, a medieval country church, stranded on this half acre, in the middle of a roundabout. Out of time, out of place. A force field of serenity surrounds it. A cherry tree at the east window. A low encircling brick wall marks the ancient boundary, no more a defense than a ring of daisies. The family vaults have their doors kicked in. Many brightly tagged gravestones. Leah and Nat and the children pass through the lych-gate and pause under the bell tower. Blue clockface brilliant in the sun. It is eleven thirty in the morning, in another century, another England. Nat uses the baby's muslin to wipe her forehead of sweat. The children, till now raucous and complaining in the heat, turn quiet. A path threads through the shady graveyard, the Victorian stones marking only the most recent layer of the dead. Natalie maneuvers the buggy over uneven ground.

– Crazy. Never seen it before. Must have driven by hundreds of times. Lee, you got that thing of water? Probably why Pauline likes it. Cos it's so old. Because you can be surer of the old ones.

Leah folds her arms flat across her bust and becomes her mother, assumes her mother's face: mouth drawn downwards, eyelids fluttering against the world's specks and their

114

determination to fly into Pauline's eyes.
Natalie, mid-glug, laughs violently, spreading water down her front.

– I wouldn't be liking the newer churches, no. I wouldn't be dying over them. You can be surer of the older ones, so you can.
– Stop it — I'm going to choke. I lived here my whole life I never knew this place even existed. All those years stuck with Marcia in that Pentecostal tin-can when we could have been here. Keisha, hear me now. I just want the spirit of the Lord to settle upon us all.

They can ridicule their mothers but they can't break the somber spell of this place. The children step gingerly between graves, they want to know if there are really and truly dead people underfoot. Leah speeds up, abandoning the path and tramping into high grass, leaving Nat equivocating with her brood upon the difference between the recently dead and the long dead. Leah stretches her arms out either side of herself. Her fingers brush the tops of the taller monuments, a broken stone urn, a crumbling cross. Soon she is behind the church. The alien past crowds round, partially legible on worn stones set at disappointed angles. Child death and lethal confinements. War and disease. Massive tablets covered in ivy, in lichen, in spots of yellow mold and moss.

Emily W____ of this parish was taken from
this life in her thirty ____ year of life
In the year of our Lord eighteen ____ seven
Leaving behind six children and a
husband Albert
Who joined her soon after in this _____

Marion ____ of this pari____
Died 17th December 1878 aged 2__ years
And also of Dora, infant daug____ of the
above
Died 11th December 1878

Take it easy for forty-eight hours.
In this terrible sun.
Take it easy, Leah Hanwell of this parish.
Only daughter of Colin Hanwell, also of
this parish.
Take it easy for the rest of your life.

Leah leans against a stone tall as herself.
Here are three figures in haut relief, almost
entirely effaced. She fits her fingers into the
mossy grooves. A lady in gathered skirts is
clutching something to her body, a feature-
less lump, something she has been given,
maybe, and two young boys in frock coats
reach out for her on either side. She is no

116

one. Time has eaten away all detail: no name no date no face no knees no feet no explanation of the mysterious gift —

– Lee, you all right?
– Hot. It's so hot.

They pass through a pair of heavy wooden doors to the interior. A service is just finishing. The queer incense smell of high church lingers. They walk round the perimeter and avoid the eyes of the faithful. Deliciously cool in here, better than air conditioning. Natalie picks up a leaflet. Congenital autodidact, always wanting to know. It must have been that break. The break made the difference. She became Natalie Blake in that brief pause in their long history, between sixteen and eighteen. Educated herself on the floor of Kensal Rise Library while Leah smoked weed all the live-long day. Natalie always picks up the leaflets, the leaflets and everything else.

– Parish founded in 938 . . . nothing of the original church remains . . . present church dates from around 1315 . . . Cromwellian bullet holes in the door, original . . .

Naomi runs ahead and climbs the font (c. 1150, Purbeck marble). Leah tries to escape the aural range of Natalie's lecture. The service ends: the parishioners begin to file out. In the doorway, the young vicar attempts to engage them. He holds a hand to his doughy waist like a nervous old woman, a flop of brown hair falls across one temple. He has a face that hopes to please but cannot owing to chinlessness. He is as he would have been in 1920 or 1880 or 1660. He is the same, but his congregation is different. Polish, Indian, African, Caribbean. The adults sharply dressed in shiny suits and clinging dresses from the market. The boys wear three-piece pinstripe, the girls clutch tiny Spanish shawls, their hair elaborately pressed and kiss-curled. The congregation pity the vicar, who is full of gentle suggestions. Let's see if we can start on time next week. Anything you can spare. Anything at all. They smile and nod, not taking him too seriously. The vicar, too, is not listening to himself. He is intent on Leah, seeking her over the heads of his fleeing flock. Light streams in from the east. Leah moves that way instinctively, toward a monument in black and white marble hung upon the wall from which she learns that IT WAS HER HAPPINESS TO MAKE HIM YE JOYFUL FATHER OF 10 SONS & 7 DAUGHTERS AND IT IS HER PIETIE TO DEDICATE THIS

MONUMENT TO YE PRESERVATION OF HIS MEMORY. HE DIED IN YE 48 YEAR OF HIS AGE. MARCH YE 24 1647. Nothing further is said of Her. Leah is drawn to put her fingers to the letters to measure their coolness. But Natalie says better not to, she says Spike don't splash the holy water WOW the same sculptor fashioned the tomb of ELIZABETH 1ST no darling not that one she was a queen darling from LONG AGO no darling from before then even but did you know it was once *W I L S D O N* meaning well meaning spring at the foot of a hill which is where this water's coming from I SAID STOP SPLASHING. Leah is suddenly so thirsty, she is made of thirst, she is only thirst. She kneels to examine the tap, reads the sign. Not Potable. Holy, but not potable.

– Mummy!
– No, not Mummy. This is somebody else. "Thought to be more powerful than the traditional Madonna, she has miraculous powers, including: the gift of serendipity, restoring lost memories, resuscitating dead babies . . ." Marcia would love this — sometimes people see visions of her in the churchyard. Marcia's always having visions. Usually of white Madonnas, though, with blond hair and nice blouses from M & S. . . .

How did she walk past it? At her back a Madonna, fashioned of jet limewood. The Madonna holds a mammoth baby in swaddling clothes. *The Christ Child* it says on the sign, his arms stretched out at either side, *his hands big with blessing* it says on the sign, but to Leah there seems no blessing in it. It looks more like accusation. The baby is cruciform; he is the shape of the thing that will destroy him. He reaches out for Leah. He reaches out to stop any escape, to the right or to the left.

– "becoming the famous shrine of Our Lady of Willesden, "The Black Madonna," destroyed in the reformation and burned, along with the ladies of Walshingham, Ipswich and Worcester — by the Lord Privy Seal." Also a Cromwell. Different Cromwell? Doesn't say. This is where decent history GCSE level teaching would have come in helpful. . . . "was shrine here since —" wait is this the original then? 1200s? Can't be. Very craply written, not clear which — NAOMI COME AWAY FROM

"How have you lived your whole life in these streets and never known me? How long did you think you could avoid me? What made you think you were exempt? Don't you know that I have been here as long as people cried out for help? Hear me: I am not like those mealy-mouthed pale Madonnas, those simpering virgins! I am older than this place! Older even than the faith that takes my name in vain! Spirit of these beech woods and phone boxes, hedgerows and lampposts, freshwater springs and tube stations, ancient yews and one-stop-shops, grazing land and 3D multiplexes. Unruly England of the real life, the animal life! Of the old church, of the new, of a time before churches. Are you feeling hot? Is it all too much? Did you hope for something else? Were you misinformed? Was there more to it than that? Or less? If we give it a different name will the weightless sensation disappear? Are your knees going? Who are you? Would you like a glass of water? Is the sky falling? Could things have been differently arranged, in a different order, in a different place?"

18.

– Oh, I used to faint a lot. A lot! They thought it was a sign of a delicate constitution, sensitive, a bit artistic. But everyone went into the nursing or secretarial back then, you see. That's simply how it was. We didn't have the opportunities.
– It was just hot.
– Because you had a lot of potential, no, listen, you did: piano, the recorder, the dancing, the thing with the . . . the . . . what's its name now, oh you know — sculpting — you liked the sculpting for a while, and the violin, you were a wonder on the violin, and lots of little things like that.
– I brought one pot home from school. I played the violin for a month.
– We made sure you had all the lessons, fifty pee here, fifty pee there, it all adds up! And we didn't always have it! That was your father — God rest him — he didn't want you to grow up feeling poor, even though we *were* poor. But you never really settled on the one thing, that's what I mean. This lawn needs watering.

Pauline stoops down suddenly, coming up with a handful of grass and earth.

– London clay. Very dry. Of course, you girls do everything differently now. You wait and wait and wait. Though what you're waiting *for* I don't know.

Almost purple with the effort, the bowl of white hair damp and flat round her face. Mothers are urgently trying to tell something to their daughters, and this urgency is precisely what repels their daughters, forcing them to turn away. Mothers are left stranded, madly holding a lump of London clay, some grass, some white tubers, a dandelion, a fat worm passing the world through itself.

– Eugh. Probably put the mud down now, Mum.

They sit together on a park bench Michel discovered some years ago. Somebody had left it in the middle of the road, up at Cricklewood Broadway. Calm as you like! Just sitting there in traffic! It looked like it had grown out of the tarmac. All other cars swerved to avoid it. Michel stopped the Mini Metro, put the seats down flat, opened the boot and wedged it in, with Pauline adding an unhelpful hand, to a chorus of car horns.

When they got it home they found it had the seal of the Royal Parks upon it. Pauline calls it the throne. Let us sit on the throne for a wee while.

– It was the heat. Olive, come here, baby.
– Not near me! I don't want my eyes going up! That's my grandchild, there. Only one I'm likely to get if things go on the way they are. I'm allergic to my own grandchild.
– Mum, enough!

They sit on the throne in silence, staring out in different directions. The problem seems to be two different conceptions of time. She knows the pull of her animal nature should, by now, be making the decisions. Perhaps she's been a city fox too long. Every new arrival — the announcements seem to come now every day — feels like a terrible betrayal. Why won't everybody stay still? She has forced a stillness in herself, but it has not stopped the world from continuing on. And then the things that happen only serve to horribly close down the possibilities of all the other things that didn't happen, and so number 37, and so the door opening at the moment that she stands there, her hand full of leaflets, and Shar saying: put those down, take my hand. Shall we run? Are you ready? Shall we run? Leave all this!

Let's be outlaws! Sleeping in hedgerows. Following the railway line till it reaches the sea. Waking up with that long black hair in her eyes, in her mouth. Phoning home from fantasy boxes that still take the old 2 pees. We're fine, don't worry. I want to stay still and to keep moving. I want this life and another. Don't look for me!

– and just trying to help, but I'll get no thanks for it. I can't tell if you're even listening to me. Anyway. It's your life.
– What d'you want with a shrine anyway?
– What d'you mean by that, a shrine? Her Ladyship? Oh, I don't bother myself about her. She's perfectly harmless. It says Anglican on the door and it's been Anglican for a thousand years. That's good enough for me. People from the colonies, and the Russiany lot, they're superstitious, and who can blame them? They've had a terrible time. Who am I to deprive a person of their comforts?

Pauline looks pointedly toward their old estate, full of people from the colonies and the Russiany lot. Today, as it has been almost all days since the sun began, the foghorn girl is out, locked in debate with whoever is on the end of her handless device. You disrespecting me? Don't disrespect me! Whatever else is to be said of her, she is of unmistakable Irish descent. Short criminal forehead, widely set eyes. There is a special contempt Pauline reserves for the fallen members of her own tribe.

– Not even the virgin could help the likes of her. Well, hello Edward, dear!
– All right there Mrs. H!
– Oh, it's good to see you, Ned. How are you love? You're looking well, considering. Not still smoking the dope, I hope.
– 'Fraid so, 'fraid so. I like the flavor.
– It'll rob you of your ambition.
– I've only got the one ambition anyway.
– And what would that be?
– Marrying you, of course. Can't rob me of that now can it?
– Oh go on with you.

Quite happy, really quite happy, and the sun thins out and purples and arranges itself in strips behind the aquamarine of the minaret and what breeze there is ripples the flag of St. George, on top of the old estate, hung from a satellite dish in preparation for the football. Maybe it doesn't matter that life never blossomed into something larger than itself. Moored to the shore she set out from, as almost all women were, once.

– Leah love, that's your phone.

Look at that: the fence on the right side

almost completely done for. The ivy from the estate invades the gaps and smothers anything Michel tries to grow, apart from the apple tree itself, which grows despite them all, unaided. She writes to the council, they don't listen, Ned never writes, nor Gloria, they live communally but she is the only one who thinks communally and oh Christ that poor homeless worm livid in the sun. Like foreskin moving forward and back, forward and back, over itself. Nobody loves me everybody hates me because I'm a wriggly worm. But who is this

   this voice

         so quiet

and so violent, right in her ear, and she thinks she must have misheard, she thinks she must be going crazy, she thinks

– Excuse me?
– You hear me? Don't be coming round this place.
– Excuse me? How did you get this number?
– That girl is my business. Don't be coming round this place pushing shit through the door, you hear me? Watch for me. I know you. You come here again you best watch for me.
– Who *is* this?
– Fuckin dyke cunt.

The worm grinds its middle together, having nothing else. Flagstone to the left of it, flagstone to the right.

– and then in Poundland the very same box — same brand, mind — is only two forty-nine! But if you shop in these places you're simply a fool to yourself, and that's all there is to be said. Leah love? Leah? Leah? Who was that? On the phone? You feeling all right?

19.

A wife's honor must be defended. It is a primal thing, he explains, referencing the great apes in a documentary. As female ape defends baby ape so male ape protects his female. Michel is very happy in his anger, they are drawn together under its canopy. It is the nicest time they've had together in months. She sits at the kitchen table clutching herself while he walks up and down waving his arms in the air like a great ape. She is a good ape, too; she wants to contribute to the greater happiness of her ape family. It is this perfectly decent desire that makes her say:

– I think so. I think it was him. It's hard to tell from a voice. Look, it's almost twenty years since I knew him at all well. But I would say: yes. If you're asking me for a hundred percent, then no, I can't say it like that but my first thought was yes that's him, that's Nathan.

So little happens in this corner of NW.

When there is a drama it's natural enough that one should want to place oneself in the picture, right at the center. It sounded like him. It really did. She tells Michel. She tells Michel all of it bar one word.

20.

On the way back from the chain supermarket where they shop, though it closed down the local grocer and pays slave wages, with new bags though they should take old bags, leaving with broccoli from Kenya and tomatoes from Chile and unfair coffee and sugary crap and the wrong newspaper.

They are not good people. They do not even have the integrity to be the sort of people who don't worry about being good people. They worry all the time. They are stuck in the middle again. They buy always Pinot Grigio or Chardonnay because these are the only words they know that relate to wine. They are attending a dinner party and for this you need to bring a bottle of wine. This much they have learned. They do not purchase ethical things because they can't afford them Michel claims and Leah says, no, it's because you can't be bothered. Privately she thinks: you want to be rich like them but you can't be bothered with their morals, whereas I am more interested in their morals than their money, and this thought, this opposition, makes her feel good. Marriage as the art of invidious comparison. And shit that's him in the phone box and if she had thought about it for more than a split second she would never have said:

– Shit that's him in the phone box.
– That's him?
– Yes, but — no, I don't know. No. I thought. Doesn't matter. Forget it.
– Leah, you just said it was him. Is it or isn't it?

Very quickly Michel is out of earshot and over there, squaring up for another invidious comparison: his compact, well-proportioned dancer's frame against a tall muscled threat, who turns, and turns out not to be Nathan, who is surely the other boy she saw with Shar, though maybe not. The cap, the hooded top, the low jeans, it's a uniform — they look the same. From where Leah stands anyway it is still all dumb show, hand gestures and primal frowns, and of course some awful potential news story that explains everything except the misery and the particulars: one youth knifed another youth, on Kilburn High Road. They had names and ages and it's terribly sad, an indictment

133

of something or another and also not good for house prices. Leah cannot breathe for fear. She is running to catch up, Olive clattering along beside her, and while she runs she finds herself noticing something that should not matter: she looks older than both of them. The boy is a boy and Michel is a man but they look the same age.

– I don't know what you're chattin about bruv but you BEST NOT STEP TO ME.
– Michel — please. Leave it, please.
– Tell your mans to step back off me.
– Don't call my house again, OK? Leave my wife alone! You understand me?
– What the fuck are you chattin' about? You want some?

They bump chests like primates; Michel is knocked back in an ignoble stumble to the pavement, landing next to his ridiculous dog, who licks him in his ear. Now his opponent towers over him and draws his foot back, preparing for a penalty kick. Leah inserts herself between the two of them, stretching out her hands to separate them, an imploring woman in an ancient story.

– Michel! Stop it! It's not him. Please — this is my husband, he's confused, please don't hurt him, please leave us alone, please.

The foot, indifferent, draws further back, for greater range. Leah begins to cry. In the corner of her eye she observes a young white couple in suits crossing the road to avoid them. No one will help. She puts her hands together in prayer.

– Please leave him alone, please. I'm pregnant — please leave us alone.

The foot retreats. A hand looms over Michel as he struggles to his feet, a hand in the shape of a gun, pointed at his head.

– Step to me again — *brrp brrp!* — you'll be gone.
– Fuck you. OK? I'm not scared of you!

In a blink the foot is drawn back once more and released into Olive's belly. She is propelled several yards into the doorway of the sweetshop. She makes a noise Leah has never heard before.

– Olive!
– You're lucky your gal came for you bruv. Otherwise.

He is already half way across the road, shouting over his shoulder.

– Otherwise what? You fucking coward! You kick my dog! I'll call the police!

– MICHEL. Don't make it worse.

She has a hand to his chest. To any by-stander it would appear that she is holding him back. Only she knows that he is not really trying to push her away. In this way the two men part, abusing each other roundly as they go, playing with the idea that they are not finished, that any moment they might turn back and set upon each other. It is only more make-believe: the presence of a woman has released them from their obligation.

21.

Leah believes in objectivity. She is a little calmer now, they are almost home. Who was that woman at the moment of crisis, screaming and weeping, begging on her knees in the street? Silly to admit it, but she had thought of herself as "brave." A fighter. Now she is introduced to a deal-maker, a pleader, a tactical liar. Please don't destroy the thing I love! And her petition had been heard, and a lesser sacrifice made in its place, and in the moment she was simply, pathetically grateful for the concession.

Afterward, too, she could not instantly put herself back together. It is Michel who holds Olive in his arms, and thumps upon their own front door while Leah goes on not being able to discover which shopping bag contains the key.

– Is she OK?
– She's fine. Unless she's hurt inside. To me she looks fine. Shocked.

– Are you OK?

The answer is in his face. Humiliation. Fury. Of course, it's harder for a man to be objective. They have the problem of pride.

– Ned!
– Guys, you OK?
– Help Lee with those bags.

They go into the kitchen and lay the beloved dog in its bed. She looks OK. Feed her? She eats. Throw a ball? She runs. Maybe she's OK, but for the humans there is still too much adrenaline and trauma to move on. Leah tells Ned the story, purging it of any possible fury or humiliation. Michel the brave! Michel the defender! She puts a hand on her husband's arm. He shrugs it off.

– She pretended she was pregnant. He took pity on us! I was lying on the floor like an idiot.
– No. You stopped it getting any worse than it needed to be.

She puts a hand on his arm again. This time he lets her.

– Do you think we should leave her tonight? I don't know. Ned, could you keep an eye out? Call if there's any problem? Or maybe we should just stay in. Cancel.

It's dinner, says Michel, I don't think we can cancel. She's OK. You're OK, baby, aren't you? You're OK? The two humans look into the animal's eyes for reassurance. Leah struggles to be objective. Wouldn't one of the humans have said the word "vet" by now if they did not fear how much money saying "vet" would entail?

22.

Hanwell never gave dinner parties. Nor did he go out for dinner. That's not true: on special occasions he took his little family to Vijay's on Willesden Lane where they took a table near the door, ate quickly, and grew self-conscious of their conversation. Nothing in Leah's childhood prepared her for the frequency with which she now attends dinner parties, most often at Natalie's house, where she and Michel are invited to provide something like local color. Neither of them know what to say to barristers and bankers, to the occasional judge. Natalie cannot believe that they are shy. Each time she blames some error of placement but each time the awkwardness remains. They are shy, whether Natalie believes it or not. They have no gift for anecdote. They look down at their plates and cut their food with great care, letting Natalie tell their stories for them, nodding to confirm points of fact, names, times, places.

Offered to the table for general dissection these anecdotes take on their own life, separate, impressive.

– or just ran. I would have run like the bloody wind and left them to it. No offense, Michel. You're very brave.
– And then did you just both go your separate ways? "Thank you, I've been your potential murderer today, now I must be off . . ."
– Ha!
– "Got a rather full day of muggings to attend to with my pretend gun."
– Ha!
– Can you pass that salsa thing? Do you think if you make a gun sign with your fingers that means you actually have a gun or that's like basically your only gun? Recession bites everyone, I suppose . . . why should gangsters be immune? Look, I've got one, too. *Brrrp!*
– Ha! Ha!
– Wait, but, sorry — you're pregnant?

Twelve people at Nat's long oak dining table stop talking and laughing and look at Leah caught wrestling the breast of a duck.

– No.
– No, it was just something she *said*, you know, to stop him.
– Very brave. Quick thinking.

Natalie's version of Leah and Michel's

anecdote is over. The conversational baton passes to others, who tell their anecdotes with more panache, linking them to matters of the wider culture, debates in the newspapers. Leah tries to explain what she does for a living to someone who doesn't care. The spinach is farm to table. Everyone comes together for a moment to complain about the evils of technology, what a disaster, especially for teenagers, yet most people have their phones laid next to their dinner plates. Pass the buttered carrots. Meanwhile parents have become old and ill at the very moment their children want to have their own babies. Many of the parents are immigrants — from Jamaica, from Ireland, from India, from China — and they can't understand why they have not yet been invited to live with their children, as is the custom, in their countries. Technology is offered as a substitute for that impossible request. Stair lifts. Pacemakers. Hip replacements. Dialysis machines. But nothing satisfies them. They worked hard so we children might live like this. They "literally" will not be happy until they've moved into our houses. They can never move into our houses. Pass the heirloom tomato salad. The thing about Islam. Let me tell you about Islam. The thing about the trouble with Islam. Everyone is suddenly an expert on Islam. But what do you think, Samhita, yeah what do you think, Samhita, what's your take on this? Samhita, the copyright lawyer. Pass the tuna. Solutions are passed across the table, strategies. Private wards. Private cinemas. Christmas abroad. A restaurant with only five tables in it. Security systems. Fences. The carriage of a 4x4 that lets you sit alone above traffic. There is a perfect isolation out there somewhere, you can get it, although it doesn't come cheap. But Leah, someone is saying, but Leah, in the end, at the end of the day, don't you just want to give your individual child the very best opportunities you can give them individually? Pass the green beans with shaved almonds. Define best. Pass the lemon tart. Whatever brings a child the greatest possibility of success. Pass the berries. Define success. Pass the crème fraîche. You think that the difference between you and me is that you want to give your child the best opportunities? Pass the dessert spoon. It's the job of the hostess to smooth things over, to point out that these arguments are still hypothetical. Why argue over the unborn? All I know is I don't want to push something the size of a watermelon out of something the size of a lemon. Nurse: bring on the drugs! Have you thought about doing it in water? Everyone says the same things in the same way. Conversations tinged with terror. Captive animals, contemplating a return to nature. Natalie is calm, having already traveled to the other side. Pass the laptop. You've got to see this, it's only two minutes long, it's hilarious.

Water shortage. Food wars. Strain A-H5N1. Manhattan slips into the sea. England freezes. Iran presses the button. A tornado blows through Kensal Rise. There must be something attractive about the idea of apocalypse. Neighborhoods reduced to scavenging zones. Setting up schools in abandoned supermarkets and churches. New groupings, new connections, multiple partners, children free of all this dull protection. On every street corner music streaming out of giant jerry-rigged sound-systems. People moving in great anonymous crowds, leaderless, in wave formations, masked, looking for food, weaponry. "Steam rushing" Caldwell, on a Sunday, running down the halls in packs, ringing every bell. Those were the days. Weren't they, Leah? Those were really the days. Pass the whisky. Because it's a facile comparison: you can't be responsible for a complex economic event in the same way you're responsible for going out on the street with the intention to steal. Pass the coffee.

It's not any coffee, it's extremely good coffee.

– It's just disappointing.
– It's so disappointing.
– Especially when you've really gone out of
your way to help somebody and they just throw
it back in your face. That's what I can't stand.
Like actually what happened with Leah — Lee
tell them about the girl.
– Sorry?
– The girl in the headscarf. Who came to the
door. It's a really sad story. All right: I'll tell
it —

It's only when they have been kissed on
both cheeks, when the heavy front door
closes, when they are released once more
into the night, that Leah and Michel come
alive. But even this camaraderie of contempt
can quickly fall apart. By the time they reach
the mouth of the tube, Leah has somehow
said too much, complained too much, and
the delicate spirit level of their relation, their
us-against-them, slips, and shows a crooked
angle.

– Don't you think they're as bored as you are?
You think you're somebody special? You think I
wake up every day so happy to see you? You're
a snob, just in the other way. Do you think you
are the only one who wants something else?
Another life?

They ride home in silence, infuriated. They walk through Willesden in silence. They come to the door in silence, both reaching for separate keys at the same time. They do comic battle at the keyhole, and Leah is the one to crack. By the time they are in the hallway they are laughing, and soon after, kissing. If only they could be alone all the time. If the world was just you and me, says Leah, we'd be happy all the time. You sound just like them, says Michel, and puts his tongue in his wife's ear.

The next morning, they arrive in the kitchen in mellow mood, in t-shirts and pants, sloping into the wide expanse of a Saturday morning. Leah goes to check the post. She sees her first. Innocent, beloved little animal, cold, not yet stiff, far from her bed, under the table in the box room, on her side. Bloody foam at her mouth. Michel! Michel! It won't come out loud enough. Or he is in the garden, admiring the tree. The doorbell goes. It is Pauline. Olive's dead! She's dead! Oh my God! She's dead! Where? Says Pauline. Show me. It's the nurse in her. And when Michel comes and sees and is no less hysterical than Leah, Leah is surprised how grateful she is for her mother's practical way of being in the world. Leah wants to cry and only to cry. Michel wants to go over and over the order of events. He wants to establish a timeline, as if this would change anything. Pauline wants to make sure the area under the table is made antiseptic and that the shoebox is buried at least one foot under the communal grass. No point asking the others, says Pauline — meaning the other occupants — they'll only say no. Hurry up now, she says, try and pull yourselves together. We need to get this done. Have some tea. Calm down. She asks: did it not occur to you she didn't bark when you came in?

23.

It could be said that one of Michel's dreams has come true: they have gone up one rung, at least in the quality and elaboration of their fear. It is in Leah's nature to blame Michel for this — their new wariness, the Chubb lock, the fact he now picks her up from the station, the way they cross the street to avoid "certain elements" and continually discuss moving out. Michel is longer at the computer, dreaming of a windfall that will transport them to another urban suburb more to his taste, which means more African, less Caribbean. To which Leah offers no comment. She is submerged, July is a lost month. She lets these little changes happen, up there, on the surface, while she walks on the bottom of the ocean. She is in terrible mourning. She is unfamiliar with the rules concerning the mourning of animals. For a cat: one week. For a dog, two will be tolerated, three is to begin to look absurd, especially in the office where — in the Caribbean spirit — all animals smaller than a donkey are considered vermin. She is mourning for her dog. She thinks the sadness will kill her. Spotting one of Olive's many twins shuffling up the Edgware Road, suffering in the heat, she is overcome. At work, Adina squints at her puffy tear-stained face. Not still the dog. Still? And if it is indeed false consciousness, if the mourning is for something other than her dog, it can make no practical difference to the mourner: it is Olive that she knew, and Olive whom she misses. Leah has become the sort of crazy person who stops other dog owners in the street to tell them her tale of woe.

Walking back from a training day in Harlesden she finds herself lost in the back streets. She takes a series of random left turns to keep moving, to lose a surely innocent hooded stranger, and then here is that strange little church again, tolling six o'clock. She goes in. Half an hour later she comes out. She does not tell Michel or anybody. She begins to do this most days. In late July, Michel insists: they must go forward. Leah agrees. They are placed on the NHS waiting list. But every morning, she locks the bathroom door and takes her little contraceptive pill. Stolen boxes from Natalie's bathroom cabinet, hidden in a drawer. She doesn't want to "go forward." For Leah, that way is not forward. She wants just him and her forever.

August comes.
August comes.

Carnival! Girls from work, boys from the salon, old school friends, Michel's cousins from south London, all walk the streets with a million others. Seeking out the good sound systems, winding their bodies close to complete strangers and each other, eating jerk, ending up in Meanwhile Gardens, stoned in the grass. Usually. Not this year. This year they finally accept Frank's annual invitation to a friend of a friend's with "an amazing carnival pad." An Italian. They turn up early on the Sunday morning, as advised, to get there before the street is closed off. They feel a bit stupid, wandering around the empty flat of people they do not know. No sign of Frank or Nat. Michel goes to help in the kitchen. Leah accepts a rum and Coke and sits in a corner chair, looking out the window, watching the police lining up along the barricades. In the corner of the room a television talks. It talks for a long time before Leah notices it, and then only because it names a local road, one street from her own.

– on Albert Road, in Kilburn, where yesterday evening hopes for a peaceful carnival weekend were marred by reports of a fatal stabbing, here, on the border of the carnival route through North West London, as people prepared for today's festivities —

Albert Road! shouts Michel, from the kitchen. Leah shouts back:

– YEAH BUT IT'S GOT NOTHING TO DO WITH CARNIVAL — IT WAS LAST NIGHT. IT'S JUST —

Michel walks through the door.

– it's just typical sensational reporting. They *want* there to be —
– Leah can I hear it please?

The television says:

– The young man, named locally as Felix Cooper, was 32 years old. He grew up in the notorious Garvey House project in Holloway, but had moved with his family to this relatively quiet corner of Kilburn, in search of a better life. Yet it was here, in Kilburn, that he was accosted by two youths early Saturday evening, moments from his own front door. It is not known if the victim knew —

– He was murdered! Why does it matter where he grew up?

I put music on now, says an Italian, and switches off the television. We need to move out, says Michel. I don't want to move, it's my home, says Leah. She accepts a kiss on her neck. No arguing, says Michel, OK? Let's try and have a nice time. I'm not arguing, says Leah. OK, but you're being naïve.

In ill temper they separate. Leah goes up one floor, to a terrace. Michel returns to the kitchen. Now the flat fills very quickly. The doorbell rings continuously. It would be easier just to leave the front door open but the host is anxious to see each guest on the videophone before they come in. People stream into the party like soldiers into triage. It's hell out there! I thought we weren't going to make it. Everyone takes turns to stand on the white stucco balconies, dancing, blowing whistles painted in Rastafarian colors at the carnival crowds, far below. Very soon Leah is drunk. She started too early. She can't find Michel. She spots Frank, not difficult to find in this crowd. They stand in the hall. The music is so loud, both outside and in, that information can only be passed sparingly. Nat's coming later. She's with the kids on one of Marcia's church floats. Sausage roll?

– So what's the secret?
– What?
– OF YOUR HAPPINESS. FRANCESCO.
– I CAN'T HEAR YOU. ARE YOU DRUNK?

They move into the kitchen where the bass can't find them. She repeats her query. We tell each other everything, he says. Punch?
The kitchen is packed. She needs water. She tries to make her way to the taps. Clean cup or glass or mug? Fags and food in the plughole. Time has not stood still during this procedure. Frank is lost. Michel is lost. Who are all these people? Why do they keep telling themselves what a good time they're all having? No need to queue for the toilets, no accumulated street filth between the toes, no six pounds for a can of Red Stripe. See! I've been telling you all these years! Perfect spot. You can see everything from here. And suddenly there's Nat, standing in the balcony alone, looking out. She turns. Frank is in the doorway. Leah is at a midpoint between them, unnoticed in the crowd. She sees the husband look at the wife, and the wife look at the husband. She sees no smile, no nod, no wave, no recognition, no communication, nothing at all. Bowls of disposable cameras in cheery colors are being distributed. The

host encourages people to record the occasion. Everyone takes turns trying on the Rasta wig. Leah surprises herself: she has a great time.

37.

– What do you mean they're not here? I dropped the camera in two hours ago. It's a one-hour service.
– I'm sorry, Madam, I can't find anything under that name.
– Hanwell, Leah. Please check again.

Leah puts both hands on the pharmacy counter.

– Are you sure it was today?
– I don't understand. Are you saying you've lost them? I was in two hours ago. Today. Monday. A man served me.
– I have no record of the name you're giving me. I just got here, Madam. Do you know who was serving you? Was it a young man or an older gentleman?
– I don't remember who served me. I know I came in here.
– Madam, there's another pharmacy at the station, are you sure it wasn't that one?

– Yes I'm sure. Hanwell, Leah. Can you look again?

A queue forms behind her. They are trying to decide if she is crazy. Sectioning is a common procedure in NW, and it is not always the people you'd think. The Indian woman in the white coat behind the counter flicks once more through her box of yellow envelopes.

– Ah — Hanwell. It was not in H. It's been put in the wrong place, you see. I'm so sorry, Madam.

She is not crazy. Photographs. Easy to forget about real photographs, their gloss and pleasure. But the first is entirely black, and so is the second; the third shows only a red aura, like a torch held beneath a sheet.

– Look, these aren't mine, I don't want these —

The fourth is Shar. Unmistakable. Shar laughing at whoever is taking the picture, pressing herself against a door, holding a little bottle of something, vodka? Underneath a dartboard. No other furniture in the filthy room. The fifth is Shar, still laughing, now sat on the floor, looking destroyed. The sixth is a skaggy redhead, skin and bone and track marks, with a fag hanging out her mouth, and if you squinted —

– I'm sorry, Madam. Let me take those, somehow we've had a mixing up.

Michel, who has been looking at shaving creams, comes over. He is not surprised. Infuriating, this perverse refusal to be either amazed or surprised.

NW, a small place.

With two pharmacies.

Photographs get mixed up.

Sounds reasonable but she can't take it reasonably. She is enraged by the possibility that he does not believe her. This is the girl! Don't you believe me? That's an insane coincidence! Her photos are in my envelope! Don't you believe me? But why should he believe her when she has lied about everything? The queue shuffles impatiently. She is shouting, and people look at her like she is mad. Michel yanks her toward the exit, the little bell over the door rings, it is all over so quickly. It is somehow the brevity of it that muddles things — those too few seconds, in which she looked and saw what was there. The girl. Her photos. My envelope. That's what happened. Like a riddle in a dream. There is no answer. Nor is there any way that she can take back what she has so loudly proclaimed, in front of all these decent local people, or to ask to see photos that are clearly not hers, again. What would people think?

■■■■

GUEST

■■■■

NW6

The man was naked, the woman dressed. It didn't look right, but the woman had somewhere to go. He lay clowning in bed, holding her wrist. She tried to put a shoe on. Under their window they heard truck doors opening, boxes of produce heaved onto tarmac. Felix sat up and looked to the car park below. He watched a man in an orange tabard, three stacked crates of apples in his arms, struggle through electric doors. Grace tapped the window with a long fake nail: "Babe — they can see you." Felix stretched. He made no effort to cover himself. "Some people shameless," noted Grace and squeezed round the bed to straighten the figurines on the windowsill. It was a dumb place to keep them — the man had knocked a few princesses over during the night, and now the woman wanted to know where "Ariel" was. The man turned back to the window. "Felix, I'm talking to you: what

161

you done with her?" "I ain't touched her. Which one is it? The ginger one?" "Shut up about ginger — she's red. She's stuck behind the thing — it's nasty down there!" It was an opportunity for manly display. Felix thrust his skinny arm behind the radiator and drew out an ex-mermaid. He held her up to the light by her hard-won feet: "Blatantly. Ginger." Grace put the doll back in place between the brown one and the blonde one. "Keep laughing," she said, "Won't be laughing when I kick you out on the street." True. The sheets were white and clean, bar the wet patch he had made himself, and the carpet worn thin from hoovering. On the only chair his clothes from the night before had already been folded and placed in a pile. The pink telephone on the glass dresser shone, and so did the glass dresser. He had known many women: he didn't think he had ever known anyone quite so female. "Lift!" He raised his backside so she could retrieve a sock. Even the bottle of perfume in her hand was shaped like a woman, a cheap knock-off from the market. He wished he could buy her the things she wanted! There were so many things she wanted. "And if you go past Wilsons on the high road — Fee, listen to me. If you go past ask Ricky — you know which one I'm talking about? Little light-skin boy with the twists. Ask 'im if he can come round and look at that sink. What's the time? Shit — I'm late." He watched her spray herself now in the hollow of her neck, the underside of her wrist, furtively, as if he was never to know she ever smelled of anything but roses and sandalwood. "Oyster card?" The man put his hands behind his head in a manful shrug. The woman sucked her teeth and went off to search the tiny lounge. It was hard to remain manful alone. He did all these sit-ups. All these sit-ups! His belly stayed concave, a curtain sucked through an open window. He picked yesterday's paper from the floor. Maybe the key was to make less effort. Hadn't the men she'd loved most cared least? "Fee, you working today?" "Nah, this week they only needed me Friday." "They need to be guaranteeing you Saturdays. That's when the work comes in. It's disrespectful. You're trained. You got your certificate. You've got to stop letting people disrespect you like that." "True," said Felix, and turned to Page Three. The woman came right up close to the man and made a sentence of words and kisses, alternating. "Never. Ignorant. Getting. Goals. Accomplished." She frowned absently at the nipples of the white woman in his newspaper which Felix — although certainly more familiar with such nipples than Grace — also found curious, so pink and tiny, like a cat's. "You ain't even done that thing have you? Fee? Have you?" "What thing?" "The list! You ain't done it have you?" Felix made a noncommittal sound, but the truth was he had not made a list of things he wanted from the universe, and privately doubted it would change anything at work. There wasn't enough work to justify five men working five days a week. He was the least experienced, the last one in. "Felix!" The beloved face appeared by the doorjamb: "Oi, it just arrived! I've got to go — it's on the sofa. Take it round your dad's, yeah?" The man wanted to object, he had his own errands to run, but they were secret errands and so he said nothing. "Go on, Fee. He'd like it. Don't get in no trouble. And listen, yeah? I'm gonna stay at Angeline's tonight and go carnival from hers. So bell me and let me know what time you're gonna reach." Felix made a face of protest. "Nah, Felix, I promised her we'd get done up together. It's tradition. She's on her own now, innit. You and me can go carnival any time. Don't be selfish. We can go Monday. We got each other — Angeline got no one. Come on, don't be like that." She kissed two fingertips and pointed them at his heart. He grinned back at her. "That's

164

it. Laters." How can you hide happiness? He listened to the front door click shut, the clatter of four flights of rotten boards taken at a clip, in heels.

"Felix! Felix Cooper. 'Sup, bruv?" A giant kid, with a foolish gappy smile and mono-brow and thick black hair sticking up the back of the t-shirt. Felix wedged the heavy envelope under his armpit and submitted to a laborious, complicated handshake. He was standing only two feet from his own front door. "Long time . . . You don't remember me innit." Felix found he disliked being punched like that, too hard, and on the shoulder, but he smiled thinly and lied: "Course I do, bruv. Long time." This satisfied the kid. He punched Felix again. "Good to see you, man! Where you headed?" Felix rubbed his eyes. "Family business. See my old man. Gotta be done." The young man laughed: "Lloyd! Used to come in for his Rizlas. Ain't seen him for *time*." Yeah, old Lloyd. Yeah, old Lloyd was all right, still up in the old estate, in Caldwell, yeah, never left. Still Rasta, yeah. Still got his Camden stall. Selling his knick-knacks. Still doing all that. Felix laughed, as he understood he was meant to, at this point. Together they looked over at the towers of Caldwell, not five hundred yards away. "Apple ain't fallen far from the tree, bruv, for real." This trigger gave up at least the surname: Khan. Of Khan's minimart, Willesden. All that family looked the same, many brothers, running the place for their father. This must be the youngest. Caldwell boys back in the day, two floors below the Coopers. He didn't remember them being especially friendly. Felix had arrived too late in Caldwell to make good friends. To do that you had to be born and bred. "Good times," said the Khan kid. To be polite, Felix agreed. "And you living back here now?" "My girl lives just there." He indicated the supermarket sign with his chin. "Felix, man, you properly *local*. I remember when you was working in there. Member when I saw you on the tills that time I was like —" "Yeah, well, I ain't there no more." Felix glared over the boy's head to the empty basketball cage across the street in which no-one had ever played basketball or ever would. "I'm in Hendon now, innit," said the kid, a little bashfully, as if it was too much good luck to confess to. "Loving it. Married. Nice girl, traditional. Little one on the way, Inshallah." He held up a twinkling ring finger for Felix to inspect. "Life is good, man. Life is good." People got to have their little victories. "Oi, Felix, you going carnival?"

166

"Yeah. Probably just Monday, though. I'm getting old, man." "Maybe I'll see you down there." Felix smiled nicely. Pointed his envelope toward Caldwell.

NO DOORBELL.

He had seen BROKEN DOORBELL many times before, also KEEP OUT. NO DOORBELL suggested a new level of surrender. Where the Post-it was peeling Felix thumbed it back down again. He knocked for a while without result: the reggae was loud enough to rattle the letterbox on its hinges. He stepped across to the kitchen window and put his mouth to the four-inch gap. Lloyd wandered into view, barefoot and bare-chested, idly munching a piece of toast. His locks were secured in a bun, a wooden spoon thrust through them like a geisha's chopstick.

"Lloyd — I been knocking. Let me in, dred." From around a dead cactus on the window-sill, Lloyd plucked a single key strung on a once-white shoelace, and passed it out to his son.

"Like a sauna in here!" Felix dropped his coat to the floor and kicked off his trainers.

In the narrow hall he remembered to give a wide berth to the first of several molten radiators, which, if you made even the faintest contact with them, burned your skin. His feet sunk into the carpet, a thick, synthetic purple pelt, unchanged in twenty years.

"Listen, I ain't staying. Got to be in town at twelve. I just brought something to show you."

Felix squeezed into the galley kitchen behind his father. Even this room was a mess of African masks and drums and the rest of that heritage whatnot. More every visit, it was piling up. A huge pot, bubbling yellow at the rim, sat on a gas ring. Felix watched Lloyd wrap a cloth round his hand and lift the lid.

"That book came — that Grace found?" He held out the envelope. "You should take all this stuff to the stall, man. Weather's good for it. You could sell it at carnival."

Lloyd dismissed his son with a hand. "No time for that nonsense. That's not my music anymore. It's just noise."

The dishes were piled high in the sink and a small hill of bed linen had been stuffed in a corner, not yet taken to the launderette. A bulb hung naked. Half a blunt smoldered in an ashtray.

"Lloyd, man . . . You need to do some cleaning. Why's the immersion on? Where's Sylvia?"

"Not here."

"What do you mean 'not here'?"

"The woman is not here. The woman has gone. She left a week ago but you ain't phoned for a week — it's news to you. Ain't news to me. She long gone. *This means freedom, this means lib-er-ty!*" These last lines came from the song presently, fortuitously, playing. Lloyd danced a woozy two-step toward Felix.

"She owed me forty quid," said Felix.

"Look at this. Gray!" Lloyd pressed his hands along his own hairline and pulled: a little nest of white hairs sprung forth. There were only seventeen years between the two men. "The woman made me *gray*. In three months she made me an old man."

Kept your flat clean. Hid the spliff till midday. Brought in a little money so you didn't come begging off me. Felix looked at his fingers.

"This is it, Fee, this is it: how can you stop people going when they want to go? How can you stop them? You can't stop them. Listen: if you can't stop a grown woman with four kids then you can't stop a stupid girl like Sylvia who's got nothing. She got *no one*." This emphasis drew his lips back

169

for a moment and he looked just like a dog. "People need to go their own way, Felix! If you love someone, set them free! Never go out with a Spanish girl, though, seriously, that is serious advice. They ain't rational. For real! Their brains ain't wired normal." Something moist fell from above onto Felix's shoulder. The constant central heating, the cooking, the lack of ventilation, caused large mold flowers to bloom on the ceiling. Scraps drifted down now and then, like petals. "Listen, I got along without your mother. I can get along now. Don't stress, man — I'll be all right. Been all right this long."

"What happened to the lampshade?"

"I woke up and she'd stripped the place. Honest to God, Felix. I should have called the police. She's probably back in fucking Madrid by now. DVD player. Bath mat. Toaster. If it weren't screwed down, believe — she took it. She took the van. How can I sell anything without the van? Tell me that."

"She owed me forty quid," said Felix again, although it was pointless. Lloyd clapped his son's face affectionately between his hands. Felix held up the envelope with the book in it.

"Why can't your fine woman come and see it though?" said Lloyd, taking the package from his son, "I want to impress her not you, man! That's the whole point, right? That's the whole point of the exercise! She wants to know a real Garvey House man. You was just born there. I lived it, bruv. Nah, I'm joking you. Let me take a piss first. There's ginger tea somewhere."

In the lounge Felix tore the envelope badly: a cloud of gray fluff exploded over the carpet. In little rusted heart-shaped frames his siblings sat on top of the TV watching him make a poor job of it. Devon aged about six, in the snow, in Garvey House, and the twins, Ruby and Tia, more recently, sitting on different concrete steps in a stairwell somewhere on Caldwell estate. Whichever way he tore the mess got worse. He took a big breath and blew, clearing the glossy back cover. Twenty-nine quid! For a book! And when would he get paid back for it? Never. Hard backed, large like an atlas. *GARVEY HOUSE: A Photographic Portrait.* Felix turned randomly to a page, Russian roulette. No bullet: a shy couple, just married, skinny, country-looking, with uneven afros and acne scars, done up in someone else's too-large wedding gear. No wedding guests, or no guests in the shot. They were celebrating alone with a half-empty bottle of Martini Rosso. He bit his lip and flicked forward.

Four handsome sistas in headscarves, covering a stretch of graffiti with a tub of fresh paint. (Color unknown. All was black and white.) In the background, broken chairs and a mattress and a boy smoking a blunt. Felix heard the toilet flush. Lloyd came back out, sniffing, suspiciously perky. He drew a freshly rolled one from his pajama bottoms and lit up. "Come on, then. Let's be having it."

This is a photographic account of a fascinating period in London's history. A mix of squat, halfway house and commune, Garvey House welcomed vulnerable young adults from the edges of

"Don't read me shit I already know. I don't need the man dem telling me what I already know. Who was there, me or he?" The book flipped itself back to the page Felix had just passed. "I knew all these girls, man. That's Anita, Prissy, that's Vicky, Queen Vicky we called her; she I don't know — fine-looking women! That little bastard at the back is Denzel Baker. Scoundrel. I knew all of them! What does it say there — ain't got my glasses."

May, 1977. The young women decorated and

redecorated. Sometimes the boys came home late and smashed the place up, perhaps out of boredom, or in the hope that Brother Raymond would pay them to fix the place up once more.

"Yeah, that's about right. Brother Raymond got Islington council funding it, and we did mess with them a bit, that's true. The boys messed things up, and the girls tried to fix it up, ha! — can't deny it. Except your mother. She messed things up, too. This was the heat-wave. We just took off the door. It was too hot! Where am I? Should be in this one. There's Marilyn! And — that's Brother Raymond. Turned the wrong way but that's him."

Felix looked closely. Garvey House spilled out into the concrete backyard. Kids barefoot, parents looking like kids themselves. Afros, headscarfs, cain rows, weird stiff wigs, a tall, skinny, spiritual-looking Rasta resting on a big stick. He could not be sure if he had a memory of this, or whether the photograph itself was creating the memory for him. When the council rehoused the Coopers, he was only eight years old. "Fee, look how fresh we were, though! Look at that shirt! Kids don't fresh it up like that anymore. Jeans hanging down your batty crease. We was fresh!" Felix had to concede it: style without money, without any means what-soever. Charity-store nylons worn sharply. Battered Clarks coming off like the finest Italian shoes. BLACK POWER sprayed in three-foot-high letters on the garden wall. Strange to see here, confirmed in black and white, what he had all his life assumed to be a self-serving exaggeration. "Let me find you a proper one of Brother Raymond. How many times I told you about Raymond! He was the reason." Lloyd flicked sloppily through the glossy pages, missing wads of photos at a time. He passed Felix the spliff; Felix declined it silently. Nine months, two weeks, three days. "If it weren't for Brother Raymond I'd be sleeping in Kings Cross to this *day*. He was a good man. He never —" "Wait up!" Felix thrust his hand into the book.

Page 37. Lloyd flat out on a stained mattress reading *The Autobiography of Malcolm X*. Broad flares and little glasses, shirtless here, too. Barely aged. Not the familiar locks but a well-kept afro, about four inches all round. "See? You never believe me: always reading, I was always reading. That's where you kids get your brains. They called me 'Professor.' Everybody did. That's why Jackie hunt me down in the first place. She wanted to get in *here*." Lloyd tapped his own temple and made a face to suggest the mysteries inside were frightening in their intensity, even to their owner. "Vampire business. She was sucking out the knowledge." Felix nodded. He tried looking more intently at the photograph. He asked after the names of three other guys in the picture — sat round a card table, smoking and playing Black Jack. "Two of them boys went down for murder. That one with the little face, can't remember his name, and him, Antoine Greene. Hard times! You lot don't even know. People now . . . That fool-man Barnes. What's he talking about? 'The struggle!' He's the one with the three-bedroom flat, isn't he? Full pension coming from the post office in a couple years. I don't need no lessons from that fool. I *seen* the struggle." Lloyd hit his fist against the wall for emphasis, and Felix's thoughts followed the reverberation to next door, "Barnesy's safe, man. He's a good guy," he said, in an automatic way, to defend a particular set of memories. Playing with Phil's daughters round by the bins, looking through Phil's fossils, growing mustard cress on cotton wool on Phil's balcony. Growing up, Felix had imagined that the adult world would be full of men like Phil Barnes. That they were as common in England as wildflowers.

"He's a fool," said Lloyd, and found his glasses between two cushions on the sofa.

Felix took control of the page-turning and quickly landed on Brother Raymond, seen clearly this time, helping to rebuild the front wall. "You see the Holloway Road, right? So where the Job Center is now — that's where it was." Brother Raymond turned out to be a small man, with a neat Trotskyite beard. "You said he was a priest." "He was!" Felix traced a finger under the caption: "Self-appointed social worker." "Listen: brother was a priest. In spirit he was a priest." Felix yawned, not too discreetly. Lloyd grew annoyed at the captions. "Yeah, sure, OK, that was Ann. So what? Ann something or another — it was thirty years ago, man! Everyone been with Ann. She was loose! So what? Who said you could take a lot of pictures? We weren't in the zoo!" Felix recognized the mood arc of the weed. Next door in the kitchen an old-fashioned tin kettle whistled on the stove. "Fee, go make us some tea."

Opening the cupboards, Felix found the honey jar on its side, sticking the box of tea to the shelf. He went to work with a damp tea towel. Lloyd shouted at him through the thin wall: "Little white geezer — I remember him! Snap snap snap, bothering us, you know? One of them who wants to get in on the struggle when it ain't even his struggle. That fool next door the same way — same mentality. We was trying to get on with our own business. Sometimes he was lucky to get out alive, you understand? Them boys weren't fooling, they were not fooling at all. Nobody said nothing about a book, though, nothing about money. The council would have wanted to know about it, you understand? If you take an image, Felix, OK? If you take an image of a man, right? That's copyrighted!" Lloyd appeared at the kitchen door, eyes bloodshot. "That's his soul in a way of speaking. How you gonna just sell that under English law? There's no way. In a public building from the council? I don't think so. Go to the library, look at the law books. Where's my money? He's selling my image on the internets? *My* image? I don't think so. Where's my rights under the English law? Put a bit of honey in mine."

From the doorway, Felix watched Lloyd settle into the old gray velour couch with his book, arrange a little pile of Hobnobs on the glass side table, the tea next to it, carefully balancing the joint at a genteel angle so the table was saved while the ash crumbled to the carpet. He considered asking his father when he'd last spoken to Devon, but chose, instead, the path of self-preservation. "Lloyd, I'm gonna chip." "You just got here!" "I know — but I gotta chip. Got shit to do." Felix slapped the doorframe in what he hoped was a cheery, conclusive way. "For who?" said Lloyd coolly, without looking up, "For you or she?" It was that particular tone, inquiring and high — and suddenly Jamaican — coiling up to Felix like a snake rising from its basket. He tried to laugh it off — "Come on now, don't start that, man" — but Lloyd knew to place his poison with precision: "I'm trying to train you up, right? It's not that you don't hear me, Felix, it's that you don't want to hear me. You're the big man these days. But let me arks you some ting: why you still chasing after the females like they can save your life? Seriously. Why? Look at Jasmine. You nah learn. The man cyan't satisfy the woman, right? Don't matter how much he gives. The woman is a black hole. I've gone deep into the literature, Felix. Biological, social, historical, every kind of oracle. The woman is a black hole. Your mudder was a black hole. Jasmine was a black hole. This one you got now is the same, and she's nice looking, too, so she's gonna suck you in *all the way* before you realize she's sucked you dry. The finer they are, the worse it is." Lloyd took a large, satisfying slurp from his tea. "You give me jokes," said Felix, weakly, and just about managed to make it out of the room.

In the hall, forcing his feet back into his Nikes, Felix heard Lloyd's hand come down hard upon a page. "Felix: come!" He returned to find his father bending the spine of the book back, pressing at the crease between two pages until it was flat. "Right there at the edge: with the flowery dress — I remember the flowers, they was purple. Hundred and twenty percent. Serious! Why you always doubting me? That's Jackie. Listen, when she was big with the girls she wore flat shoes, right? Always. Never wore flats unless she had to, right? Too vain." Lloyd reached out for his smoke, content with this logic. Felix sat on the arm of the sofa and looked down at the alleged elbow and left foot of his mother. Some hopeful muscle in him tried to flex, but it was weak from past misuse. He leaned against the wall. Lloyd moved to bring the book closer to Felix's face. It was a greenhouse in this place, it was unbearable. The walls were sweating! Lloyd slapped the page again. "That. Is. Jackie. Hundred and twenty percent." "I've got to chip," said Felix, kissed Lloyd briefly on his cheek, and fled.

The air outside was cool by comparison; he wiped his face and concentrated on breathing like a normal person. As he pulled the door to, the next flat along did the same. Phil Barnes. Sixty, now? He was trying to lift the heavy flower pot that sat outside his front door. He peered over at Felix, who smiled and pushed his cap back off his face.

"All right, Felix!"

"All right, Mr. Barnes."

"Held him on my knee. Now he calls me Mr. Barnes."

"All right, Barnesy."

"More like it. Christ, this is heavy. Don't just stand there looking like a 'youth,' Felix. Like a ne'er-do-well YOUTH. Give us a hand with this, will you?" Felix held the pot up. "That's the ticket."

Felix watched as Phil Barnes looked up and down the walkway like a secret agent, dropped a key on the floor and kicked it underneath.

"Terrible isn't it? Me, worried about my property like an old lady. Like a PLUTOCRAT. Before you know it I'll be saying things like 'You can never be too careful!' Just kill me when I get to that point, all right, Felix? Just put a bullet between my eyes." He laughed and took off his little round Lennon glasses to clean them with his t-shirt. He looked searchingly at Felix, suddenly mole-like and vulnerable. "You off to carnival, Felix?"

"Yeah. Probably. Tomorrow. Saturday today, though, innit."

"Course it is, course it is. My brain's failing me. How's your dad? Not seen him out and about much, recently."

"Lloyd's all right. Lloyd's Lloyd."

It touched Felix that Phil Barnes was kind enough to pretend, to Felix, that he, Barnes, and his neighbor of thirty years were on speaking terms. "That's eloquence, Felix! 'A word can paint a thousand pictures!' Well it can, can't it? Though thinking about it, isn't it the other way round, come to think of it: a picture can paint a thousand words?"

Felix shrugged pleasantly.

"Ignore me, Felix! I've become one of the doddering old. Must bore you to tears listening to the likes of me. I remember when I was young, I couldn't be having it, old people complaining, going on. Let the young get on with it! Have a bit faith in them! Let them do their own thing! I'm a bit anti-establishment, you know, but then I was a Mod, wasn't I. Still am, in my own way. But these days," said Phil, and put a hand on the balcony rail, "well, they just feel no hope, the young people, Felix, no hope, we've used all their resources, haven't we, used them up, well, we have! And now I'm giving you another lecture, aren't I? Run away! Run away! I'm like the 'Silver Tsunami!' You read that? It was in *The Guardian* the other week. 'Silver Tsunami.' That's me, apparently. Born between 1949 and 19 something else. Selfish baby-boomer. We've taken all the resources, you see. I said that to Amy and she said, 'Well, what have we got to bloody show for it?!' That made me laugh. She's not very politically minded, Amy, you see, but she means well. She does mean well," said Phil, and looked troubled, for he had strayed too far from small talk right to the center of things — it happened more and more these days — and now must try to return to the things that didn't matter. "How old are you now, Felix?"

Felix punched a fist into his other waiting palm. "Thirty-two. I'm getting *old*. Ain't even funny no more."

"Well, it never is, is it? That's why they complain all the time, the old. I'm beginning to have some sympathy with them, I can tell you — aches and pains. Press that button now, will you? Broken? Ah well, let's take the stairs — better for you. Those lifts are really

182

a disgrace." Felix pushed the fire door wide and held it open for Barnesy. "On the other hand they've got nothing else to do, have they, these kids? That's what gets me. That's what someone should say."

Together they made their way down the narrow breeze-block stairwell, Barnesy in front, Felix behind. From the back it was a sort of time travel to look at him, no fatter or thinner, no change in the clothes, no sign of the twenty-year distance between then and now. His fine, fair hair was turning white in a subtle silvery way, so it seemed to be simply getting blonder, and it still fell, in a young man's style, just to his shoulders, which were rounded and bear-like and soft as they always had been. He still wore a black waistcoat, undone, with a CND badge on the lapel, over an enormous white t-shirt, and elasticated jeans in a light blue wash. In his back pockets he kept a pair of soft slippers, for putting on the moment his rounds were finished. You'd see him in Rose's café on the high road, slippers on, eating his lunch. Felix had thought this an eccentric touch until he, too, delivered the post, for five months only, at the turn of the century, and found it to be the most exhausting work he'd ever done.

"They always say 'youth' don't they?" said

Phil and stopped once more, halfway down the stairs, in a thoughtful pose. Felix leaned against the handrail and waited, though he had heard this speech many times. "Never the boys from the posh bit up by the park, they're just boys, but our lot are 'youths,' our working-class lads are youths, bloody terrible isn't it? They come round here, Felix — I was trying to tell your dad, but he wasn't bothered, you know him, usually thinking more about the ladies than anything else — the police come round here asking after our kids (not our kids, literally, obviously our kids are long gone) but the community's kids, looking for information, you know. Save their big houses on the park from our kids! It's shameful, it really is. But you don't care about all that rubbish, do you, Felix, your lot? Just wanna have fun. And why shouldn't you? Leave them kids alone, I say. It's my opinion — the wife thinks I've got too many, but there you are. This new lot in here, they just don't want to know. Breaks my heart. Just watching all that reality TV, reading the rags, all that bloody rubbish, just shut your mouth and buy a new phone — that's how people are round here these days. They're not organized, they're not political — now, I used to have some good conversations with your mum way back when. Very good conversations, very interesting. She had a lot of interesting ideas, you know. Of course, I realize she was troubled, very troubled. But she had that thing most people don't have: curiosity. She might not have always got the right answers but she wanted to ask the questions. I value that in a person. We used to call each other 'Comrade' — wind your dad up! She was an interesting woman, your mum, I could talk to her — it's very hard, Felix, you see, if you are interested in ideas and all that, ideas and philosophies of the past — it's very hard to find someone round here to really talk to, that's the tragedy of the thing, really, I mean, when you think about it. Certainly I can't find anyone round here to talk to anymore. And for a woman it's even harder, you see. They can feel very trapped. Because of the patriarchy. I do feel everyone needs to have these little chats now and then. Yes, very interesting woman, your mother, very delicate. It's hard for someone like that."

"Yeah," said Felix.

"You sound doubtful. Course, I didn't know your mum very well, I'm sure . . . I know your dad hasn't got much good to say about her. I don't know. Complicated, innit. Families. You're too close to it, it's hard to see. I'll give you an analogy. See them paintings your dad sells sometimes, the dots, with the secret picture? If you stand too close, you can't see. But I'm across the room, aren't I? Different perspective. When my old man was in his residential home — dump, terrible dump — but I'll tell you, some of them nurses told me things about him I just had not a clue about. Not a clue. Knew him better than I did. In some senses. Not all. But. You see what I'm trying to say, anyway. It's a context thing, really."

Now they stepped out onto the communal grass, under a mighty sun, huge and orange in the sky.

"And your sisters, they're well are they? Still can't tell them apart, I bet."

"Those girls, man. Tia's just long. Ruby's bare lazy."

"Your words! Not my words! Let the record show!" said Phil, chuckling, and put his hands up in the air like an innocent man. "Now let me get this right: 'long' means always late, doesn't it? I think you told me that last time. See! No flies on me. I keep up with the slang. And 'bare' means 'a lot of' or 'very' or 'really.' It's an intensifier, more or less. I keep up. Helps living in here, you hear the kids talking, you stop and ask them. They look at me like I'm a mental case, as you might imagine." He sighed. Then came the difficult segue, always difficult in the same way.

"And the youngest lad? Devon? How's he doing?"

Felix nodded, to convey his respect for the question. Phil was the only person on the whole estate who ever asked after his brother. "He's all right, man. He's doing all right." They crossed the lawn in silence.

"If it wasn't for these, I tell you Felix, I sometimes think I'd be gone from here, I really would. Move to Bournemouth with all the other old bastards." He rapped the tree with a knuckle and made Felix stop under it and look up: an enclosing canopy of thick foliage, like standing under the bell skirts of a Disney princess. Felix never knew what to say about nature. He waited.

"A bit of green is very powerful, Felix. Very powerful. 'Specially in England. Even us Londoners born and bred, we need it, we go up the Heath, don't we, we crave it. Even our little park here is important. Bit of green. *In some melodious plot/ Of beechen green/ and shadows numberless* . . . Name that verse! Ode to a Nightingale! Very famous poem, that. Keats. Londoner he was, you see. But why should you know it! Who would have taught it to you! You've got your music, haven't you, your hip hop, and your rap — what's the difference between those two? I've never been sure. I have to say I can't understand the bling-bling business at all, Felix — seems very backward to me, all that focus on money. Maybe it's a symbol for something else — I can't tell. Anyway I've got my verses, at least. But I had to learn them myself! In those days, you failed the eleven plus and that was it — on your bike. That's how it used to be. What education I've got I've had to get myself. I grew up angry about it. But that's how it used to be in England for our sort of people. It's the same thing now with a different name. You should be angry about it, too, Felix, you should!"

"I'm more about the day-to-day." Felix nudged Phil Barnes in his side. "You're a proper old leftie, Barnesy, proper commie."

Laughter again, bent with laughter, hands on knees. When he reared back up Felix saw tears in his eyes.

"I am! You must think: what's he on about, half the time. Propaganda! What's he on about?" His face went slack and sentimental. "But I believe in the people, you see, Felix. I believe in them. Not that it's done me any good, but I do. I really do."

"Yes, Barnsey. Take it to the bridge," said Felix and thumped his old friend on the back.

They made their way out of the estate, up the hill, toward the street.

"I'm going up the depot, Felix. Afternoon shift. Sorting. Where're you going? You walking down the high road?"

"Nah. I'm late — I'm going into town. Best get the train. Might get this bus first."

It was right in front of them, opening its doors. Mrs. Mulherne, another Caldwell resident, was dragging a shopping bag backward out of the wrong door, her back bent, her tights wrinkled at her fragile ankles — Barnes ran forward to help her. Felix thought he'd better help, too. She felt light, almost fly-away. Women aged differently. When he was twelve Mulherne had seemed just a little too old to be running around with his dad: now she seemed like his father's mother. Next-morning glimpse of a pair of sturdy pink legs, wrapped in a ratty bath towel, dashing down the corridor to the only loo. Not the only one, either. "So brave, looking after them four wee ones by yourself. She's not good enough for you, dear. You deserve better. Everyone feels so bad for you." The Ladies of Caldwell expressing their sympathies. At bus stops, in doctors' waiting rooms, in Woolworths. Like a hit song that follows you from shop to shop. "Does everything for them kids. Die for them kids. More than I can say for her." One of them, Mrs. Steele, was his own dinner lady. A great blush whenever she saw him — and extra chips. Funny what you remember later — what you realize.

"Grace what?" "Grace. End of." "You don't have a last name?" "Not for you." At this same bus stop. Eyes on the ankles of her dark blue jeans, straightening the cuffs over and over so they sat right on her high black boots. Kiss curl cemented to her forehead. He thought he had never seen anything so beautiful. "Come on now, don't be like that. Listen: know what 'Felix' means? Happy. I bring happiness, innit? But can I ask you something? Does it bother you if I sit here? Grace? Can I speak to you? Both waiting for the same bus, innit? Might as well. But does it bother you if I sit here?" She had looked up at him finally, with manufactured eyes, the light brown kind you buy on the high road. She looked supernatural. And he had known at once: this is my happiness. I've been waiting at this bus stop all my life and my happiness has finally arrived. She spoke! "Felix — that's your name, yeah? You ain't bothering me, Felix. You would have to matter to me to bother me, you get me? Yeah. It's like that." Her bus coming over the hill. Then. Now. "Nah, wait, don't be like that, listen to me: I'm not trying to chirps you. You just struck me. I want to know you that's all. You got a face that's very . . . intensified." Lift of a movie star's eyebrow: "Is it. You got a face like somebody who chirpses girls at bus stops."

Five and innocent at this bus stop. Fourteen and drunk. Twenty-six and stoned. Twenty-nine in utter oblivion, out of his mind on coke and K: "You can't sleep here, son. You either need to move it along or we'll have to take you in to the station to sleep it off." You live in the same place long enough, you get memory overlap. "Thanks for seeing me off, Felix, love. Good to see you. Knock on my door any time. Send my love to Lloyd. I'm just downstairs and you're always welcome." Felix jumped back on the bus. He waved at Phil Barnes, who gave him a double thumbs up. He waved at Mrs. Mulherne as the bus climbed the hill and overtook her. He pressed a hand against the glass. Grace at seventy. The Tinkerbell tattoo in the base of her back, wrinkled, or expanded. But how could Grace ever be seventy? Look at her. ("And, Fee, remember: I weren't even meant to *be* there. I was meant to be at my aunt's in Wembley. Remember? That's the day I was

191

meant to be looking after her kids, but she broke her foot, she was home. So then I was like: might as well get the bus into town, do some shopping. Felix, please don't try and tell me that weren't fate. I don't care what nobody says, blatantly everything happens for a reason. Don't try and tell me that the universe didn't want me to be there, at that moment!")

Mind the gap. Felix stepped in the second carriage from the end and looked at a tube map like a tourist, taking a moment to convince himself of details no life-long Londoner should need to check: Kilburn to Baker Street (Jubilee): Baker street to Oxford Circus (Bakerloo). Other people trust themselves. A variation of the same instinct had his hand deep in his pocket clutching a piece of paper with a name on it. A train barrelled past, knocking him into the seat he'd been heading for. After a moment the two trains seemed to cruise together. He looked out now at his counterpart, in the other train. Small woman, whom he would have judged Jewish without being able to articulate any very precise reason why: dark, pretty, smiling to herself, in a blue dress from the seventies — big collar, tiny white bird print. She was frowning at his t-shirt.

Trying to figure it. He felt like it: he smiled! A broad smile that emphasized his dimples and revealed three gold teeth. The girl's little dark face pulled tight like a net bag. Her train pulled ahead, then his did.

"You're Felix? Hi! Great! You're Felix!"

He was standing outside Topshop. A tall, skinny white boy, with a lot of chestnut fringe floppy in his face. Drainpipe jeans, boxy black spectacles. He seemed to need a moment to re-arrange his brain, which Felix allowed him, taking out his tobacco and beginning to roll while the boy said, "Tom Mercer — it's just round the corner; well, a few streets over," and laughed as a way of covering his surprise. Felix did not know why his own voice so often misled on the phone.

"Shall we? I mean, can you do that and walk?"

"With one hand and running, bruv."

"Ha. Very good. This way."

But he did not seem to know how to negotiate the corner crush between Oxford and Regent streets; after a few false starts he was half a foot further back than he had been a moment ago. Felix licked a Rizla and watched the boy concede to a Peruvian holding a twelve-foot banner: BARGAIN CARPET SALE 100 YARDS. Not from London, not originally, thought Felix, who had been to Wiltshire once and returned astounded. Felix stepped in front and took control, walking through a crowd of Indian girls with luxurious black ponytails and little gold Selfridges badges pinned to their lapels. They walked against the natural flow, the white boy and Felix — it took them five minutes to cross the road. Felix diagnosed a hangover. Cracked lips and panda eyes. A delicate reaction to light.

Felix tried: "You had her long or . . . ?"

The boy looked startled. He put his hand in his fringe.

"Have I . . . ? Oh, I see. No. I mean, she was a present a few years ago, my 21st — hand-me-down from my father — he'd had her a long time . . . Not a very practical present. But you're a specialist, of course — you won't have the same sort of trouble."

"Mechanic."

"Right. My father knows your garage. He's had these cars for thirty years — longer — he knows all the specialist garages. Kilburn, isn't it?"

"Yeah."

"That's sort of Notting Hill way, isn't it?"

"Nah, not really."

"Ah, now, Felix? We'll do a left here. Escape this chaos."

They ducked down a cobbled side street. Fifty yards away, on Oxford Street, people pressed against people, dense as carnival, almost as loud. Back here all was silent, empty. Slick black doors, brass knobs, brass letterboxes, lamp-posts out of fairy stories. Old paintings in ornate gold frames, resting on easels, angled toward the street. PRICE UPON APPLICATION. Ladies' hats, each on its own perch, feathered, ready to fly. RING FOR ASSISTANCE. Shop after shop without a soul in it. At the end of this little row, Felix spotted a customer through a mullioned, glittering, window sitting on a leather pouf, trying on one of those green jackets, waxy like a tablecloth, with the tartan inside. Halfway up, the window glass became clear, revealing a big pink face, with scraps of white hair here and there, mostly in the ears. The type Felix saw all the time, especially in this part of town. A great tribe of them. Didn't mix much — kept to their own kind. THE HORSE AND HARE.

"Good pub, that pub," said Felix. It was something to say.

"My father swears by it. When he's in London it's his second home."

"Is it. I used to work round here, back in the day. Bit of film work."

"Really? Which company?"

"All about. Wardour Street and that," Felix added and regretted it at once.

"I have a cousin who's a VP at Sony, I wonder if you ever came across him? Daniel Palmer. In Soho Square?"

"Yeah, nah . . . I was just a runner, really. Here and there. Different places."

"Got you," said Tom, and looked satisfied. A small puzzle had been resolved. "I'm very interested in film — I used to dabble a bit in all that, you know, the way narrative works, how you can tell a story through images . . ." Felix put his hood up. "You in the industry, yeah?"

"Not exactly, I mean, no, not at the moment, no. I mean I'm sure I could have been, but it's a very unstable business, film. When I was in college I was really a film guy, buff, type. No, I'm sort of in the creative industries. Sort of media-related creative industry. It's hard to explain — I work for a company that creates ideas for brand consolidation? So that brands can better target receptivity for their products — cutting-edge brand manipulation, basically."

Felix stopped walking, forcing the boy to

197

stop. He looked vacantly at his unlit fag. "Like advertising?"

"Basically, yes," said Tom irritably, and then, when Felix didn't follow him: "Need a light?"

"Nah. Got one here somewhere. Like advertising campaigns?"

"Well, no not really, because — it's difficult to explain — basically we don't see campaigns as a way forward anymore. It's more about the integration of luxury brands into your everyday consciousness."

"Advertising," concluded Felix, drew his lighter out of his pocket and assumed a face of innocence.

"It's just this next right, if you'll . . ."

"Right behind you, bruv."

They walked through a grand square, and then off into a side street, although the houses here were no less grand: white-fronted and many stories high. Somewhere church bells rang. Felix slipped his hood off. "Here we are — here she is. I mean, obviously this is not the sort of thing where — sorry, Felix, will you excuse me a moment? I better take this."

The boy put his phone to his ear and sat on the black-and-white tiled steps of the nearest house, dead center between two potted orange trees. Felix walked a half circle until he was standing in the road. He crouched. She was smiling at him, but they all do that, no matter what state they're in. Frog-eye headlamps, manic grille grin. One-eyed in this case. He touched the spot where the badge should be. When the time came it would be a silver octagon, with the two letters back to back, dancing. Not plastic. Metal. It was going to be done right. He straightened up. He put his hand through the giant slash in the soft top and rubbed the fabric between his fingers: a thin, faded polyester weave. Plastic window gone anyway. The rust he didn't need to touch, he could see how bad it was. Worst at the rear left — it was like a continent there — but also pretty drastic all round the bonnet, which meant it had likely rusted through. Still: the right red. The original red. Good arch on the front wheels, square as they should be at the back, and a perfect rubber bumper — all of which marked it as authentically what it claimed to be, at least. M DGET. Easily fixed, like all of this external stuff — cosmetic. Under the hood was where the real news would be. In a funny way, the worse the news the better it was for him. Barry, at the garage: "If it moves, son, you can't afford it." He would make it move. Maybe not this month or the one after, but finally. A little impatiently he tried a door handle. He had an urge to rip through the blown-out window, taped shut with cardboard and masking tape.

"It's not a question of who feels more," the boy said. He was pulling a pebble back and forth across the tile with a foot. Felix leaned against the car. "Soph? Soph? Look, I can't talk now. Of course not! My phone was dead. No, not now. Please calm down. Soph, I'm in the middle of a thing. Soph?" The boy took the phone from his ear and looked at it curiously for a moment. He slid it back into the pocket of his coat. Felix whistled.

"Ninety-nine problems. I hear you, bruv."

"Sorry — what?"

"The car. It's got some problems."

"Well, yes," said Tom Mercer, and made an expansive gesture that meant to take in the whole vehicle. "Of course, it's clearly a project car. This is not something you're going to drive away in. Hence the price. Otherwise we'd be talking in the many thousands. Clearly a project car. Let me open it up, give you the full tour."

Felix watched Tom wrestle with the key.

"I can do that if —" began Felix. The door popped.

"Just needs a wangle. Project car, as I say. But doable." The tour turned out to be somewhat limited. "Clutch" said Tom, and

"Gears," and "Steering wheel," brushing these objects vaguely with his hand, and then, as they both looked dolefully at the moldy, curled carpet and rusted floor, the wool and wire bursting out of the stained upholstery, the hole where the radio should be, he murmured the year of manufacture.

"Year I was born," said Felix.

"Then it's fate."

Now the boy read off a series of facts from a small piece of paper he took from his pocket: "MG midget, one thousand five hundred cc Triumph 14 engine, 100,000 on the clock, manual, petrol, two-door road-ster, transmission requires —"

Felix couldn't resist: "Two doors, yeah? Got it."

Tom blushed appealingly. "My father's list. Not really a car man myself."

Felix felt moved to pat him in a friendly way on his high, bony shoulders. "Just messing with you. Can we get a look under the hood?"

It creaked open. Beneath was all the bad news he could have hoped for. The battery overwhelmed by rust, the cylinder cracked. Pistons right through to the engine block.

"Salvageable?" asked Tom. Felix looked perplexed. Tom tried again: "Can it be saved?"

"Depends. What sort of money we talking

about?"

Tom looked once more at his piece of paper. "I've been instructed around the thousand mark."

Felix laughed and reached his hand into the engine. He scratched at the rust with a fingernail.

"To be honest with you, Tom, I see these come in every day, in better condition than yours, much better — for six hundred. No-one's gonna pay six hundred for this. This one you won't be able to sell to no-one but a mechanic, I promise you."

The sun now hit the car directly: the bonnet lit up. Radiant wreck! Tom looked up, squinting.

"Good thing you're a mechanic, then, isn't it?"

There was something funny about the way he said it. Both men laughed: Felix in his big gulping way, Tom into his hand like a child. The phone in his pocket started up.

"Oh Jesus — look, it's not really any skin off my nose, but if I tell my father I took less than seven hundred I'll never hear the end of it. Personally I'd much rather be back in my bed. Excuse me a second — Soph, I'll call you back in one minute —" But he kept the phone to his ear and Felix heard more than he wanted to as Tom mimed apologies at him. At the end of the road, a happy roar rose up from a crowd at one of the pub's outdoor tables. Tom raised his eyebrows quizzically at Felix and made the "lifting a pint" gesture: Felix nodded.

"What'll you have?"
"Ginger beer, thanks."
"Ginger beer and?"
"Nah, that's it."
"Look, for me it's hair of the dog — least you can do is join me."
"Nah, I'm all right. Just ginger beer."
"My father says there's only two sentences a self-respecting Englishman should accept in this situation: *I'm on antibiotics* and *I'm an alcoholic.*"
"I'm an alcoholic."
Felix looked up from the slats of the wooden table. Tom wiped the sweat from his forehead, opened his mouth but said nothing. Felix took a moment to appreciate that his own skin could not broadcast shame so quickly nor so well. Tom's phone started up again.
Felix rose up from the bench: "Don't worry, mate, you take your call. I'll go. Pint, yeah?"
Outside it was a glorious Saturday lunchtime in late summer; inside it was ten o'clock at night on a Tuesday in October. The ceiling

black and carved into hexagons, the carpet light-absorbing and dark green. Coffin-wood furniture, ancient and heavy. One old man sat in the corner by the jukebox, in a shabby donkey jacket, with white papery skin and yellow hair and nails, rolling a cigarette — he *looked* like a cigarette. At the bar, a skinny-legged old girl perched on a stool counted and recounted four piles of twenty-pence pieces. She stopped this activity to stare frankly at Felix, who only smiled back. "All right," he said, and turned to the barmaid. The old woman sliced suddenly at the towers of coins with the side of her palm. Felix's reflexes were quick; he saved one pile from flying off the bar altogether. In his peripheral vision he saw Tom heading for the toilets. The barmaid mouthed "sorry" and screwed a finger into her temple. "No worries," said Felix. He took a cold glass in each hand. He let the barmaid put a packet of salt-and-vinegar crisps between his teeth.

"How old are you, Felix?"
"Thirty-two."
"But why d'you look younger than me?"
Felix split the bag of crisps down the seam and laid them out on the table.
"Is it. How old are you?"

"Twenty-five. I'm already losing my bloody hair."

Felix bit down on his straw and smiled round it: "My old man's the same way. No wrinkles. Genetics."

"Ah, genetics. Explanation for everything these days." Tom shielded his eyes with his hand, to make out the sun was bothering him. Felix's gaze was intense — he met your eyes no matter how you tried to avoid it — and Tom was not used to looking at even his closest friends that way, no matter a perfect stranger to whom he hoped to sell a car. He took a pair of sunglasses out of his pocket and put them on. "And how did you get from working in film to mechanic-ing, if you don't mind me asking?"

"I've done all sorts, Tom," said Felix cheerfully, and got his fingers into position to count them off. "Cheffing, that's where I started — I did a GNVQ in catering, didn't I — got quite far with that when I was younger; head chef at one point at this little Thai place in Camden, all right place; chucked that in, did a bit of painting and decorating, bit of security, you know, in the clubs, bit of retail, drove a truck delivering them crisps you're eating round the M25, worked for the Royal Mail," said Felix, with an accent so peculiar it was hard to imagine who was being impersonated. "Used to make these." He pointed at his chest. "Then got lucky, got into some stuff — you know the Cot-tes-low?" asked Felix, slowly, as a way of marking all the vital Ts. "It's a theater," he explained, abandoning all the Ts and adding an F, "near here. Was front of house for a year, box office that means. Then I was assistant backstage putting the props where they needed to be, all that — that's how I got into the film thing. Just very very lucky. Always been lucky. But then I really got deep in the drug thing, to tell you the truth, Tom, and I'm just basically picking myself up off the floor from that the past few years, so."

Tom waited for the bit about the mechanic thing — it didn't come. Like a man who has been thrown a lot of strange-shaped objects, he clung to the one that struck him first.

"You used to make t-shirts?"

Felix frowned. It was not the thing that usually interested people. He stood up and pulled at his own t-shirt so its faded message at least read straight without creases.

"I'm sorry, I don't speak — is it Polish?"

"Exactly! Says: *I Love Polish Girls*."

"Oh. Are you Polish?" asked Tom doubtfully.

That struck Felix as very funny. He fell back in his seat and was a good time repeating the question, slapping the table and laughing, while Tom took quiet sips off the head of his pint like a little bird swooping over a puddle.

"Nah, Tom, nah, not Polish. London born and bred. These I did a long time back — business venture. Five years back — know what? It's seven. Time flies, innit! Truthfully it was my old man's idea, I was more like . . . the money man," said Felix awkwardly, for it was a bold way to describe his thousand-pound stake, "Each one was in its own language. I love Spanish girls in Spanish, I love German girls in German, I love Italian girls in Italian, I love Brazilian girls in Brazilian —"

"Portuguese," said Tom, but the list continued.

"I love Norwegian girls in Norwegian, I love Swedish girls in Swedish, I love Welsh girls in Welsh — that was more of a joke one, you get me? — nah, that's harsh, but you know what I'm saying — I love Russian girls in Russian, I love Chinese girls in Chinese. But there's two types of Chinese — not many people know that, my mate Alan told me. You got to have both. I love Indian girls in Hindi, and we had a lot of different ones in Arabic, and I love African girls in I think it was Yoruba or something. Got the translations off the Internet."

"Yes," said Tom.

"Made three thousand of them and took them to Ibiza, to sell them, didn't I. Imagine you're walking through Ibiza town with a t-shirt says I love Italian Girls in Italian! You'd clean up!"

Repeating the idea, with Lloyd's enthusiasm, as Lloyd had first conveyed it to him, Felix was almost able to forget that they had not cleaned up, that he had lost his stake, along with the good job at the Thai restaurant he had given up, at Lloyd's insistence, so that he could go to Ibiza. Two thousand five hundred t-shirts still sat in boxes in Lloyd's cousin Clive's lock-up, under the railway arches of King's Cross.

"Tom, what about you?"

"What about me what?"

Felix grinned: "Don't be shy now. What would I put you down for? Everyone got a type. Let me guess: bet you like some of that Brazilian!"

Tom, somewhat dazzled by the gleaming hardware in Felix's mouth, said, "I'll say French," and wondered what the true answer was, and found it troubling.

"French girls. Right. I'll throw one of them in with the deal. Still got a few."

"Isn't it me who's making the deal?"

Felix reached over the table and patted Tom

on the shoulder.

"Course it is, Tom, course it is."

The phrase "the drug thing" still hovered over the table. Tom left it alone.

"And are you married, Felix?"

"Not yet. Planning to. That your Missus keeps belling you?"

"Christ, no. We've only been going out nine months. I'm only twenty-five!"

"I had two kids when I was your age," said Felix and flashed the screen of his phone at Tom. "That's them in their Sunday best. Felix Jr. . . . ; he's a man now himself, almost fourteen. And Whitney, she's nine."

"They're beautiful," said Tom, though he hadn't seen anything. "You must be very proud."

"I don't see much of them, to tell you the truth. They live with their Mum. We ain't together. To be honest, me and the mum don't really get on. She's one of them real . . . oppositional women."

Tom laughed, and then saw that Felix had not meant to be funny.

"Sorry — I just — well, it's a good phrase for it. I think that may be what I've got on my hands. An oppositional woman."

"Listen, if I told Jasmine: the sky's blue, she'd say it's green, you get me?" said Felix, clawing at the label on his bottle of ginger beer. "Got a lot of mental issues. Grew up in care. My mum was in care — same thing. Does something to you. Does something. I known Jasmine since we was sixteen and she was like that from *time*. Depressed, don't leave the flat for days, don't clean, place is like a pigsty, all of that. She's had a hard time. Anyway."

"Yes, that must be hard," said Tom, quietly, and took another large swig of his pint.

After that they sat in silence, both looking out upon the street, as if only accidentally sat together.

"Felix, could I maybe trouble you for one of those? Terrible roller."

Felix lit his own, nodded and silently started work on another. His phone vibrated in his pocket. He read the message and thrust the handset once more in Tom's face.

"Oi, Tom, you're an advertiser — what d'you make of that?"

Tom, who was long-sighted, drew back from the screen in order to read it: "Our records indicate you still haven't claimed compensation for your accident. You may be entitled up to £3650. To claim free reply 'CLAIM.' To opt out text 'STOP.'"

"Scam, innit."

"Oh, I should think so, yes."

"Cos how could they know if I'd had an accident? Evil. Imagine if you were old, or ill, getting that."

"Yes, said Tom, not really following, "I think they just have these . . . databases."

"Databases," said Felix and shook his head in despair, "and you reply and five quid comes off your bill. But that's the way people are these days. Everyone's looking out for themselves. My girl gave me this book, *Ten Secrets of Successful Leaders*. You read it?"

"No."

"Should read it. She was like, 'Fee, you know who reads this book? Bill Gates. The Mafia. The Royal family. Bankers. Tupac read it. Jewish people read this book. Educate yourself.' She's a smart one. I'm not even a reader but that one opened my eyes. There you go."

Tom took the cigarette and lit it and inhaled with the deep relief of a man who had given up smoking entirely only a few hours before.

"Listen — Felix, this is a bit of a weird one," said Tom, nodding at the packet of Amber Leaf between them, lowering his voice, "But you wouldn't by any chance have anything stronger? Not to buy, just a pinch. I find it takes the edge off."

Felix sighed and leaned back into his bench and began murmuring. God grant me the serenity to accept the things I cannot change, courage to change the things I can, and the wisdom to know the difference.

"Oh dear," said Tom. He cringed to the right, then somehow reversed his body and cringed to the left. "I didn't mean to —"

"You're all right. My girl thinks I've got an invisible tattoo on my forehead: PLEASE ASK ME FOR WEED. Must have one of them faces."

Tom lifted his drink and finished it off. Did this mean there was weed or there wasn't? He examined a distorted Felix through the bottom of his pint glass.

"Well, she sounds sensible," said Tom, at last. Felix passed him the finished fag.

"Come again?"

"The girl you mentioned, your girlfriend person."

Felix smiled enormously: "Oh. Grace. Yeah. She is. Never been happier in my life, Tom, to tell you the truth. Changed my life. I tell her, all the time: you're a lifesaver. And she is."

Tom held up his ringing phone and gave it the evil eye.

"I seem to be stuck with a life-destroyer."

"Nobody can do that, Tom. Only *you* have

the power to do that."

Felix was sincere, but saw he had provoked a sort of smirk in Tom, which in turn provoked in Felix a need to press his point home more strongly: "Listen, this girl changed my outlook totally. Globally. She sees my potential. And in the end, you just got to be the best you that you can be. The rest will follow naturally. I've been through it, Tom, right? So I know. The personal is eternal. Think about it."

How close to superfluous his job was these days! The slogans came pre-embedded, in people's souls. A smart thought: Tom discreetly congratulated himself for having it. He nodded at Felix deeply, satirically, samurai-style. "Thank you, Felix," he said, "I'll remember that. Best you that you can be. Personal equals eternal. You seem like a bloke who's got it all figured out." He lifted his empty glass to clink against Felix's, but Felix was not impervious to irony and left his own glass where it was.

"Seeming ain't being," he said quietly and looked away. "Listen —" He drew a folded envelope from his back pocket. "— I've got things to do, so . . ."

The boy saw he had overstepped: "Of course. Look — where were we? You need to make me an offer."

"You need to give me a reasonable price, mate."

It was only now that Tom realized he did not, after all, despise Felix's habit of over-familiarity. On the contrary, to be called "mate" at this late point in their acquaintance felt like a melancholy step down in the world. And why am I only able to enjoy things once they've passed, wondered Tom, and tried to place a mental finger upon a hazy quote from a French book, which made exactly this point, and helpfully gave the answer, too. *Candide*? Proust? Why hadn't he kept up with his French? He thought of *Pere* Mercer, on the phone, this morning: "The trouble is you don't follow through, Tom. That's always been your trouble." And of course Sophie was making essentially the same point. Some days have a depressing thematic coherence. Maybe next the cloud overhead would open up and a huge cartoon hand emerge from below, pointing at him, accompanied by a thunderous, authorial voice: TOM MERCER. EPIC FAIL. But it had already been pointed out to him — also this morning! — that this approach, too, was only another kind of trap: "Tom, dar-ling, it's really terribly narcissistic to think the whole world is against you." Listening to his mother's voice down the line he had been impressed by how calm and kind she sounded and how satisfied she was with her diagnosis of his personality. Thank God for his mother! She didn't take him seriously, and laughed when he was being funny, even when she didn't understand, as she almost never did. They were country people, his parents, and of grandparental age, for this was a second marriage for them both. They could not conceive of his daily life, did not e-mail, had never heard of Sussex University until he attended it, had no experience of either a "downstairs neighbor," a "night bus," the realities of an "unpaid internship" ("Just go in there and present a few ideas, Tom, and show them what you're worth. At the very least Charlie will listen. We worked together for seven years for Christ's sake!") or the sort of nightclub where you leave your clothes — and much else — at the door. They did not have double lives, as far as he could tell. They drank with dinner, never to excess. Where his father found Tom infuriating and inexplicable, his mother went a little gentler on him, at least allowing for the possibility that he really was suffering from some varietal of twenty-first-century intellectual ennui that made it impossible for him to take advantage of the good fortune he'd been born with. There were limits, however. One shouldn't pretend that Brixton was any sort of place to live. "But Tom: if you're feeling low, 20 Baresfield is empty until at least July. I don't know what you have against Mayfair. And you'll have somewhere to park the car without fear of it being burned to a shell in some riot." "That was twenty years ago!" "Tom, I refer you to the Aesop fable: leopard, spots." "That's not a fable!" "Honestly, I don't know why you didn't move into it in the first place." Because sometimes one wants to have the illusion that one is making one's own life, out of one's own resources. He didn't say that. He said: "Mother, your wisdom surpasseth all understanding." To which she said, "Don't be facetious. And don't make a mess!" But he was making a mess. With this girl. It was all a terrible mess.

"A reasonable price," repeated Tom and touched the side of his head, as if the strange thoughts were a misfiring synapse, and a tap to the temple might tamp them back down.

"'Cos you're talking silly money," said Felix, and began packing away his tobacco and Rizlas and phone in a manner that seemed, to Tom, to perfectly convey disappointment, not only in the failure of the deal, but in Tom himself.

"But you can't seriously be asking me to give

it to you for less than six hundred!"

Halfway through this sentence Tom recognized the strange, inappropriate plea in his own voice.

"Four hundred's more like it, bruv. My lot will tow it. That's generous! You wouldn't get that much for scrap. You'd probably have to pay that much to get it towed."

The audaciousness of this made Tom smile: "Seriously? Come on. Let's be serious."

Felix kept his poker face. Tom, still smiling, put his chin in his hand, and "thought" like a cartoon of somebody "thinking."

"Five hundred? Then we can both go home. I really can't go lower than that. It's an MG!"

"Four fifty. Ain't going no higher than that."

Tom's phone started up once more. He wore an inconclusive expression: he reminded Felix of the actors milling backstage after the matinee, with the evening performance still before them. Not fully in character, but not free of it either.

"Life-destroyer on line one. You're not easy, Felix. I can see nothing gets past Felix."

Felix withdrew the crumpled notes and began slowly counting them out into a neat pile.

So the garage lent you an MG.
Nah, dred, I bought it.

Is it. You must be doing all right.

Weren't that much. Been saving. Doing it up myself as a ~~gift for Grace~~ project for myself. A project car.

You know why you bought that though, don't you? Do you know? You don't know, do you? Do you wanna know? I'm going to impart some wisdom on you, blud, get ready. You think you know why, but you don't know . . .

Felix heard it as clearly as any actual conversation with his father: it seemed to exist on the same plane of reality. Maybe it was simply like spotting a train very early, far down the track. The boys at the garage were to pick the car up later today and have it delivered to the resident parking bays in Caldwell. To do that they would have to ask his father for a parking pass. A little after that his father would call him. The prospect of this took the shine off the triumph that should accompany purchase. The further he got down Regent Street the worse it got.

Felix, listen: you can't buy a woman. You can't buy her love. She's gonna leave you that way. Love's gonna leave you anyway so you might as well not bother with the cars and the jewels. Serious.

Felix passed in front of the Valentine kid with his leg in the air and arrow primed. Who would be happy for him? His thumb hovered over the roller ball on his phone, moving back and forth through the various digits of his siblings, but connecting with each a potential headache that made him hesitate and finally put the handset back in his pocket. Tia would have her children underfoot, and her loneliness and boredom turned easily to jealousy, even for things she cared nothing about, like cars. Ruby would only want to know what the car could do for her — when she could borrow it, where she could drive it. She lived in her twin's spare room, had nothing and no-one, and pitied herself deeply. She expected charity always, while simultaneously wanting the best of everything. Why'd you buy that wreck? Fool. Both twins had a horror of second-hand goods. Grace, too. He wouldn't be telling her anything about it until it looked like it had just rolled off the assembly line. Devon was the only one who might be interested, but you couldn't call him, you had to wait for him to call.

From Felix's pocket a digital orchestra played a piece of classical music from an aftershave advert from his childhood. He answered it joyfully, but his love sounded stressed and skipped the hellos. "Did you go see Ricky?" "Nah, sorry — forgot. I'll call him." "How you gonna call him? I ain't got his number — have you?" "When I go back I'll go past." "Downstairs called. The leak's gone through the floor." "I'll go see him, chill." "Where are you?" "At my dad's." "You show him? What did he say? Tell him I can order some more copies off the Internet. Actually let me chat to him." "Yeah, man. He's looking through it. He's into it. Told a lot of stories — you know how he is. Trip down memory lane, innit. Listen, I gotta go." "Put Lloyd on —" An ambulance passed Felix on the street. "I'm on the balcony — he's in the bathroom. Listen, I'll call you back in a bit. I gotta go." "You gotta go! I gotta work." "True!" The conversation descended into baby talk, and then briefly turned explicit. Grace was fond of proclaiming her "nastiness," although in bed she was tame, almost prudish, and in their six months together Felix had not quite managed to unite the girl on the phone and the one in his arms. "I love you, baby," she said, and Felix repeated it passionately, trying to return himself to that moment of optimism before he'd answered the phone. Weird to think she was only a few streets from him, at this moment. Her manager in the background said something about a booking for twelve at two — she was gone again without saying good-bye. Like a ghost on your shoulder and then vanished, the everyday miracle. He remembered when you turned the dial with your finger. Sometimes lines crossed and four ghosts spoke. And now Felix Jr. and his nieces spoke to videos of each other. You wait long enough, the films come true — and everybody acts like it's nothing. Still, he was glad he got to see the future. Touch and go for a while. A comic book reader, sci-fi fan, it had always been obvious, to Felix, that the future would suit him. Hollywood had nothing on Felix when it came to imagining the future. He didn't even have to go to the movies anymore, he could just walk down the street like this and see the whole damn spectacular just playing in his mind. Script by Felix Cooper. Directed by Felix Cooper. Starring Felix Cooper.

Anflex, my darling, how will you be getting home?

Particle transfer. See you in a second, my dear Gracian. In a nano-second.

Shit like that. Just rolling in his brain. Sometimes he went and told a whole film in words to Grace, and she was totally into it, and it wasn't just because she loved him: the fact was that the films in Felix's mind were blatantly better than anything people paid good money to see. Now Felix collided with a real live young man leaving a glass-walled video emporium, walking backward through the double doors while waving good-bye to his friends, still wrestling with their joysticks. Felix touched the guy gently on the elbows, and the stranger, with equal care, reached back and held Felix where his waist met his back; they both laughed lightly and apologized, called each other "Boss" before separating quickly, the stranger striding back toward Eros, and Felix onwards to Soho.

On her street he reached into his pocket, pulled out his phone, and typed: On yr St. U free? The answer came back: Door open. He had not stood on this street for three months. His phone buzzed again: Five mins please. Why not pick up cigs?

This addition was annoying: it put him back in the wrong position. He made his way over to the unventilated corner shop and spent a hot ten minutes in the queue, trying to finesse the brief speech he thought he had decided on, realizing in fact that he had decided on very little. Why did he need to come down here and say anything at all? She didn't matter anymore. News of her irrelevance should reach Soho without any effort on his part; she should just walk out of her front door and sniff it in the air. "Don't need this," said the woman at the counter. She handed him back fifty pence. Someone behind him sighed; he moved aside quickly with the shame of a Londoner who has inconvenienced, even for a moment, another Londoner. The box of fags was in his pocket. Here was the change in his hand. He couldn't remember anything about the transaction. He was sweating like a fool.

Outside he tried to calm himself and realign with the exuberant mood in the street. The sun was an incitement, collapsing day into night. Young bluds had stripped to their bare chests as if in a nightclub already. The white boys wore flip-flops and cargo shorts and drank import beers from the bottle. A small gang danced mildly in the doorway of G.A.Y, on autopilot from the night before. Felix chuckled into his chest and leaned against a lamppost to roll a fag. He had the sense that someone was watching and taking it all down ("Felix was a solid bloke, with his heart in the right place, who liked to watch the world go by") but when that fancy was finished there was nothing else for him to do. A car with tinted windows rolled by. It took a moment to put together the fearful child in the passing reflection with what he knew of his own face. He looked up and over to her door. It was open; two of the girls stood on the doorstep chatting amiably with the Somali drivers, one doorway along. Felix squared his shoulders, put a cheerful limp in his walk. ("Sometimes you got to do what you got to do!") But there was no kind of smile you could bring to these girls that would make them go easy on you. Chantelle was cutting her eyes at him when he was still twenty yards away. By the time he reached her she had already, as far as she was concerned, dispensed with greetings; she got a grip of his thin hooded top between two fingers, examined its material briefly and then released it again, like a filthy thing picked up off the floor.

"You look summery. Jesus Christ. Mr. Sunshine."

"This ain't hot to me tho. I'm skinny — I need the layers."

"Long time," said the white one with the sour face, Cherry.

"Been busy."

"Wouldn't bother with Her Majesty upstairs, if I were you: get better down here."

"Yeah, yeah, yeah," said Felix, and showed his gold teeth, but he had never been sure if upstairs truly was a separate world. Her Majesty upstairs swore it was. They used to argue about it. It didn't matter now.

"Can I go?"

They were both big girls and it was their evergreen joke not to move for him, he had to squeeze between them. Felix led with his bony shoulders.

"Like a chicken bone!"

"Pure rib!"

Cherry pinched his backside — three floors up he could still hear cackling. He rounded the last banister. Classical violins were going at it, you could hear taps running hard in the bathroom. At the threshold he was wreathed in steam.

"Felix? Darling, is that you? Door's open! Is Karenin out there? Bring the bastard in."

Karenin was on the mat. Felix gathered him sloppily into his arms. The cat's huge weight kept displacing itself: it wasn't possible to hold up its backside, belly and neck at the same time, something always fell through the gap. He whispered into its ear — "All right, K" — and stepped inside. This same fat cat in his arms, the yellowing old playbills and photos on the wall, the boxes full of sheet music for a non-existent piano, sold to a pawnshop before even Felix's time. The old-school everything. He knew it all too well. The grimy sameness, the way nothing was ever refreshed. She called them antiques. Another way of saying there's no more money. Five years! He dropped the cat down on the chaise: spring-less, the seat sunk to receive it. How did he ever come to know this place? Unknowing it would just be the restoring of things to their natural, healthy state.

"Annie? You coming out?"

"In the bath! S'heavenly. Come in!"

"Nah, you're all right. I'll wait."

"What?"

"I'LL WAIT."

"Don't be ludicrous. Bring an ashtray."

Felix looked about him. On a clothes hanger hooked to the window frame an outfit hung disembodied and flooded with light. Purple jeans, a complicated vest with safety pins on the front, some kind of tartan cape, and below on the floor a pair of yellow leather boots with heels of four or five inches, all of which would be seen by no-one except the boy from the off license who delivered her "groceries."

"Can't see no ashtray."

Piled on top of various envelopes and pages of newspapers were small mountains of spent fags and ash. It was hard to maneuver — some attempt at reorganization was under way. Towers of paper dotted the floor. It was worse than his father's situation, yet he saw now that the spirit was much the same: a large life contracted into a small space. He had never visited one then the other in quick succession like this. The sense of suffocation and impatience was identical, the longing he had to be free.

"Dear Lord — by the Pavlovas. 'The Russian bird with the long face.' Underneath her."

He would never again have to pretend to be interested in things in which he had no interest. Ballet dancers, novels, the long and torturous history of her family. He stepped over a glass coffee table to where eight photographs of Pavlova formed a diamond on the wall, echoing the pyramid of fags below, the only decoration on a small side table.

"If full, use the plastic bag on the doorknob," called Annie. "Empty into."

He did as he was told. He came into the bathroom, put the packet of fags in the ashtray and the ashtray on the lip of the bath.

"What you got them on for?"

She ran her fingertips along a pair of mother-of-pearl vintage sunglasses: "This is a terribly bright bathroom, Felix. Blinding. Could you? My hands."

What looked like a single breakfast oat sat on her bottom lip, painted over with scarlet. Felix put a cigarette in her mouth and lit it.

Even in the few months since he'd last been here the lines under her eyes seemed to have lengthened and deepened, fanning out beyond the shades. The powder she'd doused herself in gathered lumpenly here and there and made everything worse. He retreated to the toilet seat. It was the correct distance. She made a little adjustment to the costume — plumping up the big brown pile of hair, and letting the wet strands fall around her made-up face, framing it. Her narrow shoulders rose out of the bubbles, and he knew every blue vein and brown mole. She was grinning in a certain way that had started the whole thing off, the day he watched her bring up a tray of tea to the film crew on her roof, hair tied in a headscarf like one of those women in the war. The thin lips drawn back and an inch of shiny gum all round.

"How've you been, Annie?"

"Sorry?" She cupped her hand facetiously round her ear.

"How've you been?"

"How have I been? Is that the question?" She leaned back into the bubbles. "How have I been? How have I been. Well, I've been fucking desolate, really." She tapped some ash, missing the ashtray, dusting the bubbles. "Not entirely due to your disappearance, don't flatter yourself. Someone at Westminster Council has taken it upon themselves to reevaluate my claim. Because somebody else, some *citizen,* took it upon themselves to notify the council. My money's been frozen, I'm reduced to a rather tragic diet of grilled sardines. And various other necessities have been severely reduced . . ." She made the unhappy face of a child. "Guess who."

"Barrett," said Felix sullenly; he would have her in any mood but this one. He discreetly scanned the room, and soon found what he was looking for: the rolled-up twenty and the vanity mirror, peeking out from behind a leg of the old-fashioned tub.

"He's trying to bankrupt me, I suppose. So they can all just get on with charging some —"

"Russian a thousand a week," murmured Felix, matching her word for word.

"I'm sorry I'm so boring."

She stood up. If it was a challenge he was equal to it. He watched the suds slink down her body. She had a dancer's frame, with all the curves at the back. What he was now confronted with had only a pale utility to it: breasts, like two muscles, sitting high above a carriage of stringent pulleys and levers, all of it designed for a life that never happened.

"You might pass a girl a towel."

A dingy rag hung over the door. He tried to

reach around her to drape it chastely over her shoulders, but she sunk into his body, soaking him.

"Brrrr. That's cozy."

"Fuckssake!"

She whispered into his ear: "The good news is if they claim I'm out and about I might as well go out and about. *We* might as well."

Felix stepped back, got on his hands and knees and stretched an arm under the bath. "According to them I've already been out. I'm in Heaven every night dancing it up with the Twinks, without my knowledge. Sleep-living. Maybe this is the start of a whole new life for me! For God's sake, what are you doing down there? Oh, don't be such a bore, Felix. Leave that alone . . ."

Felix re-emerged holding a silver-handled mirror from a fairy tale with four thick lines of powder cut along it, crossed by a straw, like a coat of arms. Annie stretched her arms out toward him with the wrists turned up. The veins seemed bigger, bluer.

"Not even lunch time."

"On the contrary, that *is* lunch. Do you mind terribly putting it back where you found it?"

They stood either side of the toilet: the obvious gesture suggested itself. It would be one way of saying what he had to say.

"Put. It. Back. Please." Annie smiled with

all her showgirl teeth. Someone was knocking at the door. Felix spotted a wayward shiver in her eyelid, a struggle between the pretense of lightness and the reality of weight. He knew all about that struggle. He put it back. "Coming!"

She grabbed a silk Japanese thing off a hook on the door and slipped into it, folding one side into the other so as to hide a gigantic rip. It had a flock of swallows on the back, swooping from her neck down her spine to the floor. She ran out, shutting Felix in. Out of habit he opened the glass-fronted cabinet above the sink. He pushed the first row aside — Pond's Cream, Elizabeth Arden, an empty, historic bottle of Chanel No.5 — to reach the medications behind. Picked up a bottle of poxywhadya-callitrendridine, the one with the red cap which, if mixed with alcohol, had a manic-mellow buzz, like ketamine-laced Ecstacy. Worked very well with vodka. He held it in his hand. He put it back in its place. From the other room he heard her, suddenly strident: "Well, no . . . I really don't see that at all . . ."

Bored, Felix wandered in and parked himself on an uncomfortable high-backed wooden chair that once graced the antechamber of Wentworth Castle.

"I barely use the stairs. It may be a 'shared area' but I don't use it. My only traffic is the occasional deliveryman or friend coming up. Very occasional. I don't go down, I can't. Surely the people you should be talking to are the ladies downstairs, who, as we both know — I'm assuming you're a man of the world — have people stomping up and down constantly. Up, down, up, down. Like Piccadilly bloody Circus."

She stepped forward to demonstrate, with a finger, this popular right of way, and Felix got a glimpse of the man in the doorway: a big blonde, buff from the gym, in a navy suit, holding a ring binder that said Google on it.

"Miss Bedford, please, I am only doing my job."

"Sorry — what's your name? Can I see some sort of official . . ."

The blonde passed Annie a card.

"Do you have instructions to come and harass me? Do you? I don't think you do, Mr. — I can't possibly pronounce that name — I don't think you do, Erik. Because I'm afraid I don't answer to Mr. Barrett. I answer to the *actual* landlord — I'm a relative of the *actual* landlord, as in the lord of the land. He's a close relative, and I'm quite sure he wouldn't want me harassed."

Erik opened his ring binder and closed it again.

"We're the sub-agents, and we're instructed to advise the tenants that the shared areas are to be improved and the cost split between the flats. We've sent several letters to this address and received no reply."

"What a funny accent you have. Is it Swedish?"

Erik stood almost to attention: "I am from Norway."

"Oh, Norwegian! Norway. Lovely. I've never been, obviously — I never go anywhere. Felix," she said turning round, with a louche lean into the doorframe, "Erik is Norwegian."

"Is it," said Felix. He moved his jaw rigidly in impersonation of hers. She stuck her tongue out at him.

"Now Erik, is it Sweden that had all the recent trouble?"

"Excuse me?"

"I mean, Norway. Oh, you know, with the money. Hard to believe a whole nation can go bankrupt. It happened to my aunt Helen, but of course she was really asking for it. A whole country seems rather . . . careless."

"You are speaking of Iceland, I think."

"Am I? Oh, perhaps I am. I always get the Nordic ones sort of . . ." Annie tangled her fingers together.

"Miss Bedford —"

"Look, the point is, nobody wants to see this place tarted up more than me — I mean, we haven't had a film crew here since — whenever that was — and that roof is crying out to be filmed from, it really is, it's just absurd to leave it lying fallow. It's one of the best views in London. I really think it would be in your interests to make the place more attractive to outside investment. You've been very slack indeed as far as outside investment is concerned."

Erik shrank a little in his cheap suit. It didn't matter what nonsense came out of her mouth, her accent worked a spell. Felix had seen it magic her out of some unpromising corners, even when the benefits people turned up, even when the police raided the brothel downstairs while a sizable bag of heroin sat just out of sight on her night table. She could talk anybody away from her door. She could fall and fall and fall and still never quite hit the ground. Her great uncle, the earl, owned the ground, beneath this building, beneath every building on the street, the theater, the coffee houses, the McDonald's.

"The *idea* that a vulnerable woman who lives alone and barely leaves her apartment is required to pay the same amount as a group of 'business' ladies who entertain their male visitors approximately every eight minutes — I think it's incredible. Stomp stomp stomp," she shouted, and marched out a rhythm on the doorstep. "That's what's wearing the bloody carpet away. Stomp stomp stomp. Gentleman callers on the stair." Erik looked over — a little desperately — at Felix. "That," said Annie, pointing, "is not a gentleman caller. That is my boyfriend. His name is Felix Cooper. He is a filmmaker. And he does *not* live here. He lives in North West London, a dinky part of it you've probably never heard of called Willesden, and I can tell you now you'd be wrong to dismiss it actually because actually it's very interesting, very 'diverse.' Lord, what a word. And the fact is, we're both very independent people from quite different walks of life and we simply prefer to keep our independence. It's really not so unusual, is it, to have —"

Here Felix jumped up, passed his hands around Annie's waist, and drew her back into the room. With a sigh she wilted into the chaise and gave all her attention to Karenin, who looked like he considered it no less than his due. Erik opened his binder, detached a sheaf of papers and pushed them toward Felix.

"I need Miss Bedford to sign this. It obligates

her to pay her share of the works that —"
"You need it right now?"
"I need it this week, for sure."
"This is what we'll do. Leave it here, right? Come back for it, end of the week — it'll be signed, promise you."
"We have sent many letters —"
"I appreciate that — but — she's not well, boss. She ain't in her right . . . she's got this agrophobia," said Felix, an old error no amount of Annie's eye-rolling had been able to correct, maybe because his portmanteau version expressed a deeper truth: she wasn't really afraid of open spaces, she was afraid of what might happen between her and the other people in them. "Come back later, it'll be signed. I'll get it signed."
"Well, that was dull," said Annie, before the door had quite shut. "I've been thinking, Felix — ever since the sun came out — let's spend what's left of this summer on my roof. We used to love knocking around up there. This weekend, stay over — Monday's the bank holiday! Long weekend."
"It's carnival this weekend."
But this she didn't seem to hear: "Not with a lot of people. Just us. We'll make that chicken thing you like, barbecue up there. Jerk. Jerk chicken. For us two jerks."
"You eating now as well?"

Annie stopped laughing, flinched, turned her face. She crossed her hands delicately in her lap. "It's always nice to watch other people eat. I eat mushrooms. We could get some of those legal mushrooms. Do you remember? Just trying to get from here to there" — she pointed from the chair to the chaise — "took about a year. I was convinced this was France, for some reason. I felt I needed a passport to cross the room."

Felix reached for his tobacco. He would not be drawn into fond reminiscences.

"Can't buy 'em anymore. Government shut it down. Few months ago."

"Did they? How boring of them."

"Some kid in Highgate thought he was a TV and switched himself off. Jumped off that bridge. Hornsey Lane Bridge."

"Oh, Felix, that one's as old as I am — I heard that in the playground of Camden School for Girls in about 1985. 'Suicide Bridge.' It's what's called an urban myth." She walked over to him, took off his cap and rubbed his shaved head. "Let's go up there right now, and tan. Well, I'll tan. You can sweat. Inaugurate the summer."

"Annie, man: summer's almost over. I'm working. All the time."

"You don't appear to be working now."

"Usually I'd be working Saturdays."

"Well let's do another day then, you choose, make it regular, like," said Annie, in her idea of a Northern accent.

"Can't do it."

"Is it my charms he can't resist" — an American accent — "or my roof?"

"Annie — sit down, I want to talk to you. Serious."

"Talk to me on the roof!"

He tried to grab her wrist, but she quickened and passed him. He followed her into the bedroom. She had pulled down the ladder from the trapdoor in the ceiling and was already halfway up.

"No peeking!" But she made her way up in a manner that made it impossible not to, including the little white mouse-tail of a tampon's string. "Be careful — glass."

Felix emerged into light — it took a moment to see clearly. He placed his knee carefully — between one broken beer bottle and another — and pulled himself up. His hands came away covered with white flakes of sunbaked, rain-ruined wood. He had helped lay this deck, and painted it, along with a few techies and even one of the producers, because time and the budget were so tight. Everything covered in a thick white gloss to maximize the light. It was done very quickly, to service a fiction. It was never intended for use in the real world. Now she picked up a crushed cigarette packet and an empty bottle of vodka, fastidiously cramming them into an overflowing bin, as if the removal of these two items could make a serious difference to the sea of crap everywhere. Felix stepped over a sodden sleeping bag, heavy with water and filled with something, not a person, thank God. It had rained last night — there was a dewy freshness — but a serious smell was coming, and every minute of the sun made it slightly more serious. Felix headed for the far eastern corner, by the chimney, for its shade and relative unpopularity. The boards under his feet made desperate noises.

"This all needs redoing."

"Yes. But you just can't find the help these days. Once upon a time you'd get a lovely young film crew turning up, they'd pay you two thousand pounds a week, lay a deck, paint it, fuck you passionately and tell you they loved you — but that kind of service is a thing of the past, I'm afraid."

Felix put his head in his hands.

"Annie, man. You give me jokes, for real."

Annie smiled sadly: "I'm glad I still give you something, at least . . ." She righted an upturned deckchair. "Looks a bit rough at the moment, I know . . . But I've been en-tertaining — I had one of my big nights, last

Friday, such a nice time, you should have been here. I did send a text. You contrive not to see my texts. Lovely crowd, the sweetest people. Hot as Ibiza up here."

She made it sound like a society party, filled with the great and good. Felix picked up an empty bottle of Strongbow cider that had been repurposed into a bong.

"You need to stop letting people take advantage."

Annie snorted: "What nonsense!" She sat wide legged on the little bridge of bricks between the chimney stacks. "That's what people are for. They take advantage of each other. What else are they for?"

"They're only hanging round you because you've got something they want. Soho liggers. Just want somewhere to crash. And if there's free shit — bonus."

"Good. That's what I've got. Why shouldn't people take advantage of me if what I have is useful to them?" She crossed one leg over the other like a teacher reaching the substance of her lecture. "It happens that in this matter of property and drugs I am strong and they are weak. In other matters it's the other way round. The weak should take advantage of the strong, don't you think? Better that than the other way round. I want my friends to take advantage. I want them to feed off me.

I want them drinking my blood. Why not? They're my friends. What else am I to do in this place? Raise a family?"

That line of conversation Felix knew to be a trap. He swerved to avoid it.

"I'm saying they ain't your friends. They're users."

Annie fixed him with a look over her shades: "You sound very sure. Are you speaking from personal experience?"

"Why you trying to mix up my words?" He was easily flustered and it mistranslated as anger. People thought he was on the verge of hitting someone when he was only nervous, or slightly annoyed. Annie lifted a shaky finger into the air.

"Don't raise your voice at me, Felix. I hope you haven't come round here for a fight because I'm feeling really quite delicate."

Felix groaned and sat next to her on the bridge of bricks. He put his hand softly on her knee, meaning it like a father or friend, but she grabbed it and held it tightly in her own.

"Can you see? Over there? Flag's up. Somebody's home. Best view in town."

"Annie —"

"My mother was presented at the palace, you know. And my grandmother."

"Is it."

"Yes, Felix, it is. Surely I've told you that before."

"Yeah, you have, as it goes."

He worked his hand free and stood up again. "They flee from me that sometime did me seek," said Annie quietly, removed her robe and lay naked in the sun. "There's some vodka in the freezer."

"I told you I don't drink no more."

"Still?"

"I told you. That's why I ain't been round. Not just that, other reasons, too. I'm clean. You should think about it yourself."

"But darling, I am clean. Two years clean."

"Cept the coke, weed, drink, pills . . ."

"I said I'm clean, not a bloody Mormon!"

"I'm talking about doing it properly."

Annie got up on her elbows and pushed her shades into her hair: "And spend every day listening to people bang on about the time they found themselves in a bin covered with vomit? And pretend that every good time I've ever had in my life was some kind of extended adolescent delusion?" She lay back down and replaced the shades. "No thank you. Could you fetch me a vodka please? With lemon, if you can find it."

Diagonally across the street from them, on another roof terrace, a severely dressed Japanese woman — narrow black trousers and black V-neck — dropped a tray she was carrying. A glass smashed and one plate of food went flying; the other she somehow managed to hold on to. She had been heading for a small wrought-iron table at which sat a lanky Frenchman, in parodic red braces with his jeans rolled up to the calf. Now he jumped up. At the same moment a little girl ran out, looked at this domestic tragedy and put her hand over her mouth. They were all three familiar to Felix; he'd seen them many times over the years. First her alone; then he moved in. Then the baby turned up, who looked now to be four or five years old. Where had the time gone? Quite often, in good weather, he had watched the woman take pictures of her family on a proper camera set atop a tripod base.

"Oops," said Annie, "trouble in paradise."

"Annie, listen: remember that girl I was telling you about. The serious one."

"I'm afraid it really does serve them right. They couldn't just eat in their flat. That would be too much of a hardship. Instead they have to bring up each piece of individually miso-stained balsamic glaze cod fillet up on a tray, so they can eat them on the sodding terrace, all the time no doubt saying to themselves: how lucky we are to be eating on the terrace! Why, we could be in Tuscany!

Have you tried these, darling? They're tempura zucchini flowers. Japanese-Italian fusion! My own invention. Shall I photograph it? We can put it on our *blog.*"

"Annie."

"Our blog called *Jules et Kim.*"

"Me and that girl. Grace. It's serious. I'm not going to be coming round here no more."

Annie held a hand up in the air and seemed to examine her nails, though each one was lower than the finger's tip, with skin torn from either side and old blood-tracks all round the cuticles. "I see. Didn't she have another lover, too?"

"That's done with."

"I see," said Annie again, rolled onto her stomach and kicked her feet with their extraordinary arches into the air. "Age?"

Felix couldn't help but smile: "Twenty-four, coming up, I think. In November. But it ain't even about that."

"And *still* no vodka."

Felix sighed and started walking back to the trapdoor.

"I shall think of the other lover!" he heard Annie call after him as he descended. "I shall pity him! It's so important that we pity each other!"

Marlon. It was done with finally on a Sunday in February while Felix sat on Grace's stairwell, rolling a fag and shivering, peeking through the net curtain. The man had watched the other man as he trudged through the flat, collecting a bike lock, some ugly clothes, a music dock for an iPod, a pair of hair clippers. He was heavy, Marlon, not fat exactly, but soft and ungainly. He was a long time in the bathroom, re-emerging with several jars of wax and tubes of cream, at least one of which was Felix's — but Felix had won the woman and considered he could live without his Dax. After Marlon was done retrieving his things, Felix watched him as he took Grace's hands in his own like a man about to perform a religious ritual and said, "I'm thankful for the time we spent together." Poor Marlon. He really didn't have a fucking clue. He even turned up a few times after that — with mix-tapes of soca music, and handwritten notes, and tears. None of which helped his case. In the end, all the things Grace claimed to like about Marlon — that he was not a "playa," that he was gentle and awkward and not interested in money — were all the reasons she left him. Being so gentle, it was a while before he got the message. Finally he had taken his "I'm-a-male-nurse-I-find-hip-hop-too-negative-I-can-cook-curried-goat-I-want-to-move-to-Nigeria" routine back to

South London where, in Felix's opinion, it belonged.

"Fridge," said Felix to himself now and opened it — two family-sized bottles of Diet Coke, three lemons and a can of mackerel — and then remembered, and opened the freezer instead. He lifted out the bottle of vodka. He returned to the fridge and removed the least white lemon. He looked about him. The kitchen was a tiny cupboard with a cracked Belfast sink and no space to store anything and no bin. The sink was full; there were no clean glasses. A curtain-rag fluttered at the half-open window. A line of ants processed from the sink to the window and back, carrying little specks of food on their backs, with a confidence that suggested they did not expect to see tap water here in their lifetimes. Felix found a mug. He sawed at the lemon with a blunt knife. He poured the vodka. He put the top back on, replaced the bottle in the freezer and thought of how he would describe this scene of sobriety on Tuesday at seven pm to a group of fellow travellers who would appreciate its heroic quality.

Back up on the roof Annie had changed position — a cross-legged yoga pose, eyes closed — and was now wearing a green bikini. He placed the mug in front of her and she nodded, like a goddess accepting an offering.

"Where'd you get that bikini?"

"Questions, questions."

Without opening her eyes she pointed at the family on the terrace. "Now all that's left to them is to pick up the pieces. Lunch has been ruined, the Sancerre runs dry, but somehow, somehow, they'll find a way to carry on."

"Annie —"

"And what else? I've no idea what's up with you anymore. Any movement on the film front? How's your brother?"

"I left that place time ago. I'm apprenticed at this garage now, I told you."

"Vintage cars are a nice hobby. "

"Not a hobby — it's my work."

"Felix: you're a very talented filmmaker."

"Come on, man. What was my job? Getting the coffees, getting the coke. That was my job. That was it. They weren't gonna let me get no further than that, believe. Why you always going on about shit that ain't even real?"

"I just happen to feel you're very talented, that's all. And that you criminally undersell yourself."

"Leave it, man!"

Annie sighed and took the clip out of her

hair. She separated the hair into sections and started working on two long, childish plaits. "How's poor Devon doing?"

"Fine."

"You're mistaking me for one of those people who ask questions out of politeness."

"He's fine. He's got a provisional release date: 16th June."

"But that's wonderful!" cried Annie, and Felix felt a great, impractical warmth toward her. In Grace's company Devon was rarely mentioned. He was one of the "negative sources of energy" they were meant to be cleansing from their lives.

"Why 'provisional'?"

"Depends on how he acts. He has to not piss anyone off between now and then."

"If you ask me, he seems to have somewhat overpaid his debt to society for a little stick-em-up with a toy shooter."

"It weren't a toy. It was unloaded. They still call it armed robbery."

"Oh, but someone on Friday told me the funniest joke — you'd like it. Oh gosh: wording. Something like: do you know what poor people . . . ? No. Sorry, start again. Poor people — Oh God: 'In poor areas people steal your phone. In rich areas the people steal your pension.'" Felix smiled minutely. "Only, it was much better done than that."

She was shouting, without realizing it. Over on the other terrace, the Japanese woman turned and peered politely into the middle distance.

"I mean, look at this woman: she's *obsessed* with me. Look at her. She desperately wants to photograph me but can't bear to ask. It's very sad, really." Annie waved a hand at the woman and her family. "Eat your lunch! Proceed with your lives!"

Felix put himself between Annie and the view. "She's half Jamaican, half Nigerian. Her mum teaches at William Keble down Harlesden way — serious woman. She's like her mum, she's got that Nigerian education thing: focused. You'd like her."

"Hmmm."

"You know that place York's on Monmouth Street?"

"Naturally. People went there in the eighties."

"She just got promoted," said Felix, proudly. "She's like the top waitress, what do you call that again? She doesn't do the tables no more. What do you call that?"

"Maitre D."

"Yeah. Probably end up managing it. It's full every day — lots of people go there."

"Yes, but what *type* of people?" Annie put her drink to her lips and knocked it back in one. "Anything else?"

Felix got flustered again: "We got a lot in common, like . . . just a lot of things."

"Long walks in the country, red wine, the operas of Verdi, GSOH . . ." Annie held her arms wide and put her fingers together as in a yogic chant.

"She's knows what she's about. She's conscious."

Annie looked at him oddly: "That's setting the bar rather low, don't you think? I mean, bully for you she's not in a coma . . ."

Felix laughed, and spotted her grinning gummily with pleasure.

"Politically conscious, racially conscious, as in she gets it, the struggle. Conscious."

"She's awake and she understands," Annie closed her eyes and breathed deeply. "Bully for you."

But some flicker of imperiousness in her face tipped Felix over. He started shouting.

"All you know how to do is take the piss. That's all you know. What you doing that's so amazing? What you getting accomplished?"

Annie opened one startled eye: "What am I — what on earth are you talking about? I was joking, for Godssake. What exactly am I meant to be getting accomplished?"

"I'm talking about what are your goals? What do you want for your life to be like?"

"*What do I want for my life to be like?* I'm sorry, grammatically I'm finding that question extremely peculiar."

"Fuck you, Annie."

She tried to laugh this off, too, and reached out for his wrist, but he pushed her away: "Nah, but there's no point with you, is there? I'm trying to tell you where I'm going in my life, and you're just taking the piss. Pointless. You're pointless."

It came out more brutal than he'd meant. She winced.

"I think you're being very cruel. I'm only trying to understand."

Felix took it down a notch. He didn't want to be cruel. He didn't want to be seen to be cruel. He sat down next to her. He had his speech prepared, but also the sense that they were both speaking lines, that really she was as prepared as he was.

"I'm tired of living the way I been living. I been feeling like I've been in the game, at this level, and I had a good time at this level — but, come on, Annie: even you would say it's a level with a lot of demons. A lot of demons. Demons and —"

"Excuse me — you're talking to a nice Catholic girl, who —"

"Let me finish talking! For one time!"

Annie nodded mutely.

"Lost my thread now."

"Demons," said Annie.

"Right. And I've killed them. And it was hard, and now they're dead and I've completed the level, and it's time to move to the next level. It ain't even a matter of taking you to the next level. You blatantly don't want to go."

This was the speech he had prepared. Now it was out of his mouth it didn't seem to have the subtle depth it had taken on in his mind, but still he saw it had had some effect: her eyes were open and her yoga pose was over, arms unfolded, hands flat on the floor.

"You listening? Next level. People can spend their whole lives just *dwelling*. I could spend my whole life dwelling on some of the shit that's happened to me. I done that. Now it's time for the next level. I'm moving up in the game. And I'm ready for it."

"Yes, yes, I've grasped the metaphor, you don't have to keep repeating it." Annie lit a cigarette, inhaled deeply and exhaled it through her nose. "Life's not a video game, Felix — there aren't a certain number of points that send you to the next level. There isn't actually any next level. The bad news is everybody dies at the end. Game over."

The few clouds left in the sky were shunting toward Trafalgar. Felix looked up at them with what he hoped was a spiritual look upon his face. "Well, that's your opinion, innit. Everyone's entitled to their opinion."

"Mine, Nietzsche's, Sartre's, a lot of people. Felix, darling, I appreciate you coming here for this 'serious talk' and sharing your thoughts about God, but I'm quite bored of talking now and personally I'd really like to know: are we going to fuck today or not?"

She pulled playfully at his leg. He tried to get up, but she started kissing up his ankles and he soon sunk back down on his knees. It was a defeat, and he blamed her. He got her by the shoulders, not gently, and together they scrabbled to the edge of the wall, where they told themselves they couldn't be seen. He had a handful of her hair tight in his fist, and tried to land a harsh kiss but she had the knack of turning every malevolent stroke into passion. They fit together. They always had. But what was the point of fitting in this way and no other? He felt her hands on his shoulders, pushing him lower, and soon he was level with her appendix scar. She lifted her arse. He grabbed it with both hands and put his face in her crotch. Fourteen when Lloyd first explained that to eat a woman was unhygienic, a humiliation. Only at gunpoint, that was his father's opinion, and even then only if every last hair has been removed.

Annie was the first time. Years of conditioning broken in an afternoon. He wondered what Lloyd might think of him now, with his nose nestled in so much abundant straight hair, and this strange taste in his mouth.
"If it's in the way, just take it out!"

He grabbed the mouse-tail between his teeth and pulled. It came out easily. He left it like a dead thing, red on the white deck. He turned back to her and dug in with his tongue. He looked like he was frantically tunnelling somewhere and hoping to reach the other side. She tasted of iron, and when he came up for air five minutes later he imagined a ring of blood around his mouth. In fact there was only a speck; she kissed it away. The rest was quick. They were old lovers and had their familiar positions. On their knees, looking out over town, they came swiftly to reliably pleasurable, reliably separate, conclusions, that were yet somehow an anticlimax when compared to those five minutes, five minutes ago, when it had seemed possible to climb inside another person, head first, and disappear entirely.

Afterward he lay on top of her feeling the unpleasant, sweaty closeness, wondering when it would be polite to move. He did not wait very long. He rolled over onto his back. She swept her hair to one side and put

her head on his chest. They watched a police helicopter pass by on its way to Covent
Garden.

"I'm sorry," said Felix.

"Whatever for?"

Felix reached down and pulled his jeans
back up. "You still taking your thing?"

Felix saw a flash of fury pass over her face,
and also how it was contained and dispersed
in the action of opening the cigarettes, tap-
ping one out, lighting it, smiling grimly,
laughing.

"No need. More chance of being struck by
lightning. The blood just about still runs, but
trust me: the well is almost dry. Nature, the
enforcer. The destroyer! Speaking of which,
dear brother James is meant to be taking me
out to The Wolseley for a celebration of our
mutual decrepitude — he phoned up yesterday, completely natural on the phone. You'd
think we spoke every other day. Just ridiculous. But I played along, I said, 'Hello, twin
dear!' He suggests a birthday lunch — our
birthday's not till October, mind you — and
I say fine, but of course I know precisely
what he's up to, he wants me to sign the
bloody deed so he can sell out from under
me. He doesn't seem to understand that no
matter what he thinks a part of that place is
mine and who knows how much he's already

mortgaged it to pay for his little darlings'
education, up to the hilt, I'm sure, I doubt
there's a penny left in it, and we all know he
wished he'd gobbled me up in the womb, but
I'm afraid he didn't manage it and as long
as our mother is alive I really don't see why
it should be sold — where is she to go if it
is? And who's going to pay for it? That kind
of care costs money. But he's always been
like that: James has always acted like he is
an only child and I don't exist at all. Do you
know what he and Daddy used to call me
behind my back? The afterbirth. Shall we
have another drink? It's so muggy."

She lay back down on his chest. She kissed
the skin round the neck of his t-shirt. He put
his fingers in her hair.

"You should probably take one of them other
pills — the ones you take after. To be safe."

Annie made an exasperated sound.

"I don't want your babies, Felix. I can as-
sure you I'm not sitting up here like some
tragic fallen woman every night dreaming
of having your babies." She began tracing a
figure of eight with her fingernail along his
stomach. The movement looked idle but the
nail pressed in hard. "You realize of course
that if it were the other way round there
would be a law, there would be an actual
law: John versus Jen in the high court. And

John would put it to Jen that she did wilfully fuck him for five years, before dumping him without warning in the twilight of his pro-creative window, and taking up with young Jack-the-lad, only twenty-four years old and with a cock as long as my arm. The court rules in favor of John. Every time. Jen must pay damages. Huge sums. Plus six months in jail. No — nine. Poetic justice. And you wouldn't be able to —"

"You know what? I should chip." He slid her head off his body, pulled his t-shirt down and stood. She sat up and crossed her arms over her breasts. She looked in the direction of the river.

"Yes, why don't you?"

He reached down to kiss her good-bye but she jerked her head away like a child.

"Why you being like that? I've got to go, that's all." Felix felt something was off: he looked down and saw his zip was open. He pulled it closed. It occurred to him that he had said and done exactly the opposite of all he'd intended to say and do ever since he walked through her door.

"I'm sorry," he said.

"No need. I'm fine. Next time bring your Grace lady. I like conscious types. They're so much livelier. I find that most people are in a semi-vegetative state."

"I'm really sorry." Felix kissed her on the forehead.

He started walking toward the trapdoor. After a moment he heard footsteps coming up behind, and saw the flicker of her dressing gown, a few silk swallows on the wing, then a hand clamping down on his shoulder. "You know, Felix" — a dainty little voice, like a waitress reciting the specials — "not everyone wants this conventional little life you're rowing your boat toward. I like my river of fire. And when it's time for me to go I fully intend to roll off my one-person dinghy into the flames and be consumed. I'm not afraid! I've never been afraid. Most people are, you know. But I'm not like most people. You've never done anything for me and I don't need you to do anything for me." "Never done anything for you? When you was lying on this roof, dribbling out your mouth, with your eyes rolling back in your head, who was here, who put their fingers —"

Annie's nostrils flared and her face turned cruel: "Felix: what is this pathological need of yours to be the good guy? It's very dull. Frankly, you were more fun when you were my dealer. You don't have to save my life. Or anyone's life. We're all fine. We don't need you to ride in on a white horse. You're nobody's savior."

They were speaking softly enough, but putting their hands on each other, more and more violently, and pulling them off, and Felix realized it was happening, it was bad as it could be, the dreaded scene that had kept him from this place for months, and the strange thing was how precisely he knew what it was like to be Annie at this moment — he had been in Annie's role many times, with his mother, with other women — and the more he understood it the more he wanted to escape her, as if losing in the way she was losing right now was a kind of virus and pity the way you caught it.

"You act like we're in a relationship, but this ain't a relationship. I'm in a relationship — that's what I come here to tell you. But this? This ain't shit, it's nothing, it's —"

"Christ, another hideous word! God save me from 'relationships'!"

Desperate now to leave, Felix played what he believed was his trump card. "You're forty-whatever. Look at you. You're still living like this. I want to have kids. I want to get on with my life."

Annie forced out some approximation of a laugh: "You mean 'more kids,' don't you? Or are you one of these optimistic souls who feels they become a new person every seven years, once the cells have regenerated — blank page, start again — never mind who you hurt, never mind what went on before. Now it's time for my new *relationship*."

"I'm out," said Felix, and began walking away.

"What a mealy-mouthed pathetic word, 'relationship.' For people who haven't the guts to live, haven't the imagination to fill their three score and ten with anything other than —"

Felix knew better than to get into it: he had no more cards and she was anyway playing by herself. When she was like this she could have an argument with a coat-stand, with a broom. And how could he know how much she'd taken before he'd even turned up? Now he turned from her and opened the trap door and made his way down, but she followed him.

"It's what people do these days, isn't it? When they can't think of anything else to do. No politics, no ideas, no balls. Get *married.* But I've transcended all that. Long time ago. Eons ago. This idea that all your happiness lies in this other person. This idea of happiness! I'm on a different plane of consciousness, darling. I've got more balls than are dreamed of in your philosophy. I was engaged at 19, I was engaged at 23, I could be moldering in some Hampshire pile at this very moment, covering and recovering sofas with some Baron in perfect sexless harmony. That's what my people do. While your lot have a lot of babies they can't afford or take care of. I'm sure it's all perfectly delightful, but you can count me the fuck out!"

In the hall between the bedroom and lounge, Felix turned round and grabbed both her wrists. He was shaking. He hadn't realized till now what he wanted. Not just that she lose, but that she not exist.

"You're lucky that you find life easy, Felix. You're lucky that you're happy, that you know how to be happy, that you're a good person — and you want everyone to be happy and good because you are, and to find things easy because you do. Does it never occur to you some people might not find life as easy to live as you do?"

She looked triumphant. He watched her coke-jaw grinding against itself.

"My life? My life is easy?"

"I didn't say it was easy. I said you find it easy. There's a difference. That's why I like the ballet: it's hard for everybody. Felix, let go, it hurts."

Felix let go. Touching each other for so long, even in anger, made the anger unsustainable, and they both softened, and lowered

261

their voices, and looked away.

"I'm in the way, I see that. Well. No harm done. By which I mean of course: nothing but harm done."

"Every time I come round here, same drama. Same drama." Felix shook his head at the floor. "I don't get it. I never been nothing but nice to you. Why you trying to ruin my life?"

She gave him a penetrating look.

"How funny," she said, "but of course that's how it must seem to you."

After that they walked to the door quite calmly, the man slightly ahead. A stranger coming across the scene would have thought the man had tried to sell the woman a bible or set of encyclopedias, with no success. For his own part, Felix felt absolute certainty that this was the last time — the last time of passing this picture, the last time seeing that crack in the plaster — and in his mind he said a little prayer of thanks. He almost wished he could tell the woman he loved all about it, so fine an example was it of all that she had taught him. The universe wants you to be free. You must shake yourself free of the negative. The universe wants only that you ask, so that you shall receive. Behind him now he heard this woman quietly weeping. It was his cue to turn round, but he didn't, and at the threshold the weeping became a sob. He hurried to the stairs, and was a few steps down when he heard a thud on the carpet above as she went down on her knees, and he knew he was meant to feel heavy, but the truth was he felt like a man undergoing some not-yet-invented process called particle transfer, wonderfully, blissfully light.

NW6

Felix inched deeper into the carriage. He gripped the safety rail. He considered the tube map. It did not express his reality. The center was not "Oxford Circus" but the bright lights of Kilburn High Road. "Wimbledon" was the countryside, "Pimlico" pure science fiction. He put his right index finger over Pimlico's blue bar. It was nowhere. Who lived there? Who even passed through it?

Two seats came free in a bank of four. Felix roused himself and sat down. The guy opposite nodded to a loud break-beat. His friend next to him put his feet up on the seat. Pupils enormous, laughing into his neck every now again, amused by some private delirium. Felix established a private space of his own, opening his legs wide and slouching. At Finchley Road, as underground came over ground, his phone revived, bleeping to register a missed call. His thumb worked hopefully down the list. Same number, three times. It had only one physical referent in the world: a battered public call box, riveted to a wall, halfway down a concrete corridor. He had seen it many times through the reinforced glass of the visiting room. He put his mobile back into his pocket.

The thing with Devon was you wanted to talk to him, but at the same time, you didn't want to. It wasn't Devon anymore, really, but a hard-voiced stranger, who rang and said hard things, hurtful things. Jackie talking, through Devon's mouth. She was sending Devon letters. Felix learned this from Lloyd (Devon had not said; Felix had not asked). Their mother had a strange power over people — Felix did not discount witchcraft. (Jackie claimed a Ghanaian grandmother. These things were not unknown there.) She surely had a power over Felix, once upon a time. A power over the girls. But she was a person with whom there would always be a "last straw." Devon would have to learn this, as Felix and the girls had all learned it. The end for Felix was clearly marked. On that occasion it was eight years since her last "visit." The girls refused to see her. Always sentimental, Felix took her in, cautiously, promising nothing. For moral support, he asked his brother to come round. Devon began the evening at the other end of the room, standing against the wall, glaring. He ended the night cozy on the sofa, accepting Jackie's sloppy kisses all over his face. Felix softened, too. He brought down the white rum from a high shelf. Foolish. Tia called it early, as did Ruby. Lloyd. Everybody called it. Jackie's sister, Karen, said, "Listen to me: put her out your door and change the locks." But at the time it had seemed that Devon's acquiescence allowed — necessitated — Felix's. He had suffered so much more than Felix over the years, yet held no grudge.

She turned up in high summer. Many days spent smoking weed together on Hampstead Heath, laughing madly, rolling about in the grass like young lovers. Jackie, Devon, Felix. At nights they sat up drinking. "I can't believe how yellow this boy is! Look at them curls!" Emerging from the kitchen with a pack of biscuits, she told poor Devon quite casually that his father had died, some years ago — drowned. To Felix, it sounded like a tall tale. He kept quiet. In the end they were half-brothers: it wasn't his business. He had his own father, his own troubles. In the early hours she stood in the middle of the floor, as if on stage, and spoke of how lonely and miserable she'd been in England, as a young woman. This Felix had never heard; he found he wanted to hear it, although he knew perfectly well she could have exchanged this life story for any other narrative and he would have accepted it just as readily. He wanted to love her. He tried to imagine life in notorious Garvey House, being "spat at by NF kids in the grocers." She talked out her various conspiracy theories. These Felix did not interrupt. He wanted to be happy. There was one about the towers. There was one about the moon landings. The Virgin Mary was black. The planet was getting colder. 2012 would be the end of everything. She seemed to have spent the past few years in Internet cafes around the country, gathering this information. Devon followed her willingly on every point. Felix, more skeptical, let it wash over him, without comment. She had her hair tied in two thick plaits like a Red Indian, a thin gold band tied across her forehead. And lo, there would come a perfect future world with no money and no shops, just storehouses in the middle of town, with everything you needed in them and no locks on the doors. People living all together with no religion. Her eyes, he knew, had the taint of madness.

The next day she was gone, with Felix's

cashpoint card, his watch, all his chains. Two months later Devon walked into Khandi's Gem Express and Jewelry on the high road, with a kid from South Kilburn, Curtis Ainger, and a gun. Smile, you're on CCTV. Nineteen when he went in. Twenty-three this summer.

"Sorry, could you ask your friend to move his feet?"

Felix took out his earbuds. A white woman, hugely pregnant and sweating, stood over him.

"I'd like to sit down?" she said.

Felix looked at his motionless "friend" opposite, and thought it best to speak to the other one. He leaned forward. This guy had his head against the glass, oblivious and half hidden by his hood, nodding to his music. Felix touched him lightly on the knee.

"Oi, bruv — I think the lady wants to sit down."

The guy removed one can of his bulky earphones.

"What?"

"I think the lady wants to sit down."

The pregnant woman smiled tightly. It was a hot day to be in that state. Looking at her made the sweat break out across Felix's nose.

"Yeah? Why you asking me though? Why

you touching me?"

"What?"

"Why you asking me. Why don't she ask me?"

"Your man's got his feet on her seat, blud."

"But is it your business, though? Why you tryna make it your business? Who you callin' blud? I ain't your blud."

"I didn't say it was my —"

"Is it your business, though? You got a seat — you fucking get up." Felix tried to defend himself; the kid waved a hand in his face. "Shut up — fool."

The other guy opened one eye and laughed quietly. Felix stood up.

"Take mine — I'm getting off."

"*Thank* you." Felix saw how badly she was shaking, and that her eyes were watery. He angled himself out of her way, and felt the moist skin of her arms against his own. She sat down. She looked directly at the two men. Her voice was wobbly: "You should be ashamed of yourselves," she said.

They were pulling into Kilburn Station. The carriage was silent. No one looked — or they looked so quickly their glances were undetectable. Felix felt a great wave of approval, smothering and unwanted, directed toward him, and just as surely, contempt and disgust enveloping the two men and separating them, from Felix, from the rest of the carriage, from humanity. They seemed to feel it: abruptly they both stood and hustled toward the door, where Felix already stood waiting. He could hear the inevitable thrum of cusses, directed at him. The doors blessedly opened; Felix found himself shoulder-charged; he stumbled onto the platform like a clown. Laughter, close, then vanishing. He looked up to see the soles of their trainers as they took the stairs two at a time, jumped the barrier and disappeared.

Trees shaggy overhead. Hedges wild over fences. Every crack in the pavement, every tree root. The way the sun hits the top deck of the 98. The walls have grown taller outside the Jewish school, and outside the Muslim one. The Kilburn Tavern has been repainted, shiny black with gold lettering. If he hurries he may even get home before her. Lie down in that clean room, that good place. Pull her into his body. Start all over again, fresh.

Outside the Tavern, Felix spotted Hifan and Kelly eating a tray of chips at a picnic table, both of them from his year at school — he bald, she still looking fine. To get a laugh Felix high-fived Hifan, kissed Kelly on her cheek, stole a chip, and walked on, like it was all one movement, a form of dance. "What you so happy about?" Kelly called after him, and Felix shouted, "Love, shorty, L.O.V.E. LOVE!" without turning round, and did his pimp-roll walk, and enjoyed the laughter as he disappeared smoothly round the corner. Nobody to see him collide with the gray bins out the back. He steadied himself with a hand to the Tavern's back door: fancy colored glass now and a new brass doorknob. Wood floors where carpets used to be, real food instead of crisps and scratchings. About six quid for a glass of wine! Jackie wouldn't recognize it. Maybe by now she'd be one of those exiles on the steps of the betting shop, clutching a can of Special Brew, driven from the pubs by the refits. Maybe she was never that bad. It was impossible to know, with Lloyd, how much was true, how much pure venom. Felix glanced through the window to the interior: no more velvety corner booth. Where he had sat with his sisters, six little feet not even touching the ground, earnestly listening to Jackie give her leaving speech. Some new man she'd met who made her feel free. Lived in Southampton, some white guy. At seven you don't know. He didn't know that freedom was something you could feel. He thought it was something you simply were. He didn't know where Southampton was.

He loved his own father and did not want to go and live with a strange white man. Only when the conversation was almost over did it occur to Felix that she wasn't asking him to come to Southampton. Two years later, she turned up in London with a light brown baby boy. Left Devon with Lloyd and went — wherever. Wherever she went.

On Albert Road Felix fell in step behind a tall girl in tight red jeans and black spaghetti-strapped vest. She had broad shoulders and a square trunk. She had more muscles than Felix, and as she walked her muscles moved together, fluid and complicated: the way the arms attached to the back and to the backside and to the hips. Not like Grace at all, who was shorter and curvier and softer. This woman could pick Felix up and run with him all the way home, put him down on his doorstep like a baby. She wore a lot of cheap silver rings, green round their bands, and running down one forearm a tattoo of a flower with a long, winding stem. Her heels were dry and cracked. The label on her top was showing. Should he tuck it in? A trickle of sweat ran from her ear, along her neck and down her back, straight down that muscled division — strongly defined — between her left side and her right. Her phone rang. She answered it and called somebody "Baby." She turned right. Another life. Felix felt someone push two fingers hard into his back.

"Money. Phone. Now."

They were either side of him. Hoods up but perfectly visible. Same two from the train. Not much taller than he was. Not much wider, either. It had just turned six o'clock.

"NOW."

He felt himself being jostled, manhandled. He looked up at their faces. The talkative one, the one doing all the cussing, was truly a kid; the other, the silent one, was closer to Felix's own age, and too old for such foolishness. He had ashy hands, like Felix's own, and the same dull sheen to his face. Along his cheek a scar ran. He was local somehow, familiar. Felix tried turning away but they swung him back round. He swore at them at length, creatively, and looked to his right: four houses down the tall girl put a key to a lock and went inside.

"Listen, I ain't giving you nothing. Nothing!"

He found himself on the pavement. As he got back up on his knees he heard one of them say, "Big man on the train. Ain't the big man now." And instead of fear, a feel-

ing of pity came over him; he remembered
when being the big man was all that mattered. He reached into his pockets. They
could have his phone. They could have the
lone twenty in his pocket if it came to that.
He'd been mugged many times and knew
the drill. When he was younger they might
have wounded his ego; now the old fury
and humiliation were gone — they could
have it all. Everything he cared about was
elsewhere. He tried to laugh at them as he
handed over his meager valuables: "Should
have caught me two hours ago, blud. Two
hours ago I was loaded." The kid gave him
a dead-eyed look, face set in a violent pout.
It was a necessary mask, without which he
could not do what he was doing. "And the
stones," said the kid. Felix touched his ears.
Treasured zirconias, a present from Grace.

"You're dreamin'," he said.

He turned once more toward the street.
A breeze passed over the three of them,
filling their hoods and sending a cloud of
sycamore leaves spinning to the pavement.
A firm punch came to his side. Punch?
The pain sliced to the left, deep and down.
Warm liquid reversed up his throat. Over
his lips. Yet it couldn't be oblivion as long as
he could name it, and with this in mind he
said aloud what had been done to him, what

was being done to him, he tried to say it, he said nothing. Grace! Down Willesden Lane a bus came rumbling; at the same moment in which Felix glimpsed the handle and the blade he saw the 98 reopen its doors to accept the last soul in sight — a young girl in a yellow summer dress. She ran with her ticket held high above her head like the proof of something, got there just in time, cried out "Thank you!" and let the doors fold neatly behind her.

HOST

1. *These red pigtails*

There had been an event. To speak of it required the pluperfect. Keisha Blake and Leah Hanwell, the protagonists in this event, were four-year-old children. The outdoor pool — really a shallow trough in the park, one foot at its deepest end — had been full of kids, "splashing all ways, causing madness." There was no lifeguard at the time of the event, and parents were left to keep an eye as best they could. "They had a guard up the hill, in Hampstead, for them. Nothing for us." This was an interesting detail. Keisha — now ten years old and curious about the tensions between grown people — tried to get at its meaning. "Stop gazing. Lift your foot," said her mother. They sat on a bench in a shoe shop on the Kilburn High Road getting measured for a pair of dull brown shoes with a t-strap that did not express any of the joy that must surely exist in the world, despite everything. "I've got Cheryl acting wild in one corner, I got Jayden in my arms bawling, and I'm trying to see where you are, trying to keep it all together . . ." It was in this ellipsis that the event had occurred: a child nearly drowned. Yet the significance of the event lay elsewhere. "You rose up with these red pigtails in your hand. You dragged her up. You were the only one saw she was in trouble." After the event, the mother of the child, an Irish woman, thanked Marcia Blake many times, and this in itself was a kind of event. "I knew Pauline to look at but not to speak to. She was a bit snooty with me back then." Keisha could neither contradict nor verify this account — she had no memory of it. However, the foreshadowing could be considered suspicious. Her own celebrated will and foresight so firmly established, and Cheryl already wild and unreliable. Also, Jayden could not have been born at the time of the event, being five years younger than Keisha. "Keep still now," murmured Marcia, pushing the steel bar down to meet her daughter's toes.

2. *Kiwi fruit*

In the lethal quiet of the Hanwell flat a

highlight was snack-time. It was taken seriously by Mrs. Hanwell, who kept a trolley for the purpose. Three tiered with swiveling wheels of brass. It was too low to the ground to be pushed without a person bending absurdly as they did so. "There's no point bringing it all out for two, but when there's three I like to get it out." Keisha Blake sat cross-legged in front of the television with her good friend Leah Hanwell, with whom she had bonded over a dramatic event. She turned to monitor the trolley's progress: food delighted Keisha Blake and she looked forward to it above all things. Blocking the girls' view, Mrs. Hanwell now asked the television a question: "Who are all these dangerous-looking fellas in a van?" Leah turned up the volume. She pointed to the TV, at Hannibal's gleaming white hair, and then at her mother, in reality. "That hair makes you look well old," she said. Keisha tried to imagine saying something of this kind to her own mother. Silently she mourned the loss of the biscuit plate and whatever novelty was contained in those furry brown eggs. She put her feet together ready to stand up and go home. But Mrs. Hanwell did not start yelling or hitting. She only touched her bowl of hair and sighed. "It went this color when I had you."

3. Holes

The stick jammed the doors of the lift
— this had been the whole point of the
exercise. An alarm sounded. All three
children went screaming and laughing
down the stairs, up the incline, and over
the boundary wall to sit on the pavement
on the other side. Nathan Bogle pulled his
knees right up to his chin and put his arms
around them. "How many holes you got?"
he asked. Both girls were silent. "What?"
said Leah, finally. "Down there" — he
jabbed a finger at Keisha's crotch to demonstrate — "How many? You don't even
know." Keisha dared lift her eyes from the
road to her friend. Leah was hopelessly
red in the face. "Everybody knows that,"
countered Keisha Blake, trying to muster the further boldness she sensed was
required. "You should fuck off and find
out." "You don't even know," Nathan concluded, and Leah stood up suddenly and
kicked him on his ankle and shouted, "But
she does though!" and took Keisha's hand
and ran back to the flat holding hands the
whole way because they were best friends
bonded for life by a dramatic event and
everyone in Caldwell best know about it.

4. Uncertainty

They found Cheryl watching television, plaiting her own hair, from the back of her head forwards. Keisha Blake challenged her elder sister to say how many holes there were. It was not good to have Cheryl laugh at you. It was a loud, relentless laugh, fueled by the other person's mortification.

5. Philosophical disagreement

Keisha Blake was eager to replicate some of the conditions she had seen at the Hanwells'. Cup, teabag, then water, then — only then — milk. On a tea-tray. Her mother was of the opinion that anyone who is in another person's flat as often as Leah Hanwell was in the Blakes' forgoes the right to be a guest and should simply be treated as a member of the family, with all the dispensation and latitude that suggests. Cheryl took a third position: "She's always hanging round here. Don't she like her own place? What's she up in my makeup all the time for? Who does she think she is?"

"Mum, you got a tea-tray?"

"Just take it in to her. Lord!"

6. *Some answers*

Keisha Blake	**Leah Hanwell**
Purple	Yellow
Cameo, Culture Club, Bob Marley	Madonna, Culture Club, Thompson Twins
Rather have the money	Be really famous
Michael Jackson	Harrison Ford
Nobody. If I had to, Rahim.	Top secret: Nathan Bogle
Don't know	Daisies or butter-cups
Doctor or Missionary	Manager
Leah Hanwell	Keisha Blake
World peace in South Africa	No bombs
Deaf	Deaf
Hurricane	*The Lion, the Witch and the Wardrobe*
E.T.	*E.T.*

7. *Filet-O-Fish, large fries, apple pie*

It was a Caldwell assumption that plumbers did very well for themselves. Keisha saw little evidence of this. Either the personal wealth of plumbers was a myth or her father was incompetent. She had in the past prayed

284

for work for Augustus Blake, without results. Now it was almost midday on a Saturday and no news had arrived of pipes leaking or backed-up toilets. During periods of stress Augustus Blake stood on the balcony and smoked Lambert & Butlers and this he did now. Keisha could not tell if Leah felt the anxiety of the phone not-ringing in the flat as the rest of them did. The two girls lay on their bellies in front of the television set. They watched four hours of morning shows and cartoons. Each one they ridiculed in turn and spoiled for Jayden, but there was no other way of explaining to each other why they should want to watch the same things as a six-year-old boy. When the lunchtime news began, Gus came in and asked where Cheryl was.

"Out."

"More fool her."

Squeals, and a small hand-holding dance. Apart from Marcia scoring a point off the situation — "See how quick you all get your-selves ready when you're going somewhere you want to go?" — joy was unconfined, and everything colluded to extend it; Mar-cia did not make them talk to every church lady on the high road and Gus called Keisha "Madam One" and Leah "Madam Two" and did not get angry when Jayden ran ahead toward the twin arcs of the golden M.

8. *Radiography*

But on the way home they bumped into Pauline Hanwell, alone, pulling a shopping bag on wheels. It was true she looked like the actor George Peppard. Jayden held the toy of his Happy Meal up for Mrs. Hanwell's inspection. Mrs. Hanwell did not see it — she was looking at Leah. Keisha Blake looked at her friend Leah Hanwell and saw the red climbing up her throat. Mrs. Blake asked Mrs. Hanwell how she was and Mrs. Hanwell said fine and the reverse inquiry was made with the same result. Mrs. Hanwell was a general nurse at The Royal Free Hospital and Mrs. Blake a health visitor affiliated with St. Mary's, Paddington. Neither woman was in any sense a member of the bourgeoisie but neither did they consider themselves solidly of the working class either. They spoke briefly about the National Health Service, with a mixture of complaint and pride. Mrs. Hanwell told the Blakes that she was retraining to become a radiographer and Keisha could not tell if Mrs. Hanwell realized she had told them the very same thing a few days ago in front of the bins. "Now, Augustus: Colin said if you're still wanting those parking permits for your van, he can help you." Mr. Colin Hanwell worked for the council. His main responsibility was bike safety, but he had also some minimal power in the matter of parking. Keisha thought: now she is going to say she's heading to Marks & Sparks and when this was exactly what she did say Keisha experienced an unforgettable pulse of authorial omnipotence. Maybe the world really was hers for the making. "Leah," said Mrs. Hanwell, "you coming?" The gap between the posing of this question and its answer was experienced by Keisha Blake as an intolerable tension extending far beyond her ability to withstand it and almost infinite in length.

9. *Thrown*

It was clear that Keisha Blake could not start something without finishing it. If she climbed the boundary wall of Caldwell she was compelled to walk the entire wall, no matter the obstructions in her path (beer cans, branches). This compulsion, applied to other fields, manifested itself as "intelligence." Every unknown word sent her to a dictionary — in search of something like "completion" — and every book led to another book, a process which of course could never be completed. This route through early life gave her no small portion of joy, and indeed it seemed at first that her desires and her capacities were basically aligned. She wanted to read things — could not resist wanting to read things — and reading was easily done, and relatively inexpensive. On the other hand, that she should receive any praise for such reflexive habits baffled the girl, for she knew herself to be fantastically stupid about many things. Wasn't it possible that what others mistook for intelligence might in fact be only a sort of mutation of the will? She could sit in one place longer than other children, be bored for hours without complaint, and was completely devoted to filling in every last corner of the coloring books Augustus Blake sometimes brought home. She could not help her mutated will — no more than she could help the shape of her feet or the street on which she was born. She was unable to glean real satisfaction from accidents. In the child's mind a breach now appeared: between what she believed she knew of herself, *essentially,* and her essence as others seemed to understand it. She began to exist for other people, and if ever asked a question to which she did not know the answer she was wont to fold her arms across her body and look upward. As if the question itself were too obvious to truly concern her.

10. *Speak, radio*

A coincidence? Coincidence has its limitations. The DJ on Colin Hanwell's kitchen radio could not always be between tracks. He could not always be between tracks at the very moment Keisha Blake walked into the Hanwell kitchen. She made inquiries. But Leah's father, who was at the counter shelling peas from their pods, did not seem to understand the question.
"How d'you mean? There isn't any music. It's Radio 4. They just talk."
An early example of the maxim: "Truth is sometimes stranger than fiction."

11. *Push it*

It had never occurred to Keisha Blake that her friend Leah Hanwell was in possession of a particular type of personality. Like most children, theirs was a relation based on verbs, not nouns. Leah Hanwell was a person willing and available to do a variety of things that Keisha Blake was willing and available to do. Together they ran, jumped, danced, sang, bathed, colored-in, rode bikes, pushed a Valentine under Nathan Bogle's door, read magazines, shared chips, sneaked a cigarette, read Cheryl's diary, wrote the word FUCK on the first page of a Bible, tried to get *The Exorcist* out of the video shop, watched a prostitute or loose woman or a girl just crazy in love suck someone off in a phone box, found Cheryl's weed, found Cheryl's vodka, shaved Leah's forearm with Cheryl's razor, did the moonwalk, learned the obscene dance popularized by Salt-N-Pepa, and many other things of this nature. But now they were leaving Quinton Primary for Brayton Comprehensive, where everybody seemed to have a personality, and so Keisha looked at Leah and tried to ascertain the outline of her personality.

12. *Portrait*

A generous person, wide open to the entire world — with the possible exception of her own mother. Ceased eating tuna because of the dolphins, and now all meat because of animals generally. If there happened to be a homeless man sitting on the ground outside the supermarket in Cricklewood Keisha Blake had to wait until Leah Hanwell had finished bending down and speaking with the homeless man, not simply asking him if there was anything he wanted, but making conversation. If she was more curt with her own family than a homeless man this only suggested that generosity was not an infinite quantity and had to be employed strategically where it was most needed. Within Brayton she befriended everyone without distinction or boundary, but the hopeless cases did not alienate her from the popular and vice versa and how this was managed Keisha Blake had no understanding. A little of this universal good feeling spread to Keisha by association, though no one ever mistook Keisha's cerebral willfulness for her friend's generosity of spirit.

13. *Gravel*

Walking back from school with a girl called Anita, Keisha Blake and Leah Hanwell found themselves being told a terrible story. Anita's mother had been raped by a cousin in 1976 and this man was Anita's father. He had been put in jail and then got out and Anita had never met him and did not want to. Some of the family thought her father had raped her mother and some did not. It was a domestic drama but also a kind of thrilling horror because who could say if Anita's rapist father wasn't living in NW itself and/ or watching them from some vantage point at this very moment? The three girls stopped in the gravel courtyard of a church and sat on a bench. Anita cried, and Leah cried too. Anita asked: "How do I know which half of me is evil?" But parental legacy meant little to Keisha Blake; it was her solid sense that she was in no way the creation of her parents and as a result could not seriously believe that anybody else was the creation of theirs. Indeed, a non-existent father and/or mother was a persistent fantasy of hers, and the children's books she had most enjoyed always began with the protagonist inheriting a terrible freedom after some form of parental apocalypse. She made a figure of eight on the ground with her left trainer and considered the two pages she had to write about the 1804 corn laws before tomorrow morning.

14. *That obscure object of desire*

The red and white air technology of the Greek goddess of victory. Keisha Blake put her hand against the reinforced shop-front glass. Separated from happiness. It had been everywhere, the air, free for the taking, but she had only come to desire it now that she saw it thus defined, extracted, rendered visible. The infinitely available thing, now enclosed in the sole of a shoe! You had to admire the audacity. Ninety-nine quid. Maybe at Christmas.

15. *Evian*

The exact same thing had been achieved with water. When Marcia Blake spotted the bottle hiding under a bag of carrots she cussed Keisha Blake, snatched it out of the trolley and placed it back on the wrong shelf next to the jams.

16. *The new timetable*

"There: he's in your French class. And your drama class."
"Who is?"
"Nathan!"
"Bogle? So?"
"!"
"Oh my gosh, Keisha. We were *babies*. You're so dumb sometimes."

17. *GCSE*

In the office of Keisha Blake's Head of Year baseball caps and inappropriate jewelry were confiscated and hung from the wall on hooks. Keisha Blake had not been called in for a reprimand, she had come to discuss her options for a set of exams still three years in the future. She did not really want to discuss these exams, she simply wanted it to be noted that she was the kind of person who thought three years ahead about the important things in life. As she got up to leave she spotted a silver chain from which drooped a tiny pistol picked out in diamante crystals. "That's my sister's," she said. "Oh, is it?" said the teacher and looked out of the window. Keisha persisted: "She doesn't go here anymore. She got expelled." The teacher frowned. He took the necklace from the wall and passed it to Keisha. He said: "It's hard to believe that you and Cheryl Blake are even related."

18. *Sony Walkman (borrowed)*

That Keisha should be able to hear the Rebel MC in her ears and at the same time walk down Willesden Lane, was a kind of miracle and modern ecstasy, and yet there was very little space in the day for anything like ecstasy or abandon or even simple laziness, for whatever you did in life you would have to do it twice as well as they did it "just to break even," a troubling belief held simultaneously by Keisha Blake's mother and her Uncle Jeffrey, known to be "gifted" but also "beyond the pale."

19. *Detour into the perfect past tense*

(Sometimes Jeffrey — who was not a member of the church — cornered his thirteen-year-old niece and told her perplexing things. "Look it up! Look it up!" he had said, yesterday, at Cousin Gale's wedding. Keisha could only presume he was referring to a prior conversation, that had taken place many weeks earlier. Therefore he had meant: "Look up the CIA's practice of flooding poor black neighbourhoods with crack cocaine and you will see that I am right." How? Where?)

20. *Sony Walkman redux*

That two such different personalities as her mother and Uncle Jeffrey should hold an opinion simultaneously lent that opinion some force. Yet surely none of you would begrudge Keisha Blake this present pleasure of thinking to music? Oh, this outdoor soundtrack! Oh, this orchestral existence!

21. *Jane Eyre*

When being bullied Keisha Blake found it useful to remember that if you read the relevant literature or watched the pertinent movies you soon found that being bullied was practically a sign of a superior personality, and the greater the intensity of the bullying the more likely it was to be avenged at the other end of life, when qualities of the kind Keisha Blake possessed — cleverness, will-to-power — became "their own reward," and that this remained true even if the people in the literature and the movies looked nothing like you, came from a different socio-economic and historical universe, and — had they ever met you — would very likely have enslaved you or, at best, bullied you to precisely the same extent as Lorna Mackenzie who had a problem with the way you acted like you were better than everyone else.

22. *Citation*

Further confirmation of this principle was to be found in the Bible itself.

23. *Spectrum 128k*

For her fourteenth birthday Leah received a

home computer. Keisha Blake read through the accompanying booklet and was able to figure out how to program a basic series of commands so that in answer to particular prompts text would come up on the screen as if the computer itself were "talking." They did one for Mr. Hanwell:

>> **WHAT IS YOUR NAME**

"I'm to type it in here? I feel silly."

>> **COLIN ALBERT HANWELL**

>> **VERY NICE TO MEET YOU, COLIN.**

"My word! Did you do that, Keisha? How do you do these things? I can't keep up with you these days. Pauline, come and look at this, you won't believe it."

After they had finished dazzling the Hanwells, they did one for their private amusement:

>> **WHAT IS YOUR NAME?**

>> **LEAH HANWELL**

>> **OH REALLY? THAT'S JUST FUCKING FASCINATING.**

24. *The number 37*

On Sundays, Keisha Blake attended Kilburn Pentecostal with her family, minus Cheryl, and Leah often came along, not because she was in any sense a believer, but rather motivated by the generosity of spirit described above. Now a new policy revealed itself. When they reached the corner by the McDonald's Leah Hanwell said to Keisha Blake, "Actually I think I might get on the 37, go to the Lock, see that lot." "Fair enough," said Keisha Blake. There had been an attempt over the summer to mix that Camden Lock lot with this Caldwell lot, but Keisha Blake did not especially care for Baudelaire or Bukowski or Nick Drake or Sonic Youth or Joy Division or boys who looked like girls or vice versa or Anne Rice or William Burroughs or Kafka's *Metamorphosis* or CND or Glastonbury or the Situationists or *Breathless* or Samuel Beckett or Andy Warhol or a million other Camden things, and when Keisha brought a wondrous Monie Love 7-inch to play on Leah's hi-fi there was something awful in the way Leah blushed and conceded it was probably OK to dance to. They had only Prince left, and he was wearing thin.

25. *Vivre sa vie*

This sudden and violent divergence in their tastes was shocking to Keisha, and she persisted in believing that Leah's new tastes were an affectation, unrelated to anything essential in her being and largely taken up to annoy her oldest friend. "Bell me later," said Leah Hanwell and jumped on the bus's open rear end. Keisha Blake, whose celebrated will and focus did not leave her much room for angst, watched her friend ascend to the top deck in her new panda-eyed makeup and had a mauvais quart d'heure wondering whether she herself had any personality at all or was in truth only the accumulation and reflection of all the things she had read in books and seen on television.

26. *Relative time*

A number of factors — modest style of dress, early physical maturation, glasses — combined to make Keisha Blake look considerably older than she in fact was.

27. *50ml vodka*

Instead of being known as a "personality," Keisha Blake now became indirectly popular as a function. She bought alcohol for a lot of people who believed they looked too young to get it themselves, and the irrational belief in Keisha's "talent" in this area became self-fulfilling, as invested with all this belief in her infallibility she came to believe in it herself. Still, it was strange to buy booze for Leah. "It needs to be the size to fit in my back pocket." "Why?" "Because there'll be two hundred people moshing up and down and you can't be pissing around with a wine glass." As the event did not start until late, Leah first came to Keisha Blake's room to hang out and drink and talk until it was time for her to go. Probably later she would meet someone with hair in his eyes and do sex. "I saw Nathan at the chippy yesterday," said Keisha. "God, Nathan," said Leah Hanwell. "He's not coming back next term," said Keisha Blake. "They turned it into an expulsion." "That was a matter of time," said Leah Hanwell, and opened the window to have a fag. Leah drank some more and spent a long time twisting the radio knob looking for a pirate station she didn't find. At around ten fifteen p.m. Leah Hanwell said: "I don't think women can really be beautiful. I think they can be so attractive and you can want to shag them and love them and blah blah but I think really only men can be completely beautiful in the end." "You reckon?" said Keisha, and disguised her confusion by drinking deeply from her mug of tea. She was not at all sure to whom the second-person pronoun was meant to refer.

28. *Rabbit*

On the eve of her sixteenth birthday a gift was left for Keisha Blake, outside the flat in the corridor. The wrapping showed a repeating butterfly pattern. The card, unsigned, read UNWRAP IN PRIVATE, but the slant of the p and the pointy w told her it was the hand of her good friend Leah Hanwell. She retreated to the bathroom. A vibrator, neon pink with revolving beads in its gigantic tip. Keisha sat on the closed lid of the toilet and made some strategic calculations. Wrapping the dildo in a towel, she hid it in the room she shared with Cheryl, then took the box and wrapping paper down to the courtyard to the public bins by the parking bays. The following Saturday morning she began approximating the early signs of a cold, and on Sunday claimed a severe cough and stomach ache. Her mother pressed her tongue down with a fork and said it was a shame, Pastor Akinwande was going to talk on the topic of Abraham and Isaac. From the balcony Keisha Blake watched her family walk to church, not without regret: she was sincerely interested in the topic of Abraham and Isaac.

29. *Rabbit, run*

But she had also privately decided she was a different kind of believer from her mother, and could survive the occasional anthropological adventure into sin. She returned inside and raided an alarm clock and calculator for their batteries. She did not employ any mood lighting or soft music or scented candles. She did not take off her clothes. Three minutes later she'd established several things previously unknown to her: what a vaginal orgasm was; the difference between a clitoral and a vaginal orgasm, and the existence of a viscous material, produced by her body, that she had, afterward, to rinse out of the ridges along the vibrator's shaft, in the little sink in the corner of the room. She had the dildo for only a couple of weeks but in that time used it regularly, sometimes as much as several times a day, often without washing in between, and always in this business-like way, as if delegating a task to somebody else.

30. *Surplus value, schizophrenia, adolescence*

"We should go like this here," said Layla and sang a new note and Keisha made a notation. "Role models," sang Layla, in the new key, "bringing the truth, bringing the light." Keisha made a further note. "Making it right," said Layla, and then repeated the same words but sung as music, and Keisha nodded and made a further notation. Layla was genuinely musical and her voice was beautiful. Her mother was a well-known singer in Sierra Leone. Keisha could not sing and played the recorder rather badly. She had taught herself musical notation in a few weeks using piano music taken from church. As with everything that involved symbols and/or signification it had not been difficult for Keisha to do this and she did not know why that should be so or what such facility meant, nor why her sister Cheryl had not been similarly blessed, nor what she was meant to do about it or with it, or if "it" was a noun or a verb or had any material reality at all, outside of her own mind. The two girls were writing a song for the under-12 faith group that met in this back room on Thursdays after service. They were good friends, Keisha and Layla, though not as close as Keisha and Leah. The fact was they had not been bonded by a dramatic event, although in the mind of the church they belonged together in a natural and inevitable way. "Leading the way," sang Layla. Keisha made a note. She could smell her own vagina on her hands. Now Layla reverted to speaking: "Or something like, 'Sisters today, leading the way.'" Keisha made a note of this and placed parentheses around it to signify it was not yet a lyric set in stone. If these are "talents" — the ability to sing, or to quickly comprehend and reproduce musical notation — what kind of a thing is "talent"? A commodity? A gift? A prize? A reward? For what? "We follow the truth, we follow the light!" sang Layla, which had already been set in stone both musically and lyrically. With nothing to note down Keisha became anxious. Across the room hung a mirror. Two admirable young sisters, their hair still plaited by their mothers, sat on the edge of a makeshift stage, one singing and the other transforming music into its own shadow, musical notation. That's you. That's her. She is real. You are a forgery. Look closer. Look away. She is consistent. You are making it up as you go along. She must never know. "And then from here to here," sang Layla, singing these words and therefore putting the instruction itself to music. Keisha made the notation.

31. *Permission to enter*

Though they were five, the Blakes occupied a three-bed, one bathroom unit, in which only the youngest boy, Jayden, had a room of his own. As far as Keisha could make out, privacy did not seem of any importance to her brother, who was eleven, and still prone to streaks of domestic nudity, but for her own person it was a necessity, more so with every passing day, and the arrival of the dildo prompted her to reopen an old debate with her mother.

"It's a human right!" cried Keisha Blake. History GCSE module B16: *The American Civil Rights Movement*. Module D5: *The Chartists*.

"If there's a fire you'd burn up in your room," said her mother, "This Cheryl's idea? People who want locks got something to hide."

"People who want locks just want a basic human right, which is privacy, look it up," said Keisha, although with less heat this time, alarmed that her mother, in the general reach of a maternal cliché, should have gathered in the truth so precisely. She retreated to her room and thought about Jesus, another deeply godly person who was not understood as godly by the sort of clichéd people who called themselves godly, though to be fair those people were probably also sometimes godly in their own uneducated way, but only by accident, and only a bit.

32. *Difference*

A clitoral orgasm is a localized phenomena restricted to the clitoris itself. Perversely, direct stimulation of the clitoris tends not to provoke it, causing instead pain and annoyance, and sometimes an intense boredom. A vigorous and circular manipulation of the clitoris and the labia together, with a hand, is the most direct route. The resulting spasm is sharp, intensely pleasurable, but brief, like male orgasm. On the charged question of clitoral versus vaginal orgasm Keisha found herself to be an agnostic. One might as well be asked whether blue is a superior color to green.

A vaginal orgasm can be provoked by penetration, but also by simply moving one's pelvis forward and backward in a small motion while thinking about something interesting. This latter method is especially effective on a bus or a plane. There seems to be a small piece of raised flesh — about the size of a ten-pence piece — halfway up the wall of the vaginal canal on the side nearest your belly-button that is stimulated by this "rocking," but whether this is what is meant by the phrase "g-spot" and whether it is the cause of the almost unbearably pleasurable sensation, Keisha Blake could not verify one way or another. However it is achieved, what is noticeable about vaginal orgasm is its length and intensity. It is experienced as a series of spasms as if the vagina itself is opening and closing like a fist. Perhaps it is. But whether this is what is meant by the phrase "multiple orgasm" was also unclear to Keisha Blake, though it seemed typical of the unassuming tendencies of feminine descriptors to accept one "close of the fist" as an orgasm in and of itself. It was perhaps simply a phenomenological problem. If Leah Hanwell said the flower is blue and Keisha Blake said the flower is blue how could they be sure that by the word "blue" they were apprehending the same phenomena?

33. *For the prosecution.*

Marcia found Leah's gift during one of her routine sweeps. These sweeps really had Cheryl as their object — she had begun disappearing on Fridays and returning Monday — and nothing would have been easier for Keisha than to add dildo possession to her older sister's already ruined reputation. Unable to look any longer at Marcia brandishing the plastic bag, Keisha Blake threw herself face down on the bed to commence fake crying, but in the middle of this procedure found herself locked in a genuine struggle, unable to countenance blaming either her sister or Leah, but equally unable to imagine the second option — her father being informed — with which she was now being presented. Keisha Blake thought to the left and thought to the right but there was no exit, and this was very likely the first time she became aware of the problem of suicide.

"And don't tell me you bought it," said her mother, "because I don't know where you think you would have got the money." In the course of this interrogation Marcia went through most of the girls on the estate before working herself round to the painful possibility of Leah and finding the confirmation in her daughter's face.

34. *Rupture*

There followed a break between Leah Hanwell and Keisha Blake, enforced by Marcia, followed by a cooling off that could not be blamed on Marcia alone. The girls were 16. This period lasted a year and a half.

35. *Angst!*

In the absence of Leah — at school, on the streets, in Caldwell — Keisha Blake felt herself to be revealed and exposed. She had not noticed until the break that the state of "being Leah Hanwell's friend" constituted a sort of passport, lending Keisha a protected form of access in most situations. She was now relegated to the conceptual realm of "those church kids," most of whom were Nigerian or otherwise African, and did not share Keisha Blake's anthropological curiosity regarding sin nor her love of rap music. To the children of her own background she believed, rightly or wrongly, that she was an anomaly, and to the ravers and indie kids she knew for certain she was the wrong kind of outcast. It did not strike Keisha Blake that such feelings of alienation are the banal fate of adolescents everywhere. She considered herself peculiarly afflicted, and it is not an exaggeration to say that she struggled to think of anyone besides perhaps James Baldwin and Jesus who had experienced the profound isolation and loneliness she now knew to be the one and only true reality of this world.

36. *Your enemy's enemy*

In Keisha Blake's break with Leah Hanwell we must admit that Marcia Blake spied an opportunity. The break coincided with the problem of sex, which anyway could no longer be ignored. A simple ban would have backfired — they had been through all that already with Cheryl, who was presently twenty years old and six months pregnant. Pushing Keisha Blake toward Rodney Banks was Mrs. Blake's elegant solution: at exactly the moment her daughter was about to detonate, she was defused. Rodney lived on the same corridor, attended the same school. He was one of the few Caribbean children in the church. His mother, Christine, was a close friend. "You should give Rodney some time," said Marcia, passing Keisha Blake a plate to dry. "He's like you, always reading." For precisely this reason Keisha had always been wary of Rodney and keen to avoid him — as much as that was possible in a place like Caldwell — on the principle that the last thing a drowning person needs is another drowning person clinging to them.

38. *On the other hand*

Beggars cannot be choosers.

39. *Reading with Rodney*

Keisha Blake sat on Rodney Banks' bed, feet tucked underneath her. She was already five foot eight, while Rodney had stopped growing the previous summer. To be Christian to Rodney Banks, Keisha Blake tried to sit in most situations. Rodney had in his hand an abridged library copy of an infamous book by Albert Camus. Both Keisha Blake and Rodney Banks sounded the T and the S in this name, not knowing any better: such are the perils of autodidacticism. Rodney Banks was reading the text aloud, with his own skeptical running commentary. He called this "putting faith to the test." Pastor liked to recommend this muscular approach to his teenage flock, although when he did so it is unlikely that he had Camus in mind. Rodney Banks looked somewhat like Martin Luther King: the same rounded, gentle face. When he made a point that interested him, he scribbled a little illegal note on the page, which Keisha read and tried to admire. She found it hard to concentrate on the book because she was concerned about when and how the heavy petting would begin. It had happened last Friday and the Friday before, but she had not known it was going to happen until the very last moment since they were both somehow unable to refer to it verbally, or build up to it in a natural manner. Instead she had launched herself at Rodney both times and hoped for a response, which she had received, more or less. "We get into the habit of living before acquiring the habit of thinking," read Rodney, and then made a note by this sentence: "So what? (fallacious argument.)"

40. *Rumpole*

The cooling-off period between Keisha Blake and Leah Hanwell continued through their A level exams, and this was partly a pragmatic decision on Keisha Blake's part. Leah Hanwell was by this point taking the popular club amphetamine Ecstasy most weekends and Keisha did not have the faith that she herself could be involved in that life and still pass the exams she was beginning to comprehend would be essential. Which comprehension arrived partly through the efforts of a visiting careers officer. Reader: keep up! A young woman, from Barbados, new in the job, optimistic. Name unimportant. She was especially impressed by Rodney, taking him seriously and listening to him when he talked about the law. Where Rodney Banks had even got the idea of "the law" it was difficult to say. His mother was a dinner lady. His father drove a bus.

41. *Parenthetical*

(Much later in life, while taking a long walk through North West London, it occurred to Keisha Blake that the young man she had turned into a comic anecdote to be told at dinner parties was in many ways himself a miracle of self-invention, a young man with a tremendous will, far out-stripping her own.)

42. *Good place/No place*

The Baijan told Keisha Blake and Rodney Banks they must have a plan. All three were aware that Marcia Blake had her own plan: enrollment in a one-year Business Administration course at "Coles Academy," really just a corridor of office space above the old Woolworths on the Kilburn High Road. A racket, an unaccredited institution, taught by some Nairobi acquaintance of Pastor Akinwande, and requiring no move away from home.

43. *Contra*

The careers officer from Barbados chose five

institutions for Keisha Blake and Rodney Banks — the same five; they had decided they could not be parted — and showed them how to fill in the necessary forms. She wrote to Marcia on Keisha's behalf. It won't cost any money. She'll get a full council grant. There's a church. The train goes straight there, she'll be safe, she won't be the only one. Keisha Blake was advised to carry on this campaign of reassurance through the winter. Rodney was told to do the same with his mother, Christine. Keisha did not expect these campaigns to succeed. Marcia had been to the "countryside" and did not consider it a safe environment, preferring London where at least you knew what you were up against. Then in April, that "poor defenseless boy" — Marcia invariably called him that — was stabbed at an Eltham bus stop, overwhelmed by "a pack of animals." Keisha Blake, Marcia Blake, Augustus Blake, Cheryl Blake and Jayden Blake gathered round the television to watch the white boys walk free from court, swinging punches at the photographers. The boy's body was taken to Jamaica, buried in Marcia's parish.

44. *Brideshead Unvisited*

The front door was on the latch. Rodney

walked straight through into Keisha and Cheryl Blake's bedroom and said, "Where is it?" and Keisha said, "On the bed," and Rodney said, "Let me see it," and Keisha showed him the strange letter stamped with a coat of arms and said, "But if you're not going, I'm not," and Rodney said, "Just let me read it," and Keisha said, "It's only the interview offer. I'm not going to go. Anyway, it must be big money," and Rodney said, "If you get in, government pays for it. Don't you even know that?" and Cheryl said, "You two better shut up, man, baby's sleeping!" and Keisha said, "I don't even want to go!" and Rodney said, "Can I just read it please!" and after he read it, he did not mention it again, and neither did Keisha Blake. That night they went to the Swiss Cottage Odeon to see a film about a man dressed as a woman so that he could keep an eye on his children for reasons Keisha found herself too distracted to even begin to comprehend.

45. Economics

The interviews for Manchester were scheduled between ten and eleven a.m. To reach Manchester from London's Euston station would require taking a train that left well before 9:30 a.m. These trains cost one hun-

dred and three pounds return. A similar —
even more expensive — problem ruled out
Edinburgh.

46. *Pause for an abstract idea*

In households all over the world, in many
languages, this sentence usually emerges,
eventually: "I don't know you anymore."
It was always there, hiding in some private
corner of the house, biding its time. Stacked
with the cups, or squeezed between the
DVDs or another terminal format. "I don't
know you anymore!"

47. *A further pause*

In popular science magazines they give the
biological example, the regeneration of cells.
Many years after the events presently being
recounted, at a dinner in her own house,
a philosopher sitting to the right of our
heroine suggested she undertake a thought
experiment: what if your brain cells were
replaced individually with the brain cells of
another person? At what point would you
cease to be yourself? At what point would
you become another person? His breath was
nasty. He put his hand on her knee, which
she didn't remove, not wanting to make a

fuss in front of his wife. Mrs. Blake had become by that point quite extraordinarily well-behaved. The wife of the philosopher was a gray-haired QC. In the philosopher's brilliant mind she was too old to conceivably still be his wife. And yet.

48. *Residents' meeting*

At a meeting of the Caldwell residents' committee — at which Leah and Keisha, compelled by their parents, were the only young people in attendance — Keisha saw a seat free next to Leah but did not go toward it. Afterward, she tried to get away without being noticed but Leah Hanwell called from across the room and Keisha turned and found the familiar open face smiling at her, unaffected by Keisha Blake's own attempts to imaginatively traduce it.

"Hey," said Leah Hanwell.

"All right," said Keisha Blake.

They spoke of the boredom of the meeting, and of Cheryl's baby, but the other subject could not be repressed for very long.

"What did you think of Manchester? Did you see Michael Konstantinou? He was your day. But he's for Media Studies."

"We're not going there, anymore," said Keisha Blake. She put a deliberate emphasis on the plural pronoun. "It's either Bristol or Hull."

"I see Rodney in history. Never speaks a word."

Keisha, hearing this comment as a personal insult, began defending Rodney robustly. Leah looked confused and fiddled with the three rings that hung from the upper cartilage of her ear.

"No, I meant: he's got no questions, he knows it all already. Silent but deadly. You two will just fly through for sure. At least you can say C in maths. Mine's a U. A lot of them won't even consider your A levels if you failed your maths. I'm on a wing and a prayer at this point."

Keisha tried to backpedal from her overreaction by suggesting her old friend Leah Hanwell join Keisha and her new boyfriend for study sessions.

"I reckon I need to just get down to it and concentrate. It'll be OK. Would be good to see you soon, though, before the move. Pauline's loving it. I don't care, I'll be in Edinburgh by September anyway — we pray. She's acting like she's given me some big present. A new life. 'It's practically Maida Vale. Better late than never, I suppose.'" This last was done in Pauline's voice.

49. *Mobility*

The Hanwells were moving into a maison-
ette. Practically in Maida Vale. Keisha had
already heard all about it from Marcia; the
shared garden, the three bedrooms. Something called a "study."

50. *Rodney makes a note*

"Our pre-eminence: we live in the age of
comparison" (Nietzsche).

51. *Undercover*

Rodney Banks didn't cause chaos in class
nor did he speak and the combination made
him invisible, anonymous. Keisha Blake
asked him why he never spoke to the teachers. He said it was a strategy. He, like Keisha, was fond of strategies. This was one of
the things they had in common, though it
should be noted that the substance of their
strategies was quite different. Keisha meant
to charm her way through the front door.
Rodney intended to slip through the back,
unnoticed. Rodney Banks highlighted so
many passages in Machiavelli's *The Prince*
it became one block of yellow and he didn't
dare return it to the library. "The difficult

situation and the newness of my kingdom force me to do these things, and guard my borders everywhere." He always seemed to have this book with him, along with the King James, a combination in which he saw no contradiction.

52. *Parity*

By July Leah Hanwell and Keisha Blake had been offered university places. Both had lovers. (Leah's lover played the bass in a band called No No Never.) Both the universities and the lovers were of an equal standard, despite their many differences. Both girls had grown into decent-looking women with no serious health or mental problems. Neither had any interest in tanning. It was Leah's plan to spend a large part of this final NW summer under the shade of an oak tree on Hampstead Heath, with an assortment of friends, a picnic, a lot of alcohol, a little weed. She kept inviting Keisha, who longed to go. But Keisha was working part-time in a bakery on the Kilburn High Road, and when she was not in the bakery she was in church, or helping Cheryl with the baby. At the bakery she was paid three twenty-five an hour. She had to wear regulation flat black shoes with rounded toes and chunky soles, and a brown and white striped outfit topped off by a "baker's hat," with an elastic rim, under which every last strand of your hair was to be placed. It left an indentation along her forehead. She had to wash out the croissant molds and get to the donut sugar that caught in the thin gulley between the presentation case and the glass. And many other bits of drudgery. She had thought she would prefer it to clothes retail, but in the end even her great enthusiasm for sausage rolls and iced fingers could not sustain her. She kept the university's prospectus in her locker and often spent her lunch break slowly turning the glossy pages.

Every other Saturday she had a half-day and on a few occasions she managed to sneak to the heath, alone. Rodney would not enjoy the scene on the heath and could not reasonably be told about it, for this would lead to questions about the two sets of accounts Keisha was in the habit of keeping. On one side of the ledger she placed Rodney, Marcia, her siblings, the church, and Jesus Christ himself. In the other, Leah was lounging in the high grass drinking cider and asking her good friend Keisha Blake if she would take the opportunity to kill PW Botha if he happened to be standing in front of her. "I'm not capable of murder," protested Keisha Blake. "Everyone's capable of everything," insisted Leah Hanwell.

53. *Nirvana*

Leah would surely be in her room, clutching his picture, weeping. Keisha found it difficult to suppress a feeling of pleasure at this imagined scenario. Then, in the middle of the news report, Marcia said something incredible, quoting a doctor at the clinic as a source, and the next morning Keisha went directly to the library to investigate. She was infuriated to find that statistically speaking Marcia's boast was correct: our people hardly ever do that.

54. *Further education*

That autumn, Keisha Blake and Rodney Banks began attending a church in the Bristol suburbs, the Holy Spirit Ministry, identical in spirit to Kilburn Pentecostal — it came with a recommendation from Pastor. They did most of their socializing there, that first term, with an assortment of kindly people, all in their sixties and seventies. With young people of their own age they were less successful. Rodney left church literature under every door in Keisha's corridor, and after that they were avoided by fellow students and avoided them in turn. There seemed no point of entry. The students were tired of things Keisha had never heard of, and horrified by the only thing she knew well: the Bible. In the evenings Rodney and Keisha sat at either end of a small desk in Keisha's room and studied, as they had studied for their school exams, wearing earplugs and writing everything out by hand, first in draft copies, then in "best" — a habit picked up from Sunday school. There was a newly built computer center in the basement of Keisha's building that might have made their lives easier: they went in the first week to check it out. A boy in a wide fedora with a leather thong hanging from its brim sat playing Doom, that dark corridor opening on to itself over and over. The rest were either programming or using some early intra-university form of e-mail. Keisha Blake glanced over a shoulder at a chaotic-looking screen.

55. *Keisha's first visit*

Their material circumstances were quite different. Keisha occupied a 60s-build dormitory of indifferent architectural design. Leah a 19th-century terraced house, with a defunct fireplace in every room and nine housemates. Instead of a lounge, a "chill out room." Enormous speakers, no sofa. Keisha had not expected a party on her first night nor had she worn the right sort of skirt for sitting on a beanbag. The volume of techno or whatever it was made conversation a chore. Everybody was white. Leah was giving a speech and holding the fridge open. It was making the whole kitchen cold. She had been holding it open for a long time. She seemed to have forgotten why.

"Look, say you're Einstein and you're just thinking, moment to moment, and suddenly you have your big thought, about the nature of the universe or whatever. So *that* thought, it's not like the other moments, because though you've had the thought within normal time, the thought itself is basically about the nature of the universe, which is sort of infinite? So that's a different kind of moment. So Kierkegaard calls that an "instant." It's not part of normal time like the others. It's a lot of stuff like that. I have to pinch myself in class. Like: what am I doing here, with all these smart bastards? Has someone made a mistake somewhere?"

Keisha scooped some hummus up in a pita

bread and looked into her friend's dilated pupils.

"I was thinking about doing philosophy at one point," said Keisha, "but then I heard about all the maths."

"Oh, there's no maths," said Leah.

"Really? I thought there was maths."

"No," said Leah, and turned from Keisha to pull out a bottle of beer finally, "there's not."

The boy who was sleeping with Leah was also awkward. If you did not keep asking him questions about himself, or about his short films, he stopped talking and stared into space.

"About boredom," he explained.

"That sounds interesting," said Keisha Blake.

"No. The opposite. This party, full of interesting people, is a perfect example. It's totally uninteresting."

"Oh."

"They're all about boredom essentially. It's the only subject left. We're all bored. Aren't you bored?"

"In law," said Keisha Blake, "there's a lot of boring memorization. Like in medicine."

"I think we're talking about two different things," said the boy who was sleeping with Leah.

56. *Family romance*

The phone in the communal hallway rang.
Rodney nodded. Keisha stood up. When
the phone rang it was usually for Rodney or
Keisha — either Marcia or Christine — and
they took these calls interchangeably. They
were like siblings in every way, aside from
the fact they occasionally had sex with each
other. The sex itself was cozy and familiar,
without any hint of eroticism or orgasms
vaginal or clitoral. Rodney was a careful
young man, preoccupied with condoms,
terrified of pregnancy and disease. When
he finally allowed Keisha Blake to have sex
with him it turned out to be a technical
transition. She learned nothing new about
Rodney's body, or Rodney, only a lot of facts
about condoms: their relative efficacy, the
thickness of rubber, the right moment — the
safest moment — to remove them afterward.

57. *Ambition*

They were going to be lawyers, the first
people in either of their families to become
professionals. They thought life was a problem that could be solved by means of profes-
sionalization.

58. *Leah's third visit*

Springtime. Blossom overhead. Ms. Blake waited in the coach station of eagerness and hope, unable to remember why she had ever experienced any tension whatsoever with regard to her very dearest friend from home, Leah Hanwell. The coach arrived, the doors opened. Human figures with faces streamed into view, and Ms. Blake's brain sought a match between a recent memory and a material reality. Her mistake was to cling to ideas that properly belonged to previous visits. Ideas like "red hair," and "black jeans/ black boots/ black t-shirt." Fashions change. University is a time of experimentation and metamorphosis. The person who gripped her by the shoulders could no longer be mistaken for a member of a riot grrrl band or a minor Berlin artist. She was now some kind of dirty blonde warrior for the planet, with hair that was dreadlocking itself, and army trousers that would not pass an inspection.

59. *Proper names*

It was not that Ms. Blake hadn't noticed the white people walking around with the climbing equipment, or the white people huddled in stairwells discussing the best method to chain themselves to an oak tree. She had experienced her usual anthropological curiosity with regard to these matters. But she had thought it was more of an aesthetic than a protest. The details of the project were hazy in her mind. "This is Jed," said Leah, "and this is Katie and Liam and this is Paul. Guys, this is Keisha, she —" "No: Natalie." "Sorry, this is Natalie, we went to school together," said Leah. "She goes here, she's a lawyer. It's so weird to see you guys!" When Leah proceeded to offer these people a round — "No, you sit, we'll get" — Natalie Blake panicked, her budget being extremely tightly managed with no space for rounds of drinks for Crusties to whom she had never before spoken in her life. But at the bar, Leah handed over a twenty and Natalie's only job was to arrange six pints on a round tray best suited for five.

"Lee, how do you even know these people?"

"Newbury!"

60. *And the scales fell from her eyes*

It was apparently important to "keep the pressure up" if they were going to stop the government building this byroad. Rodney listened but only pointed at the books on his desk, which had the imposing heft of the law, thousands of pages long with brutal, functional covers. Leah tried a different tack: "It's basically a legal issue — there's a lot of law kids down there right now. It's good experience, Rodney, even you would agree, even Judge Rodney of the court of the world." Natalie Blake found herself smiling. She could at this moment think of no more wonderful thing than sitting up a tree with her good friend Leah Hanwell many hundreds of miles away from this claustrophobic room. Rodney raised his head from his tort casebook. He had a ruthless look on his face. "We don't care about trees, Leah," he said. "That's your luxury. We haven't got the time to care about trees."

61. *Coup de foudre*

"Mr. De Angelis, could you carry on from 'the power of habit' — top of the second page," said Professor Kirkwood, and an extraordinary young man stood up in the front row. He was not a law student, but he was here, in a "philosophy of law" lecture. He was made of parts Natalie considered mutually exclusive, and found difficult to understand together. He had a collection of unexpected freckles. His nose was very long and dramatic in a style she did not know enough to call "Roman." His hair was twisted into dreadlocks that were the opposite of Leah's, too pristine. They framed his face neatly, ending just below his chin. He wore chinos with no socks, and those shoes that have ropes threaded along the sides, a blue blazer, and a pink shirt. An indescribable accent. Like he was born on a yacht somewhere in the Caribbean and raised by Ralph Lauren.

62. *Montaigne*

In one country, virgins openly display their private parts while married women cover them. In another, male brothels exist. In yet another heavy golden rods are worn through the breasts and buttocks and after dinner men wipe their hands on their testicles. In some places they eat people. In others the fathers decide, when the children are still in the womb, which will be kept and brought up and which killed or abandoned. Kirkwood put his hand up to halt this narrative. "Naturally," he said, "all these people find their own habits to be unremarkable." A few students laughed. Natalie Blake and Rodney Banks tried to find the essay between the covers of the cheap edition they shared (they tended to buy one copy of a text book, and then, when it was finished, immediately sell it back to one of the secondhand stores by the university library). The title did not seem to be in the contents or the index, and the fact that they were still not talking to each other made cooperation difficult. "What is the lesson here for a lawyer?" asked Kirkwood. The notable young man's hand went up. Even from where Natalie Blake was sitting she could see the jewelry on his brown fingers, and an elegant watch with a crocodile-skin strap that looked older than Kirkwood. He said: "Although you may turn up in court armed with reason, we live in an unreasonable world." Natalie Blake tried to work out if this was an interesting answer. Kirkwood paused, smiled, and said: "You put a lot of faith in reason, Mr. De Angelis. But think of last week's example. Hundreds of witnesses stand in the dock: good friends, ex-teachers, ex-nurses, ex-lovers. They all say *That's Tichborne.* The man's own mother gets up there and points: *That's my son.* Reason tells us the Claimant is ten stone heavier than the man he's claiming to be. Reason tells us the real Tichborne could speak French. And yet. And when 'reason prevailed,' why did people riot in the streets? Don't put too much faith in reason.

331

Look, I think Montaigne is more skeptical. I think his point is not that you, the lawyers, are reasonable and they, the people, are unreasonable, or even that the laws the people submit to are unreasonable, but that those who submit to traditional laws have at least the defense of 'simplicity, obedience and example' — Can you see that? End of the third page? — While those who try to change them, that is, the laws, are usually terrible in some way, monstrous. We see ourselves as perfect exceptions." Natalie Blake was lost. The young man gave a slow, approving nod, the kind a man gives to his equal. His confidence seemed unwarranted, not following from anything he'd said or done. A piece of paper passed round the room. The students were asked to add their full name and from which department they hailed. Even before writing her own Natalie Blake looked for his.

63. *Reconnaissance*

Francesco De Angelis. 2nd year Economics. Universally known as "Frank." Running for African and Caribbean Soc president next month. Likely to win. Attended a "second-rate boarding school." This from someone who attended a "grammar school." Further:

"His mum's Italian or something. His dad was probably some African prince, that's usually the case."

64. *Educational parenthesis*

(Some schools you "attended." Brayton you "went" to.)

65. *8th March*

It happened that Leah's third visit coincided with a dinner for International Women's Day. A useful excuse not to see Rodney. Leah wore a green dress and Natalie wore a purple one, and they got ready together and walked to the dining hall arm in arm. The obvious pleasure they took in each other, their deep familiarity and ease in each other's company, made them more attractive as a pair than they ever could have been alone, and perfectly conscious of this fact they emphasized their similarities of height and build, and kept their long legs in stride. By the time they reached their table Natalie was quite giddy with the power of being young, almost free of a man who bored her and soon to embark on a meal of more than two courses.

66. *Menu*

Honeydew melon with tiger prawn salad
Chicken breast wrapped in pancetta with
green beans
and Juliette potatoes
Warm Chocolate fondant with vanilla bean
ice cream
Cheeses
Coffee, mints

67. *Desire*

"Who that?" asked Leah Hanwell.
"The dean," said Natalie Blake, and licked
some chocolate off her teeth. "If she stopped
speechifying we could go to the bar."
"No, the girl at the end of that table. In the
top hat."
"What?"
"Chinese or Japanese — there."
"Oh, I don't know her."
"She's so beautiful!"

68. *Valentino*

Korean. In the bar she put her hat on the
table, and as Natalie Blake spoke to someone
else in their booth, she, Natalie Blake, fre-
quently reached out for this hat and stroked

its satin brim. At her back she could hear her good friend Leah Hanwell talking to the Korean, whose name was Alice, making her laugh, and when Natalie went to the bar to buy drinks she had an unobstructed view of Leah as old-school lothario — one hand over the back of the couch, another on Alice's knee, breathing on the girl's lovely neck. Natalie Blake had seen Leah do this many times, but with boys, and there had always seemed something a little shocking and perverse in it, whereas here the relation looked natural. This thought made Natalie wonder at herself and where she was with God these days, or if she was with him at all. Unable to stop staring she made herself walk over to the jukebox and put on the song Electric Relaxation by A Tribe Called Quest in the hope that it would relax her.

69. *The invention of love: part one*

Frank was not at the bar or anywhere else in view.

70. *Partings*

On the bus back to the coach station, after what had been, let's face it, a significant visit, perhaps even approaching the status of a dramatic event, Leah Hanwell said, rather sheepishly: "Hope it was all right, me disappearing. Least you and Rodders got the room back," and this was all that was said that day about Leah Hanwell's night with Alice Nho, nor did Natalie Blake mention the fact that she had not asked Rodney to come to her room that night and never again would do so. The bus started to climb what felt like a vertical hill. Natalie Blake and Leah Hanwell were pressed back in their seats and against each other. "Really good to see you," said Leah. "You're the only person I can be all of myself with." Which comment made Natalie begin to cry, not really at the sentiment but rather out of a fearful knowledge that if reversed the statement would be rendered practically meaningless, Ms. Blake having no self to be, not with Leah, or anyone.

71. *Helping Leah get her heavy rucksack up the steps to the coach*

Natalie Blake had an urge to tell her friend about the exotic brother she had seen in Kirkwood's class. She said nothing. Quite apart from the fact that the doors were closing she feared what, precisely, the gaping socio-economic difference between Frank

De Angelis and Rodney Banks might say to her friend Leah Hanwell about her, Natalie Blake, psychologically, as a person.

72. *Romance languages*

Many of the men Natalie Blake became involved with after Rodney Banks were as socio-economically and culturally alien to her as Frank was, and were far less attractive, but still she didn't approach Frank, nor did he approach her, despite their keen awareness of each other. A poetic way of putting this would be to say:
"There was an inevitability about their road toward each other which encouraged meandering along the route."

73. *The sole author*

More prosaically, Natalie Blake was crazy busy with self-invention. She lost God so smoothly and painlessly she had to wonder what she'd ever meant by the word. She found politics and literature, music, cinema. "Found" is not the right word. She put her faith in these things, and couldn't understand why — at exactly the moment she'd discovered them — her classmates seemed to be giving them up for dead. When asked

by other students about Frank De Angelis —
she was not the only person who had noted
their fundamental compatibility — she said
that he was too full of himself and vain and
posh and racially confused and not her scene
at all, and yet the silent and invisible bond
between them strengthened, for who else
but Frank De Angelis — *or someone exactly
like Frank De Angelis* — could she ask to accompany her on the strange life journey she
was preparing to undertake?

74. *A sighting*

Five rows in front at the midnight showing
of *Black Orpheus,* looking up at his doppel-
ganger.

75. *Activism*

Natalie was cycling down University Walk
when a young man she was sleeping with
stood in her path, blocking her way. He had
a frantic look about him and at first Natalie
thought he was preparing to announce his
undying love. "Have you got half an hour?"
asked Imran, "There's something I want
you to see." Natalie wheeled her bike round
to Woodland Road and chained it up outside
Imran's halls of residence. In his small bed-

room there were two other girls from their year and a grad student she didn't know. "This is the action group," said Imran, and put a video into the player. Of course, Natalie was aware of the Bosnian conflict, but it would be fair to say that the war had not been uppermost in her mind. She told herself this was because she had no television and spent most of her time in the library. Similarly, two years earlier the existence of a country called "Rwanda" and the reality of its genocide had come to her simultaneously, in a single newspaper article. Now she sat cross-legged and watched the soldiers marching and listened to the recorded speech of the crazed man screaming, and read the subtitles about racial purity and a fantasy place called "Greater Serbia." This had just happened? Just now? At the end of history? She thought of all the times she and Leah had asked themselves — for the sake of a thought experiment — what they would have done, had they been in Berlin, in 1933. "We're going to drive an ambulance of supplies to Sarajevo," said Imran, "to help with the reconstruction. You should come." To do so would break the first commandment of Natalie Blake's family: do not put thyself in unnecessary physical peril.

For the next several weeks Natalie threw

339

herself into the organization of this trip, and made love to Imran, and thought of this period, years later, as representing a sort pinnacle of radical youthful possibility. Of sex, protest and travel, fused. That she never actually went on the trip seemed, in memory, some how less important than the fact that she had fully intended to go. (A quarrel with Imran, a few days before. He didn't call, so she didn't call.)

76. *Abandon*

Natalie Blake took out a large student loan and made a point of spending it only on frivolous things. Meals and cabs and underwear. Trying to keep up with "these people" she soon found herself with nothing again, but now when she put a debit card in the slot and hoped that five pounds would come out, she did it without the bottomless anxiety she'd once shared with Rodney Banks. She cultivated a spirit of decadence. Now that she had glimpsed the possibility of a future, an overdraft did not hold the same power of terror over her. The vision Marcia Blake had of such people, and had passed on to her daughter, came tumbling down in a riot of casual blaspheming, weed and cocaine, indolence. Were these really the people for whom the Blakes had always been on their best behavior? On the tube, in a park, in a shop. Why? Marcia: "To give them no excuse."

77. *A Sighting*

Dressed as Frantz Fanon on a staircase at a party at which Natalie herself was dressed as Angela Davis. His costume consisted of a name-tag and a white coat borrowed off a medical student. Natalie had made more effort: a dashiki and a combed out 'fro, that did not stand up well due to years of damage with a hot iron. The costume party was in the shared house of four philosophy students and the theme was Discourse Founders. His date came as Sappho.

78. *A theory about the tracking of Michelle Holland*

It is perhaps the profound way in which capitalism enters women's minds and bodies that renders "ruthless comparison" the basic mode of their relationships with others. Certainly Natalie Blake tracked the progress of Michelle Holland with a closer attention than she did her own life — without ever speaking to her. Besides Rodney, Michelle

341

was the only other person from Brayton in the university. A math prodigy. She did not have the luxury of mediocrity. Raised in the brutal high-rise towers of South Kilburn, which had nothing to recommend them, no genteel church culture, none of the pretty green areas of Caldwell nor (Natalie presumed) the intimate neighbors. What could she be but exceptional? Father in jail, mother sectioned. She lived with her grandmother. She was sensitive and sincere, awkward, defensive, lonely. It was Natalie's belief that she, Natalie Blake, didn't have to say a word to Michelle Holland to know all of this — that she could look at the way Michelle walked and know it. I am the sole author. Consequently Natalie was not at all surprised to hear of Michelle's decline and fall, halfway through the final year. No drink or drugs or bad behavior. She just stopped. (This was Natalie's interpretation.) Stopped going to lectures, studying, eating. She had been asked to pass the entirety of herself through a hole that would accept only part. (Natalie's conclusion.)

79. *The end of history*

When Natalie now thought of adult life (she hardly ever thought of it) she envisioned a

long corridor, off which came many rooms
— each with a friend in it — a communal
kitchen, a single gigantic bed in which all
would sleep and screw, a world governed
by the principles of friendship. The above
is a metaphorical figure — but it is also
a basically accurate representation of Natalie's thinking at that time. For how can
you oppress a friend? How can you cheat
on a friend? How can you ask a friend to
suffer while you thrive? In this simple way
— without marches and slogans, without
politics, without any of the mess you get rip-
ping paving stones out of the ground — the
revolution had arrived. Late to the party,
Natalie Blake now enthusiastically took her
good friend Leah Hanwell's advice and
started hugging strangers on dance-floors.
She looked at the little white pill in her
palm. What could go wrong, now we were
all friends? Remember to carry a bottle of
water. Anyway, it was all already decided.
Don't chew. Swallow. Strobe lights flash.
The beat goes on. (I will be a lawyer and
you will be a doctor and he will be a teacher
and she will be a banker and we will be art-
ists and they will be soldiers, and I will be
the first black woman and you will be the
first Arab and she will be the first Chinese
and everyone will be friends, everyone will

understand each other.) Friends are friendly to each other, friends help each other out. No one need be exceptional. Friends know the difference between solicitors and barristers, and the best place to apply, and the likelihood of being accepted, and the names of the relevant scholarships and bursaries. "You *choose* your friends, you don't choose your family." How many times did Natalie Blake hear that line?

80. *Ideology in popular entertainment*

In case anyone was in danger of forgetting, the most popular TV show in the world pressed the point home, five times a week.

81. *The Unconsoled (Leah's sixth visit)*

"Oh Jesus I just saw Rodney in Sainsbury's!" said Leah, distraught, dropping two shopping bags on the table. "I looked in his basket. He had a meat pie and two cans of ginger beer and a bottle of that hot sauce you put on everything. I came up behind him in the queue, and he pretended he'd forgotten something and hurried off. But then I saw him a few minutes later at a far end queue and he had exactly the same four items."

82. *Milk round*

A festive, chaotic scene, as well attended as the Fresher's Fair, although this time the banners were not homemade, and instead of Tolkien societies and choral clubs they had printed upon them the melodic names of law firms and the familiar names of banks. Girls in cheerleader outfits bearing the logo of a management consulting firm went round the room giving out little pots of ice cream and cans of energy drinks. Natalie Blake twisted the can in her hand to read the tag that ran round it. *Claim Your Future.* She dug into the ice cream with a little blond wood panel, and watched the green balloons of a German bank slip from their tethers and float slowly up to the ceiling. She heard Rodney's voice coming from somewhere. He was three tables along, sitting with monstrous keenness on the very edge of a plastic chair. Opposite him, an amused man in a suit and tie made notes on a clipboard.

83. *Mixed metaphors*

A year and a half later, when everyone had returned or else moved to London and Natalie was studying for the bar, Rodney Banks sent a letter c/o of Marcia Blake that began: "Keisha, you talk about following your heart, but weird how your heart always seems to know which side its bread is buttered." Frank De Angelis took this letter from Natalie Blake and kissed the side of her head. "Poor old Rodney. He's not still trying to become a lawyer, is he?"

84. *Groupthink*

A television advert for the army. A group of soldiers leap from a low helicopter to the ground. Chaotic camerawork: we're to understand these men are under attack. They run through a harsh landscape of wind and dust, through a clearing, emerging at the edge of a chasm. The wooden bridge they hoped would take them across is half-destroyed. The broken slats tumble into the ravine below. The soldiers look at the ravine, at each other, at the heavy packs they carry.

85. *Lincoln's Inn*

A crowd of new arrivals in eveningwear sat watching this advert, slouched over chairs and sofas, making boisterous conversation. Natalie Blake was a new arrival too, but more shy. She stood at the back of the rec room, trying to busy herself at the refreshment table. Now some text appeared, branded with hot irons into the screen. It was accompanied by the voice of a drill sergeant:

IF YOU'RE THINKING HOW DO *I* GET ACROSS, THE ARMY'S NOT FOR YOU.

IF YOU'RE THINKING: HOW DO *WE* GET ACROSS, GIVE US A CALL.

"I'm thinking: how are *you* getting across."

He was pointing at the television, and all around him people were laughing. She recognized his voice at once, its louche trace of Milan.

86. *Style*

The dreadlocks were gone. His dinner jacket was simple, elegant. A starched pink handkerchief peeked out of the top pocket and his socks were brightly clocked with diamonds. His Nikes were slightly outrageous and box fresh. He no longer seemed strange. (Any number of rappers now dressed like this. Money was the fashion.)

87. *The first Sponsorship Night dinner of the Michaelmas term.*

Natalie Blake was "captain" of her section. She was unsure what this meant. She stood behind her dining chair at the appointed table and waited for her sponsor, a Dr. Singh. She looked up at the vaulted ceiling. A white girl in a satin gown came and stood next to her. "Lovely, isn't it? That majestical roof fretted with golden fire! Hello, I'm Polly. I'm in your team." Next to Polly came a boy called Jonathan who said that "captain" only meant the food was served to the left of you. Portraits of the venerable dead. Heavy silverware. Fish forks. The Benchers filed into hall in their black flapping gowns and bowed. A Latin grace began. Bored, contented voices repeated alien words.

88. *The invention of love: part two*

Natalie Blake flattened her thick linen napkin over her lap and spotted Frank De Angelis running late, moving toward her table, spotting her. He looked devastating; more like *Orfeu* than ever. She was flattered by his reaction: "Blake? You look great! It's great to see you. Oh Captain my captain . . ." He did a little bow and sat down extremely close, thigh to thigh, examined the menu card, made a face. "Cottage pie. I miss Italy." "Oh, you'll survive." "You two already know each other?" asked Polly. And there was indeed something intimate about the way they spoke to each other, heads close, looking out across the room. Natalie fell so easily into the role she had to remind herself that this intimacy had not existed before tonight. It was being manufactured at this present moment, along with its history.

The bad wine flowed. An ancient Judge rose to give a speech. His eyebrows sprung owlishly from his head, and he did not neglect to mention *Twelfth Night*'s first performance or paint a bloody picture of marauding peasants burning law books: ". . . and if we look to Oman's translation of the *Anonimalle Chronicle,* we find, I'm afraid, a somewhat dispiriting portrait of the profession . . . For, upon being cornered in our own Temple Church, our not-so-noble predecessors did little to deter the angry mob. If I may quote: *It was marvelous to see how even the most aged and infirm of them scrambled off, with the agility of rats or evil spirits . . .* These days I can reassure you that beheading — in London at least! — is gratifyingly rare, and abuse of lawyers generally limited to . . ." Natalie was enthralled. The idea that her own existence might be linked to people living six hundred years past! No longer an accidental guest at the table — as she had always understood herself to be — but a host, with other hosts, continuing a tradition. "And so it falls to you," said the judge, and Frank looked over at Natalie, trying to catch her eye and yawning comically. Natalie folded her arms more firmly on the table and turned her head toward the judge. As soon as she'd done it, she felt it was a betrayal. But who was Frank De Angelis to her? And yet. She looked back at him and raised her eyebrows very slightly. He winked.

89. *Time slows down*

A Polish waitress moved discreetly round the table, seeking the vegetarians. Frank spoke, a lot, and indiscriminately, lurching from topic to topic. Where she had once seen only obnoxious entitlement Natalie now saw anxiety running straight and true beneath everything. Was it possible she made him nervous? Yet all she was doing was sitting here quietly, looking at her plate. "Your hair's different. Real? That your butter? Have you seen James Percy? Tenant, now. On the first try. You look good, Blake. You look great. Honestly, I thought you'd be gone by the time I got here. What have you been doing for a year? Here's my confession through a mouthful of bread: I've been skiing. Listen, I also fitted in the law conversion. I'm not totally the waste of space you think I am."

"I don't think you're a waste of space." "Yes, you do. No, I'll have the beef, please. But what's up with you?" Natalie Blake had not been skiing. She'd been working in a shoe shop in Brent Cross shopping center, saving money, living with her parents in Caldwell, and dreaming of winning the Mansfield scholarship, which had actually —

An apologetic Dr. Singh materialized, displacing the turbaned worthy of Natalie's imagination with a petite shaven-headed woman in her thirties, a purple silk blouse peeping out from between the folds of her gown. She sat down. The Judge finished. The applause sounded like braying.

90. *Difficulties with context*

Natalie Blake turned from flirting with Francesco De Angelis to listing all her academic achievements to Dr. Singh. Dr. Singh looked tired. She poured some water into Natalie's glass: "And what do you do for fun?" Frank leaned over: "No time for fun — sista's a slave to the wage." Surely meant as a joke, if a cack-handed one, and Natalie tried to laugh, but saw how Polly blushed and Jonathan looked down at the table. Frank tried to rescue himself by making a wider, sociological point. "Of course, we're an endangered species around here." He looked out across the room with one hand to his brow. "Wait: there's another one over there. That's about six of us all told. Numbers are low." He was drunk, and making a fool of himself. She felt for him deeply. That "us" sounded strange in his mouth — unnatural. He didn't even know how to be the thing he was. Why would he? She was so busy congratulating herself on being able to empathize with and correctly analyze the curious plight of Francesco De Angelis that it took her a moment to realize Dr. Singh was frowning at both of them.

"We have a very effective diversity scheme here," said Dr. Singh primly and turned to speak to the blonde girl on her left.

91. *Wednesday 12:45 p.m.: Advocacy*

Four students and an instructor took their places at the top of the classroom. Appellant and respondent were given Happy Family names: Mr. Fortune the Money Launderer. Mr. Torch the Arsonist. At this point Natalie Blake was forced to leave the room and seek out the toilets, to deal with her hair. The weather was unseasonably warm, she had not planned for it. Sweat leaked from the roots of her weave, fuzzing it up, and the more she thought about this the more it happened. Ambitious though she was, she was still an NW girl at heart, and could not ignore the coming crisis. She hurried down the hall. In the toilets she filled the sink with cold water, held her hair back and put her face in it. By the time she returned the only free seat was next to Francesco De Angelis. Had he kept it for her? The invention of love, part three. As she sat down, she felt his hand on her knee. Above the table he passed her a pencil.

"Sorry about the other night, Blake. Sometimes I'm an idiot. Often."

This was a phenomenon previously unknown to Natalie Blake: a man spontaneously recognizing an error and apologizing for it. Much later in their lives it occurred to Natalie Blake that her husband's candor might be only another consequence of his unusual privilege. But this afternoon she was simply disarmed by it, and grateful.

"Best be quick, you've missed a load." He began whispering the Agreed Facts in her ear, over-confidently and with enough bluff and extraneous commentary that she had to edit him in real time as she scribbled the information down, making bullet points of the grounds for appeal. "And now here comes the Junior Counsel. That's it — you're up to date." The Junior Counsel rose. Natalie turned to look at Frank in profile. He was really the most beautiful man she had ever seen. Broad, imposing. His eyes a shade lighter than his skin. She turned back to examine the Junior Counsel. He looked prepubescent. His presentation was awkward; he barely moved his eyes from a thick sheaf of A4 paper and twice called the female instructor "Your Lordship."

92. *Post Prandial*

"Where are we? Why am I here?"

"Marylebone. London doesn't begin and end on the Kilburn High Road."

"I've got my room in the Inn."

"Mary's argument."

"Frank, take me back. I don't know where I am."

"Good to be uncertain sometimes."

"We've got moot in the morning. Mate, that food was so *bad*. And too much wine. You go home, too."

"I am home. I live just here."

"No one lives here."

"O ye of little faith. It's my grandmother's. Why don't you just try to enjoy yourself for once?"

93. *Simpatica*

The only thing in the fridge was a large pink box from Fortnum & Mason. Inside were four rows of macaroons, in tasteful pastel shades. Natalie Blake brought these over to where Frank sat, shipwrecked on the kitchen "island." White space in all directions. He took the box from her and put his hands on her shoulders.

"Blake, try to relax."

"Can't relax in a yard like this."

"Inverted snobbery."

"I'm so hungry. That food was nasty. Feed me."

"Afterward."

He carried her upstairs, past paintings and lithographs, family photographs and a fainting couch in the hall. They went into a little attic room at the very top of the flat. The bed sat right under the eaves; she kept knocking her elbow against a bookshelf. Law tomes, Tolkien, a lot of 80's horror paperbacks, memoirs of businessmen and politicians. She spotted a solitary friend, *The Fire Next Time*.

"You read this?"

"I think he knew my grandmother in Paris."

"It's a good book."

"I'll believe you, Junior Counsel."

94. *The pleasures of naming*

Perhaps sex isn't of the body at all. Perhaps it is a function of language. The gestures themselves are limited — there are only so many places for so many things to go — and Rodney was in no way deficient technically. He was silent. Whereas all Frank's silly, uncontrolled, unselfconscious, embarrassing storytelling found its purpose here, in a bedroom.

95. *Post-coital*

"He was from Trinidad, he lived in South London, he worked for the trains. She says 'driver' for effect — not true. A guard. Later he worked in an office somewhere. She met him in a park. I never knew him. Harris. Really I should be 'Frank Harris.' He's dead. That's it."

Even naked he blustered. Natalie Blake maneuvered until she was on top and looked into his eyes. Boyish expressions of vulnerability, pride and fear were all still perfectly visible in the adult face. It was of course these qualities that compelled her. "Back to Milan pregnant with me. It was the Seventies. Then Puglia. Then England for school. It's not a problem, it was a great way to grow up. I loved my school." An only child. A storied family, rich though not as rich as they once were. "Once upon a time every decent family in Italy had a De Angelis gas oven . . ." No-one had known what to do with his hair. No spoken English. Dangerously pretty. Eight years old.

96. *The sole author*

"But you're making me sound like a victim, my point is I had a very good time, these were just small things, I don't really know why we're even talking about them. All your questions are leading. Rare Negroid Italian has happy childhood, learns Latin, the end. Then nothing very interesting happens between 1987 and tonight." He kissed her extravagantly. Perhaps she would always look after him, help him become a real person. After all, she was strong! Even relative weakness in Caldwell translated to impressive strength in the world. The world asked so much less of a person, and was of simpler construction.

97. *Nota bene*

Natalie did not stop to wonder whether Frank's boarding school might have done the same job for him.

98. *Sixth-month anniversary*

"Frank, I'm going downstairs, I can't work with the telly on. Can I take *Smith and Hogan*?"

"Yeah, and burn it."

"How are you going to pass this exam?"

"Ingenuity."

"What *is* that?"

"MTV Base. Music videos are the only joyful modern art form. Look at that joy."

He reached forward on the bed and put his finger over a dancing B-girl in a white shell suit. "I was in Puglia when he died. Nobody understood. *Some fat gangster? Who cares?* This was the attitude. It's not even music as far as they're concerned."

Everything he said sounded wonderful. He only lacked what the Italians call *forza,* which Natalie Blake herself would provide (see above).

99. *Frank seeks Leah*

The sun pierced through the blinds in long shadows. Natalie Blake stood in the doorway of the lounge, nervous, holding a tumbler of vodka, ready to smooth over any rupture. Leah and Frank sat side by side on his grandmother's Chesterfield. Natalie could see how Leah had grown into herself. No longer gangly: tall. No longer ginger — "auburn." The experimental period had ended. Denim skirt, hoodie, furry boots, a thick gold hoop in each ear. Back to her roots. Natalie Blake watched her boyfriend Frank De Angelis cut out crooked white lines on a glass-topped table, while her good friend Leah Hanwell rolled a twenty-pound note into a thin tube. She saw how he listened intently as Leah spoke of a man called, in her pronunciation, Me-shell. They'd just met in Ibiza. Frank was taking the task seriously. He understood that there could be no loving Natalie Blake without loving Leah Hanwell first.

"Here's something that interests me: you girls — you like your Eurotrash brothers. But isn't it true? It's a strange coincidence. There aren't that many of us. Is it a competition?"

"Look, mate: *you're* Eurotrash. He's from Guadeloupe! His dad was in the underground resistance movement thing — basically, he went on the run, the whole family had to. His dad's a school janitor in Marseilles now. His mum's Algerian. She can't read or write."

Frank dipped his head and made his mouth into a comic moue.

"Points to Hanwell. He certainly sounds like the salt of the earth. Child-of-a-free-dom-fighter. I am forced to cede the moral high ground. I am decidedly not the salt of the earth."

Leah laughed: "You're the cocaine on the mirror. The badly cut cocaine."

100. *Natalie seeks Elena*

A Mayfair lunch. A beautiful woman slips an oyster down her throat. Her phone is so slim and light it sits easily in the silk pocket of her blouse. "And he is working hard?" she asks. Elena De Angelis tapped a thin cigarette on the tablecloth and gave Natalie Blake a sideways look of fierce cunning. Before Natalie could even stutter an answer, Elena laughed. "Don't worry — I don't ask you to lie. It's not going to be the law for 'Cesco, of course it is not. But I hoped it would be a useful thing generally, for his character. It was like this for his uncle. Well. He met you. You are the first real woman he has ever brought to meet me. This is something. Tell me, is it true you have to have dinner a certain number of times in the year or you cannot be a barrister?" Natalie watched Elena tap ash

into her dinner plate. She urgently wanted
to know how this woman loved and lost a
Trinidadian train guard. "Yes," she said,
"twelve times. In the great hall. Used to be
thirty-six." Elena blew two jets of smoke
through her nostrils: "What a curious country this is!" A waiter came over and the bill
was settled somehow without any ugly grop-
ing after purses and money. "'Cesco, please
call your cousin. I said you would ring two
weeks ago, and they can't hold a position
forever. It's embarrassing."

101. *Onwards, upward*

Frank flunked the bar spectacularly, turning up forty-five minutes late, leaving ten
minutes early. Afterward the first thing he
did was call his mother. Natalie saw how
this conversation cheered him. Elena was
the kind of woman to prefer a spectacular
disaster to a conventional failure.

Leah Hanwell found a bleak flat south of
the river, in New Cross, and Natalie Blake,
out of respect for an old friendship, became
her flatmate. She read briefs on the long tri-
angulated tube rides: New Cross, Lincoln's
Inn, Marylebone. She slipped into Frank's
bed. Slipped out. Slipped in. "What time is
it?" "Eleven fifteen." "I've gotta chip!" She

tried to force herself to get up and onto a night bus, heading south. "Your principles spend more time in that dump than you do," he observed. She sank back into the pillows.

Perceptive in sudden, hard-to-predict bursts.

Goofy and always affectionate. He called a lot.

Going through the ticket barrier, the phone he'd bought her rang:

"Natalie Blake you're literally the only person in the world I can stand."

That was the year people began saying "literally."

Frank was at his desk at Durham and Macaulay Investments, betting on the future price of things he was quite unable to describe to her. More symbols, she presumed, though of a kind she couldn't decode.

102. *Save yourself*

To explain herself to herself, Natalie Blake employed a conventional image. Broad river. Turbulent water. Stepping-stones. Caldwell, exams, college, the bar — pupillage. This last gap was almost too wide to jump. There were no scholarships, and no way of earning any real money through the first half of the pupillage year. It had to be another loan, combined with the building society savings, untouched since childhood. This building society, a local concern, happened also to operate at the level of conventional images.

103. *Capitalist pigs*

He was called Peter: he had a coin-shaped slot in his back. Marcia Blake had kept the little red pocket book, and dealt with the cashiers. As certain key sums were achieved (twenty-five pounds, fifty pounds, a hundred), the child received first Peter, and then various members of the building society's branded pig family. In the Blake home these pigs were considered ornaments, and stood all together on a shelf in the lounge. Sometimes Marcia would offer a glimpse of the "credit" column with the extraordinary (untouchable) sum of 71 pounds or something like that. Natalie never touched it, and now, twenty years later, it had finally amounted to something. Ah, memories! And perhaps she even remembered handling the old one-pound paper notes? Hard to say: nostalgia is such a distorting force.
"You in this line?"
Natalie looked down at the feisty old lady at her elbow, clutching her little red book. She raised her own red book vaguely: "I think so."

But the line was an amorphous crowd of noisy NW people holding pocket books and shouting and pushing. Someone said: "We need system up in this queue, man! Always chaos in here!" Someone else: "These people don't know what is British queue."

The aluminum poles that should have been planted at intervals in the filthy carpet had not been set out. Natalie could see them piled up in a corner by the cashiers' desks.

"You now. Go!" said the old lady and Natalie Blake, uncertain whether justice had been done or no, walked up to the desk indicated, had a disturbing conversation with a teller called Doreen Bayles, made her way out of the scrum to the Kilburn high road, leaned on a bus stop and wept.

104. *One hundred and ten percent*

"I am so angry with Pastor," said Marcia, weeping. "It's so terrible, when I gave it to him in good faith, and he absolutely promised me it was one hundred and ten percent guaranteed your money back — he promised me with his hand on his heart, because it's for the church, and it's short term! We're growing the church in Laos, getting the word out over there, where the people really need it. I can't believe it because I was just going to take it out and put it back in and you weren't even going to notice because it was short term, it was just as a bridge, that's what he said, and I believed him, of course! He's a good man. I'm so angry with Pastor right now, Keisha! When I found out I went crazy for real. I'm just too trusting, this is the thing, which is the worst thing, because I think people are telling the truth when they're being very deceptive, very untruthful. It's very difficult after that to have trust. Very difficult."

105. *A romantic scene in Green Park*

Natalie had established a rule that romantic activities should be affordable for both parties. Sometimes this caused a row. Today it was unobjectionable. Weekend papers. Celebrity interviews. Movie reviews. Opinion. Lonely Hearts. Strong sun. Packed lunch. Red Stripes.

"Oh, and I talked it over with Elena — she agrees."

"There's the guard. Frank, let's just move to the grass — I'm not paying two quid for a deck chair."

"Are you listening to me? I talked with my mother. We want to give you the money."

Natalie put down the Saturday magazine,

turned from Francesco De Angelis, and pressed her face into the canvas, expecting to weep, to be "overwhelmed." Instead her face was dry, her mind strangely occupied.

106. *Parklife*

Female individual seeks male individual for loving relationship. And vice versa.

Low-status person with intellectual capital but no surplus wealth seeks high-status person of substantial surplus wealth for enjoyment of mutual advantages, including longer life-expectancy, better nutrition, fewer working hours and earlier retirement, among other benefits.

Human animal in need of food and shelter seeks human animal of opposite gender to provide her with offspring and remain with her until the independent survival of aforementioned offspring is probable.

Some genes, seeking their own survival, pursue whatever will most likely result in their replication.

107. *Let's not argue, boo*

He was still talking. He had his grown-up face on, the one he wore daily to work. She knew it was a fake. The reason he couldn't explain to her what he was doing at work was not because it was too complicated for her to understand (though it was) but because he himself didn't truly understand it. He bluffed his way through each day. She had known all along that his ego was delicate and built on uncertain foundations and she considered this trait — universal among men, as far as her own experiences went — to be a small price to pay for his aforementioned honesty and sexual openness and beauty.

". . . which then I just said to Elena: this girl gets the second-highest pass in the year — even if I didn't love her, it doesn't make *sense* to let this kind of ability go to waste for the lack of means — it doesn't make *economic* sense. Your family for whatever reason refuse to help you —"

"They don't refuse to help me, Frank — they can't!" cried Natalie Blake, and launched into a passionate defense of her family, despite the fact she was not speaking to any of them.

108. *Politics on the move*

"Cheryl could stop having children. Your brother could get a job. They could leave that money-grabbing cult. Your family make poor life choices — that's just a fact."

"You should stop talking because you really don't know what you're talking about. I don't want to talk about this on the damn tube."

It seemed that Natalie Blake and Francesco De Angelis had opposite understandings of this word "choice." Both believed their own interpretation to be objectively considered and in no way the product of their contrasting upbringings.

109. *John Donne, Lincoln's Inn, 1592*

A commotion could be heard in the clerks' room above. Polly provided a clever phrase for it: "a cockney symphony of expletives."

"Nat, what time's your flight?"

"Tomorrow morning at seven."

"Look: where would you rather be: Tuscany or West London Youth Court? I'm serious, get out of here while you still can."

They were the only two left in the pupils' room. Everyone was either in court or already in the pub.

"You can even take my last fag. Consider it part of the trousseau."

Natalie put her arms in her coat, while Polly worked the lighter, but they were not quick enough to avoid a clerk, Ian Cross, appearing at the bottom of the stairs carrying a brief.

"Oi: put that out. Concentrate. Who wants this?"

"What is it?"

Ian turned the brief over in his hands: "Junkies. Robbery. Bit of mild arson. That's young Mr. Hampton-Rowe's notes on the back of it — over at Bridgestone. He got a higher calling last minute. That Reverend Marsden fuck-up. High profile."

Natalie watched Polly blush and reach out for the brief with an imitation of mild interest: "Reverend who?"

"You're joking, aren't you? Vicar cut up a prozzie and dumped her in Camden Lock. Been wall to wall. Don't you read the papers?"

"Not those sort of papers."

"You should join the 21st century, love. There's only one kind of paper these days." As he smiled, the port wine stain around his left eye crinkled horribly. Another of Polly's clever phrases: "a whole personality constructed round a stain."

"Give it here. She can't. Nat's getting married Sunday."

"Salutations. Everyone should do it. No man is an island, I always say."

"Oh, that was you, was it? I was wondering who that was. Nat, darling, flee from here. Save yourself. Have a drink on me."

110. *Personality Parenthesis*

(Sometimes, when enjoying Pol's capsule descriptions of the personalities of others, Natalie feared that in her own — Natalie's — absence, her own — Natalie's — personality was also being encapsulated by Pol, although she could not bring herself to truly fear this possibility because at base she could not believe that she — Natalie — could ever be spoken about in the way she — Natalie — spoke about others and heard others spoken about. But for the sake of a thought experiment: what was Natalie Blake's personality constructed around?)

111. *Work drinks*

Natalie Blake hurried up the steps and past the clerks' room to avoid any other briefs. She stepped out into the slipstream of Middle Temple Lane. Everyone flowing in the same direction, toward Chancery Lane, and she fell in step, found two friends, and then two more. By the time they reached The Seven Stars they were too large a party for an inside table. The only other woman — Ameeta — offered to get the drinks and Natalie offered to help her. "Vodka shots or beer?" They had forgotten to ask. Ameeta, another working-class girl, but from Lancashire, was anxious to get it right — as working-class female pupils they were often anxious to get it right. Natalie Blake counseled for both. A few minutes later they emerged in their sensible skirt suits holding two wobbly trays sloppy with foam. The men were lined up by the railings of the Royal Courts, smoking. It was a lovely late-summer evening in London. The men whistled. The women approached.

112. *Sir Thomas More, Lincoln's Inn, 1496*

"Someone give this girl the bumps! She's getting married. Ah, the good die young. What's his name again? Francesco. An eye-tie? I move for a mistrial. Half-Trini, actually. IT'S POLITICAL CORRECTNESS GONE MAD. Seriously, though, Nat. Best of luck. We all wish you the best of luck. I don't believe in luck. Where's my invite? Yeah, where's my invite? Watch that glass! No one's invited, not even family. We want to be alone. Ooh, exclusive! Someone lift her up. Pol says he's loaded, too. Durham and Macaulay. Quickie in Islington town hall. Honeymoon in Positano. Business class. Oh, we know all about it. Oh yes, we know.

Blake's no fool. Ouch! No hitting. Point is, you're joining the other side. Enemy camp. We will be forced to continue the hunt for love in your absence. This Francesco fellow: he approve of sex after marriage? Italians tend to. Catholic, we presume. Oh, yes, we presume. Frank. Everyone just calls him Frank. He's only half-Italian. Jake, get her right leg. Ezra, get the left. Ameeta get the arse. Put me down! You're on arse duty, Ameeta, love. Objection! How come Ameeta gets the best bit? Because I *do.* Objection overruled. Why can't a gentleman refer to the posterior of a lady anymore these days? I TELL YOU IT'S POLITICAL COR-RECTNESS GONE — oh, fuck it. One two three LIFT."

The trainee barristers carried Natalie Blake across the road, whooping. Her nose came level with the arch of 16th-century doorways. So far from home!

"SHE'S GETTING MARRIED IN THE MORNING."

"Morning after. Who's that statue, up there?"

"My Latin's rusty — I have no fucking clue . . . Which way we heading? North? West! Which line do you need, Nat? The Jubilee?"

113. *Miele di Luna (two weeks)*

Sun.
Prosecco.
Sky, bleached.
Swallows. Arc. Dip.
Pebbles blue.
Pebbles red.
Elevator to the beach.
Empty beach. Sun rise. Sun set.
"You know how rare this is, in Italy?
This is what you pay for — the silence!"
Oh.
He swims. Every day.
"The water is perfect!"
Wave.
English newspapers. Two beers. Arancini.
"Is it all right if we put it on this card? We're
in room 512. I have my passport."
"Of course, Madam, you are the newlywed
suite. You mind I ask something? Where you
from?"
Wave.
The waiters wear white gloves. Obituaries.
Reviews. Cover to cover.
Rum and coke. Cheesecake.
"Can I put it straight on the room? The
other guy said it was OK. 512."
"For sure, Madam. How do you call this, in
English?"

"Binoculars. My husband likes birds. Weird saying that word."

"Binoculars?"

"Husband."

The public beach is at the tip of the peninsula. Four miles hence. Whoops. Screams. Laughter. Music from loud speakers. More bodies than sand.

Wish you were here?

Empty.

Exclusive.

"This is really like paradise!"

oh

wave

Lone family. Red umbrella. Mother, father, son. Louis.

LOOO-weee! Pink shorts. WAVE

Nowhere and nothing.

LOOO-WEEE!

Vodka cocktail.

"Have you got a pen? Do you know where they're from?"

"Paris, signora. She is American model. He is computer. French."

Louis stung by a jellyfish.

Dramatic event!

Rum Cocktail. Prawns. Chocolate cake.

"512, please."

"Madam, I promise you this is not possible.

There are no jellyfish here. We are a luxury resort. You don't swim because of this?"

"I don't swim because I can't swim."

Linguine con vongole, gin and tonic, rum cocktail.

"Signora, where you from? American?"

"512."

"This is your boyfriend swimming?"

"Husband."

"He speak very good Italian."

"He is Italian."

"And you, signora? *Dove sei?*"

114. *L'isola che non c'è*

"You should at least stand in the water one time," said Frank De Angelis, and Natalie Blake looked up at her husband's beautiful brown torso dripping with saltwater and returned to her reading. "You've been dragging those papers around since the plane." He looked over her shoulder. "What's so interesting?" She showed him the wrinkled, water-damaged page of personal advertisements. He sighed and put on his sunglasses. "'Soulmates.' *Che schifo!* I don't know why you love reading those things. They depress me. So many lonely people."

115. *The Old Bailey*

Ian Cross put his head round the pupils' door. A room full of pupils looked up hopefully. Cross looked at Natalie Blake.

"Want to see a grown jury weep? Bridgestone need a random pupil to make up the numbers. Court One, Bailey. With Johnnie Hampton-Arse. Don't worry, you won't have to do anything, just look pretty. Grab your wig."

She was excited to be chosen. It proved the efficacy of her strategy as compared to, say, Polly's. Don't get romantically involved with the star tenants of criminal sets. Do good work. Wait for your good work to be noticed. This innocence and pride was preserved right up until the moment she took her seat and spotted the victim's family in the gallery, unmistakeably Jamaican, the men in shiny gray double-breasted suits, the women in their wide-brimmed hats topped with sprays of synthetic flowers.

"Watch and learn," whispered Johnnie, rising for opening remarks.

116. *Voyeurism*

The defense was constituted along the same basic lines as transubstantiation. Someone else had used the vicar's flat to chop up Viv. Someone else had deposited her body in a series of bin bags by Camden Lock, twenty yards from his own back door. He claimed the key was freely passed among his parishioners; many people had a copy. That his sperm was found inside her was only evidence of further coincidence. (The papers had dug up a series of suspiciously similar-looking local prostitutes, all claiming to have known the vicar in the biblical sense.) "But this is not a trial about race," said Johnnie, directing the jury's attention to Natalie Blake with a slight move of his arm, "and to allow it to become one is to submit the evidential burden — your first concern, as jurors in a British court — to the guilty-cos-we-say-so principles of our lamentable gutter press." The distressed huddle of Viv's family kept clinging to each other in the gallery, but Natalie did not look at them again.

The prosecution offered a PowerPoint presentation. Grubby-looking Camden interiors. Natalie Blake sat forward in her chair. The point was the flecks of blood, but it was everything else that interested her. Four modish 60s-era white chairs, unexpected for a man of the cloth. The too-big piano in the too-small room. Mismatched sofa and ottoman, a top-of-the-range TV. Out-dated fitted kitchen with a cork floor, unfortunate, the blood soaks in. Natalie felt a nudge from the junior advocate and began taking down the pretend notes she'd been instructed to scribble.

117. *In the robing room*

As Natalie Blake turned to shuck off her gown, Johnnie Hampton-Rowe appeared behind her, put his hand on her shirt, pulling it aside with her bra. She had a delayed reaction: he was pinching her nipple before she managed to ask him what the fuck he thought he was doing. With the same sleight of hand she'd just seen in court, he turned the fact of her shouting into the crime. Backed off at once, sighing: "All right, all right, my mistake." Out of the door before she'd turned round. By the time she had collected herself and come out of the room he was at the far end of the hallway bantering with the rest of the team, discussing the next day's strategy. The junior advocate pointed at Natalie with a pen. "Pub. Seven Stars. You coming?"

118. *Emergency consultation*

Leah Hanwell arranged to meet Natalie Blake at Chancery Lane tube. She was working close by, as a gym receptionist on the Tottenham Court Road. They walked to the Hunterian Museum. It began to rain. Leah stood between two huge Palladian columns and looked up at the Latin tag etched on gray stone.

"Can't we go to the pub?"

"You'll like this."

They made their tiny donations at the desk.

"Hunter was an anatomist," explained Natalie Blake. "This was his private collection."

"Have you told Frank?"

"He wouldn't be helpful."

With no warning Natalie prodded Leah into the first atrium, as Frank had done to her a few months before. Leah didn't scream or gasp or cover her eyes with her hands. She walked right past all the noses and shins and buttocks suspended in their jars of formaldehyde. Straight to the bones of the Giant O' Brien. Put her hand flat against the glass, and smiled. Natalie Blake followed her reading from a leaflet, explaining, always explaining.

119. *Cocks*

Thick and squat and a little comical, severed a few inches after the head, or perhaps simply shrunken in death. Some circumcised, some apparently gangrenous. "Not feeling that envious," said Leah. "You?" They moved on. Past hipbones and toes, hands and lungs, brains and vaginas, mice and dogs and a monkey with a grotesque tumor on its jaw. By the time they reached the late-stage fetuses they were a little hysterical. Huge foreheads, narrow little chins, eyes closed, mouths open. Natalie Blake and Leah Hanwell made the Munch face at each other, at them. Leah knelt to look at a diseased piece of human material Natalie could not identify.

"You went to the pub."

"I sat there for twenty minutes looking at the grain of the table. They talked about the case. I left."

"You think he did the same with this Polly girl?"

"They had a 'thing.' Maybe it started the same way. Maybe he does it to everyone."

"The plot thickens. I hate plots. The gym's the same, full of cocks making drama. Drives me insane."

"What's that bit? Cancer?"

"Of the bowel. Dad's kind." Leah moved away from the jar and sat down on a little bench in the middle of the room. Natalie joined her and squeezed her hand.

"What are you going to do?" asked Leah Hanwell.

"Nothing," said Natalie Blake.

120. *Intervention*

A few weeks passed. Dr. Singh cornered Natalie Blake in the pupils' room. It was clear she had been sent as a sort of emissary. Some people upstairs — unnamed — were "concerned." Why had she stopped participating in the social life of the set? Did she feel isolated? Would it help to talk to someone who'd "been through it"? Natalie took the little card. Without realizing it she must have rolled her eyes. Dr. Singh looked wounded, and drew a finger under a line of letters: QC, OBE, PhD. "Theodora Lewis-Lane was a trail-blazer" — this was meant as an admonishment — "no us without her."

121. *Role models*

A fancy cake shop on the Gray's Inn Road. Natalie was fifteen minutes late but Theodora was twenty, demonstrating that "Jamaican Time" had not quite died out in either of them. She was fascinated by Theodora's chat-show weave (having recently abandoned her own, upon Frank's request), and the subtle, glamorous variants she bought to the female barrister's unofficial uniform: a gold satin shirt beneath the blazer; a diamante trim to the black court shoes. She was at least fifty, with the usual island gift of looking twenty years younger. Surprisingly — given her fearsome reputation — she was no more than five foot two. When Natalie slipped off her chair to shake Theodora's hand she looked disconcerted. Sitting, she reclaimed her gravitas. In an accent not found in nature — somewhere between the Queen and the speaking clock — she ordered a tremendous number of pastries before proceeding without any encouragement to tell the story of her gothic South London childhood and unlikely professional triumph. When this tale was not quite finished, Natalie Blake took a fastidiously small bite of a croissant and murmured, "I guess I just really want my work to be taken on its own merits . . ."

When she looked up from her plate, Theodora had her little hands folded in her lap.

"You don't really want to have a conversation with me, do you, Miss Blake?"

"What?"

"Let me tell you something," she said, with a sharpness that belied the fixed smile on her face, "I am the youngest silk in my generation. That is not an accident, despite what you may believe. As one learns very quickly in this profession, fortune favors the brave — but also the pragmatic. I suppose you're interested in a human rights set of some kind. Police brutality? Is that your plan?"

"I'm not sure yet," said Natalie, trying to sound bullish. She was very close to tears.

"It wasn't mine. In my day, if you went down that route people tended to associate you with your clients. I took some advice early on: 'Avoid ghetto work.' It was Judge Whaley who gave it to me. He knew better than anyone. The first generation does what the second doesn't want to do. The third is free to do what it likes. How fortunate you are. If only good fortune came with a little polite humility. Now, I believe this place does wine. Will you have a little wine?"

"I didn't mean to be rude. I'm sorry."

"It's a good tip for court: don't imagine your contempt is invisible. You'll find out as you mature that life is a two-way mirror."

"But I don't *have* contempt —"

"Calm yourself, sister. Have a glass of wine. I was just the same at your age. Hated being told."

122. *Theodora's advice*

"When I first started appearing before a judge, I kept being reprimanded from the bench. I was losing my cases and I couldn't understand why. Then I realized the following: when some floppy-haired chap from Surrey stands before these judges, all his passionate arguments read as 'pure advocacy.' He and the Judge recognize each other. They are understood by each other. Very likely went to the same school. But Whaley's passion, or mine, or yours, reads as 'aggression.' To the judge. This is his house and you are an interloper within it. And let me tell you, with a woman it's worse: 'Aggressive hysteria.' The first lesson is: turn yourself down. One notch. Two. Because this is not neutral." She passed a hand over her neat frame from her head to her lap, like a scanner. "This is never neutral."

123. *Bye noe*

hi finally
that wasn't so hard now was it
just don't like downloading things
me no like computerz
**from the internet at WORK. Weak gov
computers. One little virus**

me fear the future
and they die innit
is it
shut it blake.
That's just so fucking FASCINATING
Hello hanwell DARLING. What brings
  you to the internets this fine afternopn
noon
**woman next to me picking nose really
  getting in there**
tried to call but you no answer
delighteful.
cant take private calls in pupilf room
  what's up
big news
You got cat aids?
free may sixth?
You catch cat aids may 6th? I am free if
  not in court. I big lawyer lasy these days
  innit
Big lawyer lady jesus
shit typer
lady jesus I am getting married
!!!!!?????
on may
that's great! When did this happen???
**Six in registry same like u but irth
  actyl guests**
I'm really happy for you seriously
Actual guests.

Iz for mum really.
right
also, I really love him.
lust him.
Important to him and he wants to.
It's what people do innit.
sorry clerk one min
enough reasons?
I think I'm going to wear purple
Also for Pauline
And gold like a catholic priest
Hello?
Sorry that is really great — congrats!
Does this mesn
Mean procreation??
FUCK OFF WOMAN
☺
**FUCK OFF WITH YOUR SMILEY
  FACE**
cant believe you getting hitched
whats happening to
me too
universe?
we iz old
we're not fucking old
**at least u achieving something. I'm
  just slowly dying**
this my 2nd year as pupil. May be pupil for
  rest of
dying of boredom

life

don't know what tht means

it = not good. Most peole tenant after
   ONE YEAR

anyway boring — can I ask question and
   you not get off

offended sorry

fuck most people

haha I am so not getting off right now
can I?

when u get hitched you have to give up
   everyone else anyway.

that's the idea, isn't it?

Stupid idea.

haha

So just more people to give up.

That answer your question big lady
   jesus?

Haha yes. You iz mind reader for realz

and when all else fails:

www.adultswatchingadults.com

passes the time

you know what I'm chatting about.
   Come on girl!

Oi mate don't leave me hanging!

Sorry. Work shitstorm gotta go love you

bye noe

"bye noe"

124. *A tenancy meeting question*

Ms. Blake, would you be prepared to represent someone from the B.N.P.?

125. *Harlesden hero (with parentheses)*

Natalie Blake did not expect to be offered tenancy. To convert an external judgment into a personal choice she told herself a story about legal ethics, strong moral character and indifference to money. She told the same tale to Frank and Leah, to her family, to her fellow trainee barristers and to anyone else who inquired after her future. This was a way of making the future safe. (All Natalie's storytelling had, in the end, this aim in view.) When, contrary to her expectations, she was indeed offered tenancy, Natalie Blake was placed in an awkward position *vis-à-vis* her personal ethics and strong moral character and indifference to money (or, at least, as far as the public representations of these qualities were concerned) and was forced to refuse the offer of tenancy and take the paralegal job at R senb rg, Sl tte y & No ton that she had been talking up for several months. A tiny legal aid firm in Harlesden with half its stencilled letters peeled off.

126. *Tonya seeks Keisha*

Natalie Blake's clients called at inappropriate times. They lied. They were usually late for court, rarely wore what they had been advised to wear and refused perfectly sensible plea deals. Occasionally they threatened her life. In her first six months at RSN, three of her clients were young men who "went Brayton," although they were much younger then Natalie Blake herself. This caused her to wonder if the school had gone downhill — further downhill. She snatched lunch from the jerk place opposite McDonald's, sat on a high stool and had trouble keeping the oil off her suit. Pattie, fish dumpling and a can of ginger beer, most days. She tried to vary this menu, but at the counter any spirit of adventure abandoned her. A long-term plan existed to meet Marcia and Marcia's sister Irene, who lived nearby, for lunch, but this fantasy appointment, with its two hours of idle time and no need to read briefs, never seemed to arrive, and soon enough Natalie Blake understood that it never would. Fairly often she saw her cousin Tonya on Harlesden high street. On these occasions — despite her new status as a big lawyer lady — she experienced the same feelings of insecurity and inadequacy Tonya had compelled in her when they were children. This afternoon Tonya wore sweatpants with HONEY written across the posterior and a close-fitting denim waistcoat with a yellow bra underneath. Her fringe was purple, the hoop of her earrings brushed her shoulders. Her platform heels were red and five inches high. Despite the toddler and the baby in her double buggy Tonya retained the proportions of a super-heroine in a comic book. Natalie meanwhile was sadly "margar," as the Jamaicans say. To white people this translates as "skinny" or "athletic," and is widely considered a positive value. For Natalie it meant ultimately shapeless, a blank. Tonya's skin was never ashy but always silky and gorgeous and she was not prone to the harsh pink acne that sometimes broke out across Natalie's forehead, and was present today. Where Natalie's teeth were small and gray, Tonya's were huge, white, even, and presently on display in a giant smile. As Tonya approached, Natalie was sure she, Natalie, had dumpling oil round her mouth. But perhaps all this displacement of anxiety into the physical realm was a feminine way of simplifying a far deeper and more insoluble difference, for Natalie believed Tonya had a gift for living and Natalie herself did not seem to have this gift.

"These children are so good-looking it's criminal."

"Thank you!"

"Look at André — he blatantly knows it."

"That's his dad. His dad bought him that chain."

"Now he's like: I'm a three-year-old playa."

"You know what I'm saying! Seriously."

Underneath the smile, Natalie saw that her cousin was disappointed with this exchange, wanting, as usual, to make a deeper "connection" with Natalie, who wished to avoid precisely this intimacy and as a consequence retained a superficial and pleasant exterior with her cousin as a means of holding her at bay. Now Natalie put down André and picked up Sasha. Neither child ever seemed real to her no matter how many times Natalie felt their weight in her arms. How could Tonya be the mother of these children? How could Tonya be 26? When had Tonya stopped being 12? When would her own adulthood arrive?

"So I'm back up in Stonebridge, with my Mum. Elton and me are done, that's it. I'm finished wasting my time. It's all good, though. I'm back to school, up in Dollis Hill? College of North West London. Tourism and hospitality. Studying, studying. It's hard but I'm loving it. You're my inspiration!"

Tonya put her hand on the shoulder of Natalie's ugly navy skirt suit. Was that pity in her cousin's eyes? Natalie Blake did not exist.

"How's your mate? That nice girl. The redhead one."

"Leah. She's good. Married. Working for the council."

"Is it. That's nice. Kids?"

"No. Not yet."

"You lot are leaving it late, innit."

Tonya's hand moved from her cousin's shoulder to her head.

"What's going on up there, Keisha?"

Natalie touched her uneven parting, the dry bun, scraped back, unadorned.

"Not much. I never have time."

"I did all this myself. Microbraids. You should come by and let me do it. It's just six hours. We could make it an evening, have a good proper chat."

127. *The connection between chaos and other qualities*

At RSN Associates the law burst from broken box files, it lined the hallways, bathroom and kitchen. This chaos was unavoidable, but it was also to some extent an aesthetic, slightly exaggerated by the tenants, and intended to signify selflessness, sincerity. Natalie saw how her clients found the chaos comforting, just as the fake Queen Anne sofas and painted foxhounds of Middle Temple reassured another type of client. If you worked here it could only be for the love of the law. Only real do-gooders could possibly be this poor. Clients were directed to Jimmy's Suit Warehouse in Cricklewood for court dates. Wins were celebrated in-house, with cheap plonk, pita bread and hummus. When an RSN solicitor came to see you in your cell, they arrived by bus.

128. *"On the front line"*

Now and then, in court or in police stations, Natalie bumped into corporate solicitors she knew from university. Sometimes she spoke with them on the phone. They usually made a show of over-praising her legal ethics, strong moral character and indifference to money. Sometimes they finished with a back-handed compliment, implying that the streets where Natalie had been raised, and now returned to work, were, in their minds, a hopeless sort of place, analogous to a war zone.

129. *Return*

The commute was "killing" her. Sometimes a simple choice of vocabulary can gain traction in the world. "Killing" became the premise for a return to NW. "And what about my commute?" protested Frank De Angelis. "Jubilee line," said his wife Natalie Blake, "Kilburn to Canary Wharf." Carefully she drew up a contract, negotiated a mortgage, split the deposit in half. All for a Kilburn flat that her husband could have bought outright without blinking. When the deal went through Natalie bought a bottle of cava to celebrate. He was still at work at six when she picked up the keys, and still there at eight — and then the inevitable nine-forty-five phone call: "Sorry — all nighter. Go on without me, if you want." Motto of a marriage. Natalie Blake called Leah Hanwell: "Want to see me carry myself over the threshold?"

130. *Re-entry*

Leah turned the key in the stiff lock. Natalie crept in behind her, into adult life. Notable for its silence and privacy. The electricity was still unconnected. A clear moon lit the bare white walls. Natalie was ashamed to find herself momentarily disappointed: after camping in Frank's place all these months, this looked small. Leah did a circuit of the lounge and whistled. She was working from an older scale of measurement: twice the size of a Caldwell double.

"What's that out there?"

"Downstairs' roof. It's not a balcony, the agent said you can't —"

Leah went through the sash windows and on to the ivy-covered ledge. Natalie followed. They smoked a joint. In the driveway below a fat fox sat brazen as a cat, looking up at them.

"Your ivy," said Leah, touching it, "your brick, your window, your wall, your light-bulb, your gutter pipe."

"I share it with the bank."

"Still. That fox is with child."

Natalie thumbed the cork out. It bounced off the wall and dropped away into the dark. She took a messy swig. Leah leaned forward and wiped her friend's chin: "Cava socialist." Now watch Natalie recalibrate the conversation. It is a feminine art. She places herself halfway up a slope that has at its peak Frank's friends, all those single young men with their incomprehensible Christmas bonuses. She found it pleasing to describe this world to Leah, who knew almost nothing of it. Chelsea, Earls Court, West Hampstead. Lofts and mansion flats unsullied by children or women, empty of furniture, fringed by ghettos.

"Correction: there's always one big brown leather sofa, a huge fridge and a TV as big as this flat. And an enormous sound system. They're not home till two a.m. 'Entertaining clients.' In strip clubs, usually. It all just sits empty. Five bedrooms. One bed."

Lean flicked the end of a joint toward the fox: "Parasites."

Natalie was suddenly stricken by something she thought of as "conscience." "A lot of them are OK," she said, quickly, "nice, I mean, individually. They're funny. And they do work hard. Next time we have a dinner you should come."

"Oh, Nat. Everybody's nice. Everybody works hard. Everybody's a friend of Frank's. What's that got to do with anything?"

131. *Revisit*

People were ill.
"You remember Mrs. Iqbal? Small woman, always a bit snooty with me. Breast cancer."
People died.
"You must remember him, he lived in Locke. Tuesday he dropped dead. Ambulance took

half an hour."

People were shameful.

"Baby born two weeks ago, and they haven't let me in yet. We don't even know how many kids are in there. They don't register them."

People didn't know they were born.

"Guess how much for eggs in that market. Organic. Guess!"

People were seen.

"I seen Pauline. Leah's working for the council now. She always had such big ambitions for that child. Funny how things turn out. In a way you've done quite a bit better than her, really."

People were unseen.

"He's upstairs with Tommy. He spends all his time with him now. They only come out of that room to go and charm the ladies. Jayden and Tommy spend all their time and money charming the ladies. That's all your brother thinks about. He needs to get himself a job, that's what I keep telling him."

People were not people but merely an effect of language. You could conjure them up and kill them in a sentence.

"Owen Cafferty."

"Mum, I don't remember him."

"Owen Cafferty. Owen Cafferty! He did all the catering for church. Mustache. Owen Cafferty!"

"OK, vaguely, yes. Why?"

"Dead."

Everything was the same in the flat, yet there was a new feeling of lack. A new awareness. And lo they saw their nakedness and were ashamed. On the table Marcia laid out a fan of credit cards. As Marcia talked her daughter through the chaotic history of each card Natalie made notes as best she could. She had been brought in for an emergency consultation. She did not really know why she was taking notes. The only useful thing would be to sign a large check. This she couldn't do, in her present circumstance. She couldn't bear to ask Frank. What difference did it make if she turned figures into words?

"I'll tell you what I really need," said Marcia, "I need Jayden to get up out of here and get married, so he can run his own household, and your sister's little ones don't have to be sleeping in the room with their mother. That's what I need."

"Oh, Mum . . . Jayden's not going to ever get . . . Jayden's not interested in women, he —"

"Please don't start up that nonsense again, Keisha. Jayden's the only one of you takes care of me at all. This is how we live. Cheryl can't help anybody. She can't hardly help herself. Number three on the way. Of course I love these kids. But this is how we're living like, Keisha, to be truthful. Hand to mouth. This is it."

People were living like this. Living like that. Living like this.

132. *Domestic*

"I can't stand them living like that!" cried Natalie Blake.
"You're making unnecessary drama," said Frank.

133. *E pluribus unum*

Certainly exceptional to be taken back into the Middle Temple fold but Natalie Blake was in many ways an exceptional candidate, and several tenants at the set thought of her, informally, as their own protégé, despite having really only a glancing knowledge of her. Something about Natalie inspired patronage, as if by helping her you helped an unseen multitude.

134. *Paranoia*

A man and a woman, a couple, sat at a table opposite Natalie and Frank, having Satur-

day brunch in a café in North West London.
"It's organic," said Ameeta. She referred to
the ketchup.

"It's bad," said her husband, Imran. He was
also referring to the ketchup.

"It's not bad. It doesn't have the fourteen
spoonfuls of sugar you're used to," said
Ameeta.

"It's called flavor?" said Imran.

"Just bloody eat it or don't eat it," said
Ameeta. "Nobody cares."

Around them, at other tables, other people's
babies cried.

"I didn't say anybody cared," said Imran.

"India versus Pakistan," said Frank — he
referred, in a jocular manner, to his friends'
countries of origin — "better pray it doesn't
go nuclear."

"Ha ha," said Natalie Blake.

They continued on with their breakfast.
Breakfast tipped into brunch. They did
this once or twice a month. Today's brunch
seemed, to Natalie, a more lively occasion
than usual, and more comfortable, as if by
rejoining a commercial set and acting, at
least in part, for the interests of corpora-
tions, she had lost the final remnants of
a troubling aura that had bothered her
friends and made them cautious around
her.

The eggs came late. Frank argued chummily with the waiter until they were taken off the bill. At one point employing the phrase: "Look, we're both educated brothers." It occurred to Natalie Blake that she was not very happily married. Goofy. Made lame jokes, offended people. He was in a constant good humor, yet he was stubborn. He did not read or have any real cultural interests, aside from the old, nostalgic affection for 90s hip hop. The idea of the Caribbean bored him. When thinking of the souls of black folks he preferred to think of Africa — "Ethiopia the Shadowy and Egypt the Sphinx" — where the two strains of his DNA did noble battle in ancient stories. (He knew these stories only in vague, biblical outline.) He had ketchup by his mouth, and they had married quickly, without knowing each other particularly well. "I like her well enough," Ameeta said, "I just don't particularly trust her." Frank De Angelis would never cheat or lie or hurt Natalie Blake, not in any way. He was a physically beautiful man. Kind. "It's not tax avoidance," said Imran. "It's tax management." Happiness is not an absolute value. It is a state of comparison. Were they any unhappier than Imran and Ameeta?

Those people over there? You? "Anything with flour gives me a rash," said Frank. On the table lay a huge pile of newspaper. In Caldwell, newspaper choice had been rather important. It was a matter of pride to Marcia that the Blakes took *The Voice* and *The Daily Mirror* and no "filth." Now everyone came to brunch with their "quality" paper and a side order of trash. Tits and vicars and slebs and murder. Her mother's pieties — and by extension Natalie's own — seemed old-fashioned. "It's an insurgency," said Ameeta. Natalie pressed a knife to her egg and watched the yolk run into her beans. "Another thing of tea?" said Frank. They were all agreed that the war should not be happening. They were against war. In the mid-nineties, when Natalie Blake was sleeping with Imran, the two of them had planned a trip to Bosnia in a convoy of ambulances. "But Irie was always going to be that kind of mother," said Ameeta, "I could have told you that five years ago." Only the private realm existed now. Work and home. Marriage and children. Now they only wanted to return to their own flats and live the real life of domestic conversation and television and baths and lunch and dinner. Brunch was outside the private realm, not by much — it was just the other side of the border. But even brunch was too far from home. Brunch didn't really exist. "Can I give you a tip?" said Imran. "Start on the third episode of series two." Was it possible to feel oneself on a war footing, constantly, even at brunch? "She owns a child of every race now. She's like the United Nations of Stupid," said Frank, for one elevated oneself above an interest in "celebrity gossip" simply by commenting ironically on it. "A 'romp' with two strippers," read Ameeta. "Why's it always a 'romp'? I've never bloody 'romped' in my life." Sexual perversity was also old-fashioned: it smacked of an earlier time. It was messy, embarrassing, impractical in this economy. "I never know what's reasonable," said Imran. "Ten percent? Fifteen? Twenty?" Global consciousness. Local consciousness. Consciousness. And lo they saw their nakedness and were not ashamed. "You're fooling yourself," said Frank. "You can't get anything on the park for less than a million." The mistake was to think that the money precisely signified — or was equivalent to — a particular arrangement of bricks and mortar. The money was not for these poky terraced houses with their short back gardens. The money was for the distance the house put between you and Caldwell. "That skirt," said Natalie Blake, pointing to a picture in the supplement, "but in red."

As brunch tipped into lunch, Imran ordered pancakes like an American. After decades of disappointment, the coffee was finally real coffee. Wouldn't it be cruel to leave, now, when they'd come this far? They were all four of them providing a service for the rest of the people in the café, simply by being here. They were the "local vibrancy" to which the estate agents referred. For this reason, too, they needn't concern themselves too much with politics. They simply *were* political facts, in their very persons. "Polly not coming?" asked Frank. All four checked their phones for news of their last remaining single friend. The smooth feel of the handset in one's palm. A blinking envelope with the promise of external connection, work, engagement. Natalie Blake had become a person unsuited to self-reflection. Left to her own mental devices she quickly spiraled into self-contempt. Work suited her, and where Frank longed for weekends, she could not hide her enthusiasm for Monday mornings. She could only justify herself to herself when she worked. If only she could go to the bathroom and spend the next hour alone with her e-mail. "Working the weekend. Again," said Imran. He had the fastest connection. "Shame," said Natalie Blake.

But was it? If Polly came she would only sit down and speak of her good works — police inquests and civil litigation and international arbitration for underdog nations; recently published opinions on the legality of the war. Headhunted by a new, modern, right-on set, where she was both very well paid and morally unimpeachable. Living the dream. It was the year people began to say "living the dream," sometimes sincerely but usually ironically. Natalie Blake, who was also very well paid, found having to listen to Polly these days an almost impossible provocation.

136. *Apple blossom, 1st of March*

Surprised by beauty, in the front garden of a house on Hopefield Avenue. Had it been there yesterday? Upon closer inspection the cloud of white separated into thousands of tiny flowers with yellow centers and green bits and pink flecks. A city animal, she did not have the proper name for anything natural. She reached up to break off a blossom-heavy twig — intending a simple, carefree gesture — but the twig was sinewy and green inside and not brittle enough to snap. Once she'd begun she felt she couldn't give up (the street was not empty, she was being

observed.) She lay her briefcase on somebody's front garden wall, applied both hands
and wrestled with it. What came away finally
was less twig than branch, being connected
to several other twigs, themselves heavy with
blossom, and the vandal Natalie Blake hurried away and round the corner with it. She
was on her way to the tube. What could she
do with a branch?

137. *Train of thought*

The screenwriter Dennis Potter was interviewed on television. Sometime during the
early nineties. He was asked what it felt like
to have a few weeks to live. Natalie Blake
remembered this answer: "I look out of my
window and I see the blossom. And it's more
blossomy than it's ever been." Once she got
within network she would check the year and
whether or not that was the correct wording. Then again, perhaps the way she had
remembered it was the thing that was important. The branch lay abandoned outside
a phone box at Kilburn station. Sitting in
her tube seat, Natalie Blake moved her pelvis very subtly back and forth. Blossom was
always intensely blossomy to Natalie Blake.
Beauty created a special awareness in her.
"The difference between a moment and an

instant." She couldn't remember very much about the philosophical significance of this distinction other than that her good friend Leah Hanwell had once tried to understand it, and to make Natalie Blake understand it, a long time ago, when they were students, and far smarter than they were today. And for a brief period in 1995, perhaps a week or so, she had thought that she understood it.

138. *http://www.google.com/search?client =safari&rls=en&q=kierkegaard&ie= UTF-8&oe=UTF-8*

Such a moment has a peculiar character. It is brief and temporal indeed, like every moment; it is transient as all moments are; it is past, like every moment in the next moment. And yet it is decisive, and filled with the eternal. Such a moment ought to have a distinctive name; let us call it the *Fullness of Time.*

139. *Doublethink*

Commercial barrister Natalie Blake did pro bono death row cases in the Caribbean islands of her ancestry and instructed an accountant to tithe 10 percent of her income, to be split between charitable contributions and supporting her family. She assumed it was the remnants of her faith that made her fretful and suspicious that these good deeds were, in fact, a further, veiled, example of self-interest, representing only the assuaging of conscience. Acknowledging the root of this suspicion did nothing to disperse it. Nor did she find any relief in the person of her husband, Frank De Angelis, who objected to her actions on quite other grounds: sentimentality, wooly mindedness.

140. *Spectacle*

The Blake–De Angelises started work early and tended to finish late, and in the gaps treated each other with an exaggerated tenderness, as if the slightest applied pressure would blow the whole thing to pieces. Sometimes in the mornings their commutes aligned, briefly, until Natalie changed at Finchley Road. More often Natalie left half an hour to an hour before her husband. She liked to meet early with the pupil with whom she shared a room, Melanie, to get the jump on all the business of the day. In the evenings the couple watched television, or went on-line to plan future holidays, itself an example of bad faith for Natalie hated holidays, preferring to work. They only truly came together at weekends, in front of friends, for whom they appeared fresh and vibrant (they were only thirty years old), and full of the old good humor, like a double act that only speaks to each other when they are on stage.

141. *Listings*

It was around this time that Natalie Blake began secretly checking the website. Why does anyone begin checking a website? Anthropological curiosity. The statement "I have heard that people are on this site" is soon followed by "I can't believe that people really visit this site!" Then comes: "What kind of people would visit this site?" If the website is visited multiple times the question is answered. The problem becomes circular.

142. *Technology*

"I have it for work." "It's for work — I don't pay for it." "I've got to have it for work, and actually it makes a lot of things easier." "It's my work phone, otherwise I wouldn't even have one."

143. *The Present*

Natalie Blake, who told people she abhorred

expensive gadgets and detested the Internet, adored her phone and was helplessly, compulsively, adverbly addicted to the Internet. Though incredibly fast, her phone was still too slow. It had not finished fully downloading the new website of her chambers before the doors closed on the elevator in Covent Garden station. For the length of a twenty-minute tube ride the screen in her hand obstinately froze on the sentence

highest standards of legal representation in today's fast-changing world.

144. *Speed*

At some point we became aware of being "modern," of changing fast. Of coming after just now. John Donne was also a modern and surely saw change but we feel we are more modern and that the change is faster. Even the immutable is faster. Even blossom. While buying a samosa in the filthy shop inside Chancery Lane Station (one remnant of her upbringing was a willingness to buy food from anyone, anywhere) Natalie Blake once again checked the listings. By this point she was checking them two or three times a day, though still as a voyeur, without making a concrete contribution.

145. *Perfection*

For some reason this proposed picnic was very important to Natalie Blake, and she set about planning it meticulously. She cooked everything from scratch. She determined upon a hamper with real crockery and glasses. Even as she was ordering this stuff online she saw it was really "too much" but her course was set and she felt unable to change direction. At work she was deep into a dispute between a Chinese tech company and its British distributor. At the first video conference the Chinese Managing Director had been unable to conceal his surprise. She should not be going to a picnic. She should be in the office making her way through the other side's fresh disclosures. Natalie continued along her path. She picked an outfit. Glittering sandals and hoop earrings and bangles and a long ochre skirt and a brown vest and hair in a giant afro puff held off her face by means of one leg of a black pair of tights, cut off and knotted at the back of her head. She felt African in this outfit, although nothing she wore came from Africa except perhaps the earrings and bangles, conceptually. Her husband passed by the kitchen at the moment she was trying to force three extra Tupperware boxes into the gingham-lined hamper she had bought for the occasion.

"Jesus. That's ours?"

"She's my oldest friend, Frank."

"They'll both be in tracksuits."

"A picnic is not just weed and a supermarket sandwich. We hardly see them anymore. It's a beautiful day. I want it to be nice."

"OK."

He edged round her theatrically. Doctor avoiding a lunatic. He opened the fridge.

"Don't eat. It's a picnic. Eat at the picnic."

"When did you start baking?"

"Don't touch that. It's ginger cake. It's Jamaican."

"You know I can't eat anything with flour in it."

"It's not for you!"

He left the room silently, and it was not quite clear whether it was the beginning of a row or not. Probably he would decide later, depending on whether there was a practical advantage to be had in discord. Natalie Blake put her hands on the counter and spent a long time staring at the yellow kitchen tiles in front of her face. Who was it for? Leah? Michel?

146. *Cheryl (L.O.V.E.)*

"Just move that." With Carly screaming on her hip, Cheryl bent down to sweep the Barbie and junk mail to the floor. Natalie found a hardback annual of some kind and put the mugs of tea upon it. "Let me try and get this little one down then we can go in the living room." They sat opposite each other on their old twin beds. Natalie believed she had a memory of lying beside her sister on one of these beds, tracing spidery letters on her bare back, which Cheryl had to then guess and spell out as words. Cheryl gave Carly her bottle. She sat very straight with her third child in her arms. An adult with adult concerns. Natalie crossed her legs like a child and kept her fond memories to herself. Wasn't there something juvenile in the very idea of "fond memories"?

"Keesh, pass me that rag there. She's chucking it all up."

Pocahontas printed on the closed blind. The sun made her golden. The room was not much changed from the old days except it was now roughly divided between a boy and a girl zone; the former red, blue and Spiderman, the latter diamanté-encrusted princess pink. Natalie picked up a dumper truck and drove it up and down her thigh.

"Two against one."

Cheryl's head lifted wearily; the baby was fussy and would not settle to eating.

"Just — the pink-blue war. Poor old Ray won't survive now there's Cleo and Carly."

"Survive? What you on about?"

"Nothing. Sorry, carry on."

On every surface there balanced things upon other things with more things hanging off and wrapped around and crammed in. No Blake could ever throw anything away. It was the same in Natalie's place, except there the great towers of cheap consumer dreck were piled up behind cupboard doors, concealed by better storage.

Cheryl plucked the bottle from the child's mouth and sighed: "She ain't going down. Let's just go through."

Natalie followed her sister down the narrow hallway made almost impassable by laundry strung from a wire along both walls.

"Can I do something?"

"Yeah, take her for a minute while I have a piss. Carly, go to your auntie now."

Natalie had no fear of handling babies; she'd too much practice. She placed Carly loosely on her hip and with the other hand called Melanie to give a series of unnecessary instructions that could have easily waited until they were both in the office. She walked up and down the room as she did this, jiggling the baby, talking loudly, entirely competent, casual. The baby, seeming to sense her extraordinary competency, grew quiet and looked up at her aunt with admiring eyes in which Natalie spotted even a hint of wistfulness.

"But the thing is, yeah," said Cheryl, as she walked back in, "Jay's gone, there's plenty of space here. And I don't want to leave mum on her jacks."

"Eventually Gus is going to finish building. She's going to move back to Jamaica."

Cheryl put both hands to the base of her back and thrust her stomach out in that depressing motherly gesture Natalie felt sure she would never perform, if and when she herself became a mother. "That's way off," said Cheryl, yawning as she stretched. "He sent pictures. Not e-mail — photos in an envelope. It's a corrugated box with no roof. It's got a palm tree growing out the bathroom."

This reminder of their father's innocence, of his optimism and incompetence, made the sisters smile, and emboldened Natalie. She pressed her niece to her breast and kissed her forehead.

"I just can't stand to see you all living like this."

Cheryl sat down in their father's old chair, shook her head at the floor and laughed unpleasantly.

"There it is," she said.

Natalie Blake, who feared more than anything being made to look ridiculous — or being perceived, even for a moment, to be on the wrong side of a moral question — pretended she did not hear this and smiled at the baby and lifted the baby above her head to try and get her to giggle and when this did not work, lowered her to her lap once again. "If you hate Caldie so much, why d'you even come here? Seriously, man. No one asked you to come. Go back to your new manor. I'm busy — ain't really got the time to sit and chat with you neither. You piss me off sometimes Keisha. No, but you do."

"When I was at RSN," said Natalie firmly, in the voice she used in court, "you know how many of my clients were Caldies? There's nothing wrong with wanting to see you and the kids in a nice place somewhere."

"This is a nice place! There's a lot worse. You done all right out of it. Keisha, if I wanted to get out of here I'd get another place off the council before I come to you, to be honest."

Natalie addressed her next comment to the four-month-old.

"I don't know why your mum talks to me

like that. I'm her only sister!"

Cheryl attended to a stain on her leggings. "We ain't never been that close Keisha, come on now."

In Natalie's bag, by the door, there were three Ambien, in the inside pocket next to her wallet.

"There's four years between us," she heard herself say, in a small voice, a ludicrous voice.

"Nah but it weren't that, though," said Cheryl, without looking up.

Natalie sprung from her chair. Standing she found that holding little Carly limited her dramatic options. The child had fallen asleep on her shoulder. In a dynamic unchanged from childhood, Natalie became irate as her sister Cheryl grew calm.

"Excuse me I forgot: no-one's allowed to have friends in this fucking family."

"Family first. That's my belief. God first, then family."

"Oh, give me a fucking break. Here comes the Virgin Mary. Just because you can't locate the fathers, doesn't make them all immaculate conceptions."

Cheryl stood up and stuck a finger in her sister's face: "You need to watch your mouth, Keisha. And why you got to curse all the time, man? Get some respect."

Natalie felt tears pricking her eyes and a childish wash of self-pity overcame her entirely.

"Why am I being punished for making something of my life?"

"Oh my days. Who's punishing you, Keisha? Nobody. That's in your head. You're paranoid, man!"

Natalie Blake could not be stopped: "I work hard. I came in with no reputation, nothing. I've built up a serious practice — do you have any idea how few —"

"Did you really come round here to tell me what a big woman you are these days?"

"I came round here to try and help you."

"But no-one in here is looking for your help, Keisha! This is it! I ain't looking for you, end of."

And now they had to transfer Carly from Natalie's shoulder to her mother's, a strangely delicate operation in the middle of the carnage.

Natalie Blake cast around hopelessly for a parting shot. "You need to do something about your attitude, Cheryl. Really. You should go see someone about it, because it's really a problem."

As soon as Cheryl had the child in her arms she turned from her sister and began walking back down the corridor to the bedroom.

"Yeah, well, till you have kids you can't really chat to me, Keisha, to be honest."

147. *Listings*

On the website she was what everybody was looking for.

148. *The future*

Natalie Blake and Leah Hanwell were 28 when the first e-mails began to arrive. Over the next few years their number increased exponentially. Photo attachments of stunned-looking women with hospital tags round their wrists, babies lying on their breast, hair inexplicably soaked through. They seemed to have stepped across a chasm into another world. It was perfectly possible that her own mother was arriving at the houses of these new mothers, with her name-tag pinned to her apron, pricking their babies' feet with a needle, or sewing up the new mothers' stitches as they lay sideways on a couch. Marcia must have seen one or two of them, by the law of local averages. They were new arrivals in the neighborhood. They were not the sort of people to switch off the lights and lie on the floor. Mother and baby doing well, exhausted. It was as if no-one had ever had a baby before, in human history. And everybody said precisely this, it was the new thing to say: "It's as if no-one ever had a baby before." Natalie forwarded the emails to Leah. *It's as if no-one ever had a baby before.*

149. *Nature becomes culture*

Many things that had seemed, to their own mothers, self-evident elements of a common-sense world, now struck Natalie and Leah as either a surprise or an outrage. Physical pain. The existence of disease. The difference in procreative age between men and women. Age itself. Death.

Their own materiality was the scandal. The fact of flesh.

Natalie Blake, being strong, decided to fight. To go to war against these matters, like a soldier.

150. *Listings*

After opening an e-mail about a baby, she went to the website, and contributed to the website. She went upstairs to bed.

151. *Redact*

"Where are you going?

Natalie Blake shook her husband's hand from her shin and rose from bed. She walked down the hall to the spare bedroom and sat in front of the computer. She typed the address into the browser as smoothly as a pianist playing a scale. She removed the contribution.

152. *The past*

"Nathan?"

He sat on the bandstand in the park, smoking, with two girls and a boy. Two women and a man. But they were dressed as kids. Natalie Blake was dressed as a successful lawyer in her early thirties. Alone, he and she might have walked the perimeter of the park, and talked about the past, and perhaps she would have taken off her ugly heels and they would have sat in the grass and Natalie would have smoked his weed, and then told him to get off drugs in a motherly sort of way, and he would have nodded and smiled and promised. But in company like this she had no idea how to be.

It's well hot, said Nathan Bogle. It really is, agreed Natalie Blake.

153. *Brixton*

It was a long-standing invitation but she

hadn't called or sent a text to say she was coming. It was an impulse that struck her at Victoria Station. Fifteen minutes later she was walking down Brixton High Street, exhausted from court, still in her suit, getting in the way of merry people just starting their Friday night. She bought some flowers in a garage forecourt, and thought of all the scenes in movies where people buy flowers from garage forecourts, and of how it is almost always better to bring nothing. She found the house and rang the bell. A queeny guy with his 'fro dyed blonde answered.

"Hi. Jayden about? His sister, Nat."

"Of course you are. You look just like Angela Bassett!"

The kitchen was confusingly full. Was it the queen? Or one of the white guys? Or the Chinese guy, or the other guy?

"He's in the shower. Vodka or tea?"

"Vodka. You all heading out?"

"We just got in. The only thing to eat right now is this Jaffa cake."

154. *Force of nature*

When had she last been so drunk? There was something about being in the company of so many men with no intentions toward her that encouraged excess. She was learning many things about her little brother she had never known. He was "famous" for drinking White Russians. He'd had a crush on Nathan Bogle. He loved fantasy fiction. He could do more one-handed press-ups than any other man in the room.

The vodka ran out. They took shots of a blue drink they found in a cupboard. Natalie realized that there was no special or chosen man in this house. Jayden had managed to find for himself precisely the fluid and friendly living arrangements she herself had dreamed of so many years earlier. If it was not quite possible to feel happy for him it was because the arrangement was timeless — it did not come bound by the constrictions of time — and this in turn was the consequence of a crucial detail: no women were included within the schema. Women come bearing time. Natalie had brought time into this house. She couldn't stop mentioning the time, and worrying about it. If only she could free herself from her body and join them all at the Vauxhall Tavern, for the second wave. In reality, she had ten texts from Frank and it was time to go home. The time had come.

"And all in the same week," said Jayden, "all in the same week, she told this rude boy kid in our estate who was on my case to back off, she just ran him off, right after she came out of that last exam. Straight As. Bitch is real. Sista's a force of nature, believe!" The room was dipping and revolving. Natalie did not recognize this story. She did not think these two things had happened, at least not in the same week, perhaps not even in the same year. She certainly did not get straight As. It had occurred several times this evening, these conflicting versions, and at first she had tried to tweak or challenge them, but now she leaned back into the arms of a man called Paul and stroked his bicep. Did it matter what was true and what wasn't?

155. *Some observations concerning television*

She was watching the poor with Marcia. A reality show set on a council estate. The council estate on television was fractionally worse than the council estate in which she sat watching the show about a council estate. Every now and then Marcia pointed out how filthy were the flats of the people on television and how meticulously she took care of her own, Cheryl's mess not withstanding. "Guinness. At ten in the morning!" said Marcia. Natalie, who had not seen the show before, asked after the character arc of one of the participants. Marcia grabbed both arms of her chair and closed her eyes. "She's on crack. All she cares about is make up and clothes. Her brother is on sickness benefits but there's nothing wrong with him. He's a disgrace. The dad is in jail for thieving. The mum's a junkie." In the show poverty was understood as a personality trait. "Look at that! Look at the bathroom. Shameful. What kind of people would live like this? Did you see that?" Natalie pleaded innocence. She was checking her phone. "All you do is check that phone. Did you come round to see me or check that phone?"

Natalie looked up. A topless lad with a beer bottle in his hand ran across a scrubby patch of grass between two tower blocks and lobbed the bottle into the sole remaining window in a burned-out car. Music accompanied this action. It had a certain beauty.

"I hate the way the camera jumps all over the place like that," said Marcia. "You can't forget about the filming for a minute. Why do they always do that these days?"

This struck Natalie as a profound question.

156. *Melanie*

Natalie Blake was in her office making some

notes on an arcane detail of property law as it pertained to adverse possession when Melanie walked in, tried to speak and burst into tears. Natalie did not know what to do with a crying person. She placed a hand upon Melanie's shoulder.

"What happened?"

Melanie shook her head. Liquid came out of her nose and a bubble appeared in the corner of her mouth.

"A problem at home?"

All Natalie knew about Melanie's private realm was that her boyfriend was a policeman and there was a daughter called Rafaella. Neither the policeman nor Melanie was Italian.

"Take a tissue," said Natalie. She had a snot phobia. Melanie fell into a chair. She took a phone from her pocket. Between heaving fits of weeping she seemed to be trying to find something on it. Natalie watched her thumb, frantic on the rollerball.

"I just really need to not be here!" This problem sounded interesting, and quite unexpected coming from plain-speaking, reliable Melanie, whom Natalie often described as "her rock." (It was the year everyone was saying that such and such a person was "their rock.") But now Melanie turned blandly practical: "Not all the time! The fact is I've got Rafs and I love her and I don't want to pretend that I don't have Rafs anymore! Look at her — she's so bloody brilliant now, she's almost two."

Natalie leaned forward to peer at an image on a screen. A grand seigneur to whom a frightened peasant has come, with a confession about the harvest.

157. *On the park*

Natalie Blake was busy with the Kashmiri border dispute, at least as far as it related to importing stereos into India through Dubai on behalf of her giant Japanese electronics manufacturing client. Her husband Frank De Angelis was out entertaining clients. They were "time poor." They didn't even have time to collect their latest reward for all their hard work. Marcia kindly went to get the key before the estate agent closed, and Natalie met her mother and Leah at the front door. They whispered as they entered. It was unclear why. There were no blinds in yet and their shadows rose over the fireplace and up to the ceiling. Natalie led them around, pointing out where sofas and chairs and tables were to be placed, what would be knocked through and what kept, what carpeted and what stripped and polished. Natalie encouraged her mother and her friend to stand in front of the bay window and admire the view of the park. She recognized in herself a need for total submission.

She ran a little ahead to admire a bedroom. Look at this original cornicing. Here is a working fireplace. She waited for her mother and Leah to join her. She picked at a piece of loose plaster with a fingernail. When she had been a pupil and on the "wrong" side of a criminal case, Marcia had wanted her to "think of the victim's family." Now if she was instructed by some large multinational company, she had to listen to Leah's self-righteous, ill-informed lectures about the evils of globalization. Only Frank supported her. Only he ever seemed proud. The more high profile the case, the more it pleased him. Cheryl, years ago: "Every time I try and go back to school, Cole tries to knock me up." There but for the grace of God. Thinking of Cheryl was always helpful in moments of anxiety. At least Natalie Blake and Frank De Angelis weren't working against each other, or in competition. They were incorporated. An advert for themselves. Let me show you round this advert for myself. Here is the window, here is the door. And repeat, and repeat.

Natalie was opening the door to what she

had decided would be her office when Marcia said something probably quite innocent — "Plenty of space for a family in here" — and Natalie manufactured a row out of it and wouldn't back down. She watched her mother walk the black and white tiled hallway to the door, no longer the indomitable mistress of her childhood, but a small, gray-haired woman in a sagging woolly hat who surely deserved gentler treatment than she received.

"You all right?" said Leah.

"Yes, yes," said Natalie, "it's just the usual."

Leah found some tea-bags in a kitchen cupboard and a single cup.

"People actually think I'm early QC material. Doesn't mean anything to her. All you have to do with her is move back in. Cheryl's her angel now. They get on like a house on fire."

"You're difficult for her to understand."

"Why? What's difficult about me?"

"You have your work. You have Frank. You've got all these friends. You're getting to be so successful. You're never lonely."

Natalie tried to picture the woman being described. Leah sat down on the step.

"Trust me, Pauline's the same."

158. *Conspiracy*

Natalie Blake and Leah Hanwell were of the belief that people were willing them to reproduce. Relatives, strangers on the street, people on television, everyone. In fact the conspiracy went deeper than Hanwell imagined. Blake was a double agent. She had no intention of being made ridiculous by failing to do whatever was expected of her. For her, it was only a question of timing.

159. *In the park*

Leah was late. Natalie sat in the park café, outside, at one of the wooden tables, protected from the drizzle by a broad green umbrella. The first ten minutes she spent on her phone. Checking the listings, checking her e-mail, checking the newspapers. She put her phone in her pocket. For ten further minutes no one spoke to her and she did not speak to anyone. Squirrels and birds passed in and out of view. The longer she spent alone the more indistinct she became to herself. A liquid decanted from a jar. She saw herself slip from the bench to the ground and take the shape of an animal. Moving on all fours, she reached the end of the damp tarmac and passed over into the grass and mulch. Continuing on, quicker now, getting the hang of four-legged locomotion, moving swiftly across the lawn and the artificial hillocks, the Quiet Garden and the flowerbeds, into the bushes, across the road, and on to the railway sidings, howling.

"Sorry, sorry, sorry. Central line. Jesus, it's like a crèche out here."

Natalie looked up at the kids and chaos at every table and smiled neutrally at her friend and wondered at what point during their lunch date she should give Leah her news.

160. *Time speeds up*

There is an image system at work in the world. We wait for an experience large or brutal enough to disturb it or break it open completely, but this moment never quite arrives. Maybe it comes at the very end, when everything breaks and no more images are possible. In Africa, presumably, the images that give shape and meaning to a life, and into whose dimensions a person pours themselves — the journey from son to Chief, from daughter to protector — are drawn from the natural world and the collective imagination of the people. (When Natalie Blake said "In Africa" what she meant was "at an earlier point in time.") In that circumstance there would probably be something beautiful in the alignment between the one and the many.

Pregnancy brought Natalie only more broken images from the great mass of cultural detritus she took in every day on a number of different devices, some handheld, some not. To behave in accordance with these images bored her. To deviate from them filled her with the old anxiety. She grew anxious that she was not anxious about the things you were meant to be anxious about. Her very equanimity made her anxious. It didn't seem to fit into the system of images. She drank and ate as before and smoked on occasion. She welcomed, at last, the arrival of some shape to her dull straight lines.

Of the coming birth her old friend Layla, who had three children already, said: "Like meeting yourself at the end of a dark alley."

That was not to be for Natalie Blake. The drugs she requested were astonishing, transcendent; not quite as good as Ecstasy yet with some faint memory of the lucidity and joy of those happy days. She felt euphoric, like she'd gone clubbing and kept on clubbing instead of going home when someone more sensible suggested the night bus. She put her earphones in and danced around her hospital bed to Big Pun. It was not a very dramatic event. Hours turned to minutes. At the vital moment she was able say to herself quite calmly: "Oh, look, I'm giving birth."

Which is all to say that the brutal awareness of the real that she had so hoped for and desired — that she hadn't even realized she was counting on — failed to arrive.

161. *Otherness*

There was, however, a moment — a few minutes after the event, once the child had been washed of gunk and returned to her — that she almost thought she possibly felt it. She looked into the slick black eyes of a being not in any way identical with the entity Natalie Blake, who was, in some sense, proof that no such distinct entity existed. And yet was not this being also an attribute of Natalie Blake? An extension? At that moment she wept and felt a terrific humility.

Very soon after there were flowers and cards and photographs and friends and family who came round bearing gifts that demonstrated different degrees of taste and sense and the mysterious black-eyed other was replaced by a sweet-tempered seven-pound baby called Naomi. People came with advice. Caldwell people felt everything would be fine as long as you didn't actually throw the child down the stairs. Non-Caldwell people felt nothing would be fine unless everything was done perfectly and even then there was no guarantee. She had never been so happy to see Caldwell people. She could not place Leah Hanwell in this schema with any accuracy, as it is hardest to caricature the people you've loved best in your life. Leah came round with a soft white rabbit, and looked at Natalie as if she had passed over a chasm into another land.

162. *Evidence*

Fourteen months after her first child was born, Natalie Blake had a second. He was meant to be called Benjamin, but he arrived with a little tuft of hair on top of his head, like a spike, and they called him Spike for three days, and then recalled a romantic, childless afternoon, years earlier, spent watching a matinee revival of *She's Gotta Have It*.

Frank was joyful, and forgetful of practicalities, and for a while Natalie found she had to treat him as a third child, a fourth child — if she included the nanny — to be managed and directed along with the rest of them so that time was maximized and everybody got to where they needed to be. Only

Natalie herself was allowed to waste time, sitting at her desk, looking through digital images of her brood. This action, considered objectively, was identical to the occasions in which she had been called upon to review photographs of a crime scene. One morning Melanie caught her midway through this reverie and could not hide her delight. Hidden behind the image of Spike was another window, of listings. Natalie submitted, irritably, to a hug.

163. *Architecture as destiny*

To Leah it was *sitting room,* to Natalie *living room,* to Marcia, *lounge.* The light was always lovely. And she still liked to stand in the bay and admire her view of park. Looking around at the things she and Frank had bought and placed in this house, Natalie liked to think they told a story about their lives, in which the reality of the house itself was incidental, but it was also of course quite possible that it was the house that was the unimpeachable reality and Natalie, Frank and their daughter just a lot of human shadow-play on the wall. Shadows had been passing over the walls of this house since 1888 sitting, living, lounging. On a good day Natalie prided herself on small differences, between past residents, present neighbors and herself. Look at these African masks. Abstract of a Kingston alleyway. Minimalist table with four throne-like chairs. At other times — especially when the nanny was out with Naomi and she was alone in the living room feeding the baby — she had the defeating sense that her own shadow was identical to all the rest, and to the house next door, and the house next door to that.

All along the street that autumn the sound of babies crying kept the lights on, late into the night. In Natalie's house on the park, the shock of The Crash dislodged a little plaster in the wall in a shape of a fist and stopped plans for a basement extension. Off work and eager to feel useful, Natalie Blake waited till Spike's nap, opened a Word document and with a great sense of purpose typed the title

Following the money: A wife's account

She had a professional gift for expressing herself, and it was infuriating to listen to attacks on the radio and television upon what she thought of as the good character of her husband. As if poor Frank — whose bonus was, proportionally speaking, negligible — were no different in kind to all these epic crooks and fraudsters.

She was keen to engage him on this subject when he came home. He looked up from

436

his take-away.

"You've never asked me a single thing about work, ever."

Natalie denied this, though it was substantively true. In the name of journalism, she pursued her point.

"It shouldn't be a question of individual morals, should it? It should be a legal question of regulation."

Frank put his chopsticks down: "Why are we talking about this?"

"It's history. You're a part of it."

Frank denied being a part of history. He returned to his chow mein. Natalie Blake could not be stopped.

"A lot of our tenants write pieces online these days, for the papers. Thought pieces. I should be doing more things like that. At least it's something I can do from home."

Frank nodded at the remote control. "Can we watch TV now? I'm tired to death."

There was no relief to be found on the television.

"Turn it over," said Frank, after five minutes of the news. Natalie turned it over.

"If the city closed tomorrow," said Frank, without looking at his wife, "this country would collapse. End of story."

Upstairs the baby started crying.

Over the next few days Natalie was able

to add only two more lines to her attempt at social criticism:

I am very aware that I am not what most people have in mind when they think of a "banker's wife." I am a highly educated black woman. I am a successful lawyer.

She blamed her slow progress on Spike, but in fact the child was a good sleeper and Natalie had the Polish woman, Anna. She had plenty of time. A week later, in the course of attending to her e-mail, she caught sight of the document on her desktop and quietly moved it to a part of her computer where she would not easily stumble across it again. She watched TV in the living room and fed her child. The light failed earlier and earlier. The leaves turned brown and orange and gold. The foxes screamed. Sometimes she checked the listings. The young men on television cleared their desks. Walked out with their boxes held in front of them like shields.

164. *Semi-detached*

Each time she returned to work, the challenge was perfectly clear: make it happen so it seems like it never happened. There was much written about this phenomena in the "Woman" section of Sunday supplements, and Natalie read this material with interest. The key to it all was the management of time. Fortunately, time management was Natalie's gift. She found a great deal of time was saved by simple ambivalence. She had no strong opinions about what young children ate, wore, watched, listened to, or what kind of beverage holder they utilized to drink milk or something other than milk.

At other times she was surprised to meet herself down a dark alley. It filled her with panic and rage to see her spoiled children sat upon the floor, flicking through past images, moving images, of themselves, on their father's phone, an experience of self-awareness literally unknown in the history of human existence — outside dream and miracle — until very recently. Until just before just now.

165. *Stage directions*

Interior. Night. Artificial light.
Left and right back, high, one small window. Closed blind.
Front right, a door, ajar. Bookshelves to the right and left.
Simple desk. Folding chair. Books upon it.
Nat comes through door. Looks up at

window. Stands close to window.
Opens blind. Closes blind. Leaves. Re-
turns. Leaves.
A pause.
Returns with urgency, opens blind. Re-
moves books from chair. Sits. Stands.
Walks to door. Returns. Sits. Opens
laptop. Closes. Opens.
Types.
FRANK [mechanical tone, out of sight]
Bed. Coming? [pause] Coming?
NAT Yes. [types quickly] No. Yes.

166. *Time speeds up*

Now that there was so much work to do —
now that the whole of her life had essentially
become work — Natalie Blake felt a calm
and contentment she had previously only
experienced during the run up to university
examinations or during pre-trial. If only
she could slow the whole thing down! She
had been eight for a hundred years. She was
thirty-four for seven minutes. Quite often
she thought of a chalk diagram drawn on
a blackboard, a long time ago, when things
moved at a reasonable pace. A clock-face,
meant to signify the history of the universe
in a twelve-hour stretch. The big bang came
at midday. The dinosaurs arrived mid-after-

noon sometime. Everything that concerned humans could be accounted for in the five minutes leading up to midnight.

167. *Doubt*

Spike began to speak. His favorite thing to say was: "This is my mummy." The emphasis varied. "This is *my* mummy. This is my *mummy*. *This* is my mummy."

168. *African minimart endgame*

She had a new urge for something other than pure forward momentum. She wanted to conserve. To this end, she began going in search of the food of her childhood. On Saturday mornings, straight after visiting the enormous British supermarket, she struggled up the high road with two children in a double buggy and no help to the little African minimart to buy things like yam and salted cod and plantain. It was raining. Horizontal rain. Both children were screaming. Could there be misery loftier than hers?

Naomi threw things in the cart. Natalie threw them out. Naomi threw them in. Spike soiled himself. People looked at Natalie. She looked at them. Back and forth went the looks of paranoia and contempt. It was freezing outside, freezing inside. They managed to join a queue. Just. They only just managed it.

"I'll tell you a story, Nom-Nom, if you stop that, I'll tell you a story. Do you want to listen to my story?" asked Natalie Blake.

"No," said Naomi De Angelis.

Natalie wiped the cold sweat from her forehead with her scarf and looked up to see if anyone was admiring her maternal calm in the face of such impossible provocation. The woman in front of her in the queue came into view. She was emptying her pockets onto the counter, offering to relinquish this and that item. Her children, four of them, cringed around her legs.

Natalie Blake had completely forgotten what it was like to be poor. It was a language she'd stopped being able to speak, or even to understand.

169. *Lunch with Layla*

Her old friend Layla Thompson was now Layla Dean. She'd left the church many years earlier. She worked at a Black and Asian radio station as the head of music programming. She was married to a man who owned and ran two internet café/copy shops in Harlesden. Damien. Three children. Whenever Natalie Blake was having an argument about education (she had arguments of this kind constantly) she held up her old friend Layla as a positive example of all that she was trying to say.

When using Layla as a positive example in this manner she usually neglected to mention that she had not seen Layla for a couple of years. Layla had been having her children and Natalie had not been having children and during this period Natalie had found it difficult to have lunch with Layla, Layla's concerns seeming so myopic, so narrowly focused. Now that Natalie had children of her own it occurred to her that she would really love to have regular lunches with Layla once again. There were so many things she would be able say to Layla that she had not been able to say to anyone else. Lunch was arranged. And now she found herself speaking very fast and fully availing herself of Layla's hospitality at this beautiful soul food restaurant in Camden High Street. There was a sense in which she couldn't speak fast enough to get out all the things she wanted to say.

"'It's such a relief not to have to pretend to be interested in the news,'" said Natalie Blake, quoting another woman, and eating a small china ladle full of prawns in coconut milk broth. "And I just sat in a circle of these freaks and thought: I really don't belong here. Show me the exit. I need people I can go out dancing with." Outside, a car passed playing "Billie Jean."

"I'll come dancing with you, Natalie."

"Thank you! There's an old school hip-hop night in Farringdon somewhere, my brother told me about it. We could go next Saturday. I could get my friend Ameeta on board. Beats singing Old Macdonald."

"I like those kid classes. I used to go all the time."

"Not this one. This one's posh. But the bit I really can't deal with is when they all —" began Natalie and continued in this vein through most of the main course. Men came with punch, they came with punch. Her glass was never half empty or half filled but always filling. Men came with punch. Outside, a car passed playing "Don't Stop 'Til You Get Enough."

"What?" asked Natalie Blake. She was really too drunk to return to chambers. Her friend Layla was smiling, a little sadly. She was looking at the tablecloth.

"Nothing. You're exactly the same."

Natalie was in the middle of texting Melanie to warn her she would not be in now until tomorrow morning.

"Right. It's not like I have to become another person just because —"

"You always wanted to make it clear you
weren't like the rest of us. You're still doing
it."

A waiter came over to ask about dessert.
Natalie Blake, though eager for dessert, felt
now she could not really order one. She was
struck with dread. Her heart beat madly.
She had a schoolgirl's impulse to report
Layla Dean née Thompson to the waiter.
Layla's being horrible to me! Layla hates me!
Outside, a car passed playing "Wanna Be
Startin' Somethin'."

Layla did not look up at the waiter and
after a moment he went away. She had a
thick white napkin she was twisting in both
hands.

"Even when we used to do those songs you'd
be with me but also totally not with me.
Showing off. False. Fake. Signaling to the
boys in the audience, or whatever."

"Layla, what are you talking about?"

"And you're still doing it."

170. *In drag*

Daughter drag. Sister drag. Mother drag.
Wife drag. Court drag. Rich drag. Poor drag.
British drag. Jamaican drag. Each required

a different wardrobe. But when considering these various attitudes she struggled to
think what would be the most authentic, or
perhaps the least inauthentic.

171. *Me, myself and I*

Natalie put Naomi in her car-seat and locked
the buckle. Natalie put Spike in his car-seat
and locked the buckle. Natalie climbed up
into the giant car. Natalie closed all the windows. Natalie put on the air conditioning.
Natalie put *Reasonable Doubt* in the stereo.
Natalie instructed Frank to mute egregious
profanity as and when it arrived.

172. *Box sets*

Walking down Kilburn High Road Natalie
Blake had a strong desire to slip into the
lives of other people. It was hard to see how
this desire could be practically satisfied or
what, if anything, it really meant. "Slip into"
is an imprecise thought. Follow the Somali
kid home? Sit with the old Russian lady at
the bus-stop outside Poundland? Join the
Ukrainian gangster at his table at the cake
shop? A local tip: the bus stop outside Kilburn's Poundland is the site of many of the
more engaging conversations to be heard in

the city of London. You're welcome.

Listening was not enough. Natalie Blake wanted to know people. To be intimately involved with them.

Meanwhile:

Everyone in both Natalie's workplace and Frank's was intimately involved with the lives of a group of African-Americans, mostly male, who slung twenty-dollar vials of crack in the scrub between a concatenation of terribly designed tower blocks in a depressed and forgotten city with one of the highest murder rates in the United States. That everyone should be so intimately involved in the lives of these young men annoyed Frank, though he could not really put his finger on why, and in protest he exempted himself and his wife from what was by all accounts an ecstatic communal televisual experience.

Meanwhile:

Natalie Blake checked her listing. Replied to her replies.

173. *In the playground*

You can't smoke in a playground. It's obvious. Any half-civilized person ought to know that.

Yes, agreed Natalie. Yes, of course.

Is he still smoking? Asked the old white lady.

Natalie leaned forward on the bench. He was still smoking. About eighteen years old. He was with two other kids: a white boy with terrible acne and a very pretty girl in a gray tracksuit and neon yellow Nikes. The girl was doing what Natalie and her friends used to call "lounging" or "plotting," i.e., she sat between the white boy's legs with her elbows on his knees in a lazy summertime embrace. And they looked quite nice together, lounging on the roundabout. But it could not be denied: the smoking boy was standing on the roundabout. Smoking.

I'm going to give them all a piece of my mind. Said the old white lady. They're all off that bloody estate.

The old lady went over and at the same moment Naomi ran from the paddling pool into her mother's arms crying TOWEL TOWEL TOWEL. In case you were wondering, this was indeed the same pool in which the dramatic event had occurred, many years earlier. Natalie Blake wrapped a towel around her daughter and put plastic sandals on her feet.

The old lady returned.

Is he still smoking? He was very rude to me.

Yes. Said Natalie Blake. Still smoking.

PUT IT OUT. Shouted the old lady.

Natalie picked Naomi up in her arms and walked over to the roundabout. As she approached, a middle-aged woman, a formidable-looking Rasta in a giant Zulu hat, joined her. The two of them stood by the roundabout. The Rasta folded her arms across her chest.

You need to put that out. This is a playground. Said Natalie.

NOW. Said the Rasta. You shouldn't even be in here. I heard how you spoke to that lady. That lady is your elder. You should be ashamed of yourself.

Just put it out. Said Natalie. My child is here. Said Natalie, though she really did not have strong feelings about secondhand smoke, particularly when it was outside in the open air.

Listen if someone comes disrespecting me, said the boy, I'm gonna tell them to get off my fucking case. Did she address me respectfully though? Don't lie, cos they all heard you and no you didn't.

YOU CANNOT SMOKE IN A CHILDREN'S PLAYGROUND. Shouted the old lady. From the bench.

But why did she have to get in my face in that manner? Inquired the boy.

She has a right! Insisted the Rasta woman.

Just put it out. Said Natalie. This is a playground.

Listen, I don't do like you lot do round here. This ain't my manor. We don't do like you do here. In Queen's Park. You can't really chat to me. I'm Hackney, so.

This was an unwise move, rhetorically speaking. Even the lounging girl groaned.

Oh, NO. Said the Rasta. No you didn't. No no no. You having a laugh? *I'm Hackney?* So? SO? Listen, you can try and mess with these people but you can't mess with me, sunshine. I know you. In a deep way. I'm not Queen's Park, love, I'm HARLESDEN. Why would you talk about yourself in that way? Why would you talk about your area that way? Oh you just pissed me off, boy. I'm from Harlesden — certified youth worker. Twenty years. I am ashamed of you right now. You're the reason why we're where we are right now. Shame. Shame! Yeah yeah yeah yeah yeah yeah yeah. Said the boy. The girl laughed.

You think this is funny? Said the Rasta. Keep laughing, my sista. Where do you think this leads? Said the Rasta, to the girl.

Me? But I ain't even involved! How am I even involved?

Nowhere. Said Natalie. Nowhere. No-where. NOWHERE.

Mummy stop shouting! Said Naomi.

Natalie did not know why she was shouting. She began to fear she was making herself ridiculous.

I feel sorry for you, really. Said a previously uninvolved Indian man, who now joined the circle of judgment. You're obviously very unhappy, dissatisfied young people.

Oh my days don't you fucking start! Cried the girl. The white boy she was lounging with looked at the gathering crowd and opened his eyes very wide. He started to laugh.

You lot crease me up. He said.

How did this even get like this to this level? Asked the girl, laughing. I'm just sitting here, chillin! How am I even involved? Marcus, man, you're bait. This is on you. Next thing I know I'm on fucking Jeremy Kyle.

Why are you laughing? Asked the old white woman, who now stood with the rest, by the roundabout. I don't think this is very funny.

Oh man, this is long. Said the girl. This one's back at it now. Old Mother Hubbard's on the fucking case again. Shit is crazy!

All of this? Asked Marcus. For a fag. Is it really worth it though? Just sit down back where you was and calm yourselves. Go handle your business. Sit down, man.

Fools. Said the girl.

Just put it out, man. Said Natalie. She had not ended a sentence in "man" for quite some time.

Oi, Marcus. Said the girl. Just put that fag out please, shut this woman up. This is just getting to be ridiculous now.

You should be ashamed of yourself. Said the old white lady.

I was willing to chat with you, right? Said the Rasta. Adult to adult and try and comprehend your point of view. But you just lost me with that nonsense. Shame on you, brother. And the sad thing is I've seen where it leads.

Don't worry 'bout me. Said Marcus. I get paid. I do all right. Said Marcus.

Marcus popped his collar. This gesture was not convincing.

I get paid, I do all right. Repeated Natalie. Her lip was curled up in a snarl. I get paid, I do all right. She repeated. Yeah, sure you do. I'm a lawyer, mate. That's paid. That's really paid.

These people are fucking mental. Said the girl.

If she come over and ask me respectfully, yeah? I would have just done it. Argued Marcus. I'm actually an intelligent young man? But when someone don't respect me then they're disrespecting to me and then I'm going to step to them.

If you had any real self-respect or self-esteem, argued Natalie, one person asking you to put a cigarette out in a fucking playground would not register as an attack on your precious little ego.

A small crowd had gathered, of other parents, concerned citizens. This last point of Natalie's was a great popular success, and she sensed her victory as surely as if a jury had gasped at a cache of photographs in her hand. Easing into triumph, she accidentally locked eyes with Marcus — briefly causing her to stutter — but soon she found a void above his right shoulder and addressed all further remarks to this vanishing point. Around them the argument devolved into smaller disputes. The girl argued with the old lady. Her beau argued with the Rasta. Several people joined together with Natalie to keep yelling at poor Marcus, who by this point had finished his cigarette and looked utterly exhausted.

174. *Peach, peonies*

She couldn't find the address and walked

past it several times. It was a non-descript door with a double-glazed panel, squeezed between Habitat and Waitrose on the Finchley Road. Run-down, a 1930s block. She pressed the button and was immediately buzzed up. She stopped to examine some plastic flowers in the hall, extraordinary in their verisimilitude. Four flights, no lift. Natalie Blake stood at the inner door for a long time. In order to ring the bell she had to perform an act she later characterized to herself as "leaving her own body." Through the glass she could see peach carpet and peach walls, and a corner of the living room where a puffy white leather sofa stood, with walnut legs and arms. Opposite the sofa she spotted a matching chair and giant pouffe, done in the same style. On a hallway table sat a newspaper. She strained to see which one and concluded it was a copy of *The Daily Express,* partially obscured by an old-fashioned finger dial telephone, also in cream with a brass handle. She thought of the listing, which had described this couple as "upscale." Two bodies approached the door. She saw them clearly through the glass. Much older than they'd said. In their sixties. Awful, crepey white skin with blue veins. Everyone's seeking a BF 18–35. Why? What do they think we can do? What is it we

454

have that they want? She heard them calling: Come back!

175. *Golders Green Crematorium*

It was not difficult for Natalie Blake to get dressed for a funeral. Most of her clothes had a funereal aspect. It was harder to dress the children and she made this the focus of her anxiety, banging cupboard doors and throwing whatever got in her way to the floor.

In the car her husband Frank De Angelis asked: "Was he a good guy?"

"I don't know what that means," replied Natalie Blake.

As they pulled into the car park there was not a face in the rearview mirror that she didn't recognize, even if she lacked their names. Caldwell people, Brayton people, Kilburn people, Willesden people. Each marking a particular period. Surely she was no more than a narcissistic form of time-piece for them, too. And yet. She stepped down from her car to the courtyard. A friend of her mother's touched her arm. She moved toward the memorial garden. A man who ran the Caldwell Residents Association lay his big hand on her neck and squeezed. Was it possible not only to have contempt for the people who kept time for you? Was it also possible to love them? "You all right, Keisha?" "Natalie, good to see you." "All right, love?" "Miss Blake, long time." The weird nod of recognition people give each other at funerals. Not only was Colin Hanwell dead but a hundred people who had shared the same square mile of streets with the man now recognized that relation, which was both intimate and accidental, close and distant. Natalie had not really known Colin (it was not possible to have really known Colin) but she had known what it was to know of Colin. To have Colin be an object presented to her consciousness. So had all these others.

People spoke. People sang. And did those feet, in ancient times. Natalie was forced to come and go as each of her children kicked up a fuss. Finally the curtain opened and the coffin disappeared. Dusty Springfield. There are things you can only learn about people after they're dead. As the congregation filed out, Leah stood in the doorway with her mother. She wore a terrible long black skirt and blouse that someone must have lent her. Natalie could hear well-meaning strangers burdening Leah with long, irrelevant memories. Story-telling. "Thank you for coming," said Leah, mechanically, as each passed by. She looked very pale. No siblings. No cousins. Only Michel to help.

"Oh, Lee," exclaimed Natalie Blake, when it was her turn, and wept and held her good friend Leah Hanwell very tightly. If only someone could have forced Natalie Blake to attend a funeral every day of her life!

176. *Oblivion*

The Cranley Estate, Camden. More N than NW. A skinny man who called himself "JJ" and looked not unlike her uncle Jeffrey. And an Iranian girl, with an equally unlikely moniker: "Honey." They were in their early twenties, disasters. Natalie Blake assumed crack, but it could easily have been meth or something else again. Honey had one tooth missing. Their living room barely deserved the name. Nasty, filthy futon, TV on the whole time. The whole place stank of weed. They were sat on beanbags, barely conscious, watching *Deal or No Deal.* They did not appear nervous. JJ said: Chill here first for a bit. I just got in and I'm bushed. He did not indicate a chair. Ever accommodating, Natalie Blake found a spot on the floor between the two of them.

She tried to concentrate on the show, having never seen it before. Her phone kept beeping with texts from work. JJ had an elaborate conspiracy theory about the order of the boxes. The only thing to do was to accept the joint and let the weed take her. Quite soon she lost track of time. At some point the TV watching finished and JJ started playing a videogame: goblins and swords and elves talking nonsense. Natalie excused herself to go to the loo. She opened the wrong door, saw a leg, heard a cry. That's Kelvin, said JJ, he's crashing here right now. He works nights.

The toilet seat was see-through plexi with a goldfish print. The water out of the tap was brown. *Head and Shoulders. Radox.* Both empty.

Natalie wandered back in. JJ was busy speaking to the screen. Tell me where the friggin' grain store is. An enigmatic peasant woman smiled back at him. Natalie tried to make conversation. Had he ever done anything like this before? A few times, he said, when there's fuck all else to do. They're usually mad ugly though and I kick them out before they get in the door. Oh, said Natalie. She waited. Nothing. Honey, bored, turned to her guest. What you do Keisha? You seem nice girl. I'm a hairdresser, said Natalie Blake. Oh! Listen, she does hair. That's nice. I am from Iran. JJ made a face: Axis of Evil! Honey smacked him, but with affec-

458

tion. She stroked Natalie's face. You believe in auras, Keisha?

More weed was rolled, and smoked. At some point Natalie remembered that Frank was also working late. She texted Anna and bribed her with time-and-a-half rate to stay till eleven and put the children to bed. JJ arrived at a castle where he was set a new list of tasks. Honey started wondering aloud about some MDMA powder she'd left in a gum wrapper somewhere. Natalie said: I don't think this is going to really happen, is it? JJ said: Probably not, to be honest with you.

177. *Envy*

Leah wished Natalie Blake would speak at a charity auction for a young black women's collective Leah had helped fund. She kept going on about it. But the hall they'd managed to rent for the occasion was south of the river.

"I don't go south," protested Natalie Blake.

"It's a really good cause," insisted Leah Hanwell.

Natalie Blake thanked Leah for her introduction and stood in front of the podium. She gave a speech about time management, identifying goals, working hard, respecting oneself and one's partner, and the importance of a good education. "Anything purely based on physicality is doomed to failure," she read. "To survive, your ambitions should be in the same direction." One day she would probably find herself having to say something of this kind to Leah. Not right now, but some day. She would water it down, of course. Poor Leah.

In between the top of page two and the beginning of page three she must have been reading out loud and making sense, there must have appeared to be an unbroken continuity — no one in the audience was looking at her like she was crazy — yet she found her mind traveling to obscene tableaux. She wondered what Leah and Michel, who always seemed to have their hands on each other, did in the privacy of their bedroom. Orifices, positions, climaxes. "And it was by refusing to set myself artificial limits," explained Natalie Blake to the collective of young black women, "that I was able to reach my full potential."

178. *Beehive*

The lovely voice came through the speakers in the park café. Natalie Blake and her friend Leah Hanwell had long ago agreed that this voice sounded like London — especially its Northern and North Western zones — as if its owner were patron saint of their neighborhoods. Is a voice something you can own? Natalie's daughter and many other children were bouncing up and down and dancing to the song as their parents discreetly nodded their heads. The sun was out. Unfortunately Leah Hanwell was habitually late and soon the song had finished and Naomi was screaming about something and Spike had woken up and Leah had missed a perfectly staged demonstration of the joy of life — of family life in particular. "She's really depressed," said Natalie to Frank as they waited. "She thinks I can't see it. I see it. Completely stuck. Stasis. She can't seem to dig herself out of this hole she's in." But as soon as she'd said it the possibility confronted her that this judgment had merely arisen from the song, was really only a final verse Natalie herself had added on the spur of the moment, and that by saying it out loud she had made herself ridiculous. Frank looked up from his paper and caught her face arrested in its state of calamity. "Leah and Michel are happy-as-Larry," he said.

Some time later Natalie saw the singer interviewed on the television: "When I was growing up, I didn't think I was anything

461

special, I thought everybody could sing." Her voice was the same miracle Natalie had once heard, through a pub window, in Camden. But the woman who did or didn't own it had all but disappeared. Natalie stared at the knock-kneed girl-child, hardly there, almost nothing.

179. *Aphorism*

What a difficult thing a gift is for a woman! She'll punish herself for receiving it.

180. *All the mod cons*

Charming Primrose Hill. After much negotiation on e-mail, a daytime assignation was agreed: three o'clock. The woman opened the front door and said Phew! Weave, dressing gown, heels, beautiful, unmistakeably African. Her main objective was curling an arm around Natalie Blake and getting her into the giant house before anyone saw. Sartorially, Natalie kept to the same theme: gold hoops, denim skirt, suede boots with tassels, the hair bobble with the black and white dice, and her work clothes in a rucksack on her back. Catching herself in a huge gilt mirror in the hall she found herself convincing. At this point she was determined. At least they were attractive. Natalie Blake still believed that attraction was what mattered.

Farrow and Ball Utopia Green (matte) in the hall. African wall sculpture. Modern minimalist pieces. A gold record framed. A picture of Marley framed. Front page of a newspaper framed. A sort of horrible "good taste" everywhere. Natalie Blake looked up and saw the husband or boyfriend at the top of the stairs. He was especially handsome, with a shaved head, finely shaped. Good-looking couple, they looked like each other. Like something from an advert for American life insurance. He smiled at Natalie and showed a lot of dentistry, luminous and perfectly straight. Silky dressing gown. Cheesy. We're so pleased you're here, Keisha, we weren't sure you were for real. Can you believe she's for real? Too good to be true. Come up here Sista so I can really take you in. Soul music playing upstairs. 2009 limited-edition Bloom baby highchair, like a space station, levitating in the kitchen. MacBook Air open on the kitchen table. An older Mac closed on the stairs. He stretched out his hand. Beautiful crib you got, said Natalie Blake. You're beautiful, he said. Natalie felt his wife or girlfriend's hand on her backside.

Upstairs she was introduced to a sleigh

bed, of the kind that was fashionable about five years earlier. The shoe cupboard was open. Red soled from floor to ceiling. Above the bed they had that too-familiar tube map with the stops replaced by icons of the last millenium, gathered in cliques and movements. Natalie looked for Kilburn: Pele. On the bed an iPad played pornography, threesomes, and this was the first time Natalie had ever seen that particular piece of technology. Two girls ate each other out while a man sat on a desk with his dick in his hand. They were all German.

The beautiful African woman kept talking. Where are you from? Are you in college? What do you want to be? Don't ever give up. It's all about dreaming big. Having aspirations. Working hard. Not accepting no for an answer. Being whoever you want to be.

The more Natalie Blake stood there, fully dressed and unresponsive, the more nervous they got, the more they talked. Finally Natalie asked to go to the bathroom. En-suite. She climbed into a reclaimed Victorian bath clad in brass and porcelain from The Water Monopoly. She knew she was finished here. She lay back. Acqua di Parma. Chanel. Molton Brown. Marc Jacobs. Tommy Hilfiger. Prada. Gucci.

181. *Easter Holidays*

Anna had gone to Poland for a few days to see her family but now the volcano meant she could not return. Natalie googled. She stared at the great cloud of ash.

"You're more flexible than I am," argued Frank, and left the house. The basement was back on track. Builders were everywhere. Frank had worked hard to put things back on track. They both had. They deserved everything that was coming to them.

Got any more tea, love? Better keep these kids out of the way, they're liable to get hurt. Don't spose there's a biscuit going begging?

By ten a.m. she found herself trapped in a white painted box with two mysterious black-eyed others who seemed to want something from her that she had no way of either comprehending or providing. Men in orange tabards went back and forth. This milk is off, love. Got any jam? She gathered the children in her arms and left this building site, her kitchen. She took them to her mother's flat. To the park. To the zoo. To Kilburn market. To the African minimart. To Cricklewood Toys R Us. Home.

Naomi related this odyssey in far greater detail to her father when he came home.

"You're amazing," said Frank, and kissed

Natalie Blake's cheek. "I would have just sat around wasting my time, playing with them all day."

182. *Love in the ruins*

They were nice young men, and clearly astounded that anyone had replied to their premise. Natalie felt certain they must have posted when they were pissed. Cousins? Brothers? A 1950's semi, in Wembley, facing the North Circular, double-glazed to within an inch of its life. It was a family house with the family missing. What Brayton kids used to call a "Cornershop Villa." Natalie Blake could not explain why she knew they weren't going to kill her. She had to recognize in herself a perfectly irrational belief that whether or not a person has murderous intent toward you is one of those things "you can just tell" about people. Certainly it helped that when they opened the door they looked more scared than she did. Oh my days. I told you, Dinesh. I told you. I told you it ain't no bloke. Come in, love. Come in, Keisha. Oh my days. You're fit and all. What you saying that for! Why not? She knows and we know. She knows and we know. No surprises. Oh my days! Go that way, lovely. We ain't gonna hurt you innit we're nice boys. Oh my word, no one is gonna believe this, man. I don't even believe this. Go in there. We gonna take turns or what? What? I don't want to see you naked, bruv! That's some gay madness. Yeah but she wants to double team innit! That ain't one then another! That's two simulty-simultany-simu— at the same time. Don't you know what double team means bruv? Double team. You don't know what you're even chatting about. Double team! Shut up you joker. Natalie listened to them arguing in the hall. She sat waiting in the kitchen. A large puddle of water surrounded the freezer. All the doors said FIRE DOOR. They came back in. Shyly they suggested that everybody adjourn to a bedroom. It was peculiar how shy they were, given the circumstance. Constantly bickering. In here. Are you mental? I ain't doing it in there. Bibi sleeps in there! In there, man. Chief. Follow me, Keisha, make yourself comfortable, yeah? Dinesh man there ain't even no sheet! Go get a sheet! Stop using my name! No names. We're gonna get a sheet, wait right here don't move.

Natalie Blake lay back on the mattress. On top of the wardrobe there was a lot of boxed-up stuff. Stuff that no-one was coming back for. Surplus to requirements. There was something terribly sad about the whole place. She wished she could take the boxes down and sift through them and save whatever needed to be saved.

The door opened and the young men re-emerged in only their Calvin Kleins, one black pair, one white, like two featherweights in a boxing ring. No older than 20. They got out a laptop. The idea appeared to be like roulette. You click and a human being appears, in real time. Click again. Click again. Eighty percent of the time they got a penis. The rest were quiet girls playing with their hair, groups of students who wanted to talk, shaven-headed thugs standing in front of their national flags. On the rare occasions it was a girl they would at once started typing: GET YOUR TITS OUT. Natalie asked them: boys, why are we doing this? You've got the real thing right here. But they kept on with the Internet. It seemed to Natalie that they were stalling for time. Or maybe they couldn't do anything without the Net somewhere in the mix. You try it, Keisha, you try it, see who you get. Natalie sat at the laptop. She got a lonely boy in Israel who typed YOU NICE and took out his penis. You like being watched Keisha? Do you like it? We'll leave it there, on the dresser. How d'you want it Keisha? Just tell us and we'll do it. Anything. And still Natalie Blake knew she was in no danger. Just do what you want, said Natalie Blake.

But neither of them could really manage it at all, and soon they blamed each other. It's him! It's cos I'm looking at him, man. He's messing with my groove. Don't listen to him he ain't got no groove.

They were satisfied to play about like teenagers. Natalie became very impatient. She was not a teenager anymore. She knew what she was doing. She did not feel she had to wait around hoping to be penetrated. She could envelop. She could hold. She could release.

She sat the boy in the black Calvins on the edge of bed, rolled his foreskin down, got on him, advised him not to touch her or otherwise move unless she said so. A narrow cock but not ugly. He said: you're quite strong-minded innit Keisha. Know what you want and that. They say that about sistas don't they? And to this, Natalie Blake replied: I really couldn't give a fuck what they say. She could see the boy had no useful rhythm — it was better for both of them if he simply stayed still. She ground down on to him. Rocked. Finished very quickly, though not as quickly as his circumcised friend on the other side of the bed who gave a little groan, spurted dribblingly into his own hand and disappeared into the bathroom. Dinesh you little chief. Come back in here. Um. This is a bit weird. Where's he gone? Just you and me. You come already, yeah? Fair enough. You know what I don't think I'm gonna get there right at the moment Keisha. I feel a bit hot and bothered right now if I'm honest.

She released him. The boy flopped out of her, much reduced. She tucked it back in his pants. She started putting her clothes back on. The other one re-emerged from the loo looking sheepish. She had a spliff left over from Camden, and together they smoked it. She tried to get them to tell her something, anything, about the people who lived in this house but they wouldn't be distracted from what they called their "chirpsing." We should worship this girl man. Sista, are you ready to be worshipped? You're a goddess in my eyes. All night long baby. Till you're gonna be begging me to stop. Till six in the morning. Dinesh, man, I gotta be at work at eight.

183. *Catching up*

Natalie Blake fired Anna and hired Maria, who was Brazilian. The basement was completed. Maria moved into it. A new arena of paid time opened up. Natalie and Leah went

470

out to the Irish.

"What's up with you?" asked Leah Hanwell.

"Nothing much," said Natalie Blake. "You?"

"Same old."

Natalie told a story about a boy smoking in the park, emphasizing her own heroic opposition to persistent incivility. She told a story about how mean and miserable their mutual acquaintance Layla Dean had become, in ways intended to subtly flatter Natalie Blake herself. She told a story concerning the children's preparations for carnival, which could hardly avoid demonstrating the happy fullness of her life.

"But Cheryl wants all 'the cousins' on a church float. I don't want to go on a church float!"

Leah defended Natalie's right not to accept religion disguised as carnival fun. Leah told a story about her mother being impossible. Natalie defended Leah's right to be outraged by her mother's misdemeanors, be they ever so small. Leah told a funny story about upstairs Ned. She told a funny story about Michel's bathroom habits. Natalie noticed with anxiety that Leah's stories had no special emphasis or intention.

"Did you ever see that girl again?" asked Natalie Blake. "The one who scammed you

— who came to the door?"

"All the time," said Leah Hanwell. "I see her all the time."

They drank two bottles of white wine between them.

184. *Caught*

"What is this? 'KeishaNW@gmail.com.' What the fuck is this? Fiction?"

They stood opposite each other in the hallway. He waved a piece of paper at her. Six feet away their kids and the cousins and Cheryl and Jayden were practicing dance routines to be performed on a carnival float the following morning. Marcia was helping sew sequins and feathers on to dayglo leotards. Hearing raised voices, the many members of Natalie Blake's family paused what they were doing and looked into the hallway.

"Please let's go upstairs," said Natalie Blake. They got up one flight of stairs to the spare room, which had a charming Moroccan theme. Natalie Blake's husband held her wrist very tightly.

"Who *are* you?"

Natalie Blake tried to free her wrist.

"You have two children downstairs. You're meant to be a fucking adult. Who are you?

Is this real? Who the fuck is wildinwembley? What is that on your computer?"

"Why are you looking at my computer?" asked Natalie Blake in a small voice, a ludicrous voice.

185. *Onwards*

Frank sat on the bed with his back to her, a hand over his eyes. Natalie Blake stood up and left the spare room and closed the door. An odd sense of calm followed her downstairs. On the ground floor, in the hall, she bumped into the Brazilian girl, Maria, who regarded her with the same obtuse confusion of last week, when she'd arrived and discovered her employer to be several shades darker than she was herself.

Past the hall where her laptop sat on a side table, the screen still open for anyone to read. Past her family who called out for her. She heard Frank running down the stairs. She saw her coat slung across the banister, keys and phone in the pocket. At the door she had another chance to take something with her (on the hallway table she could see her purse, an oyster card, another set of keys). She walked out of the house with nothing and closed the front door behind her. Out of the bay window Frank De Angelis asked his wife Natalie Blake where she was going. Where she thought she was going. Where the fuck she thought she was going. "Nowhere," said Natalie Blake.

■■■■

CROSSING

■■■■

*Willesden Lane
to Kilburn High Road*

She turned left. Walked to the end of her road and the end of the next. Walked quickly away from Queen's Park. She passed into where Willesden meets Kilburn. Went by Leah's place, then Caldwell. In the old flat the kitchen window was open. A duvet cover — decorated with the logo of a football club — had been hung over the balcony to dry. Without looking where she was going, she began climbing the hill that begins in Willesden and ends in Highgate. She was making a queer keening noise, like a fox. As she crossed the road a 98 bus swung by her steeply — it looked like it might capsize — and at first it seemed to be somehow the source of the strange red and blue light coloring the white stripes of the zebra crossing. Now she saw the police car parked in its shadow, roof lights turning silently. A line of police, parked at right angles to each other, making Albert Road inaccessible to traffic. On the public side of this barrier a group of people had gathered, and a tall policeman in a turban stood in the middle of them, answering questions. But I live on Albert! said a young woman. She was carrying too many shopping bags in each hand, with more hanging from her wrists and digging into her skin. What number? asked the policeman. The woman told him. You'll have to walk round. You'll find officers at the far end who'll walk you to your door. For Christ's sake, said the woman, but after a moment she walked in the direction indicated. Can't I walk down there? asked Natalie. Incident, said the officer. He looked down at her. A big T-shirt, leggings and a pair of filthy red slippers, like a junkie. He looked at his watch. It's eight now. This road will be blocked for another hour or so. She tried to reach up on her toes to see round him. All she could see were more policemen and a white canvas tent off to the left, on the pavement opposite the bus stop. What kind of incident? He didn't answer. She was no-one. She didn't merit answering. A kid on a BMX racer said, Someone got juked innit.

She turned and walked back in the direction of Caldwell. Walking was what she did now, walking was what she was. She was nothing more or less than the phenomenon of walking. She had no name, no biography, no characteristics. They had all fled into paradox. Certain physical memories remained. She could feel the puffiness of her skin beneath her eyes and the fact that her throat was sore from shouting and yelping. She had a mark on her wrist where she had been gripped tightly. She put her hand in her hair and knew it to be wild and everywhere and that in the midst of an argument she had ripped a bit out at the right temple. She reached Caldwell's boundary wall. She walked the length of the back wall, looking down at the green verge that climbs from the low basin up to street level. She walked along the wall from one end to the other and back again. She seemed to be seeking some sign of perforation in the brick. She kept retracing the same area. She was lifting her knee to climb when a man's voice called out for her.

Keisha Blake.

Across the road and to her left. He stood beneath a horse chestnut tree with his hands thrust deep in the pockets of his hoodie.

Keisha Blake. Hold up.

He jogged across the road, fidgeting as he went: hands to nose, ears, the back of his neck.

Nathan.
You trying to break back in?

He jumped up on to the wall.

I don't know what I'm doing.
Ain't even going to ask me how I am though. That's cold.

He crouched down and looked into her face.

You don't look too good, Keisha. Reach for me.

Natalie crossed her wrists. Nathan looked at her shaking hands. He pulled her up. They jumped down to the other side together, landing lightly in the bushes. As he straightened up he looked over his shoulder at the street.

Come then.

He scrabbled down through the scrub to the small grassy area where the residents park. He leaned against an old car. Natalie made her way down more slowly, clinging to the woody parts of bushes, sliding in her slippers.

You don't look too good at all.
I don't know what I'm doing here.
Arguing with your mans innit.
Yes. How —
You don't look like you got no real problems.
Come join me. I'm flying.

Now she noticed his pupils, huge and glassy, and so she tried to put herself in the old role. It would be something to replace this absence of sensation, this nothing. She placed a hand on his shoulder. The fabric of his hoodie was stiff, unclean.

You're flying?

He made a sound in the back of his throat like a gasp. It caught at some phlegm, and he coughed a long time.

It's either fly or give it up tonight. You heading to your mum's?
No. North.
North?
Tried to get the tube at Kilburn. The road's blocked off.
Is it. Come on let's walk. This ain't the place I want to be right now. Spent nuff time in this place.

They stood in the center of Caldwell's basin. Five blocks connected by walkways and bridges and staircases, and lifts that were to be avoided almost as soon as they were built. Smith, Hobbes, Bentham, Locke, Russell. Here is the door, here is the window. And repeat, and repeat. Some of the residents had placed pretty pots of geraniums and African violets on their balconies. Others had their windows fixed with brown tape, grubby net curtains, no door number, no bell. Opposite, on the long concrete balcony that runs the length of Bentham, a fat white boy stood with a telescope on a stand, pointed down, into the car park instead of up at the moon. Nathan looked at him and stayed looking. The boy shrunk the telescope, collected the stand under his arm and hurried indoors. The smell of weed was everywhere.

Long time, Keisha.
Long time.
You got a cigarette?

Natalie put her hands on her body to demonstrate a lack of pockets. Nathan stopped where he was and pulled a loose cigarette from his own back pocket. He split it down the middle with a long thumbnail, yellow and thick, with a wide crack running down its center. Tobacco spilled into his hands. Dry black creases crossed both palms. He reached into his jeans and came back with

482

a large packet of orange Rizlas and a little baggy, held between his teeth.

Which one was you again?
Locke. You?

He nodded toward Russell.

Stand there.

Nathan got Natalie by the shoulders and moved her until she stood directly in front of him. There was some relief in becoming an object. Without making any errors she could serve as a useful buffer between the breeze and these two Rizlas being set carefully in an L construction.

Wait up one more minute. Oi: you crying?

Light passed over them and a mechanical roar; a helicopter flying low.

Yes. Sorry.
Come on Keisha now. Your man's not that harsh. He'll take you back.
He shouldn't.
People shouldn't do a lot of things they do. Ok, done.

He held out the joint, face upturned to the night sky.

No. I need to be clear in my head.

Don't pretend you're a nice girl Keisha. I known you from time. Know your family. Cheryl. Suit yourself.

He put the joint behind his ear.

Ain't just weed in there you know. Few surprises in there. Try it. We'll go plot somewhere quiet. This is it now.

He started walking. Natalie followed. Walking was what she did now. As she walked she tried to place the people back there, in the house, into the present current of her thought. But her relation with each person was now unrecognizable to her, and her imagination — due to a long process of neglect, almost as long as her life — did not have the generative power to muster an alternative future for itself. All she could envision was suburban shame, choking everything. She thought to the left and thought to the right but there was no exit. Though, perhaps, Jayden? Again she stalled. Though perhaps Jayden what?

What time is it, Keisha?
I don't know.
Should have gone from here time ago. Sometimes I don't get myself. Who's chaining me? No one. Should have gone Dalston. Too late now.

From behind a parked black taxi a boy of nine or so emerged, riding a bike without hands and with great slowness and skill. Trailing him were two more boys no older than six, and a girl of about four. They had the long faces and sloe-eyes Natalie thought of as Somalian, and their boredom was familiar to her, she remembered it. The girl kicked a dented can over and over. One of the boys had a long branch he held loosely in his hand letting it collide with whatever got in its way. They glared as they passed, and spoke their language. The stick strayed into Nathan's path. He only had to look at it for the boy to slowly raise it above their heads and away.

What are we doing? Nathan? What are we doing?
Traipsing. North.
Oh.
That's where you want to go, right?
Yes.

There is a connection between boredom and the desire for chaos. Despite many disguises and bluffs perhaps she had never stopped wanting chaos.

Got any tunes Keisha?
What?
We should go back to your yard, get some tunes. LOCKE!

485

He shouted and pointed at it, as if by naming it he had brought the block into existence.

Keisha name some Locke people.
Leah Hanwell. John-Michael. Tina Haynes. Rodney Banks.

The effort of naming made Natalie sit down exactly where she was. She lay back and put her head on the ground until the moon was all she was looking at and all that she thought.

I seen Rodney — time ago, in Wembley. Got a dry cleaners there now. Done well. He's safe, though, Rodney, still humble. He chatted with me. Some people act like they don't know you. Get up, Keisha.

Natalie got up on her elbows to look at him. She had not lain on pavement in decades.

Come on get up. Chat to me. Like usual. Go on, man.

For the second time tonight she crossed her wrists and felt herself lifted up as if she were barely there, almost nothing.

Leah. She was obsessed with you. Obsessed.
I seen her. Other things, though. Good with numbers.
Leah?

I was, man! I was good! You remember. Most people don't know me from then. You remember. Got them gold stars all day long.

You were good with everything. That's how I remember it. You had a trial.

'Zackly. Queen's Park Rangers. Everyone says they had a trial. I had a real trial.

I know you did. Your mum told my mum.

Bad tendons. I played on. No-one told me. Lot of things would be different, Keisha. Lot of things. That's how it is. That's it. I don't like to think about them days, to be truthful. At the end of the day I'm just out here on the street, grinding. Bustin' a gut, day in day out. Tryna get paid. I done some bad things Keisha I'm not gonna lie. But you know that ain't really me. You know me from back in the day.

He swiped at three beer cans and sent them clattering into the grass. They'd reached the end of nostalgia. Here the boundary wall had been partially destroyed — it looked like someone had torn it apart with their hands, brick by brick. They crossed the street, past the basketball court. Four shadowed figures stood in the far corner, the tips of their cigarettes glowing in the dark. Nathan raised a hand to the men. They raised a hand back.

Stop here. I'm gonna smoke this.
Ok me too.

He leaned into the high iron gates of the cemetery, looking in. He took the pre-rolled from behind his ear and they passed the joint back and forth and blew smoke through the bars. The something else mixed in with the tobacco had a bitter taste. Natalie's lower lip went numb. The top of her head came off. Her mouth grew rigid and slow. It became laborious to translate thought into sound or to know what thoughts could be made into sound.

> Fall back fall back fall back. Keisha, fall back.
> What?
> Move up.

Natalie found herself nudged a few feet along by his shoulder until they were standing at the furthest point between two streetlights. On the other side of the railings one spindly Victorian lamppost cast a weak glare over the flowerbeds. When Naomi was small Natalie had strapped her daughter to her chest and walked figure of eights in this cemetery hoping the child would take her afternoon nap. Local people claimed Arthur Orton was buried in here somewhere. In all her figure of eights she never found him.

> Let's go in. I want to climb in.
> Hold up. Keisha's gone crazy.

Let's go in. Come on. I'm not scared. What are you scared of? The dead?

Don't know about duppies, Keisha. Don't want to know about them.

Natalie tried to return the joint but Nathan directed it back to her mouth.

Why you even out here Keisha? You should be home.

I'm not going home.

Suit yourself.

You got kids, Nathan?

Me? Nah.

There came a gentle whirring sound, growing louder, then a screech. A bike made a sharp-angled stop in front of them. A young man with messy cane-rows, one trouser leg rolled up to the knee, leaned his bike to one side, reached over and muttered into Nathan's ear. Nathan listened for a moment, shook his head, stepped back.

Leave me, man. Too late.

The kid shrugged and put his foot to the pedal. Natalie watched the bike speed away past the old cinema.

It's just a death sentence.

What?

Kids. If they get born, they're gonna die. So

that's what you're giving them at the end of the day. See, that's why I like talking to you, Keisha, you're real. We always have deep talks you and me.

I wish we could have talked more often.

I'm on the street, Keisha. I had some bad luck. Novlene don't tell people the truth. But I'm not going to lie. You can see. Here I am. What you see is what you get.

Natalie kept looking in the direction of the boy on the bike. She had picked up the habit of being embarrassed by other people's bad luck.

I ran into Novlene, on the high road, a while back.

Smart Keisha.

What?

She tell you she don't let me in the house no more? Bet she didn't. Go on, Smart Keisha. Tell me something smart. You're a lawyer now, innit.

Yes. Barrister. It doesn't matter.

You got a wig on your head. Hammer in your hand.

No. It doesn't matter.

Nah, but you did well. My mum loves up telling me about you. Smart Keisha. Oi, look at that fox! Slinking through.

He had a little torch on the end of his phone and he shone it through the bars. The end of an ugly tail — like a bent old brush — vanished behind an oak tree.

Sneaky animals. Foxes are everywhere. If you ask me, they run tings.

The fox was scrawny and seemed to be running sideways, over the gravestones. Nathan's torch followed it as far as it could before the animal leapt into nothingness and disappeared.

How'd you get into that business?
Law?
Yeah. How'd you get into that?
I don't know. It just happened.
You was always smart. You deserve it.
That doesn't follow.
There he is again! They're fast, them foxes!
I've got to go.

The strength went from Nathan's legs. He wilted. First into the bars and then sideways into Natalie. She had not expected to be anybody else's support. Together they slid down the bars to the ground.

Jesus — you need to stop smoking.
Keisha, stay and chat with me a bit. Chat to me, Keisha.

They stretched their legs out on the pavement.

People don't chat to me no more. Look at me like they don't know me. People I used to know, people I used to run with.

He put his hand flat on his chest.

Too much speed in this thing. Heart is running. That little chief. Don't know why I ever give him my time. This is on him. Always taking shit too far. How can I stop Tyler though? Tyler should stop Tyler. I shouldn't even be chatting with you, I should be in Dalston, cos this isn't even on me, it's on him. But I'm looking at myself asking myself Nathan why you still here? Why you still here? And I don't even know why. I ain't even joking. I should just run from myself.
Calm down. Take long breaths.
Let me get myself straight, Keisha. Keep walking with me.

He slipped off his hood, took off his cap. At the nape of his neck there was a coin-sized blotch of white skin.

Come on, let's move.

He was on his feet in a second. A red and blue light passed over the cemetery wall.

What about this?
Just drop it on the ground. Come on. Be speedy.

Shoot Up Hill to Fortune Green

Where Shoot Up Hill meets Kilburn High Road they stopped, in the forecourt of the tube station.

Wait here.

Nathan left Natalie by the ticket machines and walked in the direction of the flower shop. She waited until he was out of sight and then followed, stopping by the edge of the awning. He was in the doorway of the Chinese takeaway, talking with two girls, whispering with them. One in a short lycra skirt and a hoodie, the other a small girl in a tracksuit with a headscarf that had fallen far back on her skull. The three of them stood huddled together. Something changed hands. Natalie watched him put a hand on the head of the smaller girl.

What did I just say? Don't make me say shit twice.

I ain't saying anything.

Good. Keep it that way.

Nathan stepped out of the doorway, spotted Natalie, groaned. The girls walked off in the opposite direction.

Who were those girls?

Nobody.

I know things. I used to be down the Bow Street cells every night.

Closed now. They take you down Horseferry now.

That's right, they do.

I know some things too, Keisha. I'm deep. You ain't the only smart one round here.

I see that. Who are those girls?

Let's go Shoot Up Hill then cut across.

The street was longer and wider than ever. The houses and flats are set far back on that road, they look like hide-outs, as if the people who live here still fear the highwaymen who gave the place its name. To Natalie it seemed impossible that they would ever get to the end of it.

You got money on you?

No.

We could get two tins.

I don't have anything on me, Nathan.

They walked for a time without speaking. Nathan kept close to the walls, never taking up the center of the pavement. It struck Natalie that she was no longer crying or shaking, and that dread was the hardest emotion in the world to hold on to for more than a moment. She couldn't resist this display of the textures of the world; white stone, green turf, red rust, gray slate, brown shit. It was almost pleasant, strolling to nowhere. They crossed over, Natalie Blake and Nathan Bogle, and kept climbing, past the narrow red mansion flats, up into money. The world of council flats lay far behind them, at the bottom of the hill. Victorian houses began to appear, only a few at first, then multiplying. Fresh gravel in the drives, white wooden blinds in the windows. Estate agent's hoarding strapped to the front gate.

Some of these houses are worth twenty times what they were worth a decade ago. Thirty times.

Is it.

They walked on. At intervals along the pavement the council had planted an optimistic line of plane trees, little saplings protected by a coil of plastic round their trunks. One had already been pulled up at the roots and another snapped in half.

Hampstead to Archway

That bit of the Heath where the main road runs right through and the pavement disappears. It was dark and raining softly. They walked the tarmac in single file. Natalie felt the cars very close on her right and on her left brambles and bushes. Nathan had his hood and cap to protect him. Her own half-destroyed horseshoe-braid was wet to the scalp. Now and then he offered a warning over his shoulder. Keep to the left. Dog shit. Slippy. She couldn't have asked for a better companion.

If I ruled the world!

(Imagine that.)

I'd free all my sons.

Black diamonds and pearls.

If I ruled the world!

Was the song he was singing.

The rain got heavy. They stopped in a pub's doorway, Jack Straw's Castle.

Them shoes are bait.
They're not shoes, they're slippers.
They're bait.
What's wrong with them?
Why they so red?
I don't know. I think I like red.
Yeah but why they got to be so bright? Can't run can't hide.
I'm not trying to hide. I don't think I'm hiding. Why are we hiding?
Don't ask me.

He sat down on the damp stone step. He rubbed at his eyes, sighed.

Bet there's people that live in them woods, blud.
In the Heath?
Yeah. Deep in.
Maybe. I really don't know.
Just living like animals in there. Had enough of this city. I'm tired of it right now for real. Bad luck follows me, Keisha. That's the thing. I don't follow bad luck. Bad luck follows me.
I don't believe in luck.
You should. It rules the world.

He started singing again. Singing and rapping, though the two were so low and melancholy and close in sound that Natalie could barely tell the difference.

There's that fucking 'copter again.

As he spoke, he took a packet of Golden Virginia from his pocket and flattened a Rizla on his knee. Natalie looked up. Nathan tried to tuck himself in the shadow of the doorway. Together they watched the rotating blades slice through a cover of cloud. They had smoked and smoked. She was as high as she'd ever been in her life.

This rain ain't stopping neither.

I could show you a diary. Your name. Every third line — your name. My friend Leah, her diary. That was basically my childhood — listening to her talk about you! She'd never admit it but the man she ended up marrying — he looks like you.

Is it.

It's just weird to me that you can be so vital to another person and never know it. You were so . . . loved. Why are you doing that? Don't you believe me?

Nah, it's just. That's one piece of truth my mum did speak. Everyone loves up a bredrin when he's ten. With his lickle ball'ead. All cute and lively. Everyone loves a bredrin when he's ten. After that he's a problem. Can't stay ten always.

That's a horrible thing to say to a child.

See but that's how you see it — I don't see it like that. To me it's just truth. She was trying to tell me something true. But you don't want to hear that. You want to hear some other shit. Oh Nathan I remember when you were this and that and you were all fucking sweet and shit, you get me? Nice memory. Last time I was in your yard I was ten, blud. Your mum ain't let me past the gate after that, believe.

That's not true!

Once I got fourteen she's crossing the street acting like she ain't even seen me. That's how it is in my eyes. There's no way to live in this country when you're grown. Not at all. They don't want you, your own people don't want you, no one wants you. Ain't the same for girls, it's a man ting. That's the truth of it right there.

But don't you remember —

Oh Nathan 'member this, 'member that — truthfully Keisha I don't remember. I've burned that whole business out of my brain. Different life. No use to me. I don't live in them towers no more, I'm on the streets now, different attitude. Survival. That's it. Survival. That's all there is. Talking 'bout 'we went to the same school.' And what? What do you know about my life? When you been walking in my shoes? What do you know about living the way I live, coming up the way I came up? Sit on your bench judging me. Arksing me about 'who are dem girls?' Keep your head in your own business, love. You and your fucking lezza friend. Bring her here I'll tell her too. 'You was so good at football, everybody loved you.' What good's that to me? And you go home to your green and your life and where's my green and my life? Sit on your bench. Talking out your neck about me. 'How does it feel to be a problem?' What do you know about it? What do you know about me? Nothing. Who are you, to chat to me? Nobody. No-one.

Just in front of them a little drenched bird landed on a leaf and shook itself. A passing car took the corner sharply, sending up a sheet of water.

What you crying for now? You ain't got shit to cry about.

Leave me alone. I know where I'm going. I don't need you to walk me there.

Drama. You're one of them types. Love drama.

I just want you to go. GO!

But I ain't going nowhere though. Can't run, can't hide. Look, you don't have to get all moody and that just because I talk some truth at you.

I want to be alone!

Want to feel sorry for yourself. Had some bust-up with your man. Half-caste, your man is. I seen him getting on at Kilburn with his briefcase. Look at you all sorry for yourself. You know you made it when you're crying over that shit. You give me jokes.

I don't feel sorry for myself. I don't feel anything for myself. I just want to be alone.

Yeah well you don't always get what you want.

Natalie stood up and tried to run. Almost at once she caught a soggy slipper in a divot in the road and was down on her knees.

Where you going? Give it up, man! Give it up! How many more times?

The rain fell harder than before. She saw his hand stretched out for her. She ignored it, put her hands on her right knee and sprang up. She shook her arms and legs out like a gymnast. She stood up and started walking as fast as she could but when she looked over her shoulder he was still behind her.

Hampstead Heath

I see you trying to work me out.

I'm not trying to do anything. Face front!

You finished? You take long.

There's more involved for a woman.

Best hurry up. Some geezer and his dog heading in.

What!

Nah. Chill.

I wish you'd leave me alone.

I ain't saying nothing.

But you are saying something.

Pick-er-nick time. Let's all have a pick-er-nick.

So? I used to go to picnics here. Picnics. You never had a picnic? I'm trying to describe to you what a normal life looks like.

Yeah. You love up explaining.

I used to come up here with my church.

There you go.

There you go what? You never came up here?

Nope.

Never. You never were on Hampstead Heath. When we were kids. You never came up here.

Why would I come up here?

I don't know, because it's free, because it's beautiful. Trees, fresh air, ponds, grass.

Weren't my scene.

What do you mean it wasn't your scene? It's everybody's scene! It's nature!

Calm down. Pull your knickers up.

Corner of Hornsey Lane

Stop following me. You keep talking to me. I can't hear myself think. I need to be alone now.

But I ain't in your dream Keisha. You're in mine.

I'm serious. I need you to go now.

No, but you're missing it. Listen: my dream is my dream. You get me? Your dream is your dream. You can't dream my dream. What you eat don't make me shit. You get me? That's my dream — you can't get in there.

Jesus Christ you sound like the Magic Negro.

I'm pure magic.

Just go home!

I ain't going nowhere.

If you're going to hurt me, there's no point. You're too late.

Now why would you even say that to me? We're walking nice and friendly. I'm not a bad person, Keisha. Why you acting like I'm some kind of bad man. You remember me. You know who I am.

I don't know who you are. I don't know who anybody is. Stop following me.

Why you being cold to me now? What have I done to you? I ain't done nothing to you.

Who was that girl, the little one, in the head-scarf?

Huh? Why you worrying about her?

You live with her?

That's your problem: you want to be up in everybody else's dream. We're friendly — we've been walking nice and friendly. Why're you stepping to me now?

Wasn't she at Brayton? She looked familiar to me. Is her name Shar?

Didn't know her then. That ain't her name with me.

What's her name with you?

We in court? I call my girls all sorts.

What do you do to your girls? You send them out to thieve? You pimp them out? Do you phone women up? Do you threaten them?

Whoa whoa, slow down, man. You got me twisted. Listen, me and my girls stick together. That's all you need to know. They got my back. I've got theirs. We're many but we're one. Fingers on a hand.

You hiding from someone, Nathan? Who're

you hiding from?

I ain't hiding from no-one! Who says I'm hiding?

Who is that girl, Nathan? What do you do to your girls?

You're not right in your head. You're talking some pure craziness now.

Answer the question! Be responsible for yourself! You're free!

Nah, man, that's where you're wrong. I ain't free. Ain't never been free.

We're all free!

But I don't live like you though.

What?

I don't live like you. You don't know nothing about me. Don't know nothing about my girls. We're a family.

Strange family.

Only kind there is.

Hornsey Lane

Hornsey Lane. Said Natalie Blake. This is where I was heading.

That was true. Although it could be said that it did not really become true until the moment she saw the bridge. Nathan looked around. He scratched at the sore on his neck.

No-one lives here. Who you looking to see up here? Middle of nowhere up here.

Go home, Nathan.

Natalie walked toward the bridge. The lampposts at either end were cast-iron, and their bases molded into fish with their mouths open wide. They had the tails of dragons, winding round the stem, and each lamp was topped by an orange glass orb. They glowed, they were as big as footballs. Natalie had forgotten that the bridge was not purely functional. She tried her best but could not completely ignore its beauty.

Keisha, come back here, man. I'm talking to you. Don't be like that.

Natalie stepped up onto the first little ledge, just a few inches off the ground. She had remembered only one layer of obstruction, but the six-foot barrier before her was topped by spikes, like a medieval fortification: spikes up and spikes down, an iron imitation of barbed wire. This must be how they stopped people going nowhere.

Keisha?

The view was cross-hatched. St. Paul's in one box. The Gherkin in another. Half a tree. Half a car. Cupolas, spires. Squares, rectangles, half moons, stars. It was impossible to get any sense of the whole. From up here the bus lane was a red gash through the city. The tower blocks were the only thing she could see that made any sense, separated from each other, yet communicating. From this distance they had a logic, stone posts driven into an ancient field, waiting for something to be laid on top of them, a statue, perhaps, or a platform. A man and a woman walked over and stood next to Natalie at the railing. Beautiful view, said the woman. She had a French accent. She didn't sound at all convinced by what she'd said. After a minute the couple walked back down the hill.

Keisha?

Natalie Blake looked out and down. She tried to locate the house, somewhere back down that hill, west of here. Rows of identical red brick chimneys, stretching to the suburbs. The wind picked up, shaking the trees below. She had the sense of being in the country. In the country, if a woman could not face her children, or her friends, or her family — if she were covered in shame — she would probably only need to lay herself down in a field and take her leave by merging, first with the grass underneath her, then with the mulch under that. A city child, Natalie Blake had always been naïve about country matters. Still, when it came to the city, she was not mistaken. Here nothing less than a break — a sudden and total rupture — would do. She could see the act perfectly clearly, it appeared before her like an object in her hand — and then the wind shook the trees once more and her feet touched the pavement. The act remained just that: an act, a prospect, always possible. Someone would surely soon come to this bridge and claim it, both the possibility and the act itself, as they had been doing with grim regularity ever since the bridge was built. But right at this moment there was no one left to do it.

Keisha, it's getting cold up here. I need some warmness. Come on, man. Keisha, don't be moody. Chat to me some more. Step down.

She bent over and put her hands on her knees. She was shaking with laughter. She looked up and saw Nathan frowning at her.

Listen, I'm out. I got to keep moving. You're a fucking liability. You coming or what? Asked Nathan Bogle.

Good-bye, Nathan. Said Natalie Blake.

She saw a night bus coming up the street and wished she had some money. She did not know what had been saved exactly, nor by whom.

VISITATION

The woman was naked, the man dressed. The woman had not realized that the man had somewhere to go. Outside their window came the noise of a carnival float testing its sound system, somewhere to the west, in Kensal Rise. Out in the street they call it murda. After a few bars the music stopped and was replaced by the tinkle of a passing ice cream van. Here we go round the mulberry bush. The woman sat up and looked for the letter she had left on the man's side of the bed, in the early hours of the morning. It had taken her a whole day and most of a night to "marshal her thoughts." Finally, as Monday began, she had licked the glue on the white envelope and placed it on his pillow. He had moved it to a chair, unopened. Now she watched her husband place his feet in some fine Italian tasselled loafers and draw a baseball cap down low upon his curls. "Aren't you going to open it?" asked Natalie.

"I'm going out," said Frank. The woman knelt up in an imploring position. She could hardly believe that she had awoken to find herself in the same situation as yesterday, and of the day before, that sleep could not erase it. That she would be in the same situation tomorrow. That this was her life now. Two silent enemies shepherding children to their social appointments. "I'll be out for a few hours," said the man. "When I get back I'll take the kids till seven. You should find somewhere else to be." The woman picked up the envelope and held it out to the man. "Frank, just take it with you." The man took a thin volume from a bookshelf — she was too slow to identify it — and put it in his back pocket. "Confessions are self-serving," he said. He left the room. She heard him go down the stairs, pausing briefly on the second floor. A few minutes later the front door slammed.

There was a choice of either stasis or propulsion. She got dressed quickly, dramatically, in bright blue and white, and ran down a flight of stairs. Her children met her in a hallway. Naomi was standing on an upturned box. Spike was flat on the floor on his stomach. Both were silver. Silver faces, silver sprayed clothes, foil hats. Natalie couldn't tell if this was the consequence of a dramatic event, a form of game, or something else again.

"Where's Maria?" she asked, but then answered her own question: "Bank Holiday Monday. Why're you wearing that?"

"Carnival!"

"Again? Who said both days?"

"I'm a robot. There's a competition. Maria made them. We finished up the foil."

"Both robots."

"No! Spike is a robot dog. I'm the main robot. It starts at two p.m. It is five pounds."

If she kept receiving these kinds of clear, helpful descriptions of phenomena from her children there was a possibility they might all get through the next few hours. The next few years.

"What time is it now?" Natalie's children waited for her to check her phone. "We can't stay here. It's a beautiful day. We need to get out."

Each child had their own room — there was enough space in the house for them all to sleep alone — but ignorant of the logic of capital the children insisted on sleeping together, and in the smallest room, in bunk-beds, surrounded by a mountain of their own clothes. Natalie dug through this mess looking for something suitable.

"I don't want to get changed," said Naomi.

"I don't want!" said Spike.

"But you look ridiculous," argued Natalie.

In her daughter's eyes Natalie saw her own celebrated will reflected back at her, at twice the intensity. Downstairs in the front hall she put the robot dog in the buggy and had an argument with the robot about whether or not it should be permitted to take the scooter. She lost that one, too. She closed the front door and looked up at an expensive pile of bricks and mortar. Soon it would surely be divided, have all its contents boxed and redistributed, its occupants separated, resettled. Finally a new arrangement of optimistic souls, intent on "building a life" for themselves, would cross its threshold. And in a sense it was not difficult to project oneself into the future in this way, so long as you stuck to abstractions.

Two minutes down the road, Natalie's daughter grew bored of her scooter and asked for a piggy-back. Natalie hooked the scooter to the buggy and accepted her daughter upon her back. Naomi stretched her head round so her soft cheek pressed against her mother's face and her wild hair flew in her mother's mouth.

"Why do you insist on taking the scooter

if you know you're not going to want to use it?"

The child spoke with her wet lips brushing the flesh of her mother's ear: "I don't know what I'm going to want until when I want it."

The mother looked into her children's wire baskets.

Naomi: Toothpaste, rubber ball, sticker set, a big red pitchfork, book.

Spike: Rubber ball, rubber ball, flashing plastic duck, Brillo pads, plastic sword.

Five pounds each, five items. Poundland. Natalie could remember doing this with Marcia in Woolworths, back in the day, but then it was one pound, and you got so much more for your money, and everything had to be "useful."

"I'm interested in the decision-making process here."

"I helped Spike choose. But he chose that."

"You don't want a Brillo pad, honey."

"I DO WANT."

Natalie picked up the pitchfork.

"It's for Halloween."

"Nom, it's August."

"I DO WANT!"

"Seriously," said Naomi, with a very serious look, "it's a bargain."

At the counter they were selling the *Kilburn Times* for 25 pence.

ALBERT ROAD SLAYING.
FAMILY PLEA FOR WITNESSES

On a tatty sofa a Rastafarian gentleman sat holding a picture of his adult son. Beside the father sat a beautiful young woman, clutching the left hand of the father between her own. There was a depth of misery in both these faces that Natalie found she could not look at in any sustained way. She turned over the top copy and folded the paper in half.

"And one of those," she said.

They had time to kill. Natalie had no idea what was to happen to them all after the time was killed. They walked to the pet shop. Natalie manumitted robot dog. She watched robot and robot dog run down the entrance ramp, to freedom. She unfolded the paper and tried to walk and read and push the buggy and keep an eye out for two beautiful children as they wandered about the cavernous store talking to lizards or arguing about the difference between a hamster and a gerbil. She felt an urge to call Frank — he had a stronger gift for reality than her, especially for chronology — but calling Frank would involve explaining things for which she had no explanation. Two nights ago. Six p.m.

Albert Road. Her eyes kept returning to the same block of text, trying to squeeze a little more meaning from it. She could not tell whether she was trying to insert herself into somebody else's drama — as Frank often said she was wont to do — or whether she really knew something of what had happened at that hour on that road. Now she tried to draw the word "Felix" out of the photograph within a photograph. The dimples and the cheery, laddish expression. The crisp black and yellow hooded top. It was easy to do. He was local, and she recognized him, without being able to say anything else definitive about him. Except perhaps that he looked exactly like a Felix.

She raised her head from her newspaper. She called out. Nothing. She walked to the fish, the lizards, the dogs and the cats. Nowhere. She reassured herself she wasn't the hysterical type. She walked at only a slighter faster pace back around the circuit she had just completed, calling their names in a perfectly reasonable tone. Nothing, nowhere. She abandoned the buggy and moved quickly to the counter. She asked two people a very simple question to which they replied with an infuriating lack of urgency. She went back to the fish, and the lizards, shouting. She understood that her children

were not kidnapped or murdered or likely
to be further than fifty feet from where she
was presently standing but running through
this logical series of statements did nothing
to halt the falling away of everything that
now happened inside her. She peered over
into the pit that separates people who have
known intolerable pain from people who
haven't. Instantly she was sweating all over
her body. A man in an apron came over to
tell her to calm down. She pushed past him
and ran out into the street. And it was into
this pit that she had so nearly placed Frank,
her children, her mother, Leah. Anyone who
had ever cared for her.

She took a step to the left, and stalled:
it was a direction instinct for some reason
rejected. She reversed course and ran into
the next-door warehouse, and down another
ramp into another cavern, filled with face-
less mannequins in hijab and great swathes
of black silk folded and arranged in many
square piles on long shelves. She ran without any design around the racks of fabrics
and scarfs and embroidered gowns and then
back into the street and back down the ramp
into the pet shop where she spotted them at
once, sitting on the floor right at the back in
front of the rabbit hutches.

She fell to her knees and gripped them

with both hands. She kissed them all over their faces, an offering they accepted without comment.

"Can you eat a rabbit?" asked Naomi.

"What?"

"Did you ever eat a rabbit?"

"No . . . I mean, people do. I don't. Wait — that's my phone. You shouldn't disappear like that. You freaked me out."

"Why don't you eat rabbits?"

"Honey, I don't know, I just never wanted to. Let me just answer this. Hello?"

"You eat pigs and chickens and lambs. And fish."

"You're right — it doesn't really make sense. Hello? Who's this?"

Michel. She could hear at once he was very distressed. She stood up and took a few steps backward from the children and held a finger up to signify that they should stay where they were.

"She's lying out there in the sun," said Michel. "She won't speak. I don't know what to do anymore. Why does she hate me?"

Natalie tried to calm him down. She took on Frank's role: establish chronology. But none of it made sense. Something about the pharmacy. Photographs.

"I don't understand," said Natalie Blake, a little impatiently.

"So then I ask her: what's wrong? What's really wrong? She says: 'Look in the box in the drawer.' So I look."

"And what was it?" asked Natalie, feeling that really the story was being milked for every last drop of unnecessary drama. She was eager to return to her children.

"Pills. We've been trying for a year! I don't know if she's been taking them the whole time. They got your name on them. Did you give them to her, Natalie? Why would you do that to me? What the fuck, man!"

Natalie's children came now to her side and each took a leg and starting pulling, as Natalie defended herself against the imputation of collaboration. Normally all of her energies would be in defense — she was trained in it — but as she spoke her mind traveled to what felt like open ground, where she was able to almost imagine something like her friend's pain, and in imagining it, recreate some version of it in herself.

"I'm really so sorry."

"Why does she lie to me? She's not herself. She told me she started praying. She's not herself. Ever since Olive died she's not herself."

"No, she is. She's still Leah."

"Why does she hate me?"

"Mum — let's go, Mum. Now! Let's go!"

"Leah loves you. She always has. She just doesn't want to have a baby." Clarity. Bright, blinding, free of judgment, impossible to contemplate for longer than a moment, and soon transfigured into something else. Still, for a moment it was there.

"Please come."

The three of them sat at the bus stop outside Poundland waiting for the 98. A lady in her seventies with a fetching white streak in her black hair explained how she had escaped the revolution with a Yorkshire terrier in her hand-luggage on a plane chartered by the Shah himself. Not this terrier, the one two before this one. But in a sense I really did not become a good Muslim until I came to Kilburn. This is where I really became very holy. I thought dogs were *Haraam,* said Natalie. Not my dog. Mindy-Lou is a gift from God. Let her lick your children. It's a blessing in disguise.

The bus came. Natalie sat with her forehead rumbling on the glass. The Cock Tavern. MacDonalds. The old Woolworths. The betting shop. The State Empire. Willesden Lane. The cemetery. Whoever said these were fixed coordinates to which she had to be forever faithful? How could she play them false? Freedom was absolute and everywhere, constantly moving location. You couldn't hope to find it only in the old, familiar places. Nor could you force other people to take off their clothes and give it to you like a gift. Clarity! And when I realized Mindy-Lou could actually speak to me through my mind, well, then I really had a moment, like in a story-book or a film, and I knew I would always be watched over and loved by everybody I met forever the end. OK, said Natalie, and lifted up Naomi and maneuvered the buggy to the doors. It was nice chatting with you. We get off here.

At the door Michel took Natalie's hand and led her down the hall, through the kitchen and across the grass as if it were an expedition and she wouldn't be able to find her way without him. "Maybe I should get a new dog. I don't know what she wants." He was in pieces. Such a sweet man. Natalie put a hand to her brow to block the August sun. She spotted Leah lying in the hammock in the garden, totally exposed. Here she had lain for several hours, refusing to speak. Natalie had been brought in for an emergency consultation. She tried to approach quietly with her kids, but they were dragging on her, both too hot and crying, slowing her down. Michel offered to take them into the kitchen.

They clung to their mother. "Maybe fill these," said Natalie and passed Michel two plastic drinks holders. "Kids, go. Go with Michel." She sat down on the bench across from the hammock, and said her good friend's name. Nothing. She asked Leah what the matter was. Nothing. She took her sandals off and put her bare feet in the grass. With what was left of clarity she offered her friend a selection of aphorisms, axioms and proverbs the truth content of which she could only assume from their common circulation, the way one puts one's faith in the face value of paper money. Honesty is always the best policy. Love conquers all. Each to her own.

She spoke and Leah did not stop her, but Natalie was wasting her time. She was in breach of that feminine law that states no weakness may be shown by a woman to another woman without a sacrifice of equal value being made in return. Until Natalie paid up, in the form of a newly minted story, preferably intimate, hopefully secret, she wouldn't be told anything in return nor would her good friend Leah Hanwell listen to any advice.

"Leah," cried Natalie Blake, "Leah. I'm talking to you. Leah!"

She heard Spike wailing; he was running

toward her, silver paint running down his face, and was soon upon her, and she picked him up and tried to listen and understand the injustice he believed had been done to him. Leah turned her head to Natalie very slowly. Spike was laid flat out in his mother's lap. Leah's nose was burned and peeling.

"Look at you," said Leah, "Mother and child. Look at you. You look like the fucking Madonna."

A child. Children. Not babies, not something to be merely managed any longer. Beautiful, unknowable, and not her arms or legs or any other extension of her. Natalie pressed Spike so tightly to her person he started to complain. It was knowledge as a sublime sort of gift, inadvertently given. She wanted to give her friend something of equal value in return. If candor were a thing in the world that a person could hold and retain, if it were an object, maybe Natalie Blake would have seen that the perfect gift at this moment was an honest account of her own difficulties and ambivalences, clearly stated, without disguise, embellishment or prettification. But Natalie Blake's instinct for self-defense, for self-preservation, was simply too strong.

"I'm not going to apologize for my choices,"

she said.

"Oh, God, Nat, who's asking you to? Let's just forget it. I don't want to argue with you."

"Nobody's arguing. I'm trying to understand what's really the matter with you. I don't believe you're sitting here flirting with skin cancer because you don't want a baby." Leah turned in her hammock and showed Natalie her back.

"I just don't understand why I have this life," she said, quietly.

"What?"

"You, me, all of us. Why that girl and not us. Why that poor bastard on Albert Road. It doesn't make sense to me."

Natalie frowned and folded her arms across her body. She had expected a more difficult question.

"Because we worked harder," she said, laying her head on the back of the bench to consider the wide-open sky. "We were smarter and we knew we didn't want to end up begging on other people's doorsteps. We wanted to get out. People like Bogle — they didn't want it enough. I'm sorry if you find that answer ugly, Lee, but it's the truth. This is one of the things you learn in a courtroom: people generally get what they deserve. You know, one advantage of kids is you don't have so much time to sit in hammocks getting depressed about these kinds of abstract questions. From where I'm sitting you're doing all right. You've got a husband who you love and who loves you — and he's not going to stop doing that if you just tell him the truth about what you're feeling. You've got a job, friends, family, somewhere to," said Natalie, and carried on with her bright list, but it had by this point become automatic, self-referential, and her only real thought was of Frank and how much she wanted to speak to him.

"Let's talk about something else," said Leah Hanwell.

Michel came across the lawn with Naomi, a tray of drinks, two sippy cups and a bottle of white with glasses.

"Does she speak?" he asked.

"She speaks," said Leah.

Michel poured wine for the adults.

"Please," said Leah, accepting a glass, "I don't want to do this in front of the kids. Let's talk about something else."

"I think I know what happened in Albert Road," said Natalie Blake.

First they sent an e-mail. A police website for anonymous tips. But that was anticlimactic, not very satisfying, and once it was done they stared at the screen, and felt disappointed. They decided to make the call to Kilburn Police Station.

"At the very least," said Leah Hanwell, who seemed infused with a new energy, "Nathan Bogle is a person of interest. From what you've said. Added to what we already knew. About his character. At the very least he's a person of interest."

Certainly a person of interest.

"You're right," said Natalie Blake. "It's just the right thing to do," and a few minutes later, as they went over the disparate bits of the tale once again, Leah said the same thing back to Natalie. Through the glass doors they watched the children spinning in the lawn. Leah found the number online. Natalie dialed it. It was Keisha who did the talking. Apart from the fact she drew the phone from her own pocket, the whole process reminded her of nothing so much as those calls the two good friends used to make to boys they liked, back in the day, and always in a slightly hysterical state of mind, two heads pressed together over a handset. "I got something to tell you," said Keisha Blake, disguising her voice with her voice.

ACKNOWLEDGMENTS

For creating the time: Mariya Shopova, Sharon Singh, Seeta Oosman, Freedom©, Self Control©.

For creating the author: Yvonne Bailey-Smith.

For reading the book: Simon Prosser, Georgia Garrett, Ann Godoff, Sarah Manguso, Gemma Sieff, Hilton Als, Tamara Barnett-Herrin, Devorah Baum, Sarah Kellas, Darryl Pinckney, Sarah Woolley, Daniel Kehlmann, Anelise Chen, Josh Appignanesi.

For being local: Jim Ford, Len Snow.

For knowing the law: Alison Macdonald, Matthew Ryder.

For inspiration: *The Black House,* by Colin Jones, a model for "Garvey House."

For being an ideal friend: Sarah Kellas.

For all of the above, much more, everything: Nick Laird. Thank you.

ABOUT THE AUTHOR

Zadie Smith was born in northwest London in 1975. She is the author of *White Teeth, The Autograph Man, On Beauty,* and the essay collection *Changing My Mind.*